Rio Roca Fria

Ranch land

To Davy

Bluffs

Emma
Lovell
house

Dime
Store

Parking
lot

Midnight
Pawn

Manfred's
house

Midnight
Hotel

Davy high...

TIRE REPAIR

Wedding
Chapel

Fiji's house
and the
Inquiring
Mind

E

S

Pet
cemetery

Ranch land

DAY SHIFT

DAY SHIFT

Charlaine Harris

ACE BOOKS, NEW YORK

THE BERKLEY PUBLISHING GROUP
Published by the Penguin Group
Penguin Group (USA) LLC
375 Hudson Street, New York, New York 10014

USA • Canada • UK • Ireland • Australia • New Zealand • India • South Africa • China

penguin.com

A Penguin Random House Company

This book is an original publication of The Berkley Publishing Group.

Ace Books are published by The Berkley Publishing Group.
ACE and the "A" design are trademarks of Penguin Group (USA) LLC.

Library of Congress Cataloging-in-Publication Data

Harris, Charlaine.
Day shift / Charlaine Harris.
pages ; cm. — (A novel of Midnight, Texas ; 2)
ISBN 978-0-425-26319-8 (hardback)
I. Title.
PS3558.A6427D39 2015
813'.54—dc23
2014045840

FIRST EDITION: May 2015

PRINTED IN THE UNITED STATES OF AMERICA

10 9 8 7 6 5 4 3 2 1

Cover illustration © Hugh Syme.
Cover photograph: Clouds © Mr Twister / Shutterstock.
Cover design by Judith Lagerman.
Endpaper illustration by Laura Hartman Maestro.

To the readers who are kind enough to follow me wherever I may go

ACKNOWLEDGMENTS

I need to thank Dr. Ed Uthman, Dennis DuBois, and Miller Jackson for their advice and information on various issues in this book. And, as always, thanks to Dana Cameron and Toni L. P. Kelner, aka Leigh Perry, for their helpful comments and suggestions.

It isn't the rumbling of the trucks that seizes Manfred Bernardo's attention; it is the silence that falls when their ignitions die. Big trucks often go through Midnight, slowing to stop for (or speeding up to beat) the traffic light at the intersection of the Davy highway and Witch Light Road. Since Manfred's rented house lies on Witch Light Road, he's grown used to the sound until it is simply background music. But the absence of that sound pierces his preoccupation. He's on his feet and opening the front door before he's aware of pushing back from his desk. He grabs a jacket from the rack by the door.

Glancing across the road, he sees his friend Fiji Cavanaugh come out into her front garden, which is at its bleakest in January. It's cold today, by Texas standards, but sunny. Her cat, Mr. Snuggly, a golden tabby, is at his current favorite sunning spot, the base of the pot where Fiji plans to try a gardenia. Even Mr. Snuggly is staring west.

Manfred exchanges a nod with Fiji, who is bundled in a quilted coat. He notes that today she has inexplicably arranged her hair in two dog-ears, like a six-year-old. Then he turns his attention back to the trucks. One is an equipment truck, and it's laden with building supplies: boards, bricks, electrician's wire, plumbing pipes, hardware. Two battered white vans have disgorged a clown-car number of small brown men, wearing hoodies they will surely discard as the day warms. Emerging from a Lexus, clearly in charge, is a tall white woman in tan slacks and a blue silk T-shirt. She's wearing a faux-fur vest. Her thick brown hair is gathered back into a sleek ponytail, and she wears silver earrings and a silver necklace. She also wears glasses, with big square tortoiseshell frames, and her lipstick is an aggressive red.

All these various vehicles, with their assortment of passengers, have converged around the defunct Río Roca Fría Hotel at the southwest corner of the intersection. As far as Manfred knows, it has been closed for decades. The work crews immediately start pulling the boards off the doors and windows and tossing the ancient plywood into a large skip that yet another truck has deposited on the cracked sidewalk. The workmen swarm into the dark interior of the hotel.

It reminds Manfred of a giant boot kicking a dormant anthill.

Within five minutes, Fiji has crossed the road to join him. Simultaneously, Bobo Winthrop saunters down the steps of his business and residence, Midnight Pawn, which is situated at the same intersection as the Río Roca Fría Hotel but catty-cornered to it. Manfred sees (with resignation) that Bobo is looking quietly handsome today, though he's wearing faded jeans and an ancient T-shirt with an equally ancient flannel shirt open over it. Manfred and Fiji stand with Bobo, and as they do, Manfred sees that west of the intersection, Teacher Reed has come out of Gas N Go; it's directly across the highway from the pawnshop on the east and the hotel on the south.

His statuesque wife, Madonna, is standing on the sidewalk in front of the Home Cookin Restaurant with Grady, the baby, who's wrapped in a blanket. She's holding Grady with one arm, shading her eyes with the other. Across the street from Madonna, Joe Strong and Chuy Villegas have stepped out of the Antique Gallery and Nail Salon. Joe is like his name: muscular. He looks as though he may be forty. Chuy is shorter, his dark hair is thinning a bit, and his skin is the color of toast.

Even the Rev, in his rusty black suit, emerges from his white-painted chapel to cast an unreadable look at all the activity.

We're only missing Olivia and Lemuel, Manfred thinks. Of course, Lemuel cannot come out during the day, and Olivia is gone on one of her mysterious business trips.

After a few more minutes of watching and wondering, Joe Strong takes the initiative and strolls across Witch Light Road. He threads his way through the busy men to Boss Woman, who appears to be looking over some plans on a clipboard—though Manfred is sure, reading the clues in her stance, that she is well aware of Joe's approach.

Boss Woman turns to face Joe and extends her free hand to shake his, a professional smile pasted on her face. She is able to look Joe directly in the eyes, Manfred observes. She seems to like what she sees. The well-groomed Joe is pleasant looking and has a warm manner. His mouth moves; her mouth moves. They grin at each other without sincerity. Manfred thinks, *It's like watching a ritual.* In his peripheral vision, he spies the Rev retreating into his chapel, but the rest of the Midnighters stay outside.

Bobo turns to Manfred. "Had you heard anything about this?" he asks.

"No. Believe me, I would have spread the word," Manfred tells his landlord. "This is a big thing, right?" He is aware that he feels ridiculously excited by this development in the small town where he's lived for less than a year. *Rein it in*, he advises himself. *It's not like the circus has come to town.*

And yet, in a way, it's exactly like that. Fiji's round, pretty face reflects his curiosity. Her eyes are lit up.

"What do you think?" she says, bouncing up and down on the balls of her feet. "They're going to reopen the hotel, huh? How can they even get it back up to code? It's been closed so many years. Everything will need to be ripped out and replaced. Plumbing, electricity . . . floors . . ."

Bobo nods. "I've been in there. Right after I moved here, Lem and I went in one night. There was a loose board at the back, and Lem pried it open. We had flashlights. He just wanted to show it to me."

"What was it like?" Manfred asks.

"Spooky as hell. The old reception desk with all the pigeonholes for mail is still there. The light fixtures were just hanging down with all these cobwebs on 'em. Like a horror movie. High ceilings. Wallpaper coming off in shreds. Smelled like mice. We didn't even go to the second floor. The stairs were a death trap." He smiles. "Lem remembered it when it was open. He said it was pretty nice then."

Lemuel is well over a century and a half old, so it is not surprising that he can remember the hotel in its heyday.

"So why would anyone spend the money to renovate it?" Manfred says out loud, since that is the question on all their minds. "Wouldn't it be cheaper to build a Motel 6 if you felt like Midnight could support a hotel?"

"Who wants to spend the night *here*?" Fiji asks, another question they've all thought about. "There are three motels in Davy if you go north, and at least six over in Marthasville if you go west. If you go to the interstate, there are a skadillion places to stay. Besides, Home

Cookin isn't open for breakfast." It's the only restaurant within fifteen miles.

They contemplate all those facts in silence.

"How many rooms in that hotel?" Manfred asks Bobo.

Bobo looks down at him, blue eyes narrowed in thought. "I wouldn't think more than twelve," he concludes. "The ground floor is the lobby and the kitchen and the dining room, plus there was an ancient phone booth, don't know when that went in . . . and there weren't bathrooms in the rooms . . . so, say four guest rooms on the ground floor plus a bathroom and the public rooms, and then eight on the second floor plus two bathrooms? And the third floor was storage and staff rooms, Lem said."

Fiji grabs Bobo's arm. "You said dining room?"

"Yeah," Bobo says, surprised by her agitation. "Oh. I get it. The Reeds."

"I don't know how Home Cookin keeps open, anyway. Really. Think about it. How?" Manfred spreads his open hands as he asks them.

But Bobo and Fiji ignore Manfred's question. They are just glad to have a good cook like Madonna in Midnight.

"If they *don't* open the dining room . . ." Bobo says.

"It'll be a good thing." Fiji ends his thought. "Home Cookin will be busy, Gas N Go will be busy, and maybe even Joe and Chuy will sell more antiques and do more nails."

"Huh," Manfred says. "That would be all right." Though he really feels he doesn't want anything to change in Midnight, he makes himself admit that a touch of prosperity would be good for the town. His own business is done by telephone and Internet and does not depend on foot traffic.

Manfred's cell phone rings, and he whips it out of his pocket. He doesn't have to look at the caller ID to know it's Joe, whom he's watched walking back to Chuy.

"We need to have a meeting tonight," Joe says without preamble. "Maybe Fiji can go ask the Rev, and Bobo can tell Lemuel. Is Olivia in town?"

"I don't think so. What time?"

"Here at the shop, whenever it's really dark." There's a muffled sound while Joe asks Chuy a question. "Seven o'clock good?"

"Fine, I'll tell them."

"See you then."

Manfred ends the conversation and passes along the message.

"I'll tell the Rev, but you can't ever predict what he'll do," Fiji says with a shrug.

"I'll put a note downstairs for Lemuel," Bobo says. "He'll see it the minute he gets up. Maybe Olivia will be back by then."

That night, when the work crews have gone and the tall woman, too, the inhabitants of Midnight assemble in the Antique Gallery and Nail Salon. Occasionally, they can hear Rasta yapping upstairs in the very nice apartment Joe and Chuy share. "I thought he might wake up Grady," Chuy explains. "He'll calm down in a second."

Sure enough, Rasta falls silent after everyone has filtered in. The salon area is the front right corner of the store, and the antiques, dusted and arranged attractively, take up the rest. Joe has assembled some folding chairs and an old love seat around a refreshments table. He and Chuy have made lemonade and tea, and there are a couple of bottles of wine. They've put out a cheese and cracker tray. Fiji has brought a bowl of toasted, salted pecans. Manfred tries one to be polite, then finds it hard to resist grabbing a handful.

When they all have drinks and food, they choose seats.

Madonna and Teacher settle on the love seat, with baby Grady drowsing on Madonna's chest. Madonna is regal and a little scary, and she's never been especially friendly. Her husband, Teacher, who is running Gas N Go until another buyer is in place, is the town handyman. Teacher is good at everything. Since he's been working at the convenience store full-time, projects are going undone in the town, and everyone is ready for a return to the status quo, including Teacher. Grady has started pulling up and will begin walking, and Madonna's already worried about cooking at the restaurant with him staggering around.

Joe stands in front of the motley assortment of chairs on which they've perched and begins, "Here's what I know."

They all fall silent and look attentive.

"The woman in charge is Eva Culhane. She's not the owner. She's his or her agent. I don't know who the real owner is, she was real close-mouthed about that. Here's what she told me. The hotel is going to reopen as a hotel. But the eight small rooms on the bottom floor will be made into four suites with their own bathrooms, and four rooms on the upper floor will get the same treatment. These will be residence rooms."

There is an intake of breath because so many people have questions.

"Wait," Joe says. "Wait!"

There's a little laughter, but they are all too curious or anxious to be very amused.

"The residence rooms will be for people who are in the area for a long-term job, like working for three months at Magic Portal. Or people who are waiting to get into an eldercare situation. As an aside, Eva Culhane told me that there's a waiting list for all the elder-care places in a sixty-mile radius. The remaining rooms will be conventional hotel rooms. In the family quarters, there'll be two people living there as staff. A cook will provide breakfast for residents and whoever stays at the hotel. Lunch and dinner will be cooked for permanent residents only, is what I got out of it."

Madonna's shoulders relax visibly. She gets a few diners from Magic Portal, which is an Internet company, every month. (Thanks to Magic Portal, Midnight has great Internet.) And ranchers come into Midnight every now and then for a meal. But she's in the room with her regulars, right now. More customers would be welcome. Elderly people like traditional food, which is what Madonna cooks.

"What kind of staff?" Fiji asks.

"There'll be two people in residence," Joe repeats.

"Will one of them be a nurse or some kind of medical person?" Bobo asks. "Sounds like they might need that. And they'll have to hire a maid, I would think. That's a lot of rooms to clean for one person, plus dishes, plus food prep."

"Good questions. We'll have to find out." Joe looks a little chagrined he didn't think of all this.

"Did Ms. Culhane give you a timetable?" Fiji asks.

"She said they hope to be open within six months."

There's a moment of silence.

"They must have a shitload of money," Teacher Reed says, and Bobo nods. "That's a quick turnaround."

Olivia, who'd driven in an hour earlier, speaks for the first time. She is sitting with Lemuel the vampire, her lover, and she looks exhausted. They are all ignoring the fact that Olivia's shoulder is obviously bandaged under her shirt. "We have to find out who owns the company doing the restoration," she says.

"Manfred, can you dig that up?" Joe asks.

Manfred is the most computer savvy of all the Midnight residents, but he's no hacker. He just knows his way around the Internet. "I can try," he says. Joe hands him a brochure, one that Eva Culhane had given him. It has a corporation name on it, MultiTier Living.

Olivia extends her hand silently, and Manfred hands it to her. She looks at the brochure intently before she hands it back.

When everyone has said everything they have to say (some more than once), Lemuel supports Olivia with his arm as they leave Joe and Chuy's store/salon. The remaining Midnight residents go their separate ways: Teacher, Madonna, and the sleeping Grady cross the street to walk past Home Cookin Restaurant and behind it to their double-wide, the Rev splitting off from them to go right to his bleak little cottage. He has not spoken during the whole meeting, but he has eaten cheese and crackers and the toasted pecans.

The people who live east of the Davy highway (Bobo, Manfred, Fiji) walk together, Fiji carrying a plastic container with the remaining pecans. Fiji hands the container to Bobo. "You and Manfred split those," she says. "I've got some more at home." She looks both ways before she crosses Witch Light Road. The golden tabby cat, Mr. Snuggly, is waiting for her, and Bobo and Manfred watch the woman and the cat go in the front door. Bobo says, "Hold out your hands." Manfred pulls a real cloth handkerchief from his pocket and holds it ready to catch half the salted pecans. Gathering up the corners, he nods his thanks, and Bobo splits away to go into the side door of the pawnshop, which leads to the stairs going up to his apartment.

Manfred unlocks the front door of his little house, which he rents from Bobo. He passes by his huge curving desk, crowded with computer equipment, to go through the little den (designed as a dining room) and back into the kitchen. He's full and not really thirsty, but he decides to have a cup of hot chocolate before he goes to bed, and he pulls out the extra blanket. He feels unaccountably chilled by the advent of the new people, and he wants to be warm tonight.

The next morning, Manfred sits at his computer and types "Multi-Tier Living" into his search engine. He reads the resultant description, which is too broad to be satisfying. MultiTier offers housing of all sorts, including "residence inns," and long- and short-term care facilities for the elderly and recuperating . . . at least those who don't require skilled nursing care. Manfred wades through all the bland verbiage and pictures of healthy-looking people of a certain age who are smiling at their attentive caregivers or relaxing in their small apartments. Finally, he finds another name, Chisholm Multinational.

When he searches for it, the website he finds is impressive and almost frightening in its scope. Chisholm Multinational has so many divisions he could wander through its website for hours. It's like an octopus. One tentacle is all about hotels and medical facilities: regular hotels on the high end, rehabilitation centers, nursing facilities for the care of Alzheimer's patients or people suffering from mental health issues or people going through the ravages of cancer.

Another tentacle contains various construction companies. Manfred can see that connection; you might as well build all these various structures, right? Yet another tentacle deals with janitorial work. Again, logical. You have to clean all those buildings you've erected to hold travelers and sick people.

He pushes away from his desk and decides he needs a cup of tea. He has to admire the person at the head of Chisholm Multinational, who he gathers is the grandson of the founder. He wonders if this man has any idea what all the branches of his company are doing . . . or where Midnight, Texas, is. He imagines some group of suits gathered around a large map, peering at the tiny pinpoint that is Manfred, the Rev, Fiji, Bobo, Chuy, Joe, the Reed family . . . the population of this almost-ghost town.

He feels a frisson of distaste, almost fear.

1

Five months later, Manfred Bernardo checked into Vespers, an upscale hotel on the very edge of Bonnet Park, one of the oldest and "nicest" neighborhoods in Dallas. Actually, Bonnet Park was its own little city. Manfred had thought that his clients might arrive so wired from dealing with the traffic of downtown Dallas that they might not be able to transition to a mellow séance or reading, so he'd selected Vespers first for its location, and second for its decor. The interior of Vespers combined a lot of modern lines and shades of gray with random swaths of brilliant fabric and nearly life-size sculptures of deer and lions. The deer looked startled and the lions were snarling, both reactions appropriate to finding themselves in such surroundings. Vespers played subdued techno music in the background nonstop, and all the desk staff looked as though they'd been kidnapped from a Nautica photo shoot: young, attractive, healthy, outdoorsy. They were all people who would not mind viewing their endless reflections in the other design element of Vespers—mirrors.

Manfred himself was more of an indoor kind of guy, though that was at least partly due to his occupation. Phone psychics who also had websites had to stay by the phones and the computers, so he was pale. He was also definitely not tall or pumped up. And his multiple piercings and many tattoos did not make him look hearty. But he did attract a certain kind of woman, and he did have his own brand of charm, or at least so he'd been told.

The desk clerk who checked him in and ran his credit card was not one of the women who appreciated that charm.

"And will you be wanting to make a reservation for Vespers Veneto tonight?" she asked, smiling brightly.

Though he was tempted to opt for room service, Manfred told himself that while he was in the city, he should look at as many people as he could, since there were so few in Midnight. He felt a bit starved for strangers. "Yes," he said. "That would be perfect. A reservation for one, for eight o'clock." He used the word "perfect" preemptively, hoping she would not repeat it.

"Perfect," she murmured automatically, as she entered the reservation on her keyboard. Manfred wished there were someone he could look at, to roll his eyes. Instead, he looked in the huge mirror behind the clerk, and to his utter astonishment, he *did* see someone he knew. His mouth opened to call, "Olivia!" But at that second Olivia Charity's brown eyes met his in the mirror, and she gave a tiny shake of her head.

"Did you need anything else, Mr. Bernardo?" the young clerk asked, looking at him with a bit of concern.

"No, no," he said hastily, scooping up the cardboard folder containing his plastic keycard. "Thanks," he added.

"Elevators over there," she prompted, pointing to his right. "Behind the panel of mirrors."

Of course, he grumbled to himself, while he went around the large wall to find the elevator bank. When one finally whooshed open, he could see his exasperated reflection in the mirror at the back of the elevator car. He rode up in silence. Out of habit, he looked up and down the hall when he stepped out, but he didn't see any security cameras. That didn't mean they weren't there, but he found it a little surprising in a place like Vespers, whose hauteur and prices would surely attract at least some well-heeled and famous guests.

Despite the cost, Manfred had opted for a suite so he could conduct private readings in his room. If he'd been traveling for any other reason, he would have picked a cheap motel. All he needed was a bed and a functional bathroom, preferably clean. But clients always thought better of him, and therefore themselves, if they consulted him in an obviously expensive venue.

To Manfred's approval, the living room was lavish: couch, easy chair, television, bar, and microwave, with a small round dining table and two chairs that would be perfect for his readings. The bedroom was as comfortable as he'd hoped, and the bathroom was positively over-the-top. Manfred unpacked quickly and efficiently (he'd brought an all-black wardrobe for this weekend) and put his list of bookings on the round table, together with his tarot cards, his mirror, and a velvet pad on which to place objects brought to him by clients to aid him in his readings. He was not primarily a touch psychometrist, but every now and then he got a flash of clarity.

He felt keen anticipation as he viewed the layout of familiar items. In-person readings were exciting, because he had a chance to use his true gift to the best of his ability. For that reason, the sessions were not only tiring, but occasionally frightening. He'd scheduled two in the morning, three in the afternoon for Saturday, and the same for Sunday. He'd check out Monday morning and drive back to Midnight.

But this evening, he'd relax and enjoy the change of scene and the rare luxury. This was a far cry from his little house in Midnight. In the bathroom was a claw-footed tub with a showerhead added much later, and not enough room to swing a cat. He could swing a good-sized lynx in this tiled wonder, with its multiple showerheads and double sinks. "Time to shower, change, and have a great dinner," he said happily. He'd put the glimpse of Olivia Charity out of his mind.

Manfred felt far more urbane when he went downstairs. Though he knew it was probably not the fancy-restaurant thing to do, he took his e-reader with him. He wasn't fond of staring off into space, and he was in the middle of a book about the Fox sisters, who'd founded Spiritualism. He'd also brought his cell phone.

A table-for-one diner is often in a less-than-stellar position, but Veneto wasn't busy that night. Manfred had a whole horseshoe-shaped booth to himself, his back to an identical booth facing the opposite direction. Thanks to the ubiquitous mirrors, he found he had a good view of the room and almost everyone in it. After he'd ordered, Manfred decided he could see almost too much. In his black suit, he looked like a crow in a daisy field; the other diners were in light summer colors, as befitted June.

Then in a mirror high on the wall opposite him, he spotted one other person in black, a woman. She was seated directly behind him in the booth with another woman and a man. Though Manfred got out his e-reader and turned it on, he glanced up several times because her head and shoulders seemed familiar. After the third or fourth time Manfred checked out the woman, he realized he was looking at Olivia Charity again. He'd never seen Olivia so groomed before, and he was astonished at how sophisticated and gorgeous she looked.

In Midnight, Olivia wore jeans and T-shirts and boots, very little makeup or jewelry. The Dallas version of Olivia was wearing a lot of eye makeup. Her hair was put up perfectly in a roll at the nape of her neck. Her black dress was sleeveless and sleek. She was wearing a necklace formed to look like overlapping leaves. Manfred decided it was made of jade, though he was not knowledgeable about gems.

From his position, Manfred could only glimpse Olivia's face from time to time. But her companions seemed engrossed in her conversation, so he felt free to watch them. They were both in their late fifties or even early sixties, he decided, but were definitely what you would call "well preserved." The woman was blond by courtesy, but not glaringly so. She looked like a tennis player. Her jewelry glittered.

The man had a lot of gray hair, well styled and cut, and he was wearing a suit that Manfred suspected was very expensive.

They're not talking about playing tennis, Manfred told himself. To a casual observer, the man and woman might appear to be having a pleasant conversation with Olivia, but Manfred was a keen observer by nature and trade. The couple both had the slight knowingness to their smiles, the wink-wink nudge-nudge consciousness that told him they were talking about sexual things in a public place.

Manfred was through with his meal by the time the three finished their conversation. The couple left together. In the mirror Manfred saw the woman fish something from her tiny purse and slide it over to Olivia's hand. A keycard. *Huh, I didn't expect that*, he thought. He'd always speculated about his mysterious neighbor, who had an apartment in the basement of the pawnshop next door to Manfred in Midnight.

Manfred had met Olivia during the previous year at the same time he'd met Bobo's other tenant, Lemuel Bridger. No one had ever given him much background on his neighbors, because people in Midnight weren't prone to gossiping about each other, as a rule. But gradually, Manfred had come to understand that Olivia had a mysterious job that took her out of town from time to time. And he'd observed that Olivia sometimes returned to Midnight the worse for wear. Amid other possibilities, he had considered the idea that Olivia might be a prostitute. But as he'd gotten to know her, something about the way she handled herself made him discard the idea.

Despite the way her dinner with the older couple had played out, he couldn't believe it now. *What's she up to?* he asked himself. He glanced down at his watch. After seven minutes, Olivia rose and left the restaurant. She walked right by him, but she didn't acknowledge him by so much as a twitch of an eyebrow.

Manfred left the restaurant maybe three minutes later, but he did not see Olivia at the elevator bank as he'd half expected. In fact, he didn't see her again that night. He woke once in the early morning, aware of some hubbub down the hall from his third-floor room; but it subsided, and he slept another hour.

When he stepped out of his room to go down to the hotel's coffee shop for breakfast, the police were wheeling a body in a bag out of a room closer to the elevators than his. Manfred thought, *Oh, shit. What did Olivia do?*

He stayed in his doorway until the gurneys had rolled into the staff elevator. When he ventured out and down the hall to the guest elevators, a policeman holding a clipboard asked him his name. When Manfred responded, the cop checked it off on a list. "One of the officers will talk to you later," the cop said. "You'll need to stay in the hotel until you've been interviewed."

"I'll be here." Manfred tried hard to sound appropriately somber and innocent. "I am assuming one of the guests died?"

"Two. But the officer will tell you what you need to know."

Manfred stepped into the elevator, his thoughts racing around like a mouse in a maze. He realized he'd never considered that Olivia might not be involved at all, and he'd also never considered that the body bag might contain anyone besides the man or the woman she'd dined with the night before.

When he emerged from the elevator, the calm, techno lobby of

Vespers had been overturned. Now the mirrors reflected quite a few people, mostly of the police persuasion. Manfred sighed heavily. He doubted the lobby of Vespers had ever seen so many police, uniformed or plainclothes. The staff did not look so smoothly chic today. They looked both anxious and excited.

Inside the sunny morning restaurant (Mattina), seated at a table for two, was Olivia. She looked much more like the woman he knew, in lighter makeup and a gauze blouse and khakis. He looked away elaborately (*This is not the woman I seek*), but as the hostess bustled up to seat him, Olivia jerked her head in a summons.

"I see a friend," he told the hostess, and slid into the chair opposite Olivia's. Her plate of fruit and bowl of yogurt had been sampled. As he sat, she signaled for her coffee cup to be refilled.

"My gosh, Manfred!" Olivia said, leaning forward to give him a clap on the arm. "I didn't know you were in Dallas!"

"Same here," he said at the same volume level, just loud enough to be heard by the waitstaff. "I thought I saw you last night, but then I said to myself, 'No, that just can't be Olivia!'" His voice was light, but he knew his expression was anything but. Olivia smiled at him.

The waiter arrived with the coffeepot to refresh Olivia's cup. Manfred took the opportunity to order a large breakfast. He would need the fuel.

Her face growing somber, Olivia said, "In a totally weird coincidence, I saw the Devlins last night. I haven't seen them in five years, I guess. They seemed just fine, so normal. I just can't understand it."

So the dead couple had been the Devlins.

"I never met them," Manfred said firmly and a bit more loudly than necessary. "But I saw a body being removed down the hall from me, and the policeman wouldn't tell me what had happened. Though it seems you know?"

"Yes, a horrible thing. Stuart . . . well, I hate to even say it, but apparently last night Stuart and Lucy had some kind of argument in their room, and he killed her. And then himself."

He stared at her. There was nothing in her face or eyes, no subtext. "Oh, Jesus," he said, stunned and sickened. He scrambled to recover his composure. "Did anyone hear them fighting? That's really . . . awful."

"It is," she agreed, after a gulp of coffee. "I ran into them in Veneto last night, and we ended up having dinner together. They were kind of sniping at each other, but that's the way some couples do, you know? They'd been married so long. It just seems incredible."

"It seems incredible to me, too," he said, aware that his voice was way too grim. He made another effort to relax. "So assuming the police let you go, what are your plans for the day?"

Olivia gave him a gentle smile. "I had always planned to spend another night here, and I'll stick to that. I hate to sound shallow, but I guess I'll just go on with my little shopping trip. That was my agenda for today. Now I kind of want to take my mind off them. I can't help them or change the situation, after all." She looked down at her cup and shrugged. "You know when you come to Big D, you've got to shop at the Galleria. A gal's gotta have clothes. I'll take in a movie, maybe go to a comedy club tonight. I could use a good laugh, especially after all this. You want to tag along?"

"Sorry," he said. "I'm here to work, and I'm booked up today and tomorrow." He was free both evenings, but he knew he'd need the time to recuperate. Besides, just now he didn't want to go anywhere with Olivia.

"Work?" There was a faint question in her voice.

"Private readings."

She looked at him seriously, as if she were really seeing him for the first time. "I hope you make a bundle," she said.

"That's the plan," he said, and the waiter set his plate in front of him. He was glad of the interruption. Olivia smiled at his heaped plate, but he didn't react. He poured syrup on his stuffed French toast and cut it up, hoping his appetite would return. He ate a lot on days he was working one-on-one, because the last thing he wanted was to get woozy. He dug into his food, gradually feeling hungrier since everything was delicious. Olivia drank more coffee, but he was glad she let the conversation drop so he could eat in peace. She charged her meal to her room and gathered up her cell phone and newspaper.

"Were you going to mention this to Lemuel?" Manfred asked.

She paused in pushing back her chair. "Why not?"

"Just wanted to be sure we were on the same page." If there was one person in the world Manfred did not want to keep a secret from, that person was Lemuel.

A stocky man in a sports shirt pulled up another chair to the table. Startled, Manfred looked from the man's dark face to Olivia. She looked mildly questioning and not at all alarmed.

"Manfred, this is Detective Sterling, Bonnet Park police."

"Manfred Bernardo." He shook the detective's hand. "Did you want to talk to me, or shall I scoot along?" He glanced at his watch. He had thirty minutes until he had to meet his first client.

"Just a few moments of your time," the detective said. He had a soft, conciliatory voice, contrasting sharply with a stern face. Olivia nodded and left, without a backward glance.

Great, Manfred thought. He did his best to look open and innocent. "I have an appointment soon," he said, trying to sound neutral, when Detective Sterling didn't speak immediately. "This is a working weekend, for me."

"You know Miss Charity."

"Sure. We live in the same town."

"You met here by prearrangement?"

"No." Manfred smiled. "We see plenty of each other in Midnight."

"You ate in the restaurant here in the hotel last night?"

"I did. Had an eight o'clock reservation."

"And you saw Miss Charity then?"

"I saw the back of her head, turns out. I was facing away from her, but there are mirrors all over this place. I even thought, 'She looks familiar,' but she didn't turn around, and I was reading. I didn't realize who it was until I saw her this morning."

"What was she doing?" The detective looked down at a notepad covered with scribbles, but Manfred was sure he didn't need to check someone else's account—the waiter's? Another diner's?

"Last night? Talking to an older couple. I'd never met them."

"How did they seem to be getting along, to you?"

Manfred let his surprise show. "Since I didn't think I knew any of the people, I didn't pay a lot of attention," he said. "If something out of the ordinary had happened, I'm sure I'd would remember it. Raised voices or throwing a drink . . . major drama."

"So that's all you noticed. Three people, sitting in a booth, talking. You were pretty close to them, back-to-back. You didn't hear any of the conversation? You didn't form a conclusion about how they were all getting along?"

"No. None of my business."

"Famous psychic like you, no . . . emanations?" Detective Sterling wiggled his fingers in the air to indicate something spooky. It would have entertained a five-year-old. Manfred was not amused. He'd been sure that the detective knew who and what he was the moment he'd come up to the table. He was less sure the detective had any idea at all about Olivia's means of making a living. It would have been informative and entertaining to ask Sterling, but he knew he couldn't.

Manfred smiled tolerantly (he'd had a lot of practice at that). "Not a single vibration," he said. He glanced at his watch again. "I'm sorry, I need to leave now."

"Sure, go right ahead, Mr. Bernardo. You're staying here tonight?"

"Tonight and tomorrow night, unless something happens to change my plans."

"What could happen?" Sterling seemed genuinely curious.

"My clients may not want to come to a hotel where there's an active police investigation."

"So far, everything seems to point to a murder/suicide," the detective said. "That's what the electronic keycard activity indicates. Just one entry, when they came back to their room after dinner. Though we're still checking every little fact."

"Of course. You have to be sure," Manfred echoed. Only keyed entrances would show up on the hotel's computer, he was fairly sure. The computer wouldn't register the room door being opened from the inside. Olivia hadn't used the keycard Lucy Devlin had given her.

"After all, we're not psychic like you," Detective Sterling was saying, still with that fake-jovial edge to his voice.

"Wouldn't it be handy if you were? Well, best of luck with your investigation." Manfred rose.

"So if I need to talk to you . . ."

"Give me a call." Manfred told Sterling his cell phone number, and Sterling wrote it on the pad. "I'm working, but I can spare a few minutes for the police." On that note, Manfred left the restaurant, feeling better with every step away from the detective.

He was glad to have some time to collect himself before his first client arrived. Not only did he need to push away the gnawing worry about Olivia and what she might or might not have done, but he had to prepare himself for the day to come. He looked forward to exercising his true gift with both excitement and apprehension, and the last thing he needed was to brood about the dead couple. He was worried they would contact him, and he was very grateful he hadn't met them or touched them. That would have made it easier for Stuart and Lucy Devlin to track him down from the blue hereafter.

Manfred's first and second appointments of the day went well. He was able to tell Jane Lee that her grandmother approved of Jane's fiancé, and he was able to suggest a place for Robert Hernandez to look for his mother's gold necklace. He lay down during his lunch hour with his eyes closed, and his energy level went back up.

Manfred greeted his one o'clock appointment with some pleasure. He had had sessions with Rachel Goldthorpe before. She was a longtime client who actually lived in Bonnet Park; he'd visited her home. Rachel was in her midsixties, with two daughters and a son, and several grandchildren; she loved the grandchildren and her daughters, who made her happy. Rachel had been widowed less than twelve months before. She came to Manfred because she missed her husband terribly, not least because Morton had been the only one who could handle their son, Lewis.

Manfred had actually met the Goldthorpe children, but briefly. His opinions about them had been largely formed from Rachel's anecdotes. Annelle and Roseanna, the daughters (who were now in their later thirties), seemed both loving and dutiful. But Rachel's youngest child, Lewis, was apparently batshit crazy. According to his mom, Lewis had been in and out of trouble and in and out of mental health care since he'd been fourteen. Now he was thirty-two, never married, and obsessed with his mother's possessions. After losing his last job with a property management company, he'd moved back into her pool guesthouse. From there, Lewis watched Rachel's every move and complained endlessly if she gave money to charity or even took her old clothes to Goodwill.

Today, Rachel wanted to consult with her husband, Morton, about the problem of Lewis. Manfred was fond of Rachel at least in part because he'd had great success with contacting Morton Goldthorpe, who urgently wanted to communicate with his wife. Since Morton had passed away, Manfred's sessions with Rachel had been rewarding and exciting.

When he'd sent out an e-mail blast to announce he was available for private sittings again, Rachel was among the first to make an appointment.

When Manfred answered his door, he was shocked to see how wretched his client looked. "What's wrong?" he asked, before he could think how tactless that sounded.

"I know, I know, I look bad," she said. "I'm getting over pneumonia." Rachel trudged past him and spotted the table, steered toward it. Her breathing was audible. Rachel was heavy, but she'd always been bouncy and vigorous. Today her flesh seemed to sag on her bones. There were circles under her eyes. "And then downstairs, somehow I dropped my purse. Everything went everywhere. They had to help me gather things up."

"Rachel, should you even be here?" he asked, breaking one of his own rules. He never commented on a client's appearance, pro or con.

She made an effort to smile, patting his shoulder. "I'm a lot better. This is the first time I've been out in three weeks. This morning I got my hair done and came to see you. Boy, does it feel good to be out of the house!" She patted her salt-and-pepper hair, which was arranged in its usual stiff curls. Her T-shirt read "World's Best Grandma."

"Who gave you the shirt?" Manfred said, figuring it was the kind of thing she'd like him to notice. He tried not to look as concerned as he felt.

Rachel sank into the chair with obvious relief. She pulled a refillable black bottle decorated with butterflies out of her purse and put it on the table in a handy spot. "Annelle's kids. And Roseanna's twins gave me the water bottle last Mother's Day," she said, with pride. "So much better than using a new plastic bottle every time, right? Better for the environment."

"You sure you feel up to this?" Manfred said. He didn't want to persist, but he was more than a little worried.

"I've been looking forward to this for weeks," she said firmly. "Let's get to it. I need some good in my life. Otherwise, Lewis will be the death of me. Did I tell you he'd moved into the pool house?" She took a big drink and sighed, recapping the bottle and extending her plump hands. "Ready."

Manfred sat opposite her and reached across the table to take her hands in his own. Other clients had different preferences. They wanted the tarot or the mirror, or they'd brought a loved one's possession for Manfred to hold. Rachel always wanted the touch. He wrapped her chilly fingers in his warm ones and bowed his head, his eyes closed. "Morton Goldthorpe, husband of Rachel, I'm searching for you," he said. "Rachel needs you."

"Oh, boy," she breathed. "Do I ever. That Lewis! He told me he was going to take charge of my jewelry. Take charge! Like I was an Alzheimer's person! So I had to hide my diamonds and my rubies."

Manfred heard her words from a distance. He was busy opening himself to receive Morton. But he felt relief that Rachel had hidden her jewelry. Though she dressed and looked exactly like thousands of grandmothers who passed through the doors of any given Walmart every day, Rachel was very wealthy. The late Morton had made a lot of money in real estate and had been smart enough to get out when the getting was good. Though Manfred had no idea what Rachel's bank statement would read, he knew she was well able to afford his fees, and evidently a lot of sparklies, too.

But all those considerations faded away as Manfred connected with the plane that housed the dead. His eyes were closed, so that he could see that world better: He was faced with the usual wall of billowing mist, out of which faces manifested with frightening rapidity.

And there was a face he knew approaching rapidly through the mist. Rachel's fingers felt oddly slack in his grip, but he kept his focus with ferocious intensity.

"Here he is," Manfred murmured, feeling Morton speeding through him. The spirit manifested a little differently today. Usually, Morton stopped at Manfred's fingertips, content to touch his wife through Manfred. But today Morton ripped through Manfred with such force that he passed right into his Rachel. "You will not suffer, my dearest Rachel," Manfred said, to his own surprise.

"Oh!" Rachel said dazedly, and to Manfred's ears she sounded both excited and a bit startled . . . but not frightened. Manfred's eyes flew open to look right into Rachel's, and in that flash of a moment her eyes went blank. She slumped forward onto the table.

And then her fingers relaxed completely.

Morton flowed back through Manfred. Taking Rachel with him. For five seconds Manfred couldn't see anything at all, and he felt utterly empty.

It seemed like an eternity until his vision cleared. Immediately, he noticed the limpness in Rachel's body. He knew that she was dead. He let go of her hands to wrap his arms across his chest. He shivered all over. He wanted to cry or scream or run shouting from the room, but he did none of those things.

Sometimes, as his grandmother had often said, shit just happens.

He rose to walk unsteadily to the nearest phone. He punched a number to reach the front desk. "Is there a doctor in the hotel?" he asked, hearing his voice crack. He hadn't sounded as uncertain since he was thirteen. "My guest is unconscious. In fact, I think she's dead."

2

S o what happened then?" Fiji asked him. It was three days later, and they were sitting in her little kitchen. Fiji had invited Manfred and Bobo over to share a roast for Tuesday supper. She didn't often buy expensive cuts of meat, but sirloin top roasts had been on sale at Kroger in nearby Davy, where the Midnighters went to shop. She'd cooked it traditionally, with new potatoes and carrots around the meat, and she'd made lots of gravy, and biscuits, too. It was so good that Manfred and Bobo had both had second helpings of everything.

"Then all the police who had been downstairs investigating a murder/suicide came up to my room," Manfred said grimly. "It took me about an hour to explain what Rachel and I had been doing. They assumed I was some kind of gigolo. I guess they were hoping that I'd had a connection with the couple who'd died the night before, though they'd already questioned me about that."

"Man," said Bobo. Tall, fit, blond, and with a gorgeous white-toothed smile, Bobo was much more like someone's idea of an ideal lover. In point of fact, Bobo was not vain and did not seem to be aware of how attractive he was. "With the lady in her sixties? That must have been embarrassing."

"I was too scared to be embarrassed. By that time, I figured if they only thought I'd been having an affair with Rachel, I'd be glad."

"Did you call Olivia? You said you'd seen her in the hotel." Fiji poured more iced tea into Bobo's glass.

Manfred had not discussed Olivia's connection to the murdered couple, much less his near certainty that she'd killed them both. He felt both angry with Olivia and a little frightened of her (when he thought about the Devlins), but he didn't think laying that on his friends would be right. He chose his words carefully. "I figured I'd just drag her into trouble with me if I called her. I have to admit, I really wanted to see a friendly face, so I definitely thought about it." For exactly a second. He didn't believe Olivia's face would have been too friendly if he'd involved her. And he'd had a bad moment, a second really, of thinking, *The Devlins died and now Rachel died. Coincidence?*

"And what did the cops say?" Bobo asked.

"It wasn't as bad as I thought it would be." Manfred shrugged. "Rachel didn't have a mark on her, and the hotel staff knew what I was doing, having people into my room. I didn't exactly tell them I was a psychic, but one of my appointments did."

"What about your other appointments? What did you do about them?" Fiji asked. Her mind was a great one for tangents.

"They moved me to another room. I saw two of them the next day, but two others canceled," Manfred said. He wasn't surprised, and he understood their reluctance to come into a hotel under media scrutiny, especially since they were going there to do something that would embarrass them if it became widely known. Meeting with a psychic wasn't as reputable as going to a charity dinner, say.

"Really?" Fiji was incredulous. "You were able to focus on business after that poor woman died?"

"I would have been out of there," Bobo said. "I would have been on the road back to Midnight as soon as I could pack my bags."

They looked at him expectantly.

"At first I was shook up," he admitted. "But Rachel passed so quickly, almost peacefully. After I got over the shock of it, I thought, if she had to die so young, maybe going that way was what she might have wanted. I'd never been in such close touch with a passing, not even my grandmother's. Annelle—the daughter—was at Vespers in forty-five minutes. I was so relieved. She told them how much Rachel had looked forward to the session and how happy talking to me had always made her mom. She also said that she'd begged her mother to stay home until her lungs were clear," he added more practically.

"What exactly happened?" Bobo carried his plate to the sink and rinsed it. "To make her die, I mean?"

"They're doing an autopsy. But Annelle told me Rachel had been taking medication for high blood pressure. There was more wrong with Rachel than I knew. If she'd died at home, I don't think they would have questioned her death, because she'd been under a doctor's care. I hope they got the bottle of water she drank from. Surely they did. She had a big old purse full of stuff. And it was all messed up, because she'd dropped it in the lobby, she said, and she just threw things back in there." After a minute, he added, "She said people in the lobby helped her pick up all her stuff." He tried hard not to look like he was wondering if Olivia had been there, in the lobby, being helpful.

"So what about the son, Lewis? The one you said was so crazy?" Fiji picked up Manfred's plate and took it to the sink. Surreptitiously, she dropped a scrap of roast beef into Mr. Snuggly's bowl. Though the cat hadn't been evident until then, suddenly he was there, head down and chewing. She smiled.

"That was the worst part." Manfred shuddered theatrically. "It was awful. Just when they were wheeling Rachel out, Lewis showed up, screaming and making a terrible scene. He was making an asshole out of himself, like his mom's dying was really all about him. It would have made Rachel so embarrassed. I don't mind telling you, when I heard him yelling? I asked the police if I could go to my new room."

"What was he saying?" Fiji was fascinated.

"Oh, he said I'd killed her," Manfred said bitterly. Bobo and Fiji were horrified, their mouths open, their eyes wide. "He said there'd been people following her for days. I guess those were supposed to be my many minions. Worst of all, he said that she'd been carrying a king's ransom in 'jewels'—that's what he said, jewels—in her purse, and I must have stolen them."

3

Fiji, who'd been getting the dessert plates out, paused. "You're kidding," she said, thinking of how scary that would be, being accused of something so low.

"No," said Manfred. "That part was *awful*. Maybe even worse than Rachel dying like that."

"The police didn't believe him, surely?" Fiji began to cut a cherry pie into generous triangles. *They can use the calories more than me*, she thought, and squirted whipped cream from a can into fluffy spirals on the pie. It looked pretty.

"I think it was obvious he's nuts," Manfred said. Though his words were confident, to Fiji he sounded uneasy. "And I had already told the police that Rachel had just said that she'd hidden her jewelry from Lewis."

"Did she tell you where?" Bobo asked.

"No," Manfred said. "I didn't even think of asking her. None of my business."

Bobo looked delighted to see the cherry pie. Fiji smiled at him, curbing her stupid urge to pat him on the head. Over dessert, the conversation veered away from Rachel Goldthorpe's death and the trouble it had caused Manfred to broader concerns. They talked about Midnight things: the latest curiosity a customer had brought into the pawnshop, the continuing search for a permanent manager for Gas N Go, and the way an overabundance of zucchini in Madonna's garden was affecting the cuisine of Home Cookin. Manfred seemed to feel better since he'd vented, Bobo seemed thoughtful, and Fiji herself was content in her kitchen (still sunny at seven thirty) with her company. It had been hot work cooking, but the window air conditioner kept the room at a tolerable temperature.

Fiji watched as Bobo ate all of his pie, and Manfred ate about half of his. She urged them both to take another piece home, and both the men said they would, Bobo with more enthusiasm than Manfred. She was grateful. Leaving her alone with the remains of the pie would not have been a friendly act.

Bobo offered to do the dishes, but Fiji said, "Nope, tonight's my treat. Next time, you can help."

He protested a little, but she stood firm. Bobo and Manfred thanked her profusely for the food, and then the two men left, walking across Witch Light Road side by side. Bobo was returning to his apartment above Midnight Pawn, Manfred to the house situated to the right of the pawnshop. The sun was a red streak to the west, and the sky was gathering violet shadows.

"Maybe it will rain tomorrow!" she said to Mr. Snuggly, who'd come onto the front porch with her. He licked a paw, but he suddenly raised his head and glided off into the bushes. She went back inside to clean up. While Fiji washed the dishes, she thought about Manfred's story.

And just as Manfred had, Fiji wondered about what part Olivia had played in it.

Of course, there was a lot Manfred had left out. Any fool could see that. He'd been conspicuously silent about what Olivia had actually been doing at Vespers. As Fiji scrubbed, she speculated. When you added up Olivia's mysterious absences and her closemouthed policy about her job, combined with her obviously abundant cash, it was logical to wonder if Olivia was a prostitute. Though no one in Midnight had ever said that out loud, it was easy to see they'd all considered that a possibility. But there were good reasons to doubt that hypothesis.

For one thing, Fiji knew Olivia . . . at least a little. Olivia was more than capable of taking care of herself with extreme force. Though Fiji admitted to herself that she, Fiji, was not that knowledgeable or experienced in sexual matters, Olivia didn't seem like the kind of woman who'd gladly cater to anyone else's demands. Even if her gig was as some kind of bondage dominatrix, Fiji couldn't picture Olivia putting on spike heels and spanking someone unless she chose to do so.

Plus, more logically, why would a prostitute live in Midnight? Why not live closer to her clientele? Also, how many prostitutes could afford to fly all over the country for "dates"? Not too many, Fiji guessed, though she would be the first to admit she was almost totally ignorant about the actual business of renting one's body.

And then, there was Lemuel's relationship with Olivia. Lemuel . . . how could she put it into words to herself? Men were mysterious, especially Lemuel, who had been alive for decades and decades. However, even though Lemuel seemed to be absolutely tolerant of people who had different sexual preferences from his own, Fiji felt certain that Lemuel would not consider sharing his lover with other men.

Could Olivia have been actually doing what she'd told Manfred she was doing? Staying in Dallas for the weekend to go shopping and take in some movies or a show?

Fiji realized she was shaking her head a little. Maybe yes, maybe no; but she was very inclined to settle on "No."

By the time she'd worked her way through all these thoughts, the dishes were stacked in the drainer to dry, and the counters were clean. It was full night outside, and the locusts were singing.

"It's almost bedtime," said a small, sharp voice, somewhere around the region of her ankles. She'd heard the new cat flap rattle a moment before, so he hadn't startled her, though he enjoyed it when he did.

Fiji looked down. "Yep," she said to the golden tabby. "Where've you been, Mr. Snuggly?"

"The Rev had a visitor who smelled interesting," the cat said. "And though I was very close to catching a mouse, I went to investigate."

"Thanks for your vigilance," Fiji said dryly. "Did you enjoy having company today?"

"The roast beef was good. I want some more. Manfred is very leery of me. Bobo always scratches behind my ears and on my belly," Mr. Snuggly observed. "He likes to visit me," the cat added rather smugly.

Fiji pondered that for a second. "So, who was the mysterious visitor?" she asked, squatting to stroke Mr. Snuggly's marmalade fur. She could take a hint.

"He is very tall," said Mr. Snuggly. "And he is like the Rev."

"What do you mean? In what respect?"

The cat looked up at his witch. "You know the Rev is not just an old Mexican minister, right?"

"Yes," she said.

"And you know what he is?"

"Not . . . exactly." Though she had her suspicions.

Mr. Snuggly sighed, as theatrically as a marmalade cat can sigh. "My goodness," he said, and put a paw on his food bowl, giving it a tiny significant shove. "Your great-aunt was much smarter than you are."

"If she'd been that much smarter, she'd have drowned you in a ditch," Fiji muttered, and stood, looking down at the cat with a frown on her face. When her great-aunt, Mildred Loeffler, had bequeathed Fiji the little house in Midnight and all of her witch accoutrements, her legacy had included Mr. Snuggly. While the cat had his uses, he also had the highest regard for his own comfort and convenience and a great disregard for anyone else's.

"Are you going to give me some more roast beef?" the tiny voice said. "If you're not, I'm going to take a nap before bedtime."

"You can have some with your breakfast tomorrow. You've already had supper, remember? You know what the vet said at your last checkup." Mr. Snuggly stuck his pink tongue out at Fiji, and when she scowled at him, the cat stalked from the room. She heard a squeak as the cat jumped up on her bed. She knew if she went in, she'd see him on her coverlet, curled into a compact circle against the bump of her pillow.

Fiji folded her dish towel and hung it from its rack by the sink. On a whim, she walked into the front of her house. The large front room functioned as her shop and as the meeting place for the women's group she led on Thursday nights. She crossed directly to the west window. Next door, the Reverend Emilio Sheehan's chapel sat in pristine silence. She knew the Rev was there, even though it was later than he usually stayed, because the light inside was on.

While she watched, a tall man came out of the chapel. He was followed by a small, thin man wearing a big hat; this was the Rev, and he was holding the hand of a child. Fiji could not tell if the child was a boy or a girl, only that it was unhappy.

Mr. Snuggly was suddenly at her feet. "Outside," he said urgently, and she picked him up and opened the front door. She stepped out onto her front porch. The lights at the intersection of the Davy road and Witch Light Road cast a glow over the scene.

Fiji had never seen the tall man before. He was beautifully put together: broad shoulders, narrow waist, tight ass, long legs. She was afraid her mouth would water. He was quite bald; she wondered if he was truly hairless or if he shaved his skull. As she watched, the tall man knelt, put his arms around the child, and kissed it, holding it close for a long moment.

A *leave-taking*, she thought, and felt sad. She could hear the child crying. The tall man, who'd stood to walk away, paused for a moment. She could almost feel his misery, his hesitation, his misgivings, in the droop of his massive shoulders.

He seemed to sense her presence, or perhaps he smelled her. He turned to look at her as she stood on her porch, holding the cat in her arms, the gusty wind blowing over her like a hair dryer on Warm. His eyes scanned the wooden sign in the front yard, which read THE INQUIRING MIND. She felt an impulse to call to him, to say, "I'll help!" without knowing exactly what help she could provide. But Fiji had no doubt he sensed her benevolence, because he nodded at her. Then he stiffened himself and left, climbing into a compact rental car.

Fiji thought of walking over to the Rev and the crying child. She was as close to a friend as the Rev had, as far as she knew. But she hesitated. The child was already dealing with one stranger. Would another be any help? She shook her head. The Rev would ask for her assistance if he needed it. Where the Rev was concerned, she was very, very careful. She might not know all his secrets—she didn't want to—but she knew it was wise to use the greatest restraint where he was concerned.

"I'm sleepy," complained Mr. Snuggly, and she retreated inside her house.

From the window, she watched the Rev and the child walk out of sight, going west, presumably heading to the Rev's cottage. Fiji couldn't help but feel sad at the thought of a child in the sparsely furnished living room, which was the farthest she'd ever penetrated into the Rev's domain.

She was left to wonder why the Rev had been chosen by the stranger as the caretaker of the child. She knew the Rev had not ever had a child of his own; he had told her that. The postman almost never stopped in front of his house, and Fiji could not remember ever seeing visitors there. At the chapel, yes; two or three times a month, people arranged for the interment of some beloved pet in the large fenced area behind the chapel, and every year four or five couples got married in the chapel proper. Occasionally, someone would stop in front and simply go inside to pray. But that was the extent of the Rev's communication with anyone in the outside world, as far as Fiji knew.

Though Fiji had had some experience as a babysitter while she was in her teens, it had been years since she had dealt with children of any age. But she realized now she would have to step forward.

She fell asleep that night with Mr. Snuggly curled against her, thinking of Bobo, thinking of adding green onions to the roast the next time she cooked one, thinking of the child.

4

Joe Strong, too, had watched the Rev walking back to his cottage with the child. He'd been so surprised that he'd called Chuy to their front window to see. Their apartment above the shop reflected their love of comfort and color, and Chuy heaved out of his easy chair with some reluctance. He'd been watching television, with a magazine at hand for the commercials.

But the sight was worth getting up for. "The Rev and a kid?" Chuy said. "Boy or girl?"

"I'm sure it's a boy. I wonder where he came from," Joe said after a moment of silent wonder. "Looks about four years old, don't you think?"

"Maybe. The Rev didn't steal him," Chuy said, putting his arm around Joe.

Joe kissed the top of Chuy's head. "Nope, that didn't cross my mind. If the kid stays more than overnight, he's going to need some help."

"Who, the kid or the Rev?"

"Both of them." Joe shook his head. "I have to say, I feel sorry for the kid."

They both knew the Rev was a creature of habit, and a solitary one at that. Any man the Rev's age, both silent and unsocial, was not going to be an ideal companion for a little boy—though the Reverend Emilio Sheehan was far from a typical elderly cleric, if such a person existed.

"That's what we're here for," Chuy said. "To help."

"And to fix antiques and fingernails," Joe said, laughing. "I wish I didn't love old furniture, and you didn't love decorating women. I wish we were both accountants or bounty hunters. Something less predictable."

"As long as we're happy. And we take care of each other," Chuy said, much more seriously.

"I try to take care of you," Joe said, turning to take Chuy in his arms. "How'm I doing?"

"Pretty good," Chuy said, and it was the last time he said anything sensible for a while.

The next morning, as they lay together in the old bed they'd restored, both of them reluctant to start the day, Joe said, "Lemuel went in the hotel a couple of nights ago."

"Lemuel," Chuy murmured, a note of exasperation—distaste?—in his voice. "What did he say?"

"He said it was almost finished. He couldn't believe they'd accomplished it on schedule. He believes they've poured money into what should surely be a minor project for a big company like that."

"That worries me." Chuy snuggled closer. "And I was so relaxed."

"Sorry, honey," Joe said. "But I wanted to tell you . . . he thought people would be in the hotel by next week."

"That soon. Damn."

"Yeah, I know. Could be good, could be bad."

"Why can't things just stay the same?" Chuy asked plaintively.

"Good question. Boot that one upstairs."

Chuy punched Joe in the shoulder and soon fell back to sleep.

But Joe forced himself to rise and pull on his running clothes. When he'd become conscious that the waist of his pants was getting a little tighter than he liked, he'd promised himself to resume running. This was his fourth morning in a row, and he was feeling really good about it.

He trotted down the outside stairs in the early-morning sun. The sky was clear as far as Joe could see, and a breeze was blowing steadily, for which he was grateful. Since the sidewalk (except around the hotel) was cracked and uneven, Joe ran on the road. This was normally quite safe, since vehicles on Witch Light Road were few and far between; the Davy highway was much busier. He went west out of town, waving at the only oncoming truck, driven by a local rancher named Mark Kolb. Mark lifted an index finger from the steering wheel in response.

Smiling to himself, Joe puffed along. When he'd run twenty minutes, he turned around to run back. His plan was to lengthen his run by five minutes every week. After he crossed the road to return, the sun was in his eyes, so Joe didn't see the small crowd until he was much closer to home. Stunned, he slowed, ran in place for a moment until he could evaluate what he was seeing, and then bounded up the stairs to the apartment. "Chuy, come down!" he called, and returned to the sidewalk.

There were at least five nice cars and a television crew at the Midnight Hotel. There were concrete planters full of flowers outside the main door of the hotel, which was situated on the corner. There was a banner hanging over the entrance, which Joe couldn't read until he'd walked to the corner opposite the hotel.

The banner read, Now Open!

Chuy was beside him in five minutes, fresh and clean in khakis and an oxford-cloth shirt. His dark hair was carefully combed and styled, his mustache newly trimmed, and he smelled wonderful.

"Don't hug, I'm sweaty," Joe warned him.

"No kidding," Chuy said. "Is this not crazy? How'd the Culhane woman get them to work so hard?"

"A spell?" Joe shrugged. "Plenty of money and lots of workers make for a quick completion."

"But this is incredible. And how'd she get media coverage? This is an old hotel reopening in Midnight, not a casino in Vegas!"

"Let's go listen," Joe suggested, and they crossed the street to stand just behind the gaggle of people in front of the hotel.

Eva Culhane looked even sleeker and more powerful than she had the day the redo had begun. She was all glammed up in a formfitting gray herringbone skirt and a white sleeveless blouse. Ridiculous black high-heeled sandals made the most of her legs. Her hair was loose, rippling down her back.

"That's a first," Chuy said. "The hair."

Joe nodded. "I'm trying not to worry about this. She did buy the sofa and the sideboard from us," he said. "You can't say she doesn't shop locally."

"She picked up a couple of pieces from Bobo, too."

"Oh. What?"

"Vases, some old keys that she had framed, a couple of old weapons she had shadow-boxed. Family photographs that look interesting."

"Stern woman with her hand on the shoulder of seated man with handlebar mustache?"

"Yeah, that kind of thing." Chuy shrugged. "Let's get closer."

"MultiTier Living is experimenting with this mixed residence concept," Eva Culhane was saying. "This is a small hotel, so it was one of the first on our list. We wanted to start small, to work out the bugs before we tried the concept on larger properties. We're catering to the extended-stay people, but we're including not only businesspeople who need to be close to Magic Portal for a few weeks, but the able elderly who—for one reason or another—need to have a minimum-care place to live until they can make more permanent arrangements." She paused and smiled brilliantly. "Questions?"

A reporter from the Davy paper said, "How able do these elderly people have to be?"

"Good question! Don, they have to be able to dress themselves and manage their own toilet needs," Eva Culhane said, so cozily that Joe thought she must have grown up with the reporter. "They're certainly not required to do any cleaning—or furnishing—of their own rooms. Each unit has a bedroom, a sitting room, and a bathroom. In the eldercare-designated rooms, there are features you might expect: safety bars, a panic cord, and so on. Why don't we go on the tour, and you can see for yourselves." Culhane swept open the door of the hotel and ushered in all the media: two newspaper reporters, an area magazine editor, and the film reporter, who'd come from . . .

"I don't see a station designation on his microphone or on the van," Joe said quietly. "Who would film this? What TV station would cover a hotel opening in Midnight?"

"I don't know what to think about that." Chuy looked up at his lover. "Hey, let's go home. You have to eat some breakfast before the shop opens, my rugged runner."

Joe laughed. "I'm ready for it. Maybe one egg and a granola bar."

"You're just a martyr," Chuy said, as they crossed over to the shop and started up the stairs.

After Joe had eaten and showered and gotten ready for the day, he went down to find Chuy doing Olivia Charity's fingernails. Olivia was one of Chuy's few steady customers.

"Chuy tell you about the grand opening?" Joe said, after greetings had been exchanged.

"He did," Olivia said. "I don't know if we've ever had a grand opening in Midnight. Even as far back as Lemuel can remember."

"I haven't seen him in a couple of days," Joe said, getting out his feather duster. He tried to go over all the furniture in the shop every other day, at least. The duster had been a gag gift from Chuy a couple of Christmases ago, but it had taken Joe's fancy.

"Lemuel's not here," Olivia said. Though she didn't emphasize the words, it was easy to read her unhappiness in them. "Those old books that Bobo found? Well, he couldn't translate all of them, so he's gone to find someone who can. He's on his third city."

Chuy concentrated on the job he was doing, but Joe could tell simply from the way he held his head that he was curious. But they both knew that Olivia probably would not—perhaps could not—answer a single question.

"I hope he returns soon," Joe said, which was safe enough. "Midnight's not the same without Lemuel."

Olivia turned a little to look at him. "That is the truth."

She really loves him, Joe thought, with wonder. He'd never thought of their relationship as a love affair. More as a "like attracts like" joining, like magnetized metal filings. But he hadn't figured the tenderer emotions entered into it.

He caught a glance from Chuy and understood that Chuy was thinking along the same lines.

"Maybe he won't be gone long," Chuy said. And then he changed the subject. "Olivia, do you want the little wing brushstrokes on your nails this time?"

"Sure, that was pretty," she said, but her face simply expressed indifference. As Chuy bent his head over her hand, Joe turned back to his dusting.

5

Olivia stood opposite the hotel for several minutes, her mind not made up to action. The vehicles were gone from the curb. The banner was still flapping above the doorway, but there was no one on the sidewalk. The petunias in their pots tossed their bright heads in the wind.

The wind was one thing that reminded her of home. In San Francisco, where she'd spent a significant part of her youth, the wind off the bay was a given. She had always felt good when it brushed her face. It was part of being out of her parents' compound, out of the high walls that sealed her in: or, as her father always insisted, kept her safe.

Kept her safe from everyone and everything but her family.

"Fucking assholes," she said out loud. She said that every time she thought of her parents. The words slipped out no matter where she was. Here in Midnight, it didn't make any difference. Who was there to hear, or who would question her if he did hear? But she'd startled a lot of people out in the real world. That was the way she thought of it.

Here in this little hole-in-the-road of a town, with so few people remaining that a POPULATION sign would be a joke, she'd found the most unlikely place to live and the most bizarre creature to be her lover.

He siphoned off her agitation.

There was a long list of things she liked about Lemuel Bridger. But his ability to drain her of the tension and anger that propelled her into terrible places . . . that was priceless.

And it helped him to thrive, too. Win-win.

Looking over at the reopened Midnight Hotel, she felt that familiar anger building, at least partly due to Lemuel's absence. And before she knew it, she was striding across Witch Light Road and pushing open the restored door to the lobby, which smelled like a mixture of new and old. There was the dust of decades buried deep between the refinished boards of the floor, and it added flavor to the smell of the paint and varnish and wax and the sharp tang of new nails and hardware. *This depth of scent made possible by Lem's blood,* she thought. Lem loved it when she bit him.

A bell had chimed over her head as the door opened, the electronic rendering of a real bell. In seconds, a brisk step from down the hall to the left of the registration desk announced the approach of a woman in her fifties. She had short brown hair with a lot of gray mixed in, and she had thin arms and legs and a thick middle.

"Good morning," the woman said pleasantly, walking behind the desk as if prepared to check Olivia in. "Can I help you?"

"I'm Olivia Charity." She watched the woman with the close attention of a hawk who'd glimpsed a mouse, but there wasn't any indication the woman had heard her name before. "I live here in Midnight," she continued.

"Oh, nice to meet you. I'm Lenore Whitefield."

"Will this be an old folks' home?" Olivia asked, though she'd read all the material. She just wanted to engage Mrs. Whitefield (there was a plain gold band on the woman's left hand), draw her out.

"Oh, no," Mrs. Whitefield said, smiling. "It's really a hotel for long-term renters. Shall I show you around? We do have a few rooms for what we think of as pre-assisted-living people, just places to stay if they have to leave their homes. Before an opening comes up in the facility of their choice. Not a nursing home."

Hmmmm. Very definite. Olivia was sure if Mrs. Whitefield had said, "Yes, we're a nursing home," there would have been all kinds of government involved. This way, they were skirting the issue.

"I would like to take you up on that tour," Olivia said, with a charming smile. (She knew she could be charming when she chose.) "If you have a few minutes? I have an elderly aunt who might be interested." Olivia did have an aunt, a brittle and attractive widow in her fifties, who would have rather have been shot than be called "elderly."

"Of course," Mrs. Whitefield said. "Well, down here we have the rooms equipped for her . . ." Olivia looked at one of the rooms. Though each suite was on the small side, they'd been restored with some charm and talent. The chairs were low and comfortable, the beds low and comfortable, too, and the bathrooms were designed to help people who might be having a little trouble getting up and down, with handy grab bars.

Next they visited the small dining room, where Mrs. Whitefield explained the dining policy. Through an open hatch, Olivia saw a middle-aged Latina with her hair in a net. She was chopping something on the work counter in the kitchen. There were people to cook for already?

Before she could ask a question, Mrs. Whitefield steered her into a little parlor off the lobby, sort of a common room for the residents, and pointed out the card table, television, and stack of magazines.

Back in the lobby, Mrs. Whitefield showed Olivia that a small elevator had been installed in the spot where (Olivia figured) the phone booth had been. But she chose to walk up the stairs with Mrs. Whitefield. The first rooms up there had been adapted for the modern traveler. Not only was there free Wi-Fi, there were abundant and handy outlets for charging e-readers and telephones and anything else you wanted to plug in. The televisions were flat-screen. There was a deck for your iPod. The beds were high and white and looked comfortable. There was a microwave and a coffeepot and a small refrigerator. If you were stuck with being away from home for a night or a month, you could do a lot worse than stay at the former Río Roca Fría Hotel, now reborn as simply the Midnight Hotel. There were also two more "elderly" rooms.

"So you think this multipurpose type of residence is the future thing?" Olivia said.

"Oh, definitely, especially in small towns where specialization isn't economically viable," Mrs. Whitefield said.

"You'll be working here full-time? In residence?" Olivia smiled, encouraging her companion to expound.

"Yes, I'll be here, and my husband will do the handyman-type jobs. In addition, we'll have a trained nurse stop in once a day to visit the elder residents, checking their blood pressure and so on."

"That sounds ideal," Olivia said. In fact, it did, if she had an aunt who needed to be stowed somewhere until an assisted-living place had an empty apartment. "I hope that the hotel is a great success. Whoever thought of reopening such an old place? Was it your idea?"

Mrs. Whitefield looked surprised. "Oh, honey, I don't have that kind of money," she said, laughing. "No, some big corporation has lots of projects like this, and God bless 'em, they didn't mind hiring someone like me who's been out of a job for a year, and my husband longer than that."

Desperate people whose loyalty can be bought and relied upon, Olivia thought. She came from a line of opportunists who specialized in sizing up employees that way. "That's a blessing," she said soberly.

"You bet. We get a place to live, we get to work for our living, no handouts."

"Do you have kids who'll be visiting?" Olivia said, while her face was turned away to look at the new thick curtains hanging at the window of the last room.

"We weren't blessed with children," the woman said. "But we're plenty glad for each other."

"Of course," Olivia said, infusing understanding and sympathy into her voice. "Thanks for taking the time to show me the place. I'll call my aunt's kids and tell them all about it. It looks wonderful to me."

As they went down the stairs, a heavy man in his fifties was coming in the front door with several bags weighing down his hands. Plastic grocery bags from the Kroger in Davy, Olivia noted.

"Harvey, I'm coming," Lenore Whitefield said, and hurried ahead of Olivia down the stairs. "You should have called me."

"No problem," Harvey said, though he was breathing heavily as if it pretty much *had* been a problem. "I should have parked in back and gone through the kitchen."

His wife looked as though she wanted to know why he hadn't done just that, but she took several bags from him to even out his load. She said, "Sorry, Miss Charity, I've got to get back to work. Thanks for stopping by."

Olivia said, "A pleasure to meet you, and thanks for taking me around." She left out the double doors that led onto the sidewalk by the Davy highway. An ancient pickup truck was parked there; that must be Harvey Whitefield's vehicle. Either he'd wanted his wife to see how hard he was working, or he'd wanted to get a look at Olivia, or he wasn't bright at all. Maybe all of that.

She set out walking west briskly, as if she were going to Home Cookin. She glanced down the alley. There was a battered Ford Focus parked outside what had to be the doors to the kitchen, and there was also a beautiful shiny Escalade taking up the remaining room. Was Eva Culhane still there? If not, who owned the Escalade? It was way too deluxe for the long-unemployed Whitefields.

Olivia had no sense that she was being watched, but just in case, she kept on going. She crossed Witch Light Road to go back into the Antique Gallery and Nail Salon. Joe and Chuy looked up, surprised at her return. "I took the tour, and it's really nice," she said. "You should go see it. The couple running it is called Whitefield. Lenore and Harvey."

Joe said, "Well, thanks for telling us."

Chuy grinned. "The excitement just keeps on coming."

She raised a hand in farewell. She strolled back to Midnight Pawn, going up a few steps to the door on the right of the building and entering there, turning right to go down to her apartment. She could have entered the pawnshop and spent some time talking to Bobo, but she wasn't in the mood. She was fond of her landlord, but she found him a little boring. She still couldn't believe he'd hidden those books that Lem had been looking for so hard and so long. Not that Bobo had done it maliciously; he hadn't known the smelly old volumes were important to Lemuel.

But still.

In her silent apartment, she checked her special e-mail account, the one she used only for work. Her agent said, *Everyone pleased.*

That was his usual comment, and it meant the money had been transferred as they'd specified.

But he'd added another sentence. *Other party collateral damage?*

He meant Rachel Goldthorpe. She answered immediately, *No. Coincidence. And natural?*

Right after she hit "Send" she got up to turn on the television. But she heard the ping that indicated she had e-mail. Surprised, she returned to her desk. The response read, *Sources tell me unnatural.*

"Huh," she said out loud. "But that's a big complication." Should she alert Manfred? On the whole, she thought not.

She was sorry two hours later when news crews rolled into Midnight.

Sorry she hadn't left town.

6

Manfred was deep into work mode, which meant he was visiting all his websites, taking phone calls, and churning out advice and predictions to all his followers. Not that Manfred habitually thought of them as followers—he called them clients. He never thought of himself as a confidence man, since he was the real deal. But his talent did not always manifest at the time he needed it to, so sometimes, naturally, he had to fill in.

That was the way he looked at it.

When the first knock came at the door, he raised his head, annoyed. Who could it be? Most of the people of Midnight knew his schedule, and they wouldn't come visiting during his work hours. A bit irritated, he went to the door and opened it. The *click* of a picture being taken, which reminded him of a cricket's chirp, sounded several times.

"Mr. Bernardo, is it true that Rachel Goldthorpe was in your room at Vespers when she died?"

Don't ever look furtive, his grandmother had always told him.

Manfred managed to control his pulse and his face, though inside he was scared as hell. "Yes, absolutely true," he said. "She was a longtime client of mine. I was shocked and saddened by her death." *What was this all about?*

"A client? For what service?" The newswoman, a junior one you'd send out if the story wasn't that important, looked righteous as she demanded an answer.

"I'm a psychic, as you know," Manfred said, rolling a lot of patience into his voice. And he added nothing else.

"And did Mrs. Goldthorpe discuss her jewelry with you?"

"Discuss? No," Manfred said. "She said she'd hidden it. That was all she said."

"Did you know that Lewis Goldthorpe is alleging that you stole his mother's jewelry?"

"I have no idea why he would say something like that," Manfred said. *Aside from the fact that he's a mentally ill son of a bitch.* He could see a couple of people getting out of cars in front of the pawnshop. And heading his way. "This is a complete surprise to me. If you'll excuse me, I must call my lawyer." With that, he shut the door smartly and locked it for good measure. And made for his cell phone. While he punched in a number, he closed all the curtains, providing a cheerful miscellany of colors. (He hadn't realized that curtains were supposed to match.) Manfred hated the resultant gloom, but he also didn't know how far newspeople would go to get a picture.

His landline rang. He picked it up and put it down to break the connection. Then he left it off the hook. Just at that moment, a cheerful voice answered the cell call. "Clearfork, Smith, and Barnwell! To whom may I direct your call?"

"Jess Barnwell, please," Manfred said, struggling to keep the panic out of his voice.

"Whom shall I say is calling?"

"Manfred Bernardo."

"Just one moment."

It really was just one moment before she was back on the line. "Mr. Bernardo, Mr. Barnwell is in a meeting right now, but he'll call you back the moment he's out."

Sounded like Jess had already heard some version of the news. "I'm relieved," Manfred said sincerely. "I'll be waiting. Please tell him there are news crews here."

"I will." The voice sounded sympathetic.

The knocking at the door was repeated. Manfred sat down at his computer console, but he had a hard time concentrating on his clients.

Finally the cell phone rang. Manfred snatched it up. "Jess?" he said.

"No, it's Arthur Smith. I'm outside. Can I come in?"

The sheriff of Davy County, whose area included Midnight. Manfred had met Arthur Smith months before, and he'd liked the man. "Okay, I'm coming to the door, if you're ready to jump inside," Manfred said, walking to the door.

"I'll knock two, rest, two," Smith said, hanging up.

Manfred stood at the door waiting, and then heard two quick raps, followed by a pause, then two more. He opened the door and Arthur Smith stepped quickly into the room.

Smith was in his forties, with tightly curling pale hair so light that its graying was not immediately obvious. He had wide-set blue eyes and a steady stare that could be very disconcerting. Manfred remembered that Smith had always been direct and honest with the people of Midnight when the body of Bobo's missing girlfriend had been discovered, and he was counting on that being Smith's true nature. He stood aside to avoid being photographed and also to let the sheriff enter the room quickly.

"What the hell's happened?" Manfred said. "What is this? Why are all these people here?" All his anger and fear came popping out in little explosions of words.

"I tried to get here first. But I was in court because my divorce was getting finalized, one of my deputies was working another convenience store stickup, and another one is out with a broken arm. Got thrown by his horse," said Smith.

"Okay," Manfred said. "That's kind of an unusual reason for a lawman to miss work."

"Not here, apparently," Smith said. "Mind if we sit down?"

"No, and I'm sorry about the divorce. Do you know why these people showed up? What the hell is this all about?"

"Tell me what happened in Dallas, first. Give me your version. And can I have some tea or a glass of water while you do?"

"Sure," Manfred said. He felt much calmer since the sheriff was doing his best to be low-key. He took a few deep breaths, poured Arthur Smith a glass of iced tea with a teaspoon of sugar, and settled him on the old couch in the former dining room, now Manfred's television room. It contained the couch, an armchair, and a flat-screen television set on an old credenza.

"Antiques, huh?" Smith said. He settled himself carefully on the couch.

"Just old stuff my grandmother had," Manfred said. "Not good old stuff. Just old stuff." It didn't make any difference to Manfred. As long as he was comfortable, he was happy. He said, "This is what happened in Dallas." And he told Arthur Smith exactly what had happened, with one omission—his speculations about Olivia. It helped that Smith was much more interested in the minutiae of his encounter with Rachel Goldthorpe.

"How often had you seen her before?" Smith asked.

Manfred had looked up the details soon after he'd gotten back to Midnight. Now he went to fetch the printout and handed it to his guest. "Those were the times I saw her in person," he said. "I talked to her a few times on the phone, too, but she really liked the in-person conferences."

"So what do you do at one of these conferences?" Smith leaned back with the air of someone who had all the time in the world to listen.

Manfred sighed. "The client has paid a deposit to reserve a time slot, of course."

"Of course," the sheriff said, a bit dryly.

"So when he or she gets to my hotel room, we're ready to go. I always get a suite, so the bedroom isn't visible, to keep it professional. Besides, there's almost always some kind of dining table in a suite. On that table I place several means of foreseeing the future of the client, or looking into any question he or she brings me."

Smith got out his notepad. "Like what means are those?" He was serious. Manfred was relieved. This was hard enough without dealing with the usual attitude the law showed psychics.

"Like . . . a set of tarot cards, a sort of crystal ball . . ."

"You have got to be shitting me." *Now* Smith gave him an exasperated look.

"Nope." Manfred gave him a tight smile. "Of course, I don't claim to look into it and see the future. But it *is* a helpful focus object. I can use my gift more easily if I have it in front of me."

"Your gift."

"I'm not a fraud all the time, Arthur." Manfred was nettled enough to use Smith's first name. "I'm the real deal."

"Right. Well, go on with your story."

Manfred told Smith everything in meticulous detail. He had a good memory, which was helpful in his job, and he remembered almost everything Rachel had said.

"She had a big handbag with her?"

"Yes, she did."

"What size would you say?"

Manfred shrugged and held up his hands, defining a space approximately fourteen inches by twelve inches, and four to five inches wide. "I guess around that big? It was full of stuff. She'd been sick, she told me. Pneumonia. I think she had to dig around in the purse to find her little package of tissues."

"Did she always carry a bag that large?"

Manfred tried to remember. Finally, he shrugged. "I don't notice purses, I guess."

"When she came for previous sessions with you, did she open and close her purse a lot?"

Manfred stared at him blankly for a few seconds while he plumbed his memories. "She didn't need to," he said slowly. "She got out pictures of her family the first time, I remember. A picture of her deceased husband. Morton. But she hadn't only prepaid her reservation fee, she'd prepaid in full, so she didn't need to write a check. She didn't ever ask me to do the touch psychometry. She liked the classic séance."

"Which would be what?"

Manfred sighed, but he tried to keep it quiet. He didn't like explaining himself, and he hated the incredulous looks he got from nonbelievers. But he couldn't afford to be too righteous about it; he often made up findings that were not the result of any affinity for the world of the dead but the product of astute observation of the living. He believed that painters didn't always have the inspiration for painting, writers wrote whole passages that were not muse-inspired, and that therefore it was natural that he, Manfred, didn't achieve a connection with the supernatural every time he was asked to do so. But without a product, he didn't get paid. So he did the best he could, and he always left the door open for genuine revelations. Manfred was pretty sure the sheriff wouldn't see this in the same tolerant light that another practitioner would. With an inward shrug, he began his canned explanation.

"Normally, I hold hands with the person for whom I'm doing the reading," Manfred said. "And they ask to speak to someone who's gone over. I summon that person. It's like flipping a switch to start a beacon flashing. Then I wait to see who comes. It's not always the right person. Sometimes that person isn't there. Sometimes there's someone else who has an urgent message."

Arthur Smith stared at Manfred, his hard blue eyes unblinking. It didn't take a psychic to see that he was having a hard time keeping his expression open and nonjudgmental. "All right," he said, finally. "So you're holding hands with Rachel Goldthorpe. Her purse is where?"

"I'm trying to remember. I guess," he said slowly, "that she had it on the floor by her chair. I know sometimes women will hang them on the back of the chair, if the bag has a shoulder strap. But Rachel's purse didn't." He could see her carrying it into the room. It had been a beige bag, soft leather, the squashy kind. It had had the short straps. He heard again her labored breathing, saw the pallor of her face. "She didn't set it on the table. So it must have been on the floor."

"Did anyone else come into the room during your session with Mrs. Goldthorpe?"

"Oh, no. I usually offer clients a drink from the minibar, but she didn't want anything. She had the bottle of water with her."

"She what?"

"She had a bottle of water. Not Evian or anything. A black sports bottle, with butterflies on it. Her granddaughter had decorated it for her or given it to her or something."

"What did she do with it?"

"She put it on the table. She took a big drink after she sat down. It helped relieve her cough."

"She was coughing."

"Sure. And breathing heavy. She told me she was recovering from pneumonia."

"What happened to the water?"

"I have no idea. It was sitting there when the EMTs came into the room, and after that, it kind of vanished. I was moved from that room as soon as they'd had a good look at it; I only went back in to check that they'd gotten all my stuff out, and then I was in the room next door."

"Were you by yourself in your original room, after they'd taken Mrs. Goldthorpe's body out?"

"No, the bellman was with me."

"Every second?"

"Yes," Manfred said. "They'd told him to get me out of the room. In fact, I hurried more than I wanted to because he hovered around so much."

"What had you so flustered?"

"The whole experience," Manfred said frankly. "I was so shaken up. I got obsessed with making sure I had all my power cords. Last time I stayed somewhere, I left my phone charger in the hotel room. It's inconvenient to have to get another one. Another time, I left my favorite tarot deck." He spread his hands.

"Did you look in the trash can?" Smith was leaning forward intently, his pale eyes fixed on Manfred's face. Manfred felt an absurd urge to feel all the rings in his eyebrow, make sure none of them were dangling.

"The trash? No. There was some stuff in the trash left over from the EMTs. But I didn't look through it."

"You didn't see the water bottle?"

"No. Since it was black, I guess it could have rolled somewhere, if the police didn't get it. If it was under something, I might not have noticed it."

"See the purse?"

"That I would have *definitely* noticed. I would have insisted the hotel staff hold it for a member of the family. So I guess the EMTs or the police had it. I'm really careful about stuff like that. Especially when someone as crazy as Lewis Goldthorpe is involved."

"Now that you've mentioned Lewis . . . Had you ever met him before?"

"Yes," Manfred said, with distaste. "I'd heard a lot about him from his mother. He was a source of a lot of pain and concern to her. The last time Rachel met me for a session, he followed her and began pounding on the door while I was with her. He accused me of sleeping with his mom, in really graphic terms, and that was the mildest thing he said."

"I'm a little surprised she wanted to have a session with you after that," Smith said.

"I was, too, frankly. She told me he'd been giving her a lot more trouble. Her two daughters seem so nice. I can't understand how she could have such an asshole for a son."

"You liked her?"

"Sure." Manfred felt, all over again, the outgoing flow of her spirit, the terror he'd felt when he understood what that meant. Would she have died if he hadn't contacted her husband? Had Morton come to fetch her because Manfred had called him? Or would he have been there no matter when she had died? *I wonder*, Manfred thought, *if she'd been at home in bed, would she have died at the same moment?*

"Manfred?"

"What?" His head jerked up, and he saw that Smith was looking at him with some concern. "Sorry, I was just . . . I feel bad. She was a nice lady, and I wish she were still here. I don't get to pick, though."

"You think her time had come? The wheel spun around and stopped on her name?" Arthur Smith seemed genuinely curious.

That was so close to what Manfred believed that he was startled. "Yes, that's what I think. I hope the exertion of getting out to see me wasn't too much of a strain on her. This sounds bad, but I hope if she'd been anywhere else—the doctor's office, watching a soap opera in bed, getting orange juice at the grocery store—she would have passed away at the same moment. I can't really know the answer to that. What did her autopsy say?"

"That she was an overweight and sedentary woman past her prime who'd had a bad case of pneumonia. But the tox screen isn't back yet."

"Do you think there was something in that water bottle?"

"I'm not saying anything right now, because the results haven't come back yet," Smith said firmly.

"So what is all this about?" Manfred pointed at his front door as if he could still see the media people outside.

"A lot of Mrs. Goldthorpe's jewelry is missing," Arthur Smith said. "The police got the list from her insurance agency. After her son accused you of stealing it from her purse."

Manfred could feel his mouth fall open. "You mean he was serious?" he said incredulously. "His mom just died and he's worried about her *jewelry*?"

"That's what he says."

"She said he'd planned to take it." Manfred couldn't help sounding bitter.

"What did she say? Exactly?" This was clearly the question Smith had come to ask.

"She told me that she had had to hide her jewelry from Lewis. She was angry, and she was hurt, too. She said that Lewis had told her she was senile, that he needed to keep her jewelry for her own good."

"What did you say in response?"

With a certain grimness, Manfred said, "I didn't say anything. But I thought that before she left, I would be sure to tell her to share the hiding place with her daughters. Or to rent a safe-deposit box and give a power of attorney to Annelle or Roseanna."

"It's really bad luck for you that she didn't get that advice from someone else before she saw you," Smith said. "Did she ask you to see Lewis's future?"

"I'd never try to see the future of anyone who wasn't a client," Manfred said, rather shocked. "She wanted to talk to Morton first, and he . . . took her with him."

It was Smith's turn to look incredulous. "You're saying a dead man killed his own wife."

"No!" Manfred could feel his cheeks redden. "I'm not saying that at all." He took a deep breath. "When I called Morton, he was there in a flash. I was . . . startled, really. I was actually feeling kind of proud, thinking it was my great psychic prowess that drew him with so much speed. Now, I think he was just waiting for the call. I think he knew his wife was failing, and he wanted to be with her for the transition so she wouldn't be frightened."

Manfred had the familiar experience of watching a rational man try to cope with something he believed was irrational and incredible.

"Do you . . ." Arthur Smith stopped. He took a deep breath, then cocked his head from one side to another as if he were adjusting his neck bones. "Do you think Mrs. Goldthorpe knew she was dying?"

"No," Manfred said. He didn't have to think twice about it. "She did not. She was still really engaged with life. She knew she wasn't well, but she had no idea that something was happening in her body, something so drastic that it would kill her."

"You sound real certain."

"I am real certain. By the way, I've called Jess Barnwell in Fort Worth. He's represented me before."

"Good," Arthur said. "You need a lawyer. I've heard good things about Jess Barnwell. If something about Barnwell doesn't work out, you can try Magdalena Orta Powell in Davy."

"Lot of name," Manfred said, smiling.

"Lot of lawyer."

They both stood up. "Can you get rid of these people?" Manfred asked, his head jerking to the door.

"I can try," Arthur said, without much optimism. "I'll tell them they have to stay out of the yard."

"I'd appreciate that," Manfred said, and opened the door just enough for the sheriff to exit, his hat firmly in place on his head. Manfred tried not to listen to the questions the reporters were shouting.

Lucky I work at home, he thought. He glanced at his cell phone, which had not rung yet. He was uneasy. He'd expected to hear from Barnwell before now. He called the law office again. This time the secretary told him, "I'm sorry, Mr. Bernardo, but Mr. Barnwell says you need to seek other representation. He has done work for the Goldthorpe family before, and late yesterday he was engaged by Mr. Goldthorpe."

"But Morton Goldthorpe is dead."

"Mr. Lewis Goldthorpe." The voice was carefully neutral. Then she said, "I really am sorry," and hung up.

The next phone call Manfred made was to Magdalena Orta Powell. He was beginning to feel like a rabbit trying to find a safe place to hide from the crazy fox.

He spent a certain amount of time talking to her assistant, a man named Phil Van Zandt . . . not a name you'd soon forget. From Van Zandt's voice, Manfred believed he was talking to a man in his early twenties like Manfred himself, a man who was not from "these parts."

"Could you be here tomorrow at four, Mr. Bernardo?" Van Zandt asked, in the abstracted tone of someone looking at a schedule book and a computer screen. "She should be out of court by then."

"Phil, here's my situation. I live in Midnight, and I've got report-ers camped outside my door. I can't get out of my house without run-ning the gauntlet. If I have to, I have to, but I really don't want to do that. Is there any way Ms. Powell can come to my place?"

"I can just catch her. Hold on." There was an electronic buzz. Then some music kicked on. It didn't suck.

Phil was back in less than two minutes. "She can come to you on Monday at eleven," he said. "Before you get all excited, let me tell you her fee."

After a very practical discussion, finally Manfred understood his compulsion to work hard and save money, a compulsion that had driven him for the past few months.

It was so he could pay Magdalena Orta Powell.

7

Olivia needed to get groceries. She didn't do a lot of cooking in her little apartment—microwaving was more her speed—but she was out of Windex and close to being out of toilet paper, and she'd gotten up with a hankering for a sliced apple and vanilla fruit dip. With no idea that anything odd was going on, she stepped out the side door of the pawnshop to get in her car, only to see a small crowd hovering outside Manfred's place. The sheriff's car was there, too.

She ducked right back inside. She stood fuming for a moment. Then she swiveled on her heel and went through the pawnshop door. Bobo was reading in his favorite chair, a veritable poor man's throne upholstered in velvet. He was using his e-reader today, so she knew he was following his current program of reading one hundred great mystery and suspense novels. Olivia did not know who had created the list and how the selections had been picked, but she did admire Bobo's faithfulness to his agenda.

"What's going on out there?" she asked, jerking her thumb toward the rental house.

"Good morning to you," Bobo said, putting his e-reader down reluctantly. "I'm on number twenty-seven, which happens to be Dorothy L. Sayers's *The Unpleasantness at the Bellona Club*."

Olivia was not in the mood for Bobo's cleverness. "What. Is. Going. On?" she demanded.

"Yes," said Joe, coming in the front door just in time to hear her question. "What?"

"I stood out there and listened for a minute. Manfred's been accused of being a jewel thief, and it's been hinted that he killed the old lady," Bobo said. "You should know more about it than I do, since I hear you were on the spot." He gave Olivia a very level look.

"I had nothing to do with Manfred's situation," she said immediately. "Who's accused him? Of stealing what?"

Bobo said, "I only know what I overheard the reporters saying when I put my trash can out at the curb. And I've told you that."

Joe said, "I don't believe it for a second. Manfred? Nahhh."

Olivia fumed, though she kept it under a tight lid. She was smart enough about herself to know that she felt strongest and most effective in situations in which she could take control and take action. Not always the same thing . . . but often enough. "He didn't do it," she said.

"I agree with both of you," Bobo said. "He's an honest man in a charlatan's job. I don't think he had any more to do with that than he did the murder/suicide the same weekend. In the same hotel."

There was a substantial silence.

Olivia scowled. She did not exactly feel guilty. But she didn't feel happy, either. And she hated the proximity of the newspeople. The new proprietors of the hotel were bad enough. One reason she'd settled in Midnight was to avoid scrutiny . . . and because the place felt right. "I want this to go away," she said, and she thought, *I miss Lem.*

Bobo nodded. "Sure," he said. "I do, too."

Olivia threw herself into a chair, a violently flowered padded rocker. Furniture that landed in the pawnshop tended to stay there. "So you're seriously worried that he might be arrested?"

"Yeah, I am," he said. "I don't think he's guilty of anything, but the appearance of . . . well, being a psychic, that looks fraudulent. No matter what the truth is about that, it's not right for him to be accused by the son of this woman he was trying to help. For another thing, the reporters are going to be coming in and out of town as long as there's a story, and now they even have a place to stay right here in town, if the story gains traction. And they'll be dragging up Aubrey's murder and the Lovells' disappearance." The Lovell family had run Gas N Go prior to their sudden departure from Midnight. Aubrey Hamilton, Bobo's former girlfriend, had been found dead in a riverbed north of town.

Olivia thought about the situation for a few minutes. Her eyes went from Joe's face to Bobo's. Bobo was good about letting people think, one of his many fine qualities. Before she'd gotten to know Lemuel, Olivia had wondered why she didn't feel any particular appreciation for Bobo as a man. *He's too much rose, not enough thorn,* she concluded, as she pondered ways of getting the reporters out of Midnight.

Joe said, "A few minutes ago one of the reporters came to get her nails done. She asked Chuy to hurry in case something broke in the story, but she was tired of standing outside Manfred's door. So maybe they'll just get bored and leave."

"Fat fucking chance," Olivia said, and Bobo nodded. They were far more media savvy than Joe. The tinkle of the bell over the door made them all turn in that direction.

To Olivia's utter amazement (and from their faces, Bobo's and Joe's as well), the Rev walked into Midnight Pawn. And he was holding the hand of a little boy.

Olivia could count on the fingers of one hand the times she'd seen the Rev in the pawnshop. The Rev's orbit, besides a very rare shopping trip, included his home, the Wedding Chapel and Pet Cemetery, Home Cookin Restaurant . . . and nothing else, unless there was an extreme emergency.

Therefore, this was such an emergency.

And right after the door swung shut on the Rev and the little boy, it opened again to admit Fiji, who had a basket on her arm.

"Following the Yellow Brick Road, Feej?" Bobo asked. "Hi, Rev. Hi, young man." He walked over to squat down in front of the boy.

Of course, Olivia thought, half-exasperated. *He would love kids.* "Rev," she said. "What can we do for you?" She watched Fiji flow around the Rev and come to a stop close to the boy, look at him intently. She opened the basket and out jumped Mr. Snuggly.

Mr. Snuggly immediately went to the boy and stood at his feet, looking up. The boy had dark brown hair, long and tangled. He wore denim shorts and a *Walking Dead* T-shirt, which was an unusual choice for a child his apparent age. But what was that?

"Hail, little brother," said Mr. Snuggly in his small shrill voice. With a movement too quick to track, the boy was on his knees in front of the cat, peering into his face. Suddenly, the boy smiled. It was bewitching. He looked up at Fiji, and Olivia could see that his eyes were pansy purple.

"Okay, I'm in love," Fiji said cheerfully. "Hey, kid. I'm Fiji. This is Mr. Snuggly."

"I'm Diederik," the boy said.

"I'm Bobo." Bobo extended his hand to the boy, who took it uncertainly. They shook, in an awkward way. Shaking didn't seem to be a custom with which the boy was familiar. To Olivia's surprise, Joe opened his arms and the boy stepped into them without hesitation. They hugged briefly, and the boy moved away.

"And I'm Olivia," she said, taking a step forward.

He looked up at her, and Olivia had the sensation that she was being weighed and measured. He did not extend his hand, but he gave her a respectful nod. Olivia was quite content with that, even flattered. Then something happened to the boy's face. His turned it up and rotated it as if he were following a scent.

"What's that smell?" he asked the Rev.

The Rev bent over and whispered in the boy's ear.

"Ahhhhh," the boy said, as if a suspicion had been confirmed.

The Rev straightened and looked at all of them, in turn. "Diederik's going to be staying with me for a while. His daddy's got to do a few things."

Olivia could think of at least five questions she wanted to ask, but this was the Reverend Emilio Sheehan, and he had many secrets. She knew she had better not ask any questions. It would be taken amiss. You didn't want to be on the wrong side of the Rev.

"We're glad to have you, young man," Bobo said. "You're welcome to come hang out with me here at the store any time, if the Rev has other stuff to do."

"Or with me, at the Inquiring Mind," Fiji said, as warm as melting butter.

"I can take you bow hunting," Olivia offered stiffly. She liked the way the boy had known right away she deserved respect. *Or at least I could comb your hair,* she thought. Grooming was something else Olivia understood.

"Thanks," the boy said, to all of them, and he seemed pleased, though his tone was noncommittal.

"In the meantime," the Rev said, obviously coming to his main point, "what are all these people doing in town? The hotel was bad enough." He'd taken off his dusty hat, and his thinning black hair was combed across his skull, damp with sweat.

"Sit down," Bobo suggested. "I'll tell you." They all sat, except the boy, who didn't seem much interested in what the adults were saying. He roamed around the shop making scarcely a sound, his big purple eyes taking in all the oddities and peculiarities around him, his mouth slightly open in wonder. Olivia remembered the first time she'd been in Midnight Pawn, and she could understand his fascination.

Four years ago. She'd been on her way to Dallas to get a flight to— where? Somewhere east. She'd completed a job east of Marthasville, an old rancher who wouldn't sell his land to a man with a lot of money. She almost never left from the same airport she'd flown into, and never under the same name. That day, for the first time, she'd seen the exit for Midnight and Davy on the highway.

A town called Midnight. The name had caught her fancy.

She'd been in no hurry, so she'd taken the exit. And she'd seen the closed storefronts, but the pawnshop . . . stuck at a crossroad in what seemed like to her the middle of nowhere . . . had been fascinating.

She'd had to go in.

And she'd been captivated by the cases full of old things, mysterious things. The shelves had seemed crowded with objects she had to handle. She'd looked for a long time. When Bobo, the new proprietor, had told her gently that he needed to close for an hour to get his supper, she'd driven up to eat in Davy (not trusting the Home Cookin Restaurant, wisely, because then it had been run by an old couple who had never been able to cook as well as Madonna Reed). But after a hasty hamburger and tonic water in Davy, she'd found herself going back to the pawnshop, which was so much larger inside than it appeared to be on the outside. Since it was dark by then, she'd met Lemuel.

She had never met anyone like him before. She didn't know how he'd felt about her that night, but she'd been drawn to him, powerfully. Olivia had been in the presence of hundreds of men who were better looking and richer and more powerful in a worldly way. And she'd known Lemuel for what he was immediately. But Lemuel . . . something in the age of him, the strength of him, the ruthlessness of him, drew her in.

That night, the little sign behind the cash register, which she hadn't noticed at all during her earlier visit, suddenly seemed to leap out at her. APARTMENT DOWNSTAIRS FOR RENT, with no other information. "It was waiting for the right person to read it," Lemuel had said afterward, and Olivia believed that was so.

They hadn't become lovers right away. They were both cautious people, even when biology and inclination were herding them in the same direction. It was like they took their honeymoon first, their time of learning each other, in a bubble large enough only for two.

Lost in remembering something rare, Olivia only came back to the pawnshop and the little boy when the Rev said, "When is Lem coming back, Olivia?" That was very direct, for the Rev.

Olivia said, "He's taken those books and gone to consult friends of his. Right now he's in New York." She didn't spell it out; the magic books, the ones Lemuel had been searching for in the pawnshop all those years, had been found by Bobo by sheer accident, and Lemuel was having a wonderful time looking through them. But some had been in a language so ancient Lemuel didn't have a clue as to how to translate the text, so off he'd gone, the first time he'd left Midnight for any length of time in over a hundred years.

She hadn't offered to go with him. He'd have asked her to go if he'd wanted her to, and though she'd hoped, and mentally shifted her obligations around just in case, he hadn't mentioned it.

The Rev waited, expectant.

"I don't know when he'll return," she said calmly. "When he's done what he set out to do, I suppose."

"Can you call him?"

"I can, but I won't," she said. "He's having a great time, and he deserves it."

She did not know that at all. She had heard from Lem only twice since his departure: once after he'd found no help in Atlanta, and again when he'd tracked down a possible translator in Minnesota, who'd not been able to help but had referred him to a vampire in New York.

She had told herself that to Lemuel, a week was like a moment. To her, it was like a week. Or two. And she had reminded herself that he did not like the telephone, though he knew how to use it. Lemuel had a cell phone, and from it he had texted her briefly at each stop. Nothing else.

The Rev looked grave, as if he could read her thoughts. But he didn't say anything more about Lemuel. Instead, he said, "We have to get all those people out of Midnight." He jerked his head to his right, to indicate Manfred's house. The boy had his back to the Rev. He'd wandered to the first set of shelves to stare inside a glass case at a ukulele. It appeared to be older than any of the people in the room.

"We all want that," Bobo said, between sideways looks at Diederik. Olivia knew they were all trying to figure out what made Diederik so special. "But I don't think there's a short-term way to make that happen."

Fiji was fidgeting, and finally she said, "Bobo, do you have a brush or comb handy?"

"There's one under the counter," he said, and after a moment's search she came up with a small hairbrush. She looked at it dubiously, but she took a deep breath and advanced on Diederik with a determined look.

"Come on, young man," she said. "You and this so-called brush need to meet each other." Diederik looked alarmed, but he reacted to the authority in Fiji's voice and came over to stand in front of her. She turned him around so his back was to her, and then she went to work on his dark hair. Seeing how gentle Fiji's hands were, Olivia turned a little away so she wouldn't have to watch.

The boy did look less like a feral child when Fiji had finished.

"While you're fiddling with the boy, we need to talk about the situation," the Rev said. "Olivia!"

"Yes?" Olivia straightened and looked at the older man. His clothes might be ancient, his hair thinning, and his body small, but when the Rev spoke, you listened, and you listened good.

"You have to find this missing jewelry so they know Manfred doesn't have it. Then they will leave."

"Why me?" she said angrily.

"Because you're a thief," the Rev said, and there was no judgment in his voice. "You can figure out where a thief would hide such a thing."

He could have said worse things, and they would have been true, so Olivia felt a moment of relief. But she wasn't pleased with the way everyone was carefully avoiding her eyes, and she felt the cold feeling creeping across her, the feeling she got when everyone's hand was against her.

"Why should I help Manfred?" she asked. "I hardly know him."

"Olivia," the Rev said. One word. But it was enough.

"I'll do my best," she said. "But I'd better be able to count on any help I call on the rest of you to give."

"I'll help," Fiji said instantly. Despite the fact that her attention was apparently focused on Diederik, she'd been listening. Now she pulled an elastic band from the pocket of her skirt.

Of course she'd have one, Olivia thought. *Of course she'd be ready to help.* But there was no sting to these thoughts. Olivia had finally accepted the fact that Fiji was simply that kind of person.

"I'll help however you ask me," Bobo said.

Joe hesitated for a moment. "Chuy and I will do what we can," he said cautiously. "And, of course, Rasta is always ready to help," Joe added, and everyone laughed except the Rev and the boy.

Olivia nodded to show she'd registered their offers.

Fiji had put Diederik's hair back in a neat ponytail. He looked like a different kid. He looked older.

"Rev, Diederik here needs to take a bath," Olivia said, so Fiji wouldn't have all the grooming to herself. "And he needs clean clothes."

The Rev looked at the boy as if he were seeing him for the first time. "If you say so," he said. "Diederik, I have to take care of you right. I promised your father." He turned to look at the rest of them. "The chapel will be empty for a while. Keep an eye on it. I have a funeral today at four. A cat named Meatball."

Mr. Snuggly froze in the act of licking his paw. He made a sound that was close to that of coughing. Olivia realized that the cat was laughing.

"That's worse than 'Mr. Snuggly'?" Olivia murmured. The cat gave her a disdainful look.

The Rev left without any more words, taking Diederik's hand again as if Diederik were a three-year-old instead of . . . Well, how old was he? Olivia watched the ill-assorted pair as they went to the Rev's house, presumably to put Diederik in the bathtub. She said, "You figure he's eight years old?"

Fiji frowned. "Last night I thought he was a lot younger. His clothes flapped on him."

Bobo shrugged. "I think he might be as much as eleven."

Fiji was returning Mr. Snuggly to the basket. "I'd believe eleven," she said. "And today his clothes are tight."

Joe said, "I wonder how old he'll be tomorrow." And he left without adding to his statement. They all stared after him.

"I wonder what he knows," Fiji said.

Olivia, bored with the conversation, said, "I've got to go over to talk to Manfred. I'll call him first." She went down to her apartment to get her cell phone.

When it was in her hand, she was tempted—once again—to call Lemuel.

But she didn't.

8

As he'd been instructed, Manfred was waiting at his back door to let Olivia in. She'd run across the side-by-side driveways and reached the door so swiftly that some reporters weren't sure they'd seen anyone. Manfred was able to close and lock the door behind her before any of them could make a move.

"Boy, am I glad to see you. Uh, can I get you a drink or something?" Manfred's first impression was not reassuring. Olivia the Deadly seemed irritated and tired. He had hoped for Superwoman, but he'd gotten something less. He tried to conceal his dismay.

"Yeah," she said. "Some water would be good."

They sat at the little table that he'd crammed into the kitchen and regarded each other steadily. "The Rev has appointed me to get you out of this," she said, not making any pretense at sounding happy about it.

"Why? I mean, he and I aren't exactly buddies."

"He has this kid staying with him. Diederik. There's some big mystery about him." One corner of Olivia's mouth dipped down wryly. There was always a mystery. "The Rev doesn't want reporters anywhere around this kid, is what I gather. So he wants them gone. The quickest way to do that is to solve your problem."

"Do you think . . ." Manfred trailed to a halt.

"That I can do it?" Olivia smiled, not troubling to make it a socially acceptable smile. "If anyone in Midnight can and will, it's me." She regarded the psychic. "You know I have skills, right?"

"Ah . . . I figured. But." He floundered for a moment. "The thing is, Olivia, your skill set, as far as I know, is kind of drastic."

"Awwww . . . squeamish?" The shark smile was very much in evidence. Olivia was enjoying being herself.

"Yes," Manfred admitted. "More than you, anyway. I hope we can find a way to solve this problem without doing anything . . . undoable."

"I was never as young as you." She looked away for a long moment before turning back to say, "I'm going to do this whether you approve of it or not. This is a town issue, not just your problem. So tell me what's happened."

Okay, this is what I've got to work with, Manfred told himself. "Arthur Smith was here this morning right on the heels of the newspeople. Lewis Goldthorpe's accused me of stealing jewelry from Rachel. My client who died," he added. "And as it turns out, she might not have died of natural causes. But they haven't gotten all the bloodwork results back yet."

"What do they suspect?"

"Arthur asked a lot of questions about her water bottle. I got the impression that he'd been told it might have had something in it that shouldn't have been there."

"Something you didn't drop in?" She raised an eyebrow.

"Don't make a joke of this," he said. "You know I didn't. And I'm pretty scared, in case you couldn't tell."

Manfred expected her to say something cutting, but instead,

Olivia simply nodded. "Okay, then the first step is to determine where Lewis has stashed the jewelry he says you stole. Because we're going to assume that he's hidden it. Why do you think he's doing this? And where do you think he's put it?"

"I've had a couple of hours to think about it. First, Lewis is crazy. But he's also devious and shrewd, at least according to Rachel. She talked about him a lot. Lewis and his problems were the main reason she was so hung up on keeping contact with her dead husband."

"Which you were glad to help her do." Olivia didn't exactly sneer, but Manfred thought it was a close thing.

"Yes," he said evenly. "I was glad to help her. And it was easy to reach him. He was more accessible than a lot of spirits."

Olivia's mouth crimped in a skeptical line. "All right," she said. "I'll go along with that. To get back to the subject. Why does Lewis have such a hard-on for you?"

"First, because he never liked Rachel to spend money he thought she should leave intact for him. Second, because a lot of the advice Morton gave her was about curtailing Lewis's schemes. And she followed that advice. Third, because Lewis became convinced I was angling to marry Rachel."

Olivia raised a questioning eyebrow.

"No, of course not," Manfred said. He tried a smile. "Rachel was a sweet woman, but she was older than my mother. Not my thing."

"So you believe Lewis has stolen this jewelry and pinned it on you to get even. Also so he can sell the jewelry, I presume?"

"I believe Rachel hid it to keep Lewis from stealing it from her. That's what she told me."

"So she didn't have it with her at all. When are you supposed to have gotten this jewelry?"

"Lewis is alleging that Rachel had it in her purse because she was going to get it appraised. He maintains that I rifled her purse before I called the front desk for help."

"I was in the lobby when she dropped her purse," Olivia said.

Manfred stared at her. "You were?"

"I helped her pick up everything. Me and some other people. And there was nothing like a jewelry case in there. So I know you're telling the truth. I'm going to assume you didn't even touch her purse?"

"No," Manfred said firmly. "I did not."

"I also assume the police tested it for fingerprints and didn't find yours."

"I assume the same thing."

"Since she told you she'd hidden the jewelry—what did she have, by the way?"

"She mentioned diamonds and rubies, I think."

"Okay, so she told you she'd hidden it from Lewis. Where might she have done that? It would almost certainly be at her house. When people hide things, they want to keep them close."

"Since she'd been sick and she'd been staying close to home, that would be my guess, too. I hoped she would get a safe-deposit box, but I don't think she did. She wouldn't have said 'hidden' if she'd put the jewelry in a bank. She would have told me it was safe."

Olivia nodded. "So, it's in the house. You've been there, I hope?"

"Yes." Manfred clearly didn't recall the visit with any enthusiasm. "I didn't want to go, but after our first face-to-face session, she insisted I see where Morton had lived."

"Surely that's pretty unusual?"

"Oh, absolutely. Usually, people are at least a little embarrassed about going to a psychic. But not Rachel. She wanted me to meet her family. She was so excited about being in touch with her husband again."

Olivia had a strange half smile on her face. "So you actually met the family?"

"Yeah, I told Arthur Smith about it. I met Roseanna and Annelle, the daughters. I admit I was worried about what they'd think, that they'd picture me as some kind of gigolo. Lewis made a huge deal out of not meeting me. That time." He told Olivia about the time Lewis had come pounding on the door during his next session with Rachel. "So after I met him, I wished I hadn't. And let me point out that while I was at her house, the daughters didn't bring their husbands or children. Again, I don't blame them. They didn't know what I'd be like."

"That's fascinating," Olivia said insincerely. "What I really need to know is the layout of the house."

"It's big," Manfred said. That had been the thing that had struck him most forcefully. He had never been in a house that large. "It's six thousand square feet, she told me. It's two stories. It's in a long, narrow, lot. There are surveillance cameras on the front yard and the backyard."

"Gated community?" Olivia had brought a small notepad, and now she was writing in it.

"Oh . . . no. It's in Bonnet Park, like Vespers is. But the neighborhood where Rachel lived is really old and snooty. Her house is set back from the street, with tall hedges on both sides between it and the neighbors. There's a swimming pool in back, below the terrace."

"Can you draw me a layout of the ground floor?"

Manfred thought about that. "I think so," he said. "I didn't go in every room, of course, but I did kind of a sketchy house tour. Once she got me there, Rachel wanted to show me every room. It was awkward . . . for everyone but Rachel."

Slowly, Manfred drew the plan for the ground floor, with many erasures. It contained the formal living room, a dining room, a family den, the kitchen and pantry, and a game room, plus two bathrooms; one off the game room, and one between the kitchen and the family den, with a doorway onto the hall. "The terrace and pool are off the French doors in the family den," he said, "but there's also a hall that runs the length of the house and leads right out to it. Of course, that's where the pool house is, to the right of the swimming pool. There's a U-shaped driveway out front for visitors, and a driveway that goes all the way behind the house for family. I guess there's a garage back there. I forget."

"You have a good memory," Olivia said.

"I'd never been in a house like that." He could remember how impressed he'd been and how he'd struggled to look as though he took all this absolutely for granted. He remembered, too, how hard all this space and opulence had been to reconcile with Rachel Goldthorpe, who had been such a comfortable woman to be with, just like any grandmother he'd see at a church or a Denny's.

"Okay, what about the second floor?" Olivia looked at him expectantly.

"I'm sketchier on that. I just walked through really quickly. I didn't want to scare the daughters, so I was paying more attention to having a good conversation with them, telling them a little about my own family, trying to put them at ease."

"Someday I'd like to hear about that," Olivia said.

"When you tell me about yours, I'll tell you about mine," Manfred said. Olivia gave him a very hard look, and he knew he'd hit a nerve.

"Do the best you can with the second floor," she said, pointing at the pad and paper.

So Manfred tried. "Okay, you go up the front stairs . . . then you reach a landing, and turn, and up more stairs. There's the open area over the entryway, which is two-story, and the first room on the right you come to is Lewis's room—when he was a kid. It has its own bathroom. The girls' rooms are next, and there's a bathroom in between 'em. Of course, they're not being used now. The other side of the hall is kind of the grown-up side. First, there's Morton's office. Or maybe she called it a library? It has a little bathroom. Next to it, and huge, is the master bedroom. I just peeked in there. Some of the windows overlook the side of the house, and there's a balcony, a big one, over-looking the pool at the back and the pool house. Where Lewis is staying now."

"How long ago was this?"

"Two years, maybe. It was the first time I'd been to a client's home, and the first set of one-on-one readings I'd done on my own." He smiled, a little wryly. "And in case you haven't picked up on it, I was really stunned by the size of the house. I'd never seen anything like it."

Olivia's expression was completely neutral as she looked down to the floor plans he'd drawn. Even without touching her, it was easy for Manfred to tell that she'd grown up in a house that large, or larger. She said, "The bigger the house, the more hiding places."

Manfred gave himself a moment to feel smug. He'd called that one— her voice was the voice of knowledge. "I'm sure you can pare down the possibilities," he said.

"How's that?"

"When you're hiding something, you want it under your surveil-lance, right? That's human nature. As you said earlier, she'd want to keep it close. She would hide jewelry in a place she dominated. Since Lewis had moved back, that would be a limited number of places." Manfred shrugged. "I know she liked to garden, so it's possible she hid 'em in the yard, but given her poor health in the past few weeks, I'd probably give up on everything else before I started looking outside."

"So noted. Her bedroom would be the most likely, since she would be fairly sure he wouldn't come in if she was around. He'd be in the kitchen pretty often, getting a drink or a snack. The downstairs hall bathroom would be out, since he'd use it regularly. Not the dining room or the formal living room downstairs. I'd put the probabilities in this order: her bedroom, her bathroom, Morton's office next door, then the kitchen, then the other downstairs rooms, then the empty upstairs bedrooms and bathrooms, then outside in the yard."

Manfred nodded. "That all makes sense. So what do we do?"

"I break and enter," Olivia said. "If I get lucky, we're home free. If not, I'll do some reconnaissance. Based on that, I'll make a plan. I don't think Lewis would accuse you if he were in possession of the jewels. They'd be part of the estate, and he'd get at least a third of the value of them in due course, if she divided her assets into three parts. I'm sure Rachel did hide them, as she told you, and I'm also sure he hasn't found them yet. But you can bet he'll try, when he realizes you really don't have them. Maybe he's just blaming you for their disappearance so he doesn't have to share them with his sisters."

Without further words, she was up and at the back door. She cracked it slightly and peered outside. No one had come into the backyard; evidently the sheriff's threats had been effective.

"You know," she said over her shoulder, "the easiest way out of this would be to kill Lewis."

"I'd much rather you didn't," Manfred said.

Olivia raised one shoulder and let it fall. "All right." Just as quickly as she'd arrived, Olivia departed, vanishing up the steps and into the side door of the pawnshop like smoke.

9

The Rev strode down Witch Light Road, Diederik at his heels. The boy was washed and groomed. Joe smiled from his shop window. It had been a long time since he'd been around a person so young, and he found it made him feel happy. The Rev was making his usual beeline to the Wedding Chapel and Pet Cemetery at his usual time.

Hurrying out the shop door, Joe caught up with the ill-assorted duo just as the Rev mounted the steps to the chapel. "Good morning," he said, and the Rev turned to give Joe a brisk nod. Diederik smiled. He looked like a different child with his hair brushed and his clothes clean, not to mention a scrubbed face. "Fiji?" Joe said, and the Rev nodded stiffly.

"She came by last night with some clothes for the boy," the Rev said. "They seem to fit."

"I like them," Diederik said. He had a marked accent, though Joe wasn't sure where he'd acquired it. Not Spanish or Russian, the two accents Joe knew the best.

"Rev, I wondered if you could spare Diederik this morning," Joe said, carefully. "Chuy and I could use some help in the store, and we'd enjoy having a visitor."

The Rev considered. "He's under my care," he said warningly. "You know what that means."

"Yes, sir, I know," Joe said. "And we will protect him as though he were our own."

The Rev nodded. "Then keep him close and call me if anything arises. I will come by for him." With no further ado, the older man in his rusty black turned his back on them and entered the chapel, the weathered brown door closing behind him with a *thunk*.

Diederik looked up at Joe. The boy seemed a little worried.

"You haven't met my friend Chuy," Joe said. "You'll like him. Our shop is back this way." They walked west on Witch Light Road, and then across it to the north side.

"Chuy, look who I brought with me," Joe called as they came in.

"Good," Chuy said. He was bent over the manicure station working on a customer. Joe was not too surprised to find that Fiji was getting her nails done, though that was a rare occurrence. "Chuy, this is Diederik," Joe said formally. "And you remember Miss Fiji?"

Fiji just happened to have brought a basket of muffins and a thermos of orange juice with her. When she offered some to Diederik, his whole face lit up. "We had oatmeal at the Rev's house," the boy said in his oddly accented English. "It was fine," he added politely. "But these are very good. And thank you for my clothes."

Fiji smiled. "Glad you like the muffins *and* the clothes." Chuy was painting her nails a creamy light orange, and after Diederik had consumed a muffin, he came close to watch. He was fascinated by the process. "Does your mom get manicures?" Chuy asked.

"I never saw her do that," the boy said. He looked suddenly, profoundly unhappy.

"How old are you, Diederik?" Fiji said instantly, trying to erase the unhappiness.

"I am not as old as I look, but we grow up faster than . . ." The boy hesitated. "Most people," he finished.

"You look like you're about ten years old," Fiji said, smiling. Then she looked at him again. "Or maybe older," she added.

"Oh! I'm not." Diederik laughed, but he also looked a little anxious.

Joe noticed that the boy had dodged saying whether he was older or younger, and he had to respect the boy's privacy, though he was just as curious as Fiji. They glanced at each other; Joe understood that she would not question the boy further.

After Joe had finished Fiji's manicure, he asked Diederik to sweep up around the station after wiping it down, and Diederik jumped at the chance to be useful. This was a boy who really wanted to be busy, a boy who wasn't used to sitting idle, much less kneeling in the bleak chapel with the Rev in meditation. Joe made a mental note to suggest to the Rev it was probably time to weed the pet cemetery and do the lawn mowing and bush trimming behind the chapel in the confines of the high fence. The pet cemetery was the prettiest place in Midnight, aside from Fiji's yard, which always had flowers in bloom except in the dead of winter.

"Maybe tomorrow," Fiji was saying, as if she'd read Joe's thoughts, "you can come to help me in my garden in the morning. Have you ever done yard work?"

"No, ma'am," he said.

"If I show you what weeds to pull, I'm sure you can do that. It would be a big help to me. I won't be torn between the shop and the yard." Fiji looked happy. "I'll stop by the chapel to see if I can clear that with the Rev."

Diederik looked pleased. "Thanks, and have a nice day," he said, just like a flight attendant when the passengers were exiting the plane. "Maybe I will see you tomorrow. Thank you for the muffins and orange juice." Fiji left with an empty basket.

"Whoever brought him up did it right," Chuy murmured. Diederik did a good job of cleaning the manicure station. Next he helped Joe dust all the antiques. Joe showed him a secret drawer in an old desk, which Diederik found appropriately cool. Chuy remembered he had a set of jacks left by a client's child, and after he taught Diederik how to play, the boy enjoyed it very much.

And he was unbelievably fast.

By and by, it was time for lunch. Joe and Chuy took Diederik across the street to Home Cookin and introduced him to Madonna and little Grady.

Oddly, Diederik didn't seem to know what to make of Grady, especially when he found out Grady was over a year old. Grady was going from stool to stool in front of the counter, but he didn't seem to mind being lifted into his playpen when Madonna was too busy cooking and serving to keep an eye on him. She always acknowledged offers to watch him with dignified thanks, but clearly she was sure it was her job to keep the baby from harm. Madonna was not one to share her thoughts or emotions, so it surprised everyone (but Diederik) when she said, "I am sure ready for someone to come in to manage the Gas N Go, someone permanent, so Teacher can be here to help me more."

After they'd absorbed this, Joe said, "He hasn't heard from the owners?"

"Oh, he has," she said, pouring more iced tea from the jug. "But they keep saying no one wants the job permanently, even though it'll come with the house, which the owners rented to . . . the previous family."

None of them wanted to talk about the previous manager of the filling station/store. Or his kids.

When their food came, Diederik ate every scrap on his plate. There was no conversation once the food was in front of him; he consumed it with single-minded concentration. He only paused to raise a hand to greet Fiji, who'd come in to pick up her lunch to take back to her shop. After he'd wiped his mouth with his napkin, as he saw the others doing, he seemed to be thinking hard about something.

"This is a good place," Diederik said suddenly. "Why is it hard to find someone who would live here?"

"We like it here just fine," Joe said. "But I guess, for a lot of people, there's just not enough going on, and they don't like to drive to Davy or even farther to do their serious shopping."

"But there are wide-open spaces, and you can see people coming. And there aren't many peoples," Diederik said, sweeping his arm to indicate the vastness of the country around them. His accent became more pronounced, and Joe tried to figure it out. But he hadn't traveled much. He glanced at Chuy, who gave a tiny shrug. Chuy didn't know, either. "That's wonderful. It's safer."

Fiji looked worried at the inference that Diederik was used to living in danger, but she didn't speak. Joe gave her an approving smile. He liked Fiji for her warm heart, but at the same time, it was what occasionally made her indiscreet.

It was a good moment for Bobo to come in, the sun lighting up his hair like a halo, an irony that made Joe smile. Diederik smiled when Bobo entered, too; everyone did, especially Fiji. It was the charm of the man, and Joe was sure that charm would last until Bobo was old, if he was fortunate enough to live that long.

"The reporters are getting bored hanging around Manfred's, and some of them are heading this way," Bobo said.

Diederik looked from one adult to the other, trying to figure out if he should be scared. Joe said, "Diederik, we're going to leave out the back door and drive to Davy. Have you ever had ice cream?"

The boy shook his head. "What is it?"

"Something really good," Fiji said. "You're going to have a great time."

"Explain to the Rev," Joe told Chuy. "Okay, buddy, here we go!" He extended a hand to the boy, and Diederik took it without hesitation. They made their way through the kitchen, with a wave to Madonna, and then they were outside. Joe and the boy walked back to the street, peering around the corner of Home Cookin until the little gaggle of reporters went inside. Then they crossed Witch Light Road and walked to the parking area behind the store to climb into Joe's truck. Diederik buckled his seat belt without Joe saying a word, and in short order they were headed north on the Davy highway.

Joe smiled at the boy. "I think you're really going to like ice cream," he said, and he was right.

10

The next day, Olivia turned onto Old Pioneer Street, which lay in the heart of Bonnet Park. Most of the houses on Old Pioneer had been built in the sixties and seventies, or earlier. They were positioned strategically on narrow, deep lots, and all had well-established lawns and plantings. Though many had been renovated, refurbished, and repaired, they had one thing in common: They were sizable, and they made a statement.

Eyeing the numbers on the brick pillar mailboxes, Olivia turned into the gravel drive of the third house on the right. Visitors were clearly supposed to take the right turn onto the circle around a large rosebed full of mature plants, all in bloom. Only the family or trades-men would continue to the back of the house. Or a gardener, like the young man at work on the roses. He appeared to be Hispanic and maybe nineteen. He was snipping the deadheads and tossing them into a bucket. He was very curious about Olivia's arrival. He turned to watch as she parked in front of the house.

Olivia's feet crunched on the gravel as she went up the shallow steps to the double front doors and knocked. She was a blonde at the moment, and she wore blue contacts and bright red lipstick to complement her dramatic eye makeup. Her sleeveless blouse was a bright print, and her trousers were navy blue.

"Yes?" said the maid who answered the door. She was Hispanic, and short. Her hair was thick and long and still solid black, though the wrinkles around her mouth and eyes put her in her forties. "Can I help you?" She craned a little to the side to see the young man working in the rosebed.

"I'm Rebecca Mansfield from Home Health," Olivia said, her voice solid with confidence. She waited.

"I'm Bertha," said the woman, reluctantly. "I'm the housekeeper. What can I do for you?"

"Nice to meet you, Bertha. We got a signed application from Mrs. Goldthorpe about receiving our services." She had a messenger bag slung across her chest, and a clipboard. The combined force of these authority symbols was just too much for the maid, who stepped back to let Olivia enter. The moment Olivia was inside, she moved swiftly to the center of the foyer, and her eyes got busy taking in everything. It was the scale she needed. To her pleasure, she found that Manfred's floor plan had been more detailed than she'd ever expected.

Bertha, who was clad in scrubs in lieu of a maid's uniform, said, "Miss Mansfield, Mrs. Goldthorpe passed away."

"She what?" Olivia looked at the woman, apparently shocked.

"She died of pneumonia, or something," Bertha said. "So we don't need any home health care. You want to talk to her daughter, Annelle? She's upstairs."

"Of course," said Olivia-as-Rebecca. "I'm so sorry. Ah, she did agree to our terms. . . ." Olivia felt she might not make it past Bertha if she didn't hint that money might be involved.

"Yes, ma'am. I'll get her." The maid turned to go up the stairs.

"I'll just come with you," Rebecca said. "I don't want to drag her away from whatever she's doing."

Bertha looked at her doubtfully but led Rebecca up the stairs and into the large room that was the second left after the landing. Yes, Manfred had been right. This was clearly the master bedroom. A woman who must be Annelle was standing in the doorway of a walk-in closet, looking tired and sad. She was short and plump, though not nearly as plump as her mother had been, and her hair was dark brown and graying just a bit.

Annelle was surprised to see someone she didn't know, and not pleased. "Who is this, Bertha?" she said, making a visible effort to pull herself together.

"This is Miss Mansfield from Home Health," Bertha said carefully. "Your mom must have filled out some forms?"

"Oh, for God's sake," Annelle said incredulously. "What else is going to happen? Why'd she do that?"

Bertha remained, looking curious, too. "I didn't know anything about it, Miss Annelle," she said rather smugly.

"Miss Mansfield?" Annelle was looking at her doubtfully. "I'm Annelle Kling, Mrs. Goldthorpe's daughter. I'm afraid you didn't get the news that my mom passed away very suddenly."

"Bertha just told me. I'm so sorry for intruding on your grief," Olivia lied. "We had an appointment set up with Mrs. Goldthorpe a few days ago, but when we rang the bell, no one answered, and when we left a phone message, we didn't hear back. So my office sent me by to do a wellness check. We get worried when we don't get a response from an elderly client."

"Even when they haven't signed up for your service? That's real customer devotion," Annelle said, an edge to her voice. "Or are you trying to tell me that my mom's estate owes your company money?

Because I've got to tell you, my dad's will wasn't even out of probate, and now my mom's passed away, and there's just no telling when this will all be settled."

"Not at all," Olivia said, emphatically. "She had signed a preliminary contract, but of course under the circumstances we wouldn't dream of trying to enforce . . . That's not how we do business. Her insurance policy was going to pay for it in full, anyway."

Annelle looked relieved, though Olivia got the impression it wasn't over the money situation, but all about not facing any more paperwork. "Oh, okay, good," she said. She took a deep breath, preparatory to telling Olivia good-bye, so Olivia babbled on.

"It's just that almost all of our clients are elderly—your mother was relatively young!—and so often at that age memory is not quite what it was. We worry when people that age don't respond, to put it simply."

Annelle seemed to be taken aback. "I'm sorry, I didn't mean to imply you were being . . . overzealous. We've just had people coming out of the woodwork to try to claim my mother owed them money, and all those claims have been spurious. I apologize if I seem too suspicious."

Not suspicious enough, Olivia thought. "No problem," she said. "Your mother seemed to be such a sweet lady. I'm very sorry to hear of your loss. I don't want to cause you any further trouble, but might I visit a ladies' room before I go to my next appointment?"

Annelle did her best to hide her exasperation. She was clearly anxious to get back to the painful but necessary task of cleaning out her mother's closet. "Sure," she said. "Since you're in here, you might as well use Mother's, behind that door." She pointed to a door in the north wall of the room.

"Thanks so much," Olivia said, pushing open the indicated door. She closed it firmly behind her, dumped her bag and clipboard on the vanity, and looked around. Since there was no way she would get to search the bedroom, she would look around the bathroom as long as she dared. She actually sat on the toilet while she searched the area, and after as thorough an examination as she could assay in a believable length of time, she flushed the toilet and started the water in the sink, while giving the inside of the medicine cabinet and the storage cabinet quick but intensive scans.

Nothing. Not a crack or crevice that wasn't normal building practice. No false back or revolving shelves or little holes in the floor. Though she didn't have time to go through the lower cabinet, below the sink, she had a super-quick look to verify there was nothing suspicious.

Dammit.

When she came out of the bathroom, wiser only in a negative way—she was fairly sure nothing was hidden there, and she hadn't learned anything more interesting besides the fact that Rachel Goldthorpe had had a great Mary Kay saleswoman in her neighborhood—Olivia made her good-byes and renewed her condolences to Annelle Goldthorpe Kling before going down the carpeted stairs and out to the front courtyard. She was not a hell of a lot wiser than she had been when she drove up. At least she felt more familiar with the layout. She'd confirmed that Manfred was a good observer, and she felt more comfortable with the plans he'd made of the house.

Now she had to decide what to do next.

The young gardener was still at work, though in a leisurely way, when she reemerged onto the gravel. Olivia was conscious of his stare as she opened the car door to let some of the trapped heat escape from the interior before she got in. She tossed in the messenger bag and clipboard, when her wandering thoughts were recalled by the sudden appearance of an unprepossessing and angry man. He didn't come from the front of the house, but came around the house on the gravel driveway from the backyard . . . perhaps the guesthouse? Her inner alarm system told her there was something to watch out for in this man, and she always listened to that system with great attention.

This must be Lewis Goldthorpe; he looked enough like his sister to make her guess almost a certainty, even if the first words out of his mouth hadn't been, "I'm Lewis Goldthorpe. This is my house. What are you doing here?"

Her hands clenched. It was almost impossible to resist the urge to kill him. She could do it so quickly, so cleanly, he wouldn't even know what had hit him. And that would be a better end than an asshole like this deserved, Olivia thought. Just a hard thrust of her fingers to his throat would silence him and bring him down, and then a quick twist and it would all be over. Manfred's problems, and hence the Rev's problem, would vanish. With no one to bring charges against him, Olivia was sure the missing jewelry would be found and all would be well for Manfred . . . if only this man were dead. It was a happy daydream. But there was the young gardener, who was staring for all he was worth. And then Annelle Kling was standing in the open door.

"Lewis!" Annelle called sharply. "Come here." She appeared to be biting back a long litany of things she wanted to say to her brother, and none of them were friendly.

"What's this woman doing here?" Lewis demanded. "I want to know!" He was about five foot eight, bespectacled like his sister, and blessed with a thick head of blond hair. From its careful styling, Olivia could tell it was his crowning glory. He also wore a long-sleeved dress shirt and bow tie. Olivia could see a white T-shirt underneath, through the little gaps between buttons. He was a plump man. How did he bear the layers in this heat?

"She's from a home health care agency," Annelle said, enunciating every word with care. "Evidently Mother had called them while she was ill."

"Preposterous. She would have told me. I took care of her." He turned his challenging glare to Olivia, trying and failing to look her directly in the eyes. He turned on his sister. "Have you gotten Mother's suite cleaned out yet?"

"You're not moving into the house," Annelle said, exasperation in every word. "We've gone over this and over this. We're going to sell it. God knows, Rosie and I don't want to live in it, and you can't afford to buy us out. You can stay in the pool house until we sell this place."

The gardener was as rapt as though he were watching his favorite reality show.

"You may go," Lewis told Olivia, in a patronizing way. "None of this is your concern."

The gardener was shaking his head silently, trying not to laugh.

It wasn't Olivia's concern, true, but it was interesting. Olivia smiled, making sure she looked completely benevolent. "Yes, I have to get to my next appointment." She glanced at her wrist to check the time. "I'll be late if I don't get moving." She maintained the smile as she got into the car and buckled up, relieved to feel the blast of the air-conditioning after she turned on the ignition. She managed a cheerful little finger wave at the three people staring after her as she circled the round rosebed and left the property.

When she'd reached a more mundane street, she drove through a Wendy's to get some iced tea with lemon. It tasted absolutely wonderful. She sipped it on her way to her motel, which was a far cry from Vespers. She parked around the corner from the stairs to her room and looked the lot over carefully before going to the second floor. No one had been in her room; the maid had come before she'd left that morning.

Olivia was used to being disguised, but it was a special relief to pull off the wig that had turned her into Rebecca Mansfield. She washed her face in the sink, scrubbing it with the skimpy washcloth. Divesting herself of Rebecca's clothes, she threw herself on the bed to think. Instead of plotting her next move, she thought of the almost hysterical hostility Lewis Goldthorpe had thrown at her, though he hadn't known who she was or why she was at the house. Olivia grimaced, imagining living with someone that angry and unrealistic, day after day, especially if you were elderly and sick and worried. It would be exhausting.

Olivia felt a rare moment of empathy for Rachel Goldthorpe.

She wished she had killed Lewis. What a useless waste of oxygen.

She decided to search the house that night. She had looked very carefully at the alarm system. She'd worked at an alarm company for a while, and she knew what to look for.

Olivia was certain that the maid, Bertha, didn't sleep in. A woman as unpretentious as Rachel (going by Manfred's description) would not have sleep-in staff. But Olivia hadn't survived until now without double checking, so she drove back to Rachel's neighborhood at four thirty that afternoon in her own car. At one minute after five o'clock, she watched Bertha drive away in an old Subaru. Interestingly, the gardener was with her, and they were having an animated discussion. Mother and child?

As a bonus, a moment later Olivia saw Annelle depart in a Lexus. Presumably, that left only the odious Lewis in residence in the pool house. She wished she'd managed to see the garage in back, find out what he drove. She returned to her humble motel to finalize her plan, but it remained very basic. She would break into the Goldthorpe house and search for the jewelry. And if Lewis interrupted her? Well, people got killed when they confronted burglars just about every day. No one could blame her for that, right?

Hours later, Olivia parked blocks away from Old Pioneer Street. She'd leave her car, the rental, on a more modest street, one where there were occasional pedestrians and a few other cars parked at the curb. She was still in Bonnet Park, though, so she'd taken care to be appropriately camouflaged in black jeans, a flowered T-shirt, and high-end sneakers. Her hair was braided. She strode away confidently, the messenger bag slung over her shoulder. In it were some innocent items: a thin dark sweater, a wallet (with the identification of Rebecca Mansfield, which she'd used when she'd rented the car), some keys, a broad knit hair band, things anyone might need. She had had to include a few things no innocent person would carry, though, so this was definitely the vulnerable part of her evening.

Nobody seemed to be curious tonight. A casually dressed, attractive woman out for a walk was not anything unusual in the neighborhood a few streets from Old Pioneer. Perhaps the bag was a little odd; most women wouldn't choose to take their evening walk carrying a bag. Apparently, if any of the inhabitants noticed her, they didn't find anything suspicious in her progress toward the fancier area where the Goldthorpe house stood.

Olivia didn't see a single patrol car as she walked.

In fact, she didn't see that many moving vehicles, period. Though it was Friday, Olivia estimated at least ninety percent of the people of this Dallas suburb were home. At least two or three percent of the rest were gone on their summer vacations. And a percentage of the remainder were at the movies or out having drinks. By the time Olivia reached the Goldthorpes' street, she was completely unobserved. When she reached the right driveway, she simply turned in to walk up it.

After her confident entrance, her path became more circumspect. She stepped off the crunchy gravel right away and moved silently across the grass to hide in the shadows created by a clump of bushes. She crouched and listened, closing her eyes to aid the process. Nothing moved in her immediate vicinity. After a moment, a car passed on the street, but it didn't slow or turn in. Olivia's lips turned up in a smile. Manfred had warned her there were surveillance cameras, but she had noticed this afternoon that the two in front were stationary, mounted on the front corners of the house. They were both aimed toward the front door. That left Olivia plenty of room to approach the house unseen. In her pool of shadow, she pulled on the dark cardigan and buttoned it to conceal her T-shirt. She slid the broad hair band across her forehead and neck to keep her braid from swinging. She tugged it down low over her brows. She tucked dark thin plastic gloves into her waistband. She'd need them soon, along with her lockpicks. She exhaled deeply and almost silently before she began her creepy-crawl up to the main house.

This was what Olivia lived for. Her heart beat faster, and though she didn't realize it, she was smiling. Since she knew the cameras were pointed at the front door area, she kept to the hedge as she worked her way toward the left side of the house. One of those windows would be her first attempt at entry. She hoped the front room, the formal living room, would provide her access, because that room had no furniture drawn up to the windows, a glance had told her.

If everything was tight as a drum on both sides, she'd resort to the lockpicks on one of the doors. But Olivia felt optimistic; the evening had had a good beginning. She drew parallel to the living room windows and had to leave her cover to cross the driveway and reach the shelter of the foundation plantings. The camellia bushes (she thought that was what they were) had ample space between them for her to hug the wall below the window. With some excitement she reached up to feel out the situation.

Then everything went to hell.

11

Manfred was hungry, and he was tired of feeling trapped in his house. Toward evening, the reporters began to drift away, and he felt pleased with himself. After eleven o'clock, he got into his car and drove to Davy, picking a barbecue joint called Moo and Oink, which was about the only place open this late. He had the chopped beef and the beans and the onion rings, and he enjoyed every bite. Most of all, he enjoyed being in a place that wasn't his house.

When he pulled out his wallet to pay, he saw the slip of paper with Olivia's other phone number on it, the phone in another name. As he pulled it out of his wallet, he had a sudden and clear vision. Olivia was in bad trouble; he could feel her fighting someone.

Tonight was the time she was supposed to be reconnoitering the Goldthorpe house. Manfred sat, the piece of paper in his right hand, absolutely paralyzed. Should he call her? But how could she answer, if he did? He might just make things worse.

All Manfred's pleasure in the evening had evaporated.

He looked at his watch. It was now nearly midnight. It would take him at least two hours to drive to Dallas. What did he need to take with him?

I don't need anything, he thought. *I've got my wallet and my credit cards and my driver's license. I can buy anything else I need.* This was one time when it felt good to live alone, without even a pet. Though he had no clear idea of what he would do when he got to Dallas, Manfred walked out of the restaurant and drove to the interstate. Usually, he found the Texas speed limit more than generous. Tonight, he prayed there was no state trooper concealed by the side of the road.

Along the way, he had enough sense to call Lemuel.

Lemuel answered.

Without any warning at all, Olivia had been smashed against the brick wall of the house by a man who was so strong, she'd wondered for a moment if he was a vampire. He knew about fighting, too. Olivia was used to employing her ruthlessness and agility to win a fight, but this man, whoever he was, seemed to know her capability. Her hands were pinned, one above her head and the other at her waist. His body was pressing hers against the hard surface, but there was nothing sexual about it.

Since she couldn't kill him, she went limp while she waited to find out what his intentions were. Her captor was not Lewis Goldthorpe; she was sure of that, simply from his height and his strength. Olivia realized what she *hadn't* heard. This man had not called for backup. So he was not police, not a security guard, or he would have already called for help. And if he'd been another sneak thief, he would have left before she knew he was there, to avoid confrontation.

Instead, when she went limp he forced her hands together and used a plastic zip tie to secure them. But he was trying to do too much by himself, and he didn't succeed in getting her wrists in tight proximity. She had some wiggle room. Not that that helped just at the moment, because he again used his whole body to keep her against the bricks, her hands trapped between them. He was doing something with his right hand. She heard some electronic beeps.

He'd gotten out a telephone. He'd punched two buttons.

Now he whispered, "McGuire, I've got her."

Olivia's blood turned to ice water. A moment before, she'd been cautious, waiting for more information: who this man worked for, what he planned for her. Now she knew. He'd automatically leaned a little away from her, just an inch or two, while he talked.

Olivia twisted just a little, brought her knee up sharply, and then shoved with all the power in her bound hands. Her knee landed exactly where she'd hoped it would, and he gagged and doubled over. She wheeled sideways, lifted a foot, and braced herself against the wall to kick the side of his head with all the force she could muster. She wished she'd been wearing boots. He landed on the ground on his back, and while he was fumbling to pull out a weapon, she stomped on his throat.

She knew from the feel of it she'd landed a killing blow.

She couldn't find her balance on the uneven surface. She pitched forward onto the ground beside the dying man. As he finished dying, Olivia drew herself up into a crouch. Awkwardly, she patted him down. It was no surprise that he had a knife. In the darkness, she fumbled to extricate it from its sheath. As a bonus, she felt a familiar cylindrical shape and knew he'd brought a flashlight. Yes! It was easier to free it from his belt than to work her tiny one out of her pocket. She switched it on, setting it on his stomach to shine on her hands. Even with its help, she nicked herself in the process of cutting the zip tie. Once she'd freed her hands and stanched her own bleeding with the hair band, Olivia gave herself a minute to recover. By the time her sixty seconds were up, her breathing was back to normal and her pulse had stopped hammering.

She had gathered her wits, too. Olivia used the dead man's flashlight to check that her own blood wasn't anywhere on the ground. She stuck the sawed-up zip tie in her pocket. She would take his knife, flashlight, and phone, which she found on the ground beside his body. Did he have a wallet? Yes, he did. She took that, too. No gun, which was a slight surprise.

There wasn't any way to conceal the body, so she left it where it lay. Finally, she switched off the flashlight.

Forcing herself to move stealthily, Olivia worked her way closer to the street, bush to bush, until she came to the shadowy place where she'd left her bag. She pulled down the sleeves of the sweater to cover her abraded wrists. She draped the messenger bag to cover as much of her as she could, in case there were spots she hadn't noticed.

Olivia took a few deep breaths, then started the long walk back to her car, reminding herself with every step to be wary. He'd made the call; they'd be checking. Though not twenty-five minutes had passed since she'd turned onto Old Pioneer, she felt it had been hours.

Olivia stayed in cover wherever she could—overhanging tree limbs, shadows of any kind, parked cars as she moved into the less grand streets. If she heard a vehicle approaching, she hid and remained hidden until it was past. That only happened twice. As she came closer to the street where she'd left the rental car, she abandoned the sidewalk altogether. She crouched, watching the car, from the lushly planted yard of the corner house on that block. Concealed by a cluster of yucca plants and pampas grass, Olivia watched for fifteen minutes. Nothing happened. She was just about to stand when the phone she'd confiscated began to buzz quietly.

It made her jump about a mile.

She held it up to her ear. "Falco? Where are you now?" said a familiar voice. "Did you have to hurt her? She okay? We'll be there in two."

When Olivia said nothing, the voice hesitated. Then the man said, "Isabel? Is that you?"

Gently, she placed the phone on one of the large rocks bordering the planting bed. She brought her heel down on it like a jackhammer. She was able to crack it significantly. She bent to pick it up, happy that she couldn't hear the voice anymore. Happy that she'd destroyed something that her father had paid for, though the purchaser had been his right-hand man, Ellery McGuire.

Done with waiting, Olivia strode to the rental car just as confidently as she'd left it. She climbed in as though this were part of her daily routine, and she pulled out and drove away with smooth expertise. She coasted around for an hour, checking for a tail, before she headed for her motel. She parked at the back and started up the stairs, feeling suddenly exhausted.

Somehow she was not surprised to find Lemuel sitting outside her room. "How?" she said, but he caught her up in his arms and held her close. After a second, she let herself lean on him. Then when a couple of minutes had passed, she opened her door and they went inside.

He sat by her on the bed, his arm around her. "Manfred called me directly," he said. "I was closer than he was, so I told him to turn around and go back to Midnight, if he wanted. He said he would."

"Where were you?" she asked, trying to keep her teeth from chattering.

"Here in Dallas," he said. "I had a plane layover. I can delay a night."

She started to tell Lemuel he didn't need to postpone his departure, but when she tried to make her lips move, she simply couldn't make them form those words. "I'm glad you're here," she said. "I got away from him."

"Woman, I know that," Lemuel said in his quiet voice. "Manfred gave me the address. I saw the body. Who sent him?"

"My father's right-hand man," she said. "Ellery McGuire."

Lemuel was silent. "Does he know where you are?"

"He knew I was going to that house, or at least suspected enough to put someone there. I don't know how. I'll figure it out."

"Did you get whatever you went there to get?"

"No, I never got inside. Falco caught me first. I was too cocky. On the other hand, why would I ever imagine there'd be someone waiting there for me? I had other things to worry about."

"What were you afeared of?" From time to time, you could tell Lemuel had been born in another age.

"That there might be security measures I didn't know about, or that the jerk who now lives there would catch me and I'd have to do him in . . . which wouldn't have been such a bad thing."

"But instead, someone you never expected was there waiting for you."

She nodded.

"You have no idea why?"

She shook her head. "I haven't had time to think. I was too . . . intent on getting away from the area before the body was found. I had to get to a safe place."

"You're safe now," he said, his cold lips brushing her cheek.

Suddenly she wanted the familiarity of him, the touch of him, more than anything else in the world. She turned to him, put her hands on each side of his face, brought his lips to hers.

For the first time that night, something went exactly like she'd expected. Maybe even better.

12

Manfred was rejoicing in the lifting of the siege the next day. He didn't know what had happened in Dallas to make most of his watchers withdraw, but there were only two lone reporters outside the next day. He immediately checked the Internet. His search parameter was "Goldthorpe Bonnet Park," and he got information immediately.

"Hmmm," he said. "So Lewis found a body." *Couldn't happen to a nicer guy,* he thought. "No identification. Well, well, well."

There was a quiet knock on his back door, so he was glad he was dressed and had brushed his teeth. He was sure who his caller must be. He opened the door and Olivia came in. It would be an exaggeration to say she looked like hell, but it would be accurate to say she'd looked better every other time he'd seen her.

"You just get in from Dallas?"

"Yeah." She stood facing him, her mouth tight with reluctance. "Okay, thanks for calling Lemuel. As it turned out, I didn't need him.

I got away by myself. But it was nice to have backup. Don't ever do that again."

"Sure, don't babble on and on about it," Manfred said in a friendly voice. "I didn't worry at all after getting a picture of you in danger, and I wasn't halfway to Dallas when I heard from Lemuel telling me all was well, so I only wasted half a tank of gas and some sleep. That's fine! I don't mind. Anything to help a friend."

Olivia looked more and more angry as he spoke. Just when he began to believe she might hit him, she smiled, though reluctantly. "I do thank you," she said. "But most situations, I can handle myself. I was really, really glad to see Lemuel. It was a stroke of luck that he was in Dallas, by the way. He's not there any longer."

Manfred didn't ask where Lemuel had gone. "So, are you hurt?" he asked.

"Not to speak of. Definitely not as badly as the other guy."

"I never intended anything like this." Manfred looked at her directly. "If I'd known the Rev was going to ask you for help, I would never have consented. Maybe this is a day for us being ungrateful with each other. Because I feel pretty bad that the guy is dead, Olivia."

"I feel pretty bad that he was trying to capture me to turn me over to my enemy," she retorted.

"Who is the enemy? And how does that relate to the problem with Lewis Goldthorpe?"

"I'll try to explain."

"Please do." Manfred suddenly realized he felt a little silly arguing in the middle of his kitchen, and he gestured toward the little table. A bit to his surprise, she sat. He pointed at his Keurig, and she nodded. He made her a cup of coffee, and then one for himself. There was creamer and sugar on the table, and she used both.

"I've thought about it most of the night, and this is what I think happened," she said after she'd taken a sip. "I've looked back over the news coverage of the deaths at Vespers, including Rachel's. Of course I stayed out of sight when the police and press arrived at first about the Devlins. But I think I was in the background of one of the news stories about Rachel's death, because there were several reporters there already to cover the double murder." She said this without the least trace of self-consciousness, as if she had nothing to do with the deaths of the man and his wife. "I think that I was spotted—maybe by facial recognition software. Since the story was about the huge coincidence that the same hotel had had a murder/suicide and a sudden death in the same twenty-four hours, the people looking for me covered all the bases."

"You think they're somehow hanging around the Devlin house, too?" Manfred said. He didn't know what to think. Maybe Olivia had worried herself into a mental corner.

"I wouldn't be surprised," she said. "I wondered if they'd staked out the Goldthorpe house, but after I thought about it, I decided the man, Falco, asked Lewis, or the maid, some questions about anyone who'd come by the house lately. Lewis would definitely have blabbed about the stranger who'd been there that day, the blonde who'd been asking about Rachel's application for home health care. So I think this guy was posted there just in case, and he got lucky." She smiled. "Or so he thought."

"I kind of followed that," Manfred said, after working it through. "So you have a long-standing enemy who has a lot, a *lot*, of money and persistence."

"Yeah. My dad. And most specifically, my dad's shadow, Ellery McGuire."

"Didn't see that coming," Manfred said after a moment's silence. He knew that Olivia would be angry when she realized how much she had told him; he could only blame her talkative bout on the lack of sleep and the shock.

He had no idea who his own father had been, but that had left him at liberty to imagine his father loved him and had had to be absent for some fabulous reason. At least his father had never sent a henchman to capture him. "And you told me this because?"

"Because you were able to tell I was in trouble last night. You somehow knew. How'd you do that?"

"The piece of paper with the phone number on it. You told me not to enter it in my phone. And you'd written on the paper yourself, which made it a personal object. When I held it, I knew you were in trouble."

She nodded, just a quick jerk of her head. "Okay. I won't doubt you again."

"I only get a true reading now and then," he admitted. "But I got one for you. So treasure it."

Manfred had a hundred questions he would have liked to ask Olivia, but now was not the time. There might never be a time. Somehow, he felt weirdly fonder of Olivia now, though he knew she was a killer. It was an unsettling feeling, somewhat like wanting to scratch a Bengal tiger behind the ears.

"Here's what happened at the house," Olivia said abruptly. "And by the way, good job on the floor plan."

Manfred felt absurdly pleased at the compliment. He nodded. "I have a pretty good memory," he said. "So you made it up to the second floor?"

Olivia told him about her first venture into the Goldthorpe mansion and her return trip that night.

"The guy was there to bring you to your dad? Or this McGuire?"

"He called Ellery McGuire, not my dad. It's possible my dad said something like, 'Find my daughter and bring her to me.' My dad is the man who causes things to be done. He's not picky about the method. Everyone takes cues from that. So I guess those were Ellery's orders. Otherwise, the guy could have killed me right off, and no one would have known. Being dead would be better than going back to my father."

"To you, being captured is the equivalent of being killed?"

She looked at him, surprised. Then she gave a short jerk of the head. "You're right," she said. "Or close enough."

"And Lemuel found you?"

"He'd already been to the house and back by the time I got to the motel," she said. "He rearranged the body, rather than trying to get rid of it. There was no way I could have taken the time to do that. For one thing, I wasn't sure Falco was alone."

"You thought there might be more than one guy there?"

"He was alone, but he could have had a team circling the block or parked nearby."

"So we're back where we started, at least as far as finding the jewelry I supposedly stole."

"Yeah." Olivia slumped in her chair, which made her look younger and less in control. Manfred much preferred Olivia the other way. He knew that competent, cold Olivia better.

After a moment or two, she said, "I think this means that sooner or later they're going to come check you out. They don't know why I was at the Goldthorpes', they just know I was at the hotel, but sooner or later my father'll think of looking at you."

"Should I be worried about that?" Manfred asked, trying to sound like he wasn't anxious already.

"Yes," she said. "We all should. If the Rev is flipping out about there being reporters here to cover the story you're a part of . . . he'll go ballistic if my father's people come around."

"Because they're much more scary?"

"So much more," she said, simply stating a fact. "We've got to figure out another way to get at this problem. I don't know that it'll draw them off, but we have to make progress. It's too bad we can't just . . ."

Manfred, who'd been refilling Olivia's coffee cup, looked up to find out why she'd stopped. She was staring at Manfred as though he'd sprouted a horn.

"What?" he said.

"Get her husband to tell you," Olivia said.

"What?"

"Where the damn jewelry is, of course! You're a medium. Call Rachel up, however you do it. Or her husband, what's his name?"

"Morton. I can try," Manfred said. He felt like smacking himself on the forehead. "It would help if we could get someone near to her to cooperate, but I'm sure her daughters wouldn't want anything to do with a séance. And Lewis is out of the question."

"So maybe just you and me could do it?"

"I think we need someone a little more . . . in tune," Manfred said, not quite sure how to put it.

"Someone more spiritual," Olivia said evenly.

He nodded. "Joe or Chuy," he said.

"What's spiritual about those two?" she said.

"I'm not sure what they are . . ."

"Two nice gay guys," she said.

"More than that."

She threw up her hands. "All right, then! I'll call them! Tonight, okay? Or do you have something more important to do?" Heavy on the sarcasm.

"Tonight would be fine, and we can have it here," he said, deliberately keeping his voice relaxed.

"See you then, and I'm having a nap in between," she snapped, and left as suddenly as she'd come.

13

Joe put his cell phone in his pocket and turned to Chuy. "We've been invited to a séance tonight," he said.

Chuy, who was making a salad for their lunch, finished chopping the chicken and added it to the raw spinach and the toasted pecans. He began halving the grapes. "That's a first," he said. "What do you think? Is this really something we should do?"

Joe considered it. "It's not like we didn't know there are ghosts all around us," he said. "We see them every day."

Chuy tilted the cutting board to add the grapes. "Bacos?" he asked. "I'm assuming it was Manfred who called?"

"Yes to the Bacos, and no to Manfred," Joe said. "Here's the surprise. It was Olivia." He gave Chuy his *amazed* face, and Chuy laughed. But then he said, "Poor Olivia."

Joe nodded. "I think we should help them out. It's not like they ever asked us for anything."

Chuy began drizzling on a honey-based dressing. "All right, sweetie. By the way, have you been over to the hotel yet?"

"Not since you and I took the tour with Ms. Whatever."

"There are three old people in there, and two geek-type people doing contract work with Magic Portal. There's one man whose purpose I can't discern."

They sat down at the table and Joe served himself from the bowl. "This looks great, Chuy. Do you think we need to do anything about this one man?"

"I think we need to find out what he's up to. We have to protect the boy."

"We do," Joe agreed. "Okay, I'll see what's up at the hotel."

"Good. I have an appointment this afternoon, Myra Shellenbarger."

"She's fun," Joe said, smiling. "She knows everything going on in a twenty-mile radius."

"Or farther. And she's not afraid to name names." Chuy smiled back. "I like her. What you see is what you get."

"It can be tiring knowing so many people with hidden depths," Joe said. "Some days, shallow is good. This salad is great, by the way."

"Got it out of *Southwest Cooking*," Chuy said. "I left out the roasted corn."

After that, the talk turned to cooking, and whether the U.S. Postal Service would stop delivering on Saturdays, and where Lemuel might be in his research project to discover more about the magic books he'd finally found, the ones that Bobo had hidden without meaning to.

There was not a reporter in sight when they strolled down to Manfred's house just after dark. They glanced over at the newly rechristened Midnight Hotel.

"It's still strange to see it lit up," Chuy said. He was holding Joe's hand. This was one of the good things about living in Midnight.

"But kind of nice. Sometimes when I look into the past, I can see all the stores here, busy and bustling. People all around."

"Horses in the streets." Chuy chuckled. "And the smell of them. And people who don't bathe."

"Do you ever wish we could see the future?" Joe asked. "There's so much of the past that lives with us still."

"No," Chuy said instantly. He stopped walking and faced Joe, taking Joe's free hand. "I would go mad," he said, meaning every word.

Joe's eyes met Chuy's. "Then that won't ever happen," he said quietly. "The past is burden enough." After a second, they began walking again. "I saw Mildred today," Joe said, clearly changing the subject. "She was letting Hattie Barnes in the back door."

"Mildred," Chuy said, a wealth of rueful comments in the one word. "What a woman, so mistaken in some ways and so ahead of her time in others."

"She certainly left her house to the right person, though I doubt she ever imagined Fiji would be stronger than Mildred herself ever was. If I remember correctly, Mildred considered Fiji the best of a weak lot."

Chuy shook his head. "Mildred couldn't imagine the scope of Fiji's power."

"And Fiji herself doesn't know it yet." The two were both smiling when Manfred answered the door.

"Glad you all were able to make it," he said. "Please, come in. You want some water or lemonade? I've got some wine, but I don't advocate drinking any alcohol before an attempt to get in touch with those who've gone ahead."

"I'm sure you're right," Joe said, trying not to cast a sideways glance at Chuy, with whom he'd split a bottle of wine at dinner. "I don't believe I need anything. Chuy?"

Chuy shook his head. "Is Olivia here yet?" he asked. "I haven't seen her today."

"I'm here," she called from the kitchen, and Joe followed Manfred into his alleged kitchen. Joe looked around, trying to suppress his dismay. He couldn't imagine cooking in the depressing and outdated little room.

"Do you cook much, Manfred?" Chuy said, managing to make his tone only inquisitive.

"No, I'm a microwave kind of guy," Manfred said. "You cook, Olivia?"

"No," she said, with a little astonishment in her voice. As if she couldn't believe they were talking about something so unimportant when there was business to be done.

Joe sighed. He realized that once again, he was being reminded to be grateful for the love and nurturing of Chuy, who loved to cook and considered the preparation of good food to be an important part of his day. "So, we're here to contact the dead," he said. "Mrs. Goldthorpe, I assume?"

"Yeah," Olivia said. Joe drew near enough to see that Olivia's face was bruised.

"You're okay?" he asked.

"You should see the other guy," she said, without a smile.

Chuy put his hand on Olivia's shoulder, and she did not pull away. She even seemed, after a moment, to relax just a little.

"So what's the procedure?" Joe asked.

"You sound interested," Manfred said.

"I am. I've never done this before," Joe said. He didn't need to contact the dead, since he could see them all the time, but he didn't add that.

"I'm glad you're open to the experience," Manfred said briskly. "I've pulled this table out so there's room for all of us."

So at least the kitchen doesn't always look this crammed, Joe thought.

"We all sit around it and hold hands. I'll try to summon Rachel. If she won't come, I'll try to reach her husband, Morton. He may not be willing since I don't have Rachel to use as an attraction, but I can try."

"The son accuses you of theft?" Chuy said.

Manfred nodded.

"Then we'll do our best," Joe said, and took Olivia's left hand with his right, and Manfred's right hand with his own left. Across the table, Chuy linked hands, too. Their eyes met, and in his partner's, Joe saw almost infinite patience.

Olivia did not look excited or interested. She looked intent. And deep past that intensity and committal to move forward, Joe saw pain and suffering and rage. He sighed. One day Olivia would explode from this volatile combination, like a bomb. She was dealing out pain and violence to get rid of the rage, and probably Lemuel's energy leeching helped. But the more violence Olivia dealt, the less effective it was in controlling the rage.

Manfred said, "Olivia, you need to relax."

She took some deep breaths and managed to contain herself. "All right," she said. "All right." The tension dropped a few degrees, and Manfred's power began to flow between their linked hands. It was strong and pure, and it glistened. Joe could see it, almost taste it. Joe began to see faces in that power, spirits drawn close by it. It seemed funny to him that Manfred could only sense the presence of the dead, when they were so visible to him and Chuy.

Not everyone came back, of course. Bobo's girlfriend Aubrey hadn't, and she'd been a murder victim. It was a fact that those who'd met violent deaths were much more likely to walk forever as ghosts. Joe had figured he'd see Aubrey striding across the barren land to reach the river or coming into the shop to play her irritating flirtation games.

But meeting up with the ghost of her murderer had been a much more painful prospect. Luckily Joe hadn't seen that one, either.

Joe made himself look at the faces forming nearby. Mildred, well, that made sense. And he recognized the homeless man who'd roamed around Midnight for ten years, attracted by the town but scared of it, too. He saw a Native American woman who had something urgent to say, and she muttered it through Manfred's lips . . . but in a language they couldn't understand. Olivia's eyes showed white all around at hearing Manfred speak in tongues, as it must have seemed to her.

Then Rachel Goldthorpe said, "I'm sorry he's giving you trouble." The other three hadn't ever heard her voice, but they never doubted this was the dead woman.

Manfred was even sitting like someone else, Joe realized. His shoulders were slumped with age and illness, and he was a little back from the table as though there were more of him to accommodate. *She must have been a heavy woman,* Joe thought.

Silence reigned, and Joe thought, *None of us know what to do. We all thought Manfred would question the spirit, if she appeared.* They hadn't foreseen it was possible that Rachel might inhabit the psychic.

Joe said, "Rachel, where did you hide the jewelry?" He was not frightened of the dead, but he was uncertain how to handle the situation, which was a first for him.

Rachel said, via Manfred, "In Morton's study. Where Lewis will never look. He and his dad never got along." She shook Manfred's head sadly.

"Where in the study?" Joe asked, trying not to sound impatient.

"Inside . . ." It was like a cell phone had dropped the call.

"Inside *what?*" Olivia snapped.

"I see the world . . ." Rachel whispered, and then Manfred was back in his body. His eyes opened. He looked from one of them to another. "I feel like something happened," he said. "Tell me what it was."

"Are ghosts always irritating and vague? Is that part of dying?" Olivia said.

Chuy released her hand. "Olivia," he said reprovingly.

"Well, it was exasperating," she said. "At least now we know which room."

"Could someone tell me what happened?" Manfred looked from face to face.

Joe said, "Rachel paid us a visit. She said she'd put the jewelry in Morton's study, because Lewis and Morton didn't get along. Inside something."

"Inside what?"

"She didn't tell us that. We lost the connection before she could specify. She said something about the world. How do you feel?"

"That's the first time I've ever been taken over like that," Manfred said. "Interesting experience, and a little too personal for me." He seemed excited about the possession, rather than exhausted or terrified, which was what Joe would have expected.

"That was an interesting experience for all of us," Chuy said. "I thought we'd be here for hours trying to summon a spirit, and she popped into you like a hand into a puppet."

"I'm not sure I like that analogy," Manfred said. "But I'll accept it. I was definitely somewhere else."

Olivia stared at Manfred. "I couldn't do that," she said. "I couldn't lose control like that."

"Then the chances are overwhelmingly good that you won't," Manfred said. "Usually, the spirits visit people who are open to the experience. I hate to sound all abracadabra, but it's true. I have a theory or two about why spirits are so vague."

"Let's hear them." Olivia got up and leaned against the kitchen wall. She seemed too restless to sit any longer.

"I think maybe they lose their hold on specifics about the world, in the first place. If you were in a whole new situation and had no contact with the universe you'd known all your life, you might not remember every little thing, either. If we can talk to a spirit, they're sticking around because they haven't reached their final destination, for whatever reason. But they aren't *in the world* any longer, so a lot of worldly stuff no longer seems important to them. My alternate theory? They do it to aggravate us. Because if they aggravate us, they're still important to us and interacting with us and affecting us."

"Interesting," said Joe. "In this instance, identifying the room and using the qualifying 'inside' may be specific enough. I don't suppose there's any way you can just go to the house and tell the daughters that's where you suspect the jewelry is hidden?"

"No," Manfred said. "Because they'll say, 'How did you know?' And I'd have to answer one of three things: 'A little bird told me.' Or, 'Your mom's spirit possessed me and told my friends.' Or, 'I know it's there because I hid it there.' Guess which one they'd believe?"

"But at least the jewelry would be found, and the case would go away," Joe said.

"Leaving my reputation ruined. Psychics don't have much reputation as it is, and you can imagine that my business would sink like a stone if it was widely believed I'd robbed an elderly lady out of her sparklies and then tried to return them when I'd gotten caught out."

"Plus, Lewis the asshole would go unpunished," Olivia said. She pulled herself away from the wall and walked around the little room, unable to be still any longer.

"Olivia, you need not fear about that," Chuy said. "In the end, Lewis will get whatever he has earned."

Olivia gave Chuy a very skeptical look. "Right," she said. She laughed, but it was a laugh that sounded anything but amused. "I would never have thought you, of all people, would say that."

"Why?"

"Because you and Joe have faced such ugliness, being together," she said, obviously editing as she spoke.

Joe looked at Chuy. "We try not to judge," Joe said quietly. "There's always a chance for redemption."

"If that's what you have to tell yourselves so you can live with all the assholes, so be it," Olivia said. "But I don't have to." Her eyes were lit with the fire burning in her. To Joe and Chuy, it was visible.

Manfred said, "Who needs a glass of water?" The passion of the conversation clearly made him uncomfortable.

"That's right, just sweep it under the rug," Olivia said, turning on him.

"After being inhabited by a lady in her sixties, I feel I can do without any more upset tonight," Manfred said, an edge to his voice.

"I see your point," Olivia said stiffly, after a moment. "I'll go back to my place. We'll make another plan. I'll check in with the Rev. How's the little boy doing?"

"Not so little. He's growing," said Chuy. "Visibly," he added.

"He's taller than he was when he got here," Joe said.

They all looked at each other.

"I was going to say, 'How is that possible?'" Manfred shrugged. "I should know better."

14

On Monday morning, Manfred was at his window as the Rev and Diederik went from the Rev's cottage to the chapel. He had his phone in his hand as he watched them make their way down the newly restored sidewalk. A couple of old people, one with a walker, were taking their constitutionals around the hotel. Both of the senior citizens stopped in their tracks as the oddly assorted duo went by.

The new citizens of Midnight were probably gaping because the Rev was wearing the same rusty black suit, black hat, and string tie he always wore, along with his ancient cowboy boots and his threadbare white shirt. (His face did not look as old as his clothes, but it was deeply grooved.) But the boy was at least two inches taller than he had been mere days before; consequently, his clothes were straining at the seams.

"Well, damn," Manfred said to himself. "We've got to get that boy more clothes. The Rev's been wearing the same thing for years. He'll never notice the kid needs something new." He called Fiji. "I don't know how much you know about kids' sizes," he began, "but the Rev's visitor has to have something that fits."

"I just got him some shorts and T-shirts," she said, surprised.

"They're too small now," Manfred said.

She hung up, and Manfred watched as she burst out her front door and walked over to the chapel. The Rev and Diederik were just crossing the chapel yard to the steps, the boy looking anything but enthusiastic. Fiji stopped dead at the sight of Diederik, and then she marched toward them. The wind had picked up, and Manfred smiled to see her hair and her skirt frisk in the air like banners. She planted herself in front of the Rev. Manfred watched her mouth moving. The Rev was standing stock-still, stiff with unhappiness at being intercepted on his appointed round. But then her words caused the old man to look behind him at the boy, and he appeared a bit surprised at what he was seeing.

Fiji's arms waved a little, and the Rev nodded, and then he entered the chapel and the boy followed Fiji over to her house. As they walked through Fiji's front yard, the boy looked around him at all the flowers, blooming gloriously, and the bushes, lush and green despite the Texas heat. Finally he spotted the cat, Mr. Snuggly, and Manfred watched Diederik's face light up. He scooped up the cat and carried him in the house, Mr. Snuggly's face visible over the boy's shoulder like a fuzzy golden thundercloud.

Manfred laughed. It was the best he'd felt in days.

Then Manfred pondered the meaning of the boy's accelerated growth. He didn't have a clue. He wondered when Diederik's father would return. He hoped it would happen before Diederik was six feet tall.

Manfred got a personal phone call about an hour later, just when he'd gotten into his stride on his professional phone site. "Hi, Mr. Bernardo, Phil Van Zandt here," said a man's voice. "From Magdalena Orta Powell's office," it added helpfully.

"Oh, sure! Sorry, I was deep in the work zone," Manfred said. "What's up?"

"I'm sorry to say the police department in Bonnet Park wants to question you," Phil Van Zandt said sympathetically. "They called Ms. Powell. She's made an appointment there for two this afternoon, which will give you enough time to drive there, stopping for a quick lunch." *Because only barbarians skip lunch,* his voice implied.

"Okay, I'll try to be there," Manfred said, trying to rearrange his day mentally.

"Ohhhhhh . . . there mustn't be any 'try' about it, Mr. Bernardo. You can be there at two, right? Or Ms. Powell will have to call them to reschedule. And that'll mean she has to rejigger her whole afternoon."

"Or you do."

"Well, yes, but that's my job. So you can make it?"

Manfred glanced at the clock he kept on the desk. "Yes, I can make it," he said. "Headquarters of the Bonnet Park police?"

"Yes, right, need the address?"

"Thanks." Manfred scribbled it down. "I'd better get started."

"No problem," said the obliging Phil. "Hope all goes well."

Cryptic, but pleasant.

Manfred logged out and checked his pockets to make sure he had everything. Unfortunately, he had no good-luck charm to include. Fiji was walking up to his front door as he went out.

"I was going to ask if you'd go with me to Marthasville to buy Diederik some more clothes," she said.

"Sorry, I have to go in to the police station in Bonnet Park with my lawyer," he said. "The police want to question me."

Fiji said, "Here, then." She put her hands on either side of Manfred's head, and her lips moved. The pressure of her small hands was intense and felt somehow hot, as though she'd rubbed her hands together briskly before applying them.

"What was that for?" he asked, when her hands were back by her sides.

"That was to make your words believable," she said, grinning. "I tried it out last week on a policeman who stopped me because my tags had expired."

"It worked?"

"You betcha. I didn't get a ticket. And I did go right to Davy and get new tags the next day."

"So, does my believability expire?"

"No spell lasts forever without reinforcement," she said. "Not that I know of, anyway."

He got into his car feeling a bit . . . jaunty, which was an adjective he'd never thought of applying to himself. He had a good lawyer *and* a good witch *and* a kick-ass adventuress on his side. He listened to NPR on his drive to Bonnet Park, convinced it would make him feel smarter. The Dallas traffic almost popped the balloon of his confidence, but he negotiated it with some finesse and pulled into the visitor's lot ten minutes early.

As if she'd planned it to the second, a Lexus pulled in beside him, and out of it stepped Magdalena Orta Powell. It must be her; she looked like a distinguished lawyer. He decided she was in her mid-forties. Her hair was short and styled perfectly, her makeup was good but understated, her skirt was a beige cotton blend and fitted her curves unapologetically, and the short-sleeved brown and white patterned blouse with its big brown buttons was attractive but definitely on the ladylike side. Her brown heels were attention-grabbers. Manfred felt certain he could not have taken a single step wearing them.

"Mr. Bernardo?" She shook his hand. Her grip was firm, but she didn't squeeze. She stood back and gave him a head-to-toe scan. Manfred had wisely eschewed his public "all black" look for his police visit, instead wearing a pair of khakis and a white linen shirt

with subdued palm trees all over it. "No jewelry aside from the piercings, good," she said. "The piercings are bad enough."

"But they'll believe me," Manfred said confidently. He didn't know
what Fiji had done to him, but he wished he could pay her to come
over and do it every morning.

"Are you on drugs?" his lawyer asked sharply.

"I never use drugs," he said. "And what do I call you? I can't say
'Magdalena Orta Powell!' every time I want to get your attention."

"Ms. Powell will do just fine," she said. "Shall we dance?" She pointed
up the walkway to the glass doors into the public safety building. "This
is less intimidating than going into the Dallas police headquarters," she
added, "but don't be fooled. This is professional law enforcement, and
they hate having a messy case on their hands."

"I haven't done anything wrong," he said, with great certainty.

"I wish I could guarantee that meant you wouldn't end up in jail."

He did feel a twinge of concern for a moment, but then it floated
away on the tide of his conviction that he would convince the police
that he was the most upright citizen they'd ever met.

"Detective," he was saying a few minutes later when they'd been
ushered back to an interrogation room. He stood and shook the detective's hand.

"You know each other?" Ms. Powell didn't get up, but she nodded
to the detective as if she'd met him before.

"We met at the hotel, Vespers, right, Mr. Bernardo?" Detective
Sterling sat down opposite them.

Manfred gave him a much closer look than he'd given when he'd
first met the detective. Sterling was dark and stocky, and his close-cut
hair was graying. He'd put on a pair of glasses with metal rims, which
glinted in the overhead light, giving him a strangely old-fashioned
look. Another man entered at that moment and took the seat by
Sterling. They were wearing what amounted to a uniform: white

short-sleeved shirts, blue patterned ties, and khakis. But the other detective was very tall, at least five inches over six feet, and older, too, with snowy hair. He did not wear glasses, and his blue eyes were sharp and intent in a weathered, red, lined face.

Yet Manfred was not afraid. He could feel Ms. Powell tense, though, and she said, "Well, a detective who does *not* seem to have met my client yet. Hi, Tom."

Tom smiled at Ms. Powell. "Maggie. Hey, buddy, I'm Tom Freemont."

Manfred smiled back at him as they shook hands. "Good to meet you, Detective. What can I do for you all today?"

"You've gotten all kind of snarled up in something, Mr. Bernardo," said Detective Sterling. *Just us good and simple folks, trying to understand.* "We need to straighten that out, make sure we understand exactly what's happening."

Manfred tried to look intelligently interested.

Ms. Powell said, "Are you charging my client with anything?"

"No, not at the present time."

"Then what do you need to know about? What crime are you thinking he may have committed? Because I sure haven't heard of anything. Did not Rachel Goldthorpe die of natural causes?"

"We're still waiting for the test results to come back. Maybe a combination of age, weight, high blood pressure, and a bad case of pneumonia all wound up together and killed her." Detective Freemont flipped open a folder and glanced at the contents. "We have to say there was no immediately obvious cause of death."

"So you don't think my client had anything to do with the death of Mrs. Goldthorpe."

"I didn't say that."

"So you believe she was murdered?"

"We don't know at the present. But, all right, at this time we don't suspect Mr. Bernardo of murder," Freemont said baldly.

"Then what?" Magdalena Orta Powell looked puzzled and vexed. She pulled it off beautifully.

"There are the charges leveled by Lewis."

"You charging Mr. Bernardo with theft? Do you seriously think Ms. Goldthorpe brought a purse full of jewelry to a séance with her late husband?"

"She might have." Freemont tilted his chair, waving his hand in an "anything's possible" gesture.

"Right. And when she slumps over dead, my client's first impulse would be to go through her purse? No, I don't think so! He calls downstairs, like anyone would do. His first concern was Mrs. Goldthorpe."

"That's what he says," Detective Sterling said, stopping just short of insulting sarcasm.

"Do you have any evidence at all that suggests any different?" Ms. Powell's eyes were practically shooting fire. Manfred was proud of her. He was positive that she was defending him brilliantly.

"No, we don't," Detective Sterling said. "But we find it strange that his friend"—and here he poked his finger in the air in Manfred's direction—"was sitting with two people who later that evening died in an apparent murder/suicide, while Mr. Bernardo's guest, the very next day, died in his room."

"There's no connection whatever," Manfred said calmly. He knew they would believe him. "I didn't know someone I knew from Midnight was going to be there. I don't think Olivia knew the couple very well. And the next day, while I was having clients in my room, she went shopping, at least as far as I know. I've scarcely seen her since then. You haven't been by to ask her any questions about their deaths, or she'd have told me. And you know I didn't kill poor Rachel. I didn't know she had jewelry to hide until she told me that day during our session." And here his voice sharpened. "Why was my name even leaked to the press? There's no evidence at all that I've ever done anything wrong!"

Only Ms. Powell's hand on his arm stopped Manfred from rolling forward. He stopped talking then. But he didn't lower his gaze, and he waited to hear what they would have to say.

"All right," Sterling said finally. He pulled off his glasses and polished them with a pocket handkerchief he conjured out of nowhere. "Well, I've got to say you put forth a convincing argument, Mr. Bernardo."

Yes! You go, Fiji! Manfred thought.

"Where were you last night, Mr. Bernardo?"

"At home," he said promptly.

"Did you go out at all?"

"Nope. The night before, I had some friends in," he said.

"Who?"

"Actually, Olivia Charity. And Joe Strong and Chuy Villegas, who also live in Midnight."

"And the night before that?"

Manfred knew this was the question they really wanted to ask, because of the body at the Goldthorpe house. "I went out to eat," he said. "Then I went home."

"Where did you eat? It any good?"

Oh, come on! Manfred thought. He got out his wallet and pulled out the receipt from Moo and Oink. "I don't usually keep receipts," he said, "but I haven't cleaned out my wallet lately."

Freemont leaned over to take the receipt from Manfred, and the detectives gave it a very serious look. They wouldn't be able to get past the time and date stamp. Sterling sighed.

Freemont said, "So you contend that you were at Vespers for your . . ." He looked down at a paper. "*Client* weekend, the same weekend your friend from this tiny, tiny town is there, completely by coincidence. Also by coincidence, the people you both meet happen to die."

It did sound fishy, put that way.

"He doesn't contend that, he states it," Ms. Powell said calmly. "Because that is exactly what happened. He never met the couple who died so tragically. His acquaintance, Olivia Charity, never met Rachel Goldthorpe, at least not to my client's knowledge. This is all nothing more than coincidence, the kind the world is always throwing at us. Mr. Bernardo has never seen Mrs. Goldthorpe's allegedly missing jewelry. You can hardly charge my client with her death when you don't know what killed her. So that's the end of this conversation." Ms. Powell got smoothly to her feet. Following her lead, so did Manfred. "This was a long way for my client to drive to answer a few questions he's answered before." Nobly, she did not mention her own inconvenience, because she would get paid for it. "I trust you won't demand his presence again."

"Only if the tox screen shows something," Freemont said, suddenly sounding bored. He stood, too, towering over them. "And you ought to know, that little shit Lewis Goldthorpe plans on dragging your client through as much mud as he can."

Ms. Powell and Manfred left the Bonnet Park police/fire station within an hour of entering it. Manfred realized he was now much poorer, but since he was walking out a free man, the price was fair. Ms. Powell was silent until they reached her car. Then she said, "I think we should bring action against Lewis Goldthorpe."

"Won't that just draw more attention to a bad situation?"

"Depends on what he accuses you of. If he tells the world you're a thief, you may be sorry you didn't get a preemptive strike in."

"It would be best for me if this just went away. Any more time in the news, and my reputation's going to be terrible, anyway. If there's any big exposé on me because of this publicity, I'm not going to come out looking good. And frankly, I'm as nice a guy as they come in the psychic business."

"Interesting way to put it." The lawyer looked at him.

He shrugged. "But so true."

"Why do you think Lewis Goldthorpe is gunning for you?"

"Because Mom always liked me best."

When Ms. Powell looked blank, Manfred said, "Because his mother never got along with Lewis, and she did with me. She didn't know me very well, so that made it easy. If she'd really spent a lot of time with me, it might have been a different story. But I didn't want her possessions, I got along fine with her husband because he was dead, I listened to all her stories because she was a nice lady, and I believe in an afterlife, like she did."

"Whereas Lewis . . . ?"

"Fought with her husband when he was alive, badgered her about anything she planned to leave her children, didn't believe in any psychic help I could offer her, and wasn't at all interested in his nieces and nephews. Plus, he doesn't really believe in life after death."

"So you think that's all it takes to keep a woman's attention and loyalty? Not coveting her possessions? Listening to her stories?"

"Whoa! I think we just veered off the course. I wasn't saying that at all. I was saying that was why Rachel was glad to talk to me rather than her own son. I was less demanding and more accepting."

Ms. Powell took a deep breath and visibly calmed herself. "Sorry," she said.

"You're going through a rough patch in your own life," Manfred observed.

"Not hard to tell," she said, and smiled ruefully. "Sorry for being unprofessional. I'm back in lawyer mode now."

"Has Lewis actually accused me with the police?"

"Yes, he has."

"So why haven't I been arrested?"

"Because there's no evidence to prove you took her jewelry."

"Then why can't his allegations be ignored?"

"Because her jewelry still isn't around, and though they don't really believe him, it's possible he's right."

"So I'm over a barrel until the jewelry is found. My situation is completely the same. Why did they call me in here?"

She was looking off into the distance. Her eyes went to his face. "Fishing expedition," she said. "A waste of my time and your money."

Manfred looked at her doubtfully. "My time is money, too," he pointed out. He couldn't help but feel a little offended.

"I'll bet it's not as valuable as mine," she said.

And he was sure that when he got his bill, he would agree.

As he drove back to Midnight, Manfred thought about the bottom line on this little "fishing expedition." The detectives didn't know anything new, he hadn't completely dispelled their suspicions—though he was convinced he'd weakened them—and he'd lost hours of work time.

On the plus side, he'd gotten to know his lawyer, and he found himself much more confident he'd stay out of jail.

Magdalena Orta Powell was not exactly what he'd expected, and he was pretty sure she felt the same about him.

15

Olivia had gotten a phone call from Lemuel during the middle hours of the night. Lemuel did not like the telephone, but he had overcome his natural aversion to call her because he knew it would make her feel better. The conversation had been brief.

"Olivia, I am now in New Orleans."

She was silent for a second, dismayed at how relieved she was to hear his voice. "You learning a lot about the books?" she said, when her silence made her uncomfortable.

"I have found a woman who is knowledgeable. A female vampire."

"Great. Are you feeling . . . Have you gotten enough food?" Olivia was always cautious about being explicit on the telephone. She knew how easily someone could listen in.

"There is abundance here," Lemuel assured her. "I need only walk into a bar."

She smiled. "And do you have an idea of how long you'll be gone?"

"Not as of yet."

"Then let me know when you're coming back." She hesitated. "It feels strange to walk past your apartment, since I know you're not in it. It feels funny that you're not here."

"I miss you, too. Be careful and vigilant."

"Good-bye."

And he'd hung up without saying good-bye in return. That was Lemuel's conversational style. She was satisfied with the conversation, though she had to repress a twinge of unease, bordering on jealousy, that Lemuel's source for information about the long-lost and mysterious books was a female, and a vampire. Lemuel was more susceptible to women than men as bedmates, though he would take energy or blood from anyone except small children. Having two sources of sustenance was like being a hybrid car.

He preferred the energy, because it was easier and cleaner to acquire, and he could sip it from many people. Taking blood left an obvious mark, and sometimes a body, because it was certainly possible to get carried away on the odd occasion. In the same way, though he preferred sex with women, he'd had connections with men, he'd told her quite casually. "Weren't too many women around," he'd said, during her favorite together time—postsex. "And vampires like me don't have the gift of the glamour."

There had been a lot of questions Olivia had wanted to ask, but in the interest of appearing tolerant and sophisticated, she had not. And she had realized the next day, while Lemuel was in his day sleep, that no matter how curious she might be about Lemuel's past and how he'd managed to live his life under his strange circumstances, the most important thing to her was that she had him now. Lemuel was not "hers," like her car or her bed was hers. And she knew he would outlive her, barring extraordinary circumstances. But he was hers in a way no one else had ever been; that certainty gave her a fixed point.

Her cell phone rang, the secret one. The caller would be her agent or someone preapproved.

A man said, "Is this Rebecca?"

"I can get a message to her."

"I have a job for her."

"Who and where?"

"My bitch of an ex-wife has a family heirloom. She's holding it for ransom. If I want it back, I have to make concessions in having my kids on the weekends. If I have it, I can tell her to go to hell and I'd see my kids more often."

"I don't need to know why. I need her name and address and a description of the item. Details about her routine."

There was a pause. "Sure. Where can I send all that?"

Olivia gave him an address in Oklahoma.

"Okay. How do I pay you?"

"You already know that." What was he trying to pull? The money went to her agent first, and he took his cut. Then he sent the bulk of it to her account, which wasn't in America. Lemuel had asked her once how she could be sure her agent was honest. "I know where he lives," she'd told him.

"When . . . ?"

"Soon. I'll call you at this number when I've gotten it."

And she hung up, as abruptly as Lemuel had. That thought made her smile. But the smile faded immediately as she thought over the man's story. She didn't believe him, at least not entirely. He had tailored it to make her feel good about the theft. He might be a terrible father, and his soon-to-be-ex-wife a paragon of virtue. But it didn't make any difference to Olivia. She was not a social worker. She took the side she was paid to take.

She would not go to check the mailbox for another two or three days. It was a long drive. Maybe, in the interim, she could take care of Manfred's problem. Then the Rev would be off her back, the news media would never again come to Midnight, and the mysterious fast-growing boy—whoever he was—would be safe. And when Lemuel returned, he would not be spotted by anyone who shouldn't come to Midnight.

She went out that day, stopping by Manfred's to see if he'd gotten any more news. He told her about his visit with the Bonnet Park police the day before and about his new esteem for his lawyer. "There aren't any reporters here today at all," he said, casting a look out the front windows. "I guess I'm not news since the more exciting developments at Rachel's house. Yee-haw."

"Don't relax. All it'll take is another accusation by Lewis Goldthorpe, and you're back on the hot plate," she said. She came to the window to look out herself.

A car pulled up in front of Manfred's little house.

"Who . . . ? Oh, shit," he said, with heartfelt disgust.

"I shouldn't have said anything." Olivia's lips curled back as she watched a man and a woman get out of the aged car. The man was Lewis Goldthorpe. The woman was a news blogger, and her site had gathered a certain amount of attention from people who liked their news on a screen and on the sensational side. Olivia had seen her on a minor national show. "That's PNGirl. You know, Paranormal Girl."

"She's asked me for interviews before. Should I answer the door?" Manfred said.

"Only if you want her to take your picture and put it on the Internet," Olivia said. "And you know Lewis is going to scream and holler." She glanced sideways (and a little down) at Manfred. "This is going to make the Rev furious."

"Maybe he won't find out," her companion said feebly.

Olivia snorted. "Right," she said, loading the word down with contempt. "See?"

The door to the chapel opened. The gaunt, small figure of the Rev was clearly visible for a moment, another person right behind him. Then the chapel door shut.

"Was that the boy?" Manfred said.

"Yep." Olivia thought of sneaking out the back of the house to give Lewis a flat tire, but that would only mean he'd stay in Midnight longer. "If he'd come by himself," she said, "I could have taken care of this whole situation."

She expected Manfred to say something angry and decisive, but when she glanced over at him, he just looked exasperated. "Because finding his car here, and Lewis missing, would sure let me off the hook," he said, in the manner of one speaking to an idiot.

"Of course I would take care of the car," she snapped. She was offended at the suggestion she could not make someone disappear in a professional manner.

"But he didn't come by himself, because he doesn't really want to talk to me person-to-person," Manfred pointed out. "He wants to rant at me in front of a witness, to emphasize how terribly I exploited his poor sainted mother. He wants to ruin me, because his mother turned to me when she'd reached the end of her tether with him."

"Okay, Mr. Insightful, so what's our next step? By the way, knowing why he's doing it doesn't really help a lot."

Manfred looked down. He appeared to be counting to ten. Olivia smiled.

"We still have to get the jewelry back," Manfred said. "And I think we have to show that it was there all the time. Then he'll have no more excuse to harass me. Or if he drums something up, no one will credit it."

"I can't gain entry again by a ruse," Olivia said. The knocking at the door had begun, and they both stepped away from the window, retreating farther into the house to the former dining room. "I've tried to break in at night, and that didn't work. I could try it again. This time, maybe, there won't be anyone there waiting on me."

Though since Falco had died, Olivia's father had to be sure she'd been in the area. Maybe other men were just hanging around waiting for her. Maybe they would come to Manfred's place of residence to look for her now. To try to find what connection he had with her. At least her name hadn't been in the paper; she'd finally tracked down the article online.

"Or we could ask Fiji if she could help," Manfred was saying when she pulled herself out of the abyss.

Olivia felt her mouth fall open. "Fiji? You've got to be kidding me. She can't break and enter."

"She wouldn't go about it the same as you," he said. "I don't think you know how powerful Fiji is. You don't know what she can do."

"And you do?"

He nodded.

Olivia felt piqued. "In what way?" she demanded.

"Olivia! You *know* she's a witch."

"Yeah, yeah. And?"

"Do you know how good a witch she really is?"

Olivia reconsidered the first answer that almost flew out of her mouth. Instead, she said, "I guess I can hardly be a big skeptic since I sleep with an energy-draining vampire."

"Good point. Anyway, she might come up with a solution that we haven't thought of."

"We can't cross the road until Lewis and his pet journalist are gone."

Without a word, Manfred turned on the television and they watched the news, ignoring the sound of persistent knocking at the front door. Then at the back.

There was unrest in the Baltic, refugees were dying in Africa, and the stock market wasn't doing well. Just another wonderful day on the news circuit. In a ludicrous attempt to make the future seem less grim, nutritionists had discovered that cheese curd was a miracle food.

Olivia said, "I've never even seen a cheese curd."

"Me, either."

That was the extent of their conversation until the knocking stopped and they heard a car drive away.

Manfred called Fiji right away. "We're coming over, okay?" he said.

Olivia heard her say, "Sure. It's so hot. Want some iced tea?"

16

"Was that the guy?" Fiji asked as she opened her door. They'd passed an exiting customer as they'd come in, a smiling white-haired lady who'd wished them a good day. She'd been carrying a cloth shopping bag, and it looked heavy.

"She sure looked happy," Manfred said, glancing after the old woman, who'd climbed into an aged Cadillac.

"Yes," Fiji said. "She did." She waited, looking pleasant.

"Yes, that was the amazing Lewis and a blogger who's evidently a big name if you love the Internet. Oh, your spell worked great at the police station," Manfred said.

"Good!" She turned to lead the way in. The shop area was less crowded; when some of Fiji's display cases had been destroyed the previous year, she'd liked the look when the room had been cleaned up. When she'd gotten her insurance payment, she'd added more wall shelves and fewer freestanding cabinets. Now Fiji retrieved her office chair from behind the counter and rolled it out to the two upholstered chairs flanking a little wicker table. On the table was a tray with a pitcher of tea and a plate of cookies.

Olivia and Manfred both helped themselves, though Olivia looked as if she were thinking sarcastic thoughts.

"What did your visitors want?" Fiji asked.

Manfred said, "Here's our problem." He went on to explain (in what he felt were clear terms): the charges by Lewis, the consequences of Lewis's harassment to the whole community, and (to Olivia's anger) the attack she'd faced at the Goldthorpe house.

Fiji said, "Well, I feel like Don Corleone when the undertaker comes to see him about the rape of his daughter."

Manfred began laughing, then stopped in midcackle. "You mean, we should have come to you first? That you could have taken care of it better than we have from the get-go?" Olivia was not laughing a bit.

Fiji smiled. "Hey, don't push the analogy too far. I just meant it's appealing to have someone ask me for help instead of treat me like an extra appendix."

"I've seen what you can do," Manfred said. "With great respect."

Fiji nodded, her eyes on Olivia. After a moment, Olivia nodded in agreement. Fiji's shoulders relaxed, and Manfred saw that he hadn't read the situation right, at all. Fiji had been very anxious about what they'd come to her for, and his request had been a relief. He had to wonder what she'd thought he might say instead.

"So what you know is: No one stole the jewelry. It's in the library in Rachel's house. It's inside something, maybe one of the books, but there are hundreds of books in the library. And also, Olivia's enemies are hot on her trail, the people she came here to hide from."

Olivia looked surprised for a second, and then she said, "Exactly. But I'm not completely sure which enemy has found me."

"You're rich in enemies." Fiji made the comment with a complete lack of judgment.

"There are plenty of people who want to find me, for whatever reason."

"You don't want to talk about why."

"No."

She's so damaged, Manfred thought. This image of Olivia was far more disturbing than her tough-woman exterior. It gave him the creeps. He took a bite of cookie. Oatmeal, with raisins and spice. He said, "These are great," indistinctly.

Fiji smiled at him before shifting her attention back to Olivia. "Do you have any ideas about how I can help you?"

"Not specifically, no," Olivia said. "But we need to get in the house to search. I went once in disguise, but Lewis might recognize me, no matter how well I disguise myself. Lewis is very suspicious. If I watch to make sure he leaves, I don't think the maid would let me come in under any pretext, much less give me the time to rummage around in an upstairs room. There was a gardener, too, who seemed pretty interested in everything that went on. There's no explanation or disguise that would give me the freedom to search."

"And this hidden jewelry needs to be found by the police, and the hint as to where it is can't come from Manfred."

"Right," Manfred said. "If it came from me, the big question would be 'How?' I can't answer that in a way that would satisfy a policeman."

"I guess I could freeze the maid when she answered the door," Fiji said. "She'd stay that way for about seven minutes. Would that be enough time?"

Olivia's mouth was hanging open.

"I'm afraid not," Manfred said. "We probably need at least forty-five minutes, since we don't have that much information."

"Can you try another séance to see if you can learn something more specific?" Fiji asked.

"I can try, but I don't have any guarantee that'll be successful."

"Frozen?" Olivia said.

"Not frozen cold, but frozen in the moment," Fiji explained. "As in, she couldn't move. On the other hand, she'd remember what had happened to her. That's usually not good, unless the person really needs to be taught a lesson."

Diederik came into the shop. They all looked at him, and then Manfred said, "Damn." Diederik now looked perhaps thirteen.

"I bought those clothes yesterday," Fiji said. "Yesterday. Or maybe the day before? But . . ."

"Damn," said Manfred. Again.

"If you have any more?" Diederik said. The boy looked embarrassed.

"I do," she said, looking only mildly pleased with herself. "Go look in the bag on my guest bed. Where you changed the last time."

Diederik looked vastly relieved. As he passed Fiji, he bent to give her a kiss on the cheek. "Thank you," he said. His voice was breaking.

"What the hell," Olivia said, very quietly. "I hadn't gotten past the 'frozen' yet. And now we have a teenager instead of a little boy. *What the hell.*"

"I don't know why he's growing so fast," Fiji said, quietly. She leaned forward. "The Rev isn't saying anything. I don't know if he expected this or not. Or maybe the dad left Diederik here because he knew what was going to happen?" She rolled her eyes. "Be that as it may, the last thing we need is *anyone's* eyes on Midnight."

The bell over the door chimed. One of the old men from the hotel came in, a wizened man who was God knows how far up in years. He carried a cane, he was slightly bent, and he had wispy white hair protruding at all angles from under his straw hat. Manfred had seen him on the sidewalk outside the hotel, walking very slowly. He recognized the hat and the hair.

"Lady, is that your boy?" he asked Fiji, in a very hoarse voice.

"Why do you want to know?" Fiji said, standing up, in as polite a tone as anyone had ever asked a rude question.

"He's growing all over the place! You better put a weight on his head! Someone's gonna call the TV stations."

Manfred said, "Are you the only one at the hotel who's noticed?" He could tell from the expressions on the faces of Olivia and Fiji that they were as astonished—and wary—as he was. None of them had spoken to any of the hotel residents. Manfred had thought, *They're only in Midnight temporarily*, and he hadn't put himself out to speak to any of the old people the few times he'd encountered them.

"Hell, no!" the old man huffed in his hoarse, wheezy tone. "We all have. We ain't dead. We're old. We got nothing to do but watch. You understand me?"

"We understand you," Olivia said.

"Can I have one of them cookies?" He hobbled closer to the table, and Manfred stood to offer him the chair. "Thanks, sonny, don't mind sitting for a minute." He backed up to the chair and lowered himself into it.

"Please have one," Fiji said. "And some tea." She fetched another glass and handed the old man a cookie on a napkin.

It was not pleasant to watch the old man eat the cookie, though he seemed to enjoy it a lot. "We're always getting healthy shit for breakfast, oatmeal and egg whites," he said, spraying a few crumbs. "Makes you want something with a lot of sugar and fat in it."

"I'm Fiji Cavanaugh. I made those, and I'm glad you like them."

"We got two women down at the hotel, they want to know if they can come to your Thursday night shindig," he said. "Your class."

Manfred thought Fiji looked completely taken aback. "Of course. Do they need help getting down here?"

"Mamie does. Suzie rolls along like a tank."

"I'll be sure they get here and get back," Fiji said. "Maybe my friends Manfred and Olivia here can help."

The old man turned his beady eyes on them. "You're the tough girl from the pawnshop," he said. He turned his gaze on Manfred. "And you're the phone psychic guy?"

Manfred nodded.

"I'm Tommy," the man said, extending a wrinkled hand scattered with age spots. "Tommy Quick. Ain't so quick no more. Used to be Carlo Bustamente, back in the day."

"Wow," Manfred said. "Early days of Vegas, right?"

The old man wheezed with laughter and withdrew his hand from Manfred's. "There hasn't been any late days of Vegas!"

Fiji and Olivia cast questioning glances Manfred's way, but he waved a hand. The rest of the story would have to wait for Tommy's departure. "So, how'd you come to be in Midnight?" he asked. "Did you lose a bet or something?"

The wheezy laugh again. "You might say that, or you might say I got lucky, sonny," Tommy told Manfred. "I'll tell you about it. So I'm in a terrible dive in Vegas, see, the kind you wouldn't want your mom to stay in. Not that I know your mom, but I'm just saying. It was a place so bad that only broke old people, like us, or broke young people, like your average little criminal, would choose to live there."

They realized he was waiting for an acknowledgment, and they all nodded like puppets. "Anyways," Tommy went on, "this woman come by the place we're staying. Now, we've been praying we won't get stabbed every time we go out to get groceries, you understand?"

He paused again, waiting. They nodded obediently. "This woman says there's a place in the boonies in Texas where we can live, eat three meals a day, have our rooms cleaned, be comfortable. We says,

'What's the catch?' And she says, 'The catch is, it's in the boonies in Texas.'" He laughed again.

Manfred could manage only a weak smile. But Fiji grinned. "So you agreed, then?" Fiji said encouragingly.

"Yeah, me and Mamie and Suzie. The next thing we knew, we were in the Midnight Hotel and being trotted out for every visitor. There's one other old guy, Shorty Horowitz. He was in the hotel next to ours, but we only knew him by sight. He was the only other guy broken-down enough to take this cockamamie offer."

Manfred exchanged glances with Fiji and Olivia. That was a lot of glances. He could tell that like him, they didn't know what to make of this. "Are you supposed to do anything in exchange for this safe place to live?" Manfred asked, finally.

"They haven't told us nothing yet." Tommy was completely unsurprised by the question. "Except to act happy if we got asked any questions. If we're supposed to do something, it must not be anything urgent. We're bored. We got nothing to do. So the reason I came down here was, what's up with the kid?"

Diederik came out in his new clothes, denim shorts and a striped T-shirt, and waited shyly for them to notice him.

"You look great!" said Fiji. "I'll have to run out this afternoon to get you some more in case you grow again."

The boy, who was less of a boy every day, smiled back at her. "You are most kind," he said in his odd accent. "I will be glad to repay you with work."

"I'll be sure to save all my odd jobs for you, young man," she said. "In fact, tell the Rev I've asked you over to work for me and to have lunch with me."

His olive face lit up with pleasure, and the boy hurried out of the shop and over to the chapel.

"Weird," said Tommy, shaking his head. "He's the opposite of a dwarf, huh?"

"We don't know what's up with the kid," Manfred said. "But we figure no one else needs to be concerned about it."

"I gotcha. So this is one of those things the Whitefields don't need to know about?"

"They don't know . . ." Olivia's voice trailed off.

"They don't know we ain't genuine old people waiting for a nursing home with a loving family and some money?"

"Right."

"I don't think so. Mamie, she told the woman—Lenore—she told her, 'You got us for the duration, sweetie,' and Mrs. Whitefield, she says, 'Just until you get a bed in Whispering Creek, Miss Mamie.' But we ain't got no one going to pay for us to live at Whispering Creek, which from the brochures in the lobby is one of those really high-end nursing homes. Like a spa."

"So how do you feel about that?" Fiji said.

"I liked you until you said that, sister," the old man said. "I want you to know how I feel about something, I'll tell you. This place is dead, but it's safe. And it gets more and more interesting. That old man in the hat? His suit looks older'n me. The boy keeps growing overnight. The two men who run the antiques store—hey, are they a couple? Ain't we modern here? Suzie made it over to the pawnshop; she says the guy who runs it is a hunk and there's all kinds of weird shit inside. Oh, and your cat came down yesterday, Fiji. He walked all around having a good look like he was thinking about buying the place. Then that Eva Culhane came in, and Harvey and Lenore ran up to stick their noses up her ass, and she said, 'No pets! This is a pet-free zone!'"

"Oh, no," Fiji said. She looked around the room. Mr. Snuggly was not in sight. He was a wise cat. "So what else did Eva Culhane do?"

"I think she was just checking to make sure we was all still alive." Tommy laughed his wheezy laugh. "She was the one scooped us up in Vegas."

"Really?" Olivia looked as though that was very interesting. But she clearly didn't know what to make of it.

"This was fun," said Tommy Quick, né Bustamente. "If you want to come down and visit, bring some of them muffins. Scones. Whatever." He heaved himself to his feet and carefully made his way out. They heard him going down the steps slowly, and Fiji got up to make sure he reached the sidewalk without falling.

"Okay, he's on his way back to the hotel," she said, resuming her seat. "That was interesting."

"You haven't read any stories on the history of Las Vegas, I take it," Manfred said.

Olivia and Fiji shook their heads in unison.

"Not in the earliest mob days, but not far after, Tommy Quick was a knee-breaker for organized crime," Manfred said.

"You know this how?"

"My grandmother had a storefront in Las Vegas once upon a time," he said. "She was full of stories. And that got me interested, so I read some books."

"I wasn't even worried about the hotel," Fiji said. "Now I have to worry about the hotel." She threw up her hands. "Every damn thing is a problem here. And my cat! He's lucky they didn't kick him or run him over. He crossed the Davy highway by himself! Idiot!"

"I've done it before," said a sour little voice. Mr. Snuggly emerged from behind Fiji's counter. He strolled over to the group of humans and paused to sit by the little table, his fluffy tail wrapped neatly around his legs. "I look and look and look, and then I run very fast." Olivia, not a fan of the cat, glared at him, and he returned the look. She glanced away first.

"Why?" Fiji said. "Why did you go down there?"

"I knew they were real old people, but not helpless old people. I wanted to find out why they were here. I wanted to know if they were magic." Mr. Snuggly began licking a paw.

"Are they?" Manfred asked, tired of being left out of the conversation, even if it was with a cat.

"No. Not at all. They are old. They've done bad things. They're not mean. One of them is dotty. That's right, isn't it? That's what Aunt Mildred used to say. Dotty."

Fiji looked taken aback. Apparently, she hadn't ever heard the cat refer to her own great-aunt as "Aunt Mildred."

"Sure, that's right," Manfred said quickly. "No magic there, huh?"

"None," said Mr. Snuggly emphatically. "Plenty of ghosts at the hotel, of course. And lots of misdirection."

"What does that mean?" Olivia glared down at Mr. Snuggly, who met her eyes without any problem at all.

"I'm going to take a nap now," the cat said, and went back behind the counter, presumably to jump in the padded cat bed Fiji had put under the counter.

Manfred was having a hard time picking up the thread of the plan they'd been considering before Diederik, Tommy, and Mr. Snuggly had intervened. He put his head in his hands.

"The boy is growing at twenty times the normal speed," he said. "An old hoodlum just popped in to promise us he'd keep silent in return for scones. Mr. Snuggly has uncovered bad doings at the hotel. And I still need to clear my name of these bogus theft charges, which draw attention to Midnight, and therefore to all this other shit that should remain secret."

"That's a good summary," Fiji said brightly.

Olivia said, "Let's get back to the part where you were freezing someone."

"Bertha, the maid," Manfred said helpfully. "And then you and I run up the stairs, Olivia, and we search the study lickety-split. We find the jewelry, we call the police, and it's all over."

"Except we have to explain to the police how we knew where to search." Olivia had gotten up to pace back and forth in the limited space. At every turn, she fixed her eyes scornfully on a glass dolphin or a stained-glass rainbow. "And the maid can tell the police that Fiji did something to paralyze her."

"Okay," said Fiji. "So . . . we go when she's not there. Right after she leaves work."

"No one will be there to answer the door," Manfred said. "Lewis lives in the pool house. Even if Lewis is in the house and decides to open the door, he knows me. And if you froze him, he'd squawk till the cows come home."

"We're talking ourselves into believing this is impossible." Fiji's generous mouth skewed to one side as she thought.

"Too bad Lemuel's not here," Manfred said. "He could hypnotize Lewis into showing the police where the jewelry's hidden after we find it."

"Yeah, because that's what Lem lives for, to make your life easier," Olivia snapped. "For your information, Lem can't do that."

Taken aback by her vehemence, Manfred stared at her. "I'm sorry," he said, wondering what he was apologizing for. But he knew it didn't make any difference, that just saying the words was important. He braced himself for another scathing remark, but to his astonishment, Olivia relaxed.

"I'm just missing him," she said, not looking at either of them.

Apologies are contagious, Manfred noted. He also observed that both he and Fiji were a little embarrassed at Olivia's moment of tenderness. He considered patting Olivia on the shoulder, but he felt he might lose his arm if he did—or even worse, somehow, he feared she might be grateful.

Just then, Fiji's pocket made a squealing sound, and they all looked down at it, Fiji included. She pulled out her phone and said, "Hello?" Suddenly, she flushed from her throat to her eyes. "Oh, hi," she said, and turned her back on Olivia and Manfred to walk briskly down the hall to her kitchen. They could still hear her, but she had the illusion of privacy, Manfred figured.

"Yeah, I had a good time, too," she was saying, and Olivia raised her eyebrows. She glanced over at the pawnshop and back to Manfred. He shook his head vigorously. Whoever her caller was, it wasn't Bobo Winthrop, which would have been wonderful.

"I'm pretty sure he would have told me," Manfred whispered.

"What's he futzing around for?" Olivia hissed. "She's not gonna wait forever! A woman has needs!"

"Okay, I can do that," Fiji was saying. "Then I'll look forward to it. Sure, seafood is fine." Her voice got louder as she apparently began walking back to the shop from the kitchen. "See you then." And she was punching the "end" button on her phone as she rejoined them.

"Who's the guy?" Olivia said. "Anyone we know?" Manfred admired Olivia's perfectly light tone.

"You remember the bouncer at the Cartoon Saloon?"

"From when we all went there? Sure. The good-looking guy?"

"Yeah." Fiji seemed a little proud of that. "So, I called him after a couple of weeks, because I was tired of staying at home." That last was added a little defiantly. "And we've been going out from time to time."

"Bouncers get nights off?" Manfred had no idea what a professional bouncer could expect in the way of downtime, but he felt he had to say something.

"He has a day job as an EMT during the week, and he's a bouncer on weekends," Fiji said. "We're going to Little Fishes in Marthasville tomorrow night. And a movie." She took a deep breath. "Back to the original problem. Sorry for the interruption."

"If I were in an action movie," Manfred said, after a long pause, "I'd put some of that plastic explosive on the door of the Goldthorpe house, blow it up, race in dodging bullets, and sweep all of the books out of the shelves in the library, so the first thing the police saw when they came in would be all the missing stuff."

"I have no idea where to get plastique, I have no idea how to use it, I don't know who would be shooting at you since no one's living in the house, and we aren't sure that the library is actually full of books, or that the jewelry is in one." Olivia stood up. "If I had to check all the books, I'd pick an atlas first, because of the 'world' reference. This is getting us nowhere. I'm going to go walk and think." She left.

"Ahhhh . . . okay," Manfred said. He stretched and rotated, feeling stiff physically and full of cobwebs mentally. "When I come up with a plan, I'll get back with you, Fiji. Thanks for letting us brainstorm here, even if nothing came of it . . . yet."

Fiji, who had settled back into the office chair, didn't budge. "All right. I'll think about it, too. Maybe I'll come up with something."

"That would be great," Manfred said. "What's bad for me turns out to be bad for Midnight, too. Have a good time on your date."

She nodded, and Mr. Snuggly appeared to jump into her lap and curl up in a contented golden ball. She scratched behind his ears. He began purring, loud enough for the sound to reach Manfred. For once, Mr. Snuggly sounded like an absolutely normal cat.

Manfred crossed the porch and walked down the flagstone path to the sidewalk. He was glad to leave Fiji's shop because he was disappointed they hadn't made a plan. As he crossed Witch Light Road, he admitted to himself that he was also dismayed that Olivia was not acting like Olivia ought to act—tough, callous, decisive. Fiji was behaving in a confusing way, too; they all knew (except the man most concerned) that for years she had carried a huge flaming torch for Bobo Winthrop, who regarded the witch as his best buddy. Yet she was going out with the bouncer, whom Manfred remembered as a very tough guy.

To cap off Manfred's unsettled feeling, when he stopped at the end of his driveway to open his mailbox, he found a bill from Magdalena Orta Powell. He opened it and winced when he saw the bottom line. He sat down at his computer to work with renewed dedication. *If I ever have to go to court over this,* he thought, *I might as well forget ever buying a new car. Or my own house.* He wondered what Magdalena's house looked like. Perhaps the plumbing was made of gold.

Manfred reminded himself that while his car was humble, it was paid for, that he didn't need a house, and that adding a room to the lawyer's house was better than being in jail.

Much better.

17

Joe went farther on his morning run than he'd ever gone. He enjoyed the quiet time for thinking, not that there was exactly a cacophony in Midnight or that Chuy's conversation was not welcome. But sometimes the solitude of running was just what he needed. This morning, with the sun already blazing on his back, Joe was thinking of their little Peke, Rasta, and of all Rasta's health problems. The dog was getting older, and Joe knew there would be hard times ahead. He and Chuy had not aged, or at least not that Joe could perceive, in many, many, years.

That didn't mean they were invulnerable. Just as Joe was thinking of the previous week when Chuy had cut himself with a kitchen knife, Joe looked down, saw a rattlesnake right in front of him, and tried to leap sideways in midstride.

Joe realized three things as he lay by the side of the road. First, the snake had not been a diamondback at all, but a gopher snake. He still would not have wanted to tread on it, but it wouldn't have injected him with poison. Second, he had landed poorly and his ankle was hurting like a bitch. And third, there was no one coming in any direction.

"Okay," Joe said out loud. "Okay. First, I have to sit up." His palms and elbows were scraped and bleeding. That was minor but uncomfortable. Joe rolled onto his knees and pushed up. He glanced around for the snake, but it was gone.

Sometimes Joe saw a rancher or a commuter to Magic Portal on his morning run, but today was not one of those days. He hobbled back into Midnight, struggling not to say any of the words that popped into his head. The pain tempted him to break a promise he and Chuy had made to each other long ago. Joe looked up at the blue sky, at a vulture floating on the thermals far above, his wings spread wide. He took a deep breath, restraining himself. A promise was a promise. He limped on.

The first person to spot him was the boy Diederik, who was standing outside the Rev's cottage. Diederik came running to Joe's aid, seeming delighted to have something to do.

"You need help, yes?" the boy said.

"Yes," Joe said. "I definitely need help."

He found it was very easy to put his arm around the boy's offered shoulder. The boy was almost as tall as Joe now.

"How are you feeling?" he asked Diederik, only realizing it was odd that he was the one asking the question as the words left his mouth.

"Very strange," the boy said. "I feel like there are two people in me."

Joe didn't understand, but he didn't have to, to see the boy's distress. He said, "I know you miss your father."

"He hoped to be back by now," Diederik said, trying to sound matter-of-fact, but failing. "I don't think he will be back in time." They were making progress on the sidewalk, and they crossed the road to the shop, Joe gasping with the effort. Diederik was feeling Joe's weight after a few steps.

"The Rev's trying hard to take good care of you," Joe said.

"I miss my father and my mother," Diederik said breathlessly. "But my father told me to be brave and he would return."

Joe had no reply to that.

Chuy was reading a magazine at his workstation when Joe and Diederik made their awkward entrance, and his eyes widened as he looked from one to another.

"Mr. Joe saw a snake," Diederik said simply. "And he fell down."

"Pretty much in a nutshell," Joe said, trying to smile.

"Let me see," Chuy said, kneeling at Joe's feet. Joe, feeling a little ridiculous—but also ridiculously glad to see Chuy—held out the injured limb. Chuy got the running shoe off quickly and as gently as possible, but the pulling and tugging made Joe gasp. The ankle was already discolored and swollen.

Chuy said, "I'll run upstairs to get an ice pack." His glance went over to Diederik. "And some clothes for the boy. For tomorrow." He hurried out the front door to go up the outside stairs. Not for the first time, Joe reflected how nice it would be if their stairs were inside the building, like the ones in the pawnshop. He distracted himself by imagining the project. Maybe this winter . . . ?

Diederik moved restlessly, and Joe realized it was past time to get his weight off the boy. "Help me over to the chair," Joe said. "We'll both feel better."

Diederik helped Joe into one of the manicure chairs. Joe didn't want to collapse onto one of the antiques in his sweaty condition. And the plastic chair rolled, a huge plus. Following Joe's directions, the boy wheeled the other manicure chair over to prop Joe's foot on. Then Diederik regarded Joe with a fascinated gaze until Chuy returned, his arms full.

First, Chuy wrapped the injured ankle in a washcloth, then put cold packs around it and secured them with an elastic bandage. He gave Joe a bottle of water, some ibuprofen, and a hug. Then he handed a pair of his own shorts and a T-shirt to Diederik. "For tomorrow," he said.

"I don't think I can grow any more," Diederik said. "I am almost as big as you gentlemen!" He smiled. "But I'm grateful for the clothes."

If anything could distract Joe from the pain in his ankle, this was it. "He looked about eleven the day after he got here," he whispered. "Now he could be fifteen."

"I've never seen anything like it," Chuy said, his voice low. "Diederik, where is the Rev?" he said, in a louder tone.

"He is digging a grave," the boy said. "I offered to do it for him, but he said I could take a walk, that it was his sacred duty. And Miss Fiji, she didn't have anything for me to do this morning, and no more muffins or cookies." He looked at Chuy hopefully.

"Oh," Chuy said. "Hmmm. I've got some English muffins. You could have them with butter and jelly."

"I'm always hungry," Diederik said simply.

"Then you watch Joe while I go fix them." Chuy went out the front door to mount the stairs again.

Joe's ankle was subsiding to a dull throb now. He figured nothing was broken.

"Is everyone in Midnight like me?" Diederik said suddenly.

"No, only the Rev," Joe said. He would have enjoyed some quiet, but the boy was too restless for that. "We've never seen anyone like you, either," he added, his eyes closed while he shifted the chairs around in an attempt to be more comfortable. "You're growing so fast. I've seen you look at Grady. Most kids grow like him, not like you."

"Am I very—peculiar?" Diederik had to grope for a word that would fit. His accent was not as pronounced as it had been when he'd first gotten to Midnight. In the few days he'd been in residence, his speech had grown, right along with everything else about him.

"Peculiar?" Joe thought about it. "No. Not in the sense of weird or bizarre. But I don't think there are many like you around."

Diederik fidgeted and finally went to seek out the broom and dustpan. He swept the already-clean area around Chuy's workstation, and then the English muffins came downstairs borne by Chuy, along with a thermos of juice. Diederik fell on the muffins like he was starving, and he drank all the juice. He sat in one of the antique chairs very neatly and promptly fell asleep.

"Where's Rasta?" Joe asked abruptly. The men exchanged startled glances.

"He was in here with me when you two came in!" Chuy leaped to his feet and began looking around. "You don't think he got out when I went upstairs?"

"Maybe Mr. Snuggly sneaked in," Joe said. Rasta and Mr. Snuggly had a long-running feud, though more often than not Rasta barked and danced around when Mr. Snuggly came near. He'd never hidden before.

Joe called, "Rasta! Here, boy!" with a kind of hushed urgency. He didn't want to wake the boy.

They heard a pitiful whine.

"Look," Chuy said, pointing to an old desk about ten feet away. A tiny face peered from behind the furniture, ears back.

"He's scared," Joe said, recognizing the look and attitude.

"Of what?"

Joe reached out a hand to touch Chuy's arm. When Chuy looked down at him, Joe nodded toward the sleeping boy. "Him."

They were thoughtful for a while. No one came into the store to disturb them, and the phone didn't ring. None of the old people from the hotel stopped by, which was something of a relief. Visits from the newcomers formed an increasingly frequent (and not always welcome) part of the day. The boy slept on. From time to time, he twitched in his sleep or his hand went to his face as if something about it bothered him.

"He's like the Rev," Joe said finally, so quietly Chuy had to strain to hear him.

"But the Rev is the only one left."

"He thought so. What if he was wrong?"

"So the boy is about to . . ." Chuy's eyes widened.

"Yes," breathed Joe. "Go look on the computer." Chuy left most of the electronic work to Joe, but he could search for a calendar as well as anyone.

"Full moon in three nights," he said. "What can we do to get ready?"

Joe shrugged. "We can stay upstairs and bolt the door," he said. They fell silent and looked at Diederik.

18

Olivia was in the chapel. She could count on one hand the times she'd entered the old building. She realized now that she hadn't been missing anything. The chapel had been built from thick planks, perhaps hand-cut, she speculated, looking at them now. It was a very basic rectangular building with a pitched roof and a steeple slapped on top. It was painted white inside and out, but it was just about due another coat. Inside, the wood floors had been painted, too, a dark gray. The benches that served as the pews were sturdy but a bit splintery. There was electricity, of a very basic sort, though the Rev didn't often turn the bare bulb on. There was an altar. There was no stained glass, no beautiful vestments or altar cloths, no candles or incense. But there were three paintings, the old one above the altar that had always been there, and two Grandma Moses–style oils depicting two stories from the Bible: Daniel in the lions' den, and Noah and the ark. The new paintings were donations from Bobo. The owner, whom

Bobo had told the Rev was the artist himself, had never redeemed the artworks, and Bobo had thought they would suit the Rev.

Bobo had been right.

The Rev had been gazing at them in a fascinated way when Olivia had entered.

Now the Reverend Emilio Sheehan was sitting on a bench facing Olivia, and they were staring at each other. The Rev, small and dark and wiry, was as tough as shoe leather. Though Olivia considered herself just as formidable, she was a little anxious. She could not remember ever having a one-on-one conversation with the Rev.

But she knew he didn't do small talk, and she was not good at it, either, so she went straight to the point.

"I know everyone likes Fiji better," she said. "And I know she's a better person than me."

The Rev cocked his head to one side and waited. His dark eyes were bright in the gloomy interior of the chapel.

"But I have my own strengths and weaknesses," she said.

He nodded. "You're a fighter," he said.

She took a deep breath. "My father is one of the richest men in America."

The Rev's expression didn't change. "And?" he said. The syllable came out cracked and harsh, like the croaking of raven.

"And you know what this man did to me when I was a little girl?"

The Rev seemed, almost undetectably, to brace himself to hear something distasteful. "Fucked you?"

"Nope. That would have been straightforward. He let my mom do things with me. Rent me out to her little boyfriends. He pretended he didn't know." Her lips twisted in disgust. "She charged them to have sex with me. It was like Monopoly money to her. I was like the little shoe or the iron." Her shoulders compacted, her body hunched in on itself. She appeared about half her size.

The Monopoly references did not seem to register with the Rev. "She living? Able to pay?"

"Now there's a question that makes sense," Olivia said. "No, she's not. She was the first person I killed."

"What did you do with her?" The Rev asked this question with an almost professional interest.

"I took her boat out," she said. "I tossed her in the ocean. I hope the fishes ate her."

"Something surely did," the Rev said. He approved of that.

She said, greatly daring, "Is that what you do with the bodies?"

"No," the Rev said, after a laden pause. "Not unless it's at the full moon, some instance of self-defense. I'm no cannibal."

"Gotcha," she said, puzzled by his words, but getting that he was offended. "My point is—I kill people who need killing, and it doesn't seem to bother me. I could say my parents made me that way, but that sounds like I think I need an excuse. I don't."

"Dead insides," the Rev said, by way of diagnosis.

"Exactly." She seemed relieved to find someone who understood. "I have to wonder how you can be a reverend, and yet you do these things?"

"Hide the bodies of killers? Dispense justice to those who threaten the peace of this place?"

In a nutshell, Olivia thought. She nodded.

"Because that's why I'm here," he said. "I can't say no different than that. The God of Moses and Abraham put me here to preserve and protect Midnight. That's my job. And I'll do it to the best of my ability." He gave her a sharp nod in return, to tell her the subject was closed.

"I'm trying to help Manfred solve his problem," she said. "But so far, we haven't gotten anywhere. Do you have any advice?"

"Use every resource available," he told her. "You haven't done that yet. That's quieter. But if that don't work, go in strong and hard." And the way he leaned back after he spoke, Olivia knew that was all he was going to say. She thought of a dozen other questions, but she'd reached his limit.

"All right, then," she said. "I'm doing the best I can."

"Then that's all you need to worry about, Olivia." The Rev extended his hand, holding it over her head but not touching it. In his creaking, cracking voice, he said, "God over the serpents and animals and creatures of the land and water, bless this thy servant, Olivia. Give her strength and courage to complete her purpose. Amen."

Feeling oddly better, as if she'd been given a blank check, Olivia rose to her feet and left the chapel.

She had had an idea.

She went over to Manfred's. He gestured her in and dashed back to his computer and telephone console. He picked up the phone and had it at his ear like lightning. "No, Mandy, I don't think you need to do that," he said. "No, I definitely think a more conservative approach . . . Why? Because if you jump ahead of your stars, you're going to cancel out the advice they're giving you. Wait to see what the vet has to tell you before . . . Yes, I'm sure. Wait, and you'll be rewarded with valuable information." After a few more minutes of reassurances, he hung up. "Wanted to have her dog put to sleep because she found a lump on the dog's chest," he said. "No signs, no symptoms of anything wrong. Wanted to spare the dog pain."

"Speaking of animals," she said, "I was just over looking at the Rev's new paintings. And asking his advice."

He made a face and rubbed his eyes with both hands. "Thanks for letting me know that you don't give a damn about what I'm doing," he said. He put his hands down and looked at her. "What's up?" He sounded tired.

Olivia didn't understand what he was blathering about. "While I talked to the Rev, I had an idea. Lewis doesn't know me as Olivia, but there's a faint chance he might recognize me, and Bertha or the gardener might, too. Despite the wig. Lewis knows you by sight. Fiji's not good at subterfuge. We ruled out her bespelling someone. But what about the old people?"

"Tommy and the people at the hotel?" Manfred was not too swift today, Olivia thought, because he seemed slow to hop on the bandwagon. "What about them?"

"We'll take them to the Goldthorpe house," Olivia said. "They might have known Rachel or her husband. You know how most people think old people all look alike? I'm willing to bet that Lewis won't know they're *not* friends of his mother's or father's."

"They're way older," Manfred said. Olivia thought he seemed a little huffy, and she could not think why. "Rachel was in her early sixties. Tommy and his buddies have to be twenty years older, give or take five years."

"Morton was older than Rachel, right? Maybe they were his friends."

"Okay, assume we say they were. Assume these old people, whom we hardly know, agree to pretend they knew Morton. So what?"

"We get in in the daytime. No breaking in." Olivia smiled broadly. "See, we've sent a letter ahead of time, telling Lewis that Mr. Quick had loaned some books to his old friend Morton Goldthorpe. He's heard Morton passed, and he's coming to collect the books. We take Tommy and one of the other oldies posing as his wife. That way we get into the library and have a look at what's there."

"You think Lewis will let us get that far? You've met him. Did he seem like a guy who would let in a stranger without a fight?"

"Maybe not, but we'll have the old people with us, so what can he do about it?"

"He's crazy bad and rude, Olivia. You can't count on him to act like a guy with social skills. And especially if I were anywhere near. Lewis wouldn't piss on me if I were on fire."

"I had this idea in a church. So it's got to be a good one, if we just fine-tune it a little." She was not completely serious, but she could visualize this all falling into place, and she thought it was the beginning of a real plan. She was frustrated that Manfred couldn't seem to see its promise. "Manfred, it's all confusion to the enemy!"

He smiled, a bit reluctantly. "That's true," he said. "But it sounds kind of sketchy, to say the least. Who will go with them?"

"Do you think we could talk Joe into it?"

"Joe . . . why him?"

"Because he just inspires a feeling of reliability. You trust him. Right?"

"That's true. He's the most likable resident of Midnight, with the possible exception of Bobo. What about Bobo?"

"He can't leave work," she said. "Let me review the domino effect we have going. Teacher used to take over during the day if Bobo wanted off. But now Teacher's stuck in the convenience store until the owners find a permanent replacement. Lem isn't here to keep the pawnshop open at night, so I've been filling in for him, though I can't do it every night. I have my own business to conduct."

"We should ask Bobo first, though."

"Why are you being so freaking stubborn?"

"Because I know Bobo better, that's all."

"All right. Go over there and ask him." Olivia marched into Manfred's TV area and sat on the couch. She was obviously prepared to wait until kingdom come.

Manfred glanced at his telephone, and its light was blinking merrily. "I have to work," he said. "I have bills to pay."

"Like your lawyer bill? It's only going to get higher if we don't close this thing down."

"I'll be right back." Manfred knew when to accept the situation. He was over at the pawnshop in less than a minute.

Though the day outside was bright and cloudless and blindingly hot, the inside of the pawnshop was dark and cool. Bobo was behind the high counter, sitting on a stool and typing on the keyboard.

"Guns," he explained. "The paperwork on guns. Never ending."

"Bobo, I have a favor to ask you."

"I'm kind of stretched thin now, Manfred, but you can ask."

Now that Manfred's eyes were accustomed to the dusky light, he could see that Bobo looked tired and that his sleepy goodwill was simply sleepy. Suddenly, Manfred felt selfish. He was asking his land-lord and friend to do something that was both an imposition and an inconvenience.

"Never mind," he said.

Bobo smiled. "Well, okay. Normally I'd bug you to find out what you needed, but having Teacher stuck in place at the convenience store and Lemuel gone at the same time is running me ragged. And of course, this is the time when the shop's gotten busy, for a reason I can't even begin to understand." As if to underline his words, the bell on the door chimed as a burly man came in carrying a guitar case. Bobo glanced at the wall of musical instruments on display and sighed. "Be right with you," he called.

"It's cool," Manfred said. "You've got a lot on your plate right now." He turned to go.

"Hey," Bobo said abruptly. "Is it true that Fiji is going out with the bouncer from Cartoon Saloon?"

"So she says."

"But he seems a little . . ." Bobo's voice trailed off, and he waved a hand to convey what his words could not.

"A little what?" Manfred said, curious to see what Bobo would come up with.

"A little tough," Bobo said.

This was interesting. "Yeah, well, bouncer," Manfred said cautiously. "She says he's also an EMT."

"I just hope he's a good guy. He seems all wrong for her."

"Fiji's healthy and pretty. You can't expect her to sit home by herself."

And this time Manfred left, but he was smiling to himself.

19

Olivia took care to be sitting on the same spot on the couch when she saw Manfred returning, though of course she'd been looking around while he was gone. She could tell from the way he walked that she would get her way.

"All right, we'll ask Joe," Manfred said as he came in. "Maybe we can eat at Home Cookin tonight and talk about it. That way I won't miss any more time off work."

"So ahead of time, I need to ask the oldies if they're willing."

"Go right ahead. Since this whole crazy idea is based on them saying yes for some unknown reason."

"Unknown reason, hell," Olivia said. "They'll do it for money, same as anyone else."

"And think of something to call them besides the oldies," Manfred called as she let herself out.

Olivia, the bit firmly between her teeth, felt purposeful and much more cheerful. She pulled her hair back into a ponytail as she walked to the hotel. She felt the beginning of a trickle of sweat on her back, knew it would roll with an unpleasant ticklish feeling down the crack between her hips. She found she was looking forward to talking to Tommy again. He was a rascal, through and through.

Olivia liked old people. It surprised her to realize this, and she wondered if it had something to do with her relationship with Lemuel, who was the oldest person she'd ever met . . . though perhaps calling him a person was a bit of a stretch.

But then she remembered her father's mother. She'd liked Grandmother. There had been a few moments in her childhood that hadn't actually sucked, and the times she'd gotten to stay with her grandmother had contained all those moments. So she walked into the hotel with pleasant anticipation. Two old women were sitting in the lobby, which contained several comfortable chairs and a table or two. One of the women was knitting, and the other was listening to an iPod. They both looked up with interest as she came to a stop in front of them.

"I'm Olivia Charity," she said. "I met Tommy the other day. I believe you ladies must be Mamie and Suzie?"

Mamie turned out to be the knitter, and Suzie the listener. Mamie had to use a walker, and Olivia discovered quickly that her conversation tended to wander away from time to time. Mamie's knit pants hung on her, and her shoes were orthopedic, but she wore makeup, by God, and her hair was white and curly like a lamb's coat. Suzie was (to Olivia's surprise) of Asian descent, though her speech was purely American. Her thick gray hair was cut short at her earlobes, and her eyeglasses were decorated with rhinestones. Suzie was wearing a red T-shirt and white crops with red sandals. She looked as if she were about to go on a Golden Age cruise.

"Yeah," Suzie said, when Olivia introduced herself, "Tommy told us about you. I'll go get him." Suzie was able to walk on her own with relative ease.

Left alone with Mamie, Olivia asked her how she liked the hotel.

"It's safer than the Five Aces," Mamie said. Her eyes were a faded blue, and her eyelids looked very thin and delicate with their trace of blue eye shadow. "We were going to get murdered in our beds there. Or right out in the street."

"So you were glad to move?"

"Glad? Well, I don't think 'glad' really covers it . . . I never have liked Texas. I loved Vegas. But I wanted to live, more than I wanted to be in Nevada." She looked at Olivia with close attention. "I expect you'll be that way, too."

"Probably," Olivia said. But it was a creepy thing to think about, and she was relieved when Tommy and Suzie returned, Tommy moving slowly with his cane and Suzie in possession of a bit of news. "We have asked if we can use what Mrs. Whitefield calls the parlor," she said. "Mrs. Whitefield said yes."

Olivia was relieved. The lobby was wide open, and there were several doors behind which could lurk any number of listeners. At the moment, there was no one there besides them and a sleeping man in the chair in the corner of the room, a newspaper half off his lap. He was several decades younger than the people Olivia had come to see. In fact, he seemed to be Olivia's age.

"That's Shorty's grandson," Tommy said, pointing with his cane. "He came in late, couple of days ago. He jumped out of his car and ran into the hotel like he was on fire."

"Shush," said Mamie. "You'll wake him up. I think Shorty's having his visit with the nurse."

"Then this guy ought to be in his own room!" Tommy said. He seemed to be in a grumpy mood. Olivia wondered if Suzie had woken him from his own nap.

The parlor turned out to be a small room leading off the south side of the lobby. Olivia glanced back, and she saw that the younger man's eyes were wide open and fixed on her. He hadn't been asleep at all. He hadn't wanted to talk to the old ladies, so he'd been feigning. He looked faintly amused, and as his eyes met hers, he winked. She almost smiled. *His eyes are gorgeous,* she thought. Brown and large and emphasized with perfectly arched dark eyebrows, he looked like someone out of an old Spanish painting. And as she thought this, he batted those long eyelashes at her. She smiled and shook her head and followed her old people.

Then she thought, *It's just like he knew what I was thinking.* And she frowned. *Exactly like he knew.*

Exactly.

She put this thought on her mental back burner as she explained Manfred's problem to Mamie, Suzie, and Tommy. And then she sketched in the plan she'd devised to solve it.

"Seems pretty weak, but I want to get out of this place for a day, so I'll say yes," said Tommy. "Girls?"

"He won't hurt us?" Mamie said cautiously.

"No. If our friend Joe can't go with you, another one of us will. We won't let you get hurt."

"What about stairs?" Mamie was being sure all her obstacles could be overcome.

"There are three steps up to the front door, and a flight of stairs inside. But there's an elevator." Olivia remembered seeing what had certainly seemed like an elevator door when she'd gone up the stairs, right beside the library. "I'll make sure," she said, though how she was going to do that she couldn't imagine at the moment.

"So," said Suzie, after an expectant pause, "what's in it for us?"

On her walk over, Olivia had anticipated the question. "Two hundred dollars apiece," she said.

"Two fifty," Tommy said.

"Two twenty-five."

"Done," Mamie said, in her faint voice.

"Do I have to square this with Mrs. Whitefield?" Olivia asked.

"She ain't our keeper," Tommy said. "We can go where we want."

"Long as we tell her we're missing a meal," Suzie said. "By the way, it would be nice to have a lunch or dinner somewhere else, while we're making this big trip of yours. And not at our own expense."

"Done," Olivia said. After all, everyone had to eat. "I'll come back and let you know, when we've finalized our arrangements."

"And we want to go to the library in Davy," Mamie said unexpectedly. "We need something to read, and they got the audiobooks there, we called to ask."

Olivia was not much of a reader herself, but she approved of it as a pastime, so she said, "I'll see if they have some kind of bookmobile, and if they don't, I'll take you myself."

There were nods all around, and it seemed they'd struck a bargain.

"A real pleasure dealing with you, Olivia," Tommy said.

When she exited through the lobby, Mr. Big Eyes was nowhere in sight. As Olivia walked back to the pawnshop, she felt well pleased with the day. Forward progress was always a good thing. Even a weak plan was better than no plan. And anything would do to fill in the time until Lemuel returned, especially since she hadn't had a chance to start working on the proposal she'd received days before.

Olivia took a shower before she walked down to dinner to meet with Joe. Since the Home Cookin restaurant was the only place to eat in Midnight, it was fortunate for the Midnighters that Madonna Reed was an excellent cook of the home-style variety. Tonight, Madonna was experimenting with a chicken potpie, which meant that she'd had a lot of leftover vegetables and chicken. Since the menu at Home Cookin stayed pretty steady, a change was interesting.

Olivia met up with Manfred on the way through the door. Joe was waiting for them, and Chuy with him, which was no surprise.

Rasta was sitting in Chuy's lap. The Peke often came to meals with his humans, though Madonna had forbidden any feeding from the table or plate. Joe and Chuy had pretended to be shocked she'd think such a thing was possible. Instead of sitting at the big table in the center of the little restaurant, the usual spot for all town residents (and until the hotel had reopened they could all fit around it), the four settled in one of the booths against the west wall, which signaled they had something to talk about.

A teen boy from one of the ranches to the south of Midnight was working as a combination busboy/waiter. He hurried to bring them water and to take their drink orders. Chuy put Rasta down on the floor and pretended he wasn't curious when Joe said, "What do you all want to talk about?"

Manfred said, "It's like this. You know about my situation. With the law and with Lewis Goldthorpe."

Joe and Chuy nodded.

"And you heard what Rachel said at the séance." They nodded again.

"So Olivia has come up with a plan."

Joe listened patiently as Manfred explained. Then Olivia told them about her bargain with Suzie, Mamie, and Tommy. Chuy, after he'd grasped the outline of the proposal, sighed and looked down at his cutlery.

"I can't do it," Joe said. "I'm sorry, but I can't go with the old people."

Whatever Olivia had expected, it wasn't a flat refusal.

"What—why?" she said, shocked.

"Olivia, we can't be involved in this. Unless there's a direct threat to us or our town."

Olivia opened her mouth to protest. Chuy held up his hand.

"We aren't what we once were. But we still have rules," Chuy said.

"This *is* a direct threat," Olivia argued.

"Not to us," Joe said.

"Not to Midnight," Chuy said.

"How is this different from Connor Lovell?" she asked. She did not raise her voice, but her intensity was laserlike.

Manfred inhaled sharply. He had not wanted to ever hear that name again. He knew Olivia had made a misstep.

"Let it go," he told her. "Olivia, that's their right."

"Okay, then," she said, struggling to regain her composure.

Manfred noticed uneasily that Joe's eyes, normally a calm, boring brown, were sort of glowy. Chuy's, too. Rasta had leaped up beside Chuy. He was relieved to see that the dog's eyes looked absolutely normal. "We'll make another plan, guys. No problem," he said, in a brave attempt at a cheerful voice.

There was a lull in the conversation, during which they all took a step back from being upset.

Manfred said, "Olivia, didn't you tell me that you were looking for a desk for your apartment?"

Olivia took the cue. "Thanks for reminding me. Joe, I do need a desk, if one comes in that's not too fragile or pricey."

"I did get a fauxtique desk yesterday," Joe said, smiling. "Probably from the nineteen sixties and very sturdy. I don't know if we could get it down the stairs to your place, though. We'd have to come around to the side, take it straight in the east door. . . ."

They embarked on a technical discussion about moving the desk.

"Maybe I can use my high school math skills for once," Manfred said. "I knew there was a reason I had to take it."

They were able to have a decent dinner together, though Manfred became distracted by trying to figure out another plan. He yearned to be out from under his situation the way a man in the desert yearns to spot a palm tree.

Olivia elbowed him when he was thinking vaguely about

suing Lewis for slander. Or some other defamation. "What?" he asked her.

There was a stranger inside the doorway.

"That's Mr. Big Eyes, Shorty Horowitz's grandson," she said.

The stranger waited to be seated, and Manfred called, "Just take a seat anywhere. Madonna or the kid will be with you in a second." He nodded and took one of the tables for two along the front wall. Unfortunately, it was the Rev's table.

"Any one but that one!" Olivia said. He raised his eyebrows and pointed to the one nearest the door. They all nodded.

Olivia muttered, "I could kick myself. I should have thought that at him, to see if he'd react. I know he heard me thinking about how pretty his eyes are, at the hotel."

The man was looking down at his silverware rather pointedly.

"He *can* hear my thoughts," she said to Manfred.

Joe and Chuy had gone to the counter to talk to Madonna for a moment, while the new boy was coming to their booth with the credit card and charge slip.

"I've met a person who could do that, before," Manfred said.

"You're kidding."

"Not at all." Manfred signed the slip and got out of the booth to walk to the newcomer's table. Mr. Big Eyes looked up, unsurprised.

"Hi," Manfred said. He hesitated. "Do you, by any chance, know a waitress in Louisiana? Works in a bar in a little town called Bon Temps?"

The difference in the newcomer's face was comical. He looked startled, alarmed, and panicky in quick succession. "Why do you want to know?" he said, with unconvincing indifference.

"Because I know her, too, and my friend here believes you share a trait with her."

Olivia, who'd been right on his heels, stepped up to Manfred's side.

"I'm Olivia Charity," she said. "I hear you're Shorty Horowitz's grandson?"

"Your buddies told you," the newcomer said. He was tall and lean, and he looked as if he'd spent a lot of his life looking behind him and around corners, waiting for an attack. "Yeah, I'm Rick Horowitz."

"Manfred Bernardo." Manfred held out his hand, and somewhat reluctantly, Rick shook it. When he let Manfred's hand go, he looked a little surprised.

"So you do know Sookie," he said. "You're a friend?"

"Yes, I am," Manfred said. "Olivia, I'll tell you about her someday."

"Is everyone in this town different?" Rick said, keeping his voice low.

Manfred smiled. "Brother, you have no idea," he said. "If you're going to be in town for a few days, drop in to see me. You can't spend your whole time in the hotel."

Olivia said, "We don't see too many new faces here, Rick."

The newcomer looked from one of them to the other. He seemed to come to a conclusion. "Please," he said. "If we're going to know each other beyond saying hello, you can call me Barry."

Rick—or rather, Barry—told Manfred he'd visit the next morning. He'd glanced down at his cell phone at a weather screen, and then told them he needed to order.

"You have somewhere to be tonight," Manfred said.

"Not exactly," Barry said. "I don't stay out after sunset in Texas."

They both regarded him with some astonishment. When he didn't expand on this statement, Manfred said, "Sure. Well, see you around." With the new busboy hovering to take Barry's order, they waved and left Home Cookin.

"Doesn't stay out after sunset in Texas?" Olivia muttered to Manfred as they walked home.

"I don't blame him," Manfred said. "I think he's vampire-phobic."

"Just in Texas?"

"He hasn't told us the whole truth about anything but that. He's really worried about vampires. I guess it's lucky Lemuel isn't around."

Olivia obviously disagreed, but she said, "There aren't any other vampires in a two-hundred-mile radius of Midnight. Did you know that? This Rick, rechristened Barry, might be glad to hear it."

"No," Manfred said, very surprised. "I never realized . . . well, okay. Interesting. Listen, what do you think of asking this new guy to step into Joe's place in your plan?"

"You have that much confidence in him after knowing him for ten minutes?"

"Would you quit your bitching? Who else are we going to find?"

To Manfred's surprise, she laughed. "I wish I could think of someone. You're chipper all of a sudden."

"It's interesting having someone new in town," he said. "And I think you're right. From what I get from him, I'm almost certain he's a telepath, so that's even more interesting. Kind of unnerving, though."

"To have someone know what you're thinking? Damn straight, it's unnerving. Did I understand you were telling him you knew another telepath? You kept that one close to your chest."

"You have more secrets than I do."

"No shit, Sherlock."

Manfred laughed again. "I haven't heard anyone say that in years."

"My grandmother . . ." But then Olivia clamped down on whatever she'd thought of telling him, somewhat to Manfred's disappointment.

"Too many people know too much here, anyway," she muttered.

"I have to take over the pawnshop now." She hurried up the front steps of the pawnshop and the CLOSED sign flipped over to OPEN.

Bobo popped out of Midnight Pawn almost as soon as Olivia went in. "Hey, buddy," he said easily. "I'm just about to go grab some supper before Home Cookin closes. Sometimes Madonna doesn't want Dillon around anymore, so she sends him home."

"Dillon?"

"Dillon Braithwaite. The new kid. The waiter."

"Only you would know his name," Manfred said.

"You didn't ask him who he was?" Bobo seemed surprised and a little reproachful.

"Never occurred to me," Manfred said with absolute honesty. "I'd never do that in a city, so I never thought of doing it here."

"Well . . . gosh." Bobo shook his head and hurried off to get some food. From Dillon the waiter.

As he stopped by his mailbox and retrieved a hefty bundle of envelopes, Manfred wondered if his lack of curiosity about the boy made him a bad person. Did he routinely ignore waitstaff? He shrugged. He couldn't work up a lot of concern about it.

From the size of the bundle, Manfred did realize he hadn't opened his mail in a couple of days. He sat at his desk, conveniently handy to a trash basket, to sort through it. He pitched several ads, two offers for credit cards, one letter from a local cemetery offering to give him a tour and sell him a plot at a reasonable cost for his final resting place, and one Hallmark card from his mother, who wanted him to know that she was "Thinking of You." Though Manfred loved his mother, he couldn't say that he gave her a lot of thought in return. But he did need to call her. He was overdue in his duty. He glanced at his calendar and saw that he hadn't talked to her for three weeks.

He dug out his cell phone and placed the call, knowing that if he didn't do it right at this moment, he'd put it off again. Rain Bernardo picked up on the first ring.

"Hi, Mom," he said. She responded with almost embarrassing fervor. He thanked her for the card, told her he was working long hours as usual, told her he still liked his house and the town, and came very close to telling her about Rachel. But the enormity of the gap between his life and hers seemed so wide; there would have to be so much fill-in before he could talk across it. In the end, he told her nothing new.

But she had news for him. "I'm getting married," she said, almost defiantly.

For a second, Manfred was too stunned to say anything. "Wow, that's great!" he blurted, desperately trying to fill the silence. "Gary, I'm assuming."

"Yes, of course, Gary."

"When will it be?"

"We're just going to slip off some weekend soon," she said evasively.

"I'll come," he said, absolutely certain that he must make the effort. He owed his mother that much. "Just let me know for sure."

"Well, we haven't set a date yet," she said.

"What are you not telling me?"

"Oh, son, you're so sharp." She sighed. "The thing is, Gary's kids aren't as . . . agreeable to the idea as you are."

"Why not? You're one of the nicest women I ever met," Manfred said honestly.

She laughed, but only a little. "That sounds like you came up to me at a party or something, instead of me being your mom."

"Uh-huh," he said. He waited.

"Well, the thing is, they . . . oh, they're just silly, stupid people," she said, in a burst of anger that was as unexpected as it was refreshing.

"Me," he said, suddenly understanding. "They don't like me."

"They don't even know you," she said, and the anger was still there, full force. "They just don't like the idea of you. A psychic. Isn't that stupid?"

"It's an excuse," Manfred said. He'd had more experience with human beings than some people three times his age. "They just don't want their dad to get married, to you or anyone else. I can bet that if I were super-wealthy, they wouldn't have any objections at all to what I do."

"I hate to think that, but I have to say there's something to it," Rain said.

"Mom, you're just barely over forty, so you can have a long and happy marriage with Gary. Go for it." Rain had been unmarried and in her teens when she'd had Manfred, and she would never talk about his father. If his grandmother, Xylda, had known, she hadn't said a word. Manfred thought she didn't know who her daughter had been sleeping with, or she'd have found a way to let him know without actually telling him. Xylda had loved him, maybe more than she'd loved her own daughter, Rain, but she'd loved drama most of all.

"I do deserve to be happy," Rain said now, as if she'd been told that but was just now believing it. "I am going to marry Gary. And if we decide not to tell his kids in advance, we may not tell you, either. We'll just go do it."

Since he'd already told her that was what he wanted, Manfred could only repeat that he agreed and wished her luck. "Tell me when it's done," he said. "I love you, Mom. If Gary's the guy you want, go for it."

When he hung up, after having the whole conversation with Rain several times, Manfred sat back in his chair and worried for a minute or two. Gary and his mother had been dating six years, but those were years that Manfred had not been around much, since he'd been living mostly with his grandmother. He realized that he didn't know Gary very well. Presumably his mother did, and that was what was important. Should he check Gary out? But Rain had dated the man for a long time. If she hadn't found out if he had a criminal record in that length of time, she didn't want to know.

Manfred decided to leave well enough alone.

It would be strange when his mother had a last name that was different from his.

Once he had thought of that, he realized he couldn't, for the life of him, remember Gary's last name. He laughed out loud. The great psychic couldn't remember his mom's future name. *Redding. That was it.*

Having settled that, Manfred gave the subject no more thought. Instead, energized by his interest in the new guy, Rick (or Barry) Horowitz, he settled in to work for over an hour before knocking off to watch some television. He figured he'd made back what he'd had to pay Magdalena Orta Powell . . . but he'd thought of something else he needed from her. And he knew he couldn't get it in a straightforward way.

He found the bill and cover letter he'd received from Powell's office. He examined it carefully.

Then he started comparing fonts in his Word program.

"I sent a letter to Rachel's house," he told Olivia the next morning, after he'd been to the Davy post office. He knew he sounded smug, but he was feeling pretty optimistic. Ever since Fiji had laid the "confidence" spell on him, he'd had these moments of sheer . . . rightness. Like he *couldn't* do the wrong thing and every idea he had was a good one. "It'll be delivered tomorrow, and Lewis will have to sign for it."

Should he be worrying about this? He didn't know, and he only realized theoretically that he should care.

"Why?" she said blankly.

"I duplicated Magdalena's letterhead. Her letter tells Lewis that the old folks are coming and they should be allowed access to search for possessions of theirs in the library."

"Show me," she said.

So he did, smiling all the while. "Pretty damn official, huh?"

Olivia looked at the "letter" very carefully. "You idiot," she said, but she didn't sound furious, which Manfred took as a compliment.

"Sounds good, doesn't it?"

"When did you get the idea that lawyers talked like this?"

"What, you know a lot about lawyer talk?"

"I know more than you do, apparently." She reread the letter. "However, this isn't bad, and Lewis may swallow it. It gives us a kind of layer of credibility. Unless he calls Ms. Powell. Didn't think of that, did you?"

Manfred felt that he should be crestfallen, but he wasn't. "He won't. He'll be so angry he'll be getting ready to repel the boarders. So he'll get the letter tomorrow. And we should plan on going to the house the next day, or tomorrow afternoon, even. What do you think would suit the old folks best?"

Olivia said, "Say we leave here day after tomorrow at nine. We'll have to stop at least once, because they'll have to pee. We get to Dallas, take them to a Golden Corral or an Outback or something, and then go to Bonnet Park. We'll get to the Goldthorpe house between one and two, give or take. And we'll spend about an hour there. We should be able to have them back by dinner."

Manfred had been confident she'd end up being glad about his taking the initiative. "Now we have to enlist Barry. We'll have to take two cars. He can ride with one of us, and the other will drive the old people."

"I'll go talk to him," she said.

"I'll go over to Fiji's," Manfred said, to his own surprise. "I haven't seen her today."

As Olivia set off for the hotel, Manfred crossed Witch Light Road to see Midnight's own witch.

As soon as he saw her, he felt completely sober.

20

Fiji was crying. It made something inside Manfred twist and cringe. For a second he stood, shocked, and then he said, "That Travis! Last night! Did he hurt you?"

Fiji looked as surprised as a weeping woman could. "No! Are you kidding? I would have killed him if he had."

Manfred felt a relief so intense that he had to sit down in one of the wicker chairs. "Then what?" he said. "What's wrong?"

"I didn't have a good time," she said. She was making a desperate attempt to stop crying, and it wasn't doing her voice any favors. Her words kind of hiccupped out.

"Lots of dates are like that," he said, having to suppress an impulse to laugh.

"How the hell would I know?"

"Why wouldn't you?"

"Oh, Manfred," she said disgustedly.

He was bewildered.

"Seriously," he said. "I don't see why you wouldn't know that. Did you just date one guy all through high school or something?"

"I'm fat," she said, as one stated the obvious.

"Not so," Manfred said instantly. "You have a woman's body, a butt and boobs." He started to say, "And even if you were, you're still pretty," but he had enough sense to shut up while he was ahead.

She looked both embarrassed and flattered. "Nice of you to say so."

"I speak the truth, grasshopper," he said seriously. He had no idea what that reference was, but his grandmother had always thought it was funny. Fiji seemed to find it so, too. "So anyway, what was wrong about your date with Travis, since we're agreeing that nothing's wrong with the way you look?"

She sighed heavily. "We just don't seem to have anything in common." She propped herself on her elbows and swabbed her face with a tissue. "We always talk about the Cartoon Saloon and the crazy people who come in there. He asks me how things are with the shop, and I say okay. Last night, he asked me who actually comes to my shop."

"And you told him?"

"I told him I sold alternative-lifestyle things for women, mostly, and led classes in how to find your inner strength, and that I was a witch and sold some stuff pertaining to witchcraft. So my clientele is mostly women. And I'm a practitioner as well."

"And he said?"

"And I quote, 'Oooooh, spooky lady!' He didn't really seem to know how to react aside from that. He asked me if I had any tattoos."

"You told him you were a witch, and that's all he could think of to say?" Manfred smiled, just a little, and in a second he and Fiji were laughing out loud.

"I know," she said. "I know! But at the moment, it wasn't funny at all, it felt like the kiss of death!"

"How'd it go after that?" Manfred was trying not to laugh any more. He was a bit surprised the bouncer hadn't had a chance to find out about Fiji's tattoos firsthand.

"Pretty dire. I didn't know how to talk about the price beef was fetching and calf roping or bull riding—he loves the rodeo—and he didn't know what to make of Midnight. He told me about his last shift with the ambulance, when a guy had a heart attack and then he'd had to pull a baby out of a wreck. Finally we got down to what television shows we watched, and I kind of feel like it's all over if that's the main topic you can come up with. Not that you can't find out a lot about people from that," she added, in case that was Manfred's fallback position when he was on a date.

"I've talked about television, I admit it freely," he said, trying to keep a straight face, but they started laughing again.

"It was *awful*," Fiji said. "Assuming he ever calls again, I think I'll give it a pass. That's what I get for going out with someone who had nothing but hotness going for him."

"Hey, it could have turned out good."

"Yeah, but . . . it didn't. I lost a few hours of time. And a little of my self-respect. And I never discovered if the hotness was all attitude."

"I ran into Bobo the other evening, and he knew you were going out with Travis McNamara."

"Yes, I told him," she said, in a voice so even you could have put a level on it. She shrugged. "He seemed pleased." She was trying as hard as she could to look neutral about that, but in fact the feelings chased across her face. Defiant, angry, sad.

"He was pretty worried about it. He thought Travis was too rough for you."

Looking much more cheerful, she sat up straight, took a deep breath, and said, "Thanks for coming over and listening to my crap. I'll bet there was something you wanted to talk about?"

"That confidence you gave me. It was great."

Fiji brightened even more. "I'm so glad! It was something new I was trying out. How long before it wore off?"

"That's the only problem. I'm still getting, like, flashbacks," he said, trying not to sound uneasy. "I can't tell if some plan I have is actually a good idea, or if I just think so because I'm under the spell. Kind of like Olivia thinking she's had a good idea if she has it in the chapel."

Fiji looked thoughtful. "Okay . . . what you're saying is it's working too well? That you feel you might have lost your judgment?"

He nodded vigorously. "Exactly."

"So I need to temper it somehow." Fiji pulled out the old notebook she kept in a drawer under the counter and got a pen from the caddy on her desk. "And you're having flashbacks. So I need to cut down on the . . ." Her voice trailed off as she wrote a few more words. "Thanks, Manfred. I appreciate the feedback."

"Have you met the new guy yet?"

"What new guy?"

"He may tell you his name is Rick, but he also says it's Barry. Horowitz. He came in the middle of the night two nights ago. He's the grandson of one of the residents."

"And he's staying?" She was still waiting for the pertinence of the new guy to manifest itself.

"For a while, at least," Manfred said. "He's unusual, Fiji. Even for here."

Diederik came in, looking hopeful. Fiji immediately put a plate up on the counter, piled with homemade biscuits covered with plastic wrap. "Oh, thank you," the boy said. He was even more appreciative when Fiji put a knife, a dish of butter, and some jam beside the biscuits.

They were both giving him a careful once-over. "I don't think you grew as much," Manfred said. "It's slowing down."

"I did get some bigger clothes, just in case, but I believe you're right," Fiji said, pushing the plate closer to Diederik, who unwrapped the biscuits with speed. He remembered to offer them to Manfred, but when Manfred shook his head, the boy looked relieved and dug in. Fiji put a glass of juice beside the plate, and Diederik drained it at a gulp.

"What does the Rev feed you?" Manfred asked.

"Oatmeal every morning. But some bacon also, this morning." Diederik's answer was not very clear.

"I don't know where you put it," Manfred said.

Fiji looked a little forlorn, as if she well understood the compulsion to eat, but Diederik said, "I'm always hungry. Always. I hope it won't be like this forever!"

"I'm just guessing, but I don't think it will be," Fiji said. "Do you expect your father will come back soon?" She glanced at the calendar on her desk anxiously.

"Yes, after he completes his job," Diederik said. He pushed the plate away from him, abruptly uninterested. "My aunt couldn't keep me anymore. My mother died."

Manfred could tell Fiji was as unnerved as he was. He picked up a wisp of a picture from the boy's head. "Did you have a brother or sister?" he asked.

"I had an older sister. But she died before she was born, my mother told me." Diederik looked suddenly forlorn.

"I'm so sorry," Manfred said. It was definitely time to change the subject. "Listen, Diederik, when you finish doing whatever Fiji has lined up for you to do, can you come over to my place? I have a computer game you might enjoy."

"Oh, yes," the boy said, his smile back in place.

Manfred gave a wave of his hand and turned to leave. As he went through the door, he saw Bobo walking across the street to

Fiji's. "Leaving the store without a master?" he called, thinking with pleasure of how glad Fiji would be to see Bobo.

"I got a sign on the door with my phone number on it," Bobo said. "I'm going nuts waiting for Lemuel to come back and Teacher to be relieved from convenience store duty. I hope he's making good money."

"No one seems to know who actually owns the convenience store. Except Teacher."

"I never asked," Bobo said with a shrug.

Manfred sat down at his computer and got back to work. He thought about taking the time to research who owned the store. But he would miss a day of work, going to Bonnet Park on his mission. With a sigh, he returned to solving the problems of people he didn't know and might never meet. His own concerns would have to wait.

21

When Olivia entered the hotel, all the inhabitants were arguing. She stood back and listened for a while, a little amused and a lot exasperated. One of the "temporary residents" who was doing some contract work for Magic Portal, the computer business located east of Davy and Midnight, had returned to the hotel to find that (apparently) Shorty Horowitz had picked the lock to his room and (this was definite) was asleep on his bed. Shorty Horowitz, a short and round man with more white hair bristling out of his ears and nostrils than on his head, was irate, the temporary resident was even more irate, and Barry Horowitz was trying to calm everyone down, including Lenore Whitefield, who looked completely rattled. Harvey Whitefield was not in evidence.

"My grandfather got confused and thought he was getting into his own room," Barry was saying. Olivia was the only one who noticed he hadn't consulted with the old man before he said this.

"And he picks the locks in his own place?" was the first thing that popped out of the other man's mouth. A young man about Barry's age, he was wearing a ratty T-shirt and jeans, but he was making some serious money if his accessories were any indication. The wallet in his back pocket was so thick with plastic that (if Olivia had been given to worrying about people) she would have had concerns for his spine. He had a very cool watch on his wrist. The sunglasses propped up on his head were high-end Oakleys.

"Nobody else is gonna do it!" Shorty bleated, and Olivia had to stifle a grin.

"Why don't you have keycards like everyone else in this century?" Mr. Temporary snarled at Mrs. Whitefield.

Olivia thought it was interesting that the man's rudeness stiffened Lenore Whitefield's spine.

"It wouldn't be in keeping with the age of the hotel," she retorted. "Mr. Lattimore, nothing in your room was taken or harmed. Mr. Horowitz is obviously a senior citizen with some memory issues. I'm sure you got an unpleasant surprise, but the incident is over, with no one hurt. And no property damage."

Olivia decided there was more to the woman than she'd imagined. The wind went out of Lattimore's sails, and he deflated completely after threatening to have Magic Portal find him a room somewhere else, to which Mrs. Whitefield responded, "Good luck with that."

The hall cleared abruptly.

Lattimore stomped into his room and shut the door, making sure to shoot the dead bolt so that everyone could hear it. Barry guided Shorty downstairs to his own room, with Olivia following at a discreet distance. Finally, Barry emerged from Shorty's room. He looked frazzled. He did not seem surprised that Olivia was waiting for him. She said, "I came to talk to you."

"I figured. To what do I owe the honor?"

"I have a business proposition for you."

"Does it involve vampires in any way?"

"Not to my knowledge."

"Then I'm all ears."

Shorty's room was at the rear of the hall. On their way to the lobby area, Olivia saw Tommy, Mamie, and Suzie playing cards in Tommy's room with the door virtuously open. "I'll talk to you all later," she called. They nodded, barely lifting their heads from their cards.

Barry brought her a can of Coke. Olivia popped the top to be sociable, though carbonated beverages were not her drink of choice.

"You seem to understand old people," she began, wanting to start on a positive note.

"I understood that I needed to come find out what was happening when I got to Shorty's apartment in Nevada and found out he'd gone," Barry said grimly. "As you saw just now, my grandfather has memory glitches. He seems to have managed to cover that up from the people who lured him here. Evidently, he told them that he had no living relatives. The Whitefields were some kind of surprised when I tracked him down."

"I didn't know any of that," Olivia said, after an appreciable pause.

"I know," he said.

"The other three were brought here the same way, but at least they all knew each other," Olivia said. "No wonder your grandfather is so disoriented." He was in a strange land with strange people.

"In all fairness, this is a lot nicer than the apartment he was in," Barry said. "And someone's watching him all the time, though maybe not closely enough, as I discovered today. But since no one at all was minding him before, this is still better. But I need to know why he was brought here, who brought him, what they want."

This was an issue Olivia had planned to investigate after she'd solved Manfred's problems, so she wasn't best pleased at having it pushed to the forefront of the agenda. But she accepted it as inevitable. "You can't take care of him, I gather?"

"I don't see how," Barry said. "I haven't settled anywhere in years, and I can't stay in Texas."

"You have some history here in this state?"

"Most of it bad," he said gloomily.

"I take it you have vampire trouble."

He nodded. "You could say that. I would rather have done anything than follow Shorty's trail to Texas, but all my roads seem to lead back here. I had a hell of a lot of bad luck in Dallas, mostly due to my own stupidity. The vampire population here has . . . Well, they're prejudiced against me, let me just say."

"There's only one in this area. And he's unusual. And he's not here at the moment."

"That gives me exactly one drop of relief, into a bucket of worry."

"Plus, in the summer, a lot of the vamps have started migrating."

"Sure. Somewhere where the days aren't so long." Barry sounded very familiar with vampire habits.

"You're not a hunter, are you?"

He snorted. "Do I look like a fool with a death wish?"

She shook her head. "No, but people don't always look like what they are. No one would look at you and say, 'He's a telepath.'"

"We're definitely not common," he said offhandedly.

"There are many more?" She didn't disguise her surprise.

"At least one more." He obviously wasn't going to talk about that. "What do you need?" He'd been relaxed, chatty, but no longer.

"All right," she said, with equal briskness. "I need you to go with Tommy, Suzie, and Mamie tomorrow on a little road trip to a fancy house in a suburb of Dallas. Manfred and I will go with you most of the way, but we're not going to the house in question. We'll fill you in on everything at length, so you're prepared. But what we need you to do, if you agree, is get in the house, get the older people up to the room designated as the library, and look at it as hard as you can while you're there. There's something hidden there, and we need to know where to start to look. Now that I know what you can do, I also want you to get as close to the man named Lewis as you can. Get everything you can out of his mind. And tell us what you see."

"How much?" was all Barry asked.

Naturally, Olivia was curious about Barry's need for money. He was able-bodied, personable, not stupid. But actually, it didn't matter.

"No," he said. "It doesn't."

Having a telepath around was a two-edged sword. "Interesting," Olivia said, after an appreciable pause. "I'm so used to assuming my mind is opaque that I simply hadn't applied your particular skill to me."

"Yeah, it wins me friends everywhere."

"But you haven't really tried to conceal it."

"Not here. It's effing weird. Everywhere else I've been, my whole life, my primary purpose has been concealing what I am. But here . . . not so much."

"Let me ask you . . ."

"What?"

"You've been in the diner."

"Yeah."

"What's the deal with the Reeds?"

"What do you mean?" He was hedging. She didn't have to be a telepath to see that.

"I've always wondered about them. Why are they here? They're so . . . I started to say, *normal*. But there has to be a reason for them to be here. It's not simply chance." Olivia really did want to know.

"Would you like me to tell them things about you?"

Olivia leaned forward, ready to break his neck if she had to. "What do you think?" she whispered.

"Then I'm not going to tell you things about them."

Olivia forced herself to relax. She hadn't realized until this moment how much she didn't trust the Reeds, and his reaction somehow reinforced that feeling. "Fair enough," she said.

"So. You never answered. How much?"

"Five hundred," she said. She had that much in her room, and she could go by the ATM in Davy to get more. Manfred would repay her.

"Seven fifty."

"Six hundred."

"Six fifty," he countered.

"Done," she said.

He stood to extend his hand to her, and she also stood to shake his. When she touched him, she had the same feeling she'd had when she'd first touched Lemuel. "Not completely human," she said.

"What?"

"You heard me." She smiled, glad that she'd been able to shake him up in return for the unpleasant surprise he'd given her.

Barry smiled back. "Sorry about your psycho mom," he said, and walked away.

"Tomorrow morning, bright and early," she called after him. She would not let him have the last word.

She was tougher than that. She was always tougher than that.

22

The day of the Bonnet Park field trip didn't start well on any level. Manfred, Olivia, and Barry were up and ready by the designated time, and Olivia and Manfred both took their cars over to the hotel. Mamie, Suzie, and Tommy were up, which was good, and they'd had breakfast, which was good, but Mamie had had a bad night and she was hurting.

"I can't go," she said. "I just can't face a long drive. My hip hurts too bad today, dammit. I want to get out of this hole and see some life."

Manfred agreed with her assessment. Mamie looked frail and pale, and she moved with obvious difficulty. But Tommy and Suzie argued and cajoled and wasted time trying to persuade their friend to go with them. It was a relief to Manfred when Mamie remained adamant.

Then Lenore Whitefield became an obstacle. She was startled and dismayed to discover that "her" old people had planned an excursion. It was obvious she'd never imagined they might want to be anywhere else, and she was uncertain about whether she could allow it.

"Allow it?" Olivia stood with her hands on her hips. "Are they in jail? Do they have to bring notes from their parents?"

Lenore flushed. "Miss Charity, you're being difficult on purpose. Of course not, but they're in my care, and I'm responsible for their well-being."

"Last I heard, I was an adult and responsible for myself," Tommy said pugnaciously. "I'm no baby sucking on a tit." Suzie nodded vigorously.

Lenore grew even redder. "No need for that kind of talk, Tommy. You'll miss your nurse's visit."

"I ain't dying today," Tommy said. The force of his personality was too much for Lenore. She literally threw up her hands.

"All right, go on," she said. "Please don't try to do too much, and please take all your medication before you go."

"We'll have them back this evening," Manfred said, trying to placate the woman. He had an uneasy feeling that if Lenore called Eva Culhane, they'd never leave the building, because from the little he'd seen of Culhane, she was formidable. Since his first conversation with Tommy, he'd been aware there was something wrong with the setup at the Midnight Hotel.

Instead of pleading with the old people, why didn't Lenore call the families of the residents? Because they didn't have families, and they'd been selected to live in Midnight because of that. They'd been picked because they'd be grateful. Shorty wouldn't be there if he'd been coherent enough to remember he had a grandson.

Manfred had been so overwhelmed with his own problems that he hadn't even tried to figure out why the hotel had reopened. As he ushered Tommy and Suzie out to the waiting cars, he realized he needed to spare some of his worry time for the situation at the Midnight Hotel.

Barry could have told him that he and Olivia were thinking parallel thoughts.

Manfred *wasn't* ready to be met with a firm refusal by Olivia when he suggested Barry ride with her.

"No," she said. "He goes with you. He stays with you. I don't like him in my head. I'll take the first lap with Tommy and Suzie."

Manfred couldn't take any more upset that morning. "All right," he said. "Fine. Call me when they need to stop. Hey, there's a Cracker Barrel in a reasonable location for lunch. I checked the Internet last night."

"And all old people love Cracker Barrel? That's what you're saying, sonny?" Tommy protested from Olivia's front passenger seat.

"I do," Suzie said as she buckled her seat belt in the back. "Let's stop there!"

"They do have good breakfast, and you can get it all day," Tommy said thoughtfully.

"Apparently these two old people *do* love Cracker Barrel," Olivia said. Manfred could tell she was holding some irritation in with an effort, and that was another worry.

"So why's she so mad at you?" Manfred asked Barry, once they were actually on their way.

"She didn't want me to be able to read her mind. But I can't block out specific people. No one wants me to be able to dip in their head," Barry said reasonably. "But they want to know what everyone else is thinking."

"Were you born able to read minds?"

"Yeah. It's not an easy thing to grow up that way. To put it mildly. Especially when you're little and you repeat what you hear without understanding there are going to be consequences."

Manfred tried to imagine that, but he found himself so dismayed by the prospect that he could only say, "That's *awful*."

"Tell me about it." Barry laughed, but not like it was really funny.

"Like I told you," Manfred said, concentrating on the road ahead, where a pickup had just pulled slowly into his lane. "I've met another telepath. But I never thought about what being a mind-reading kid would be like. Damn."

"You know Sookie, you said."

Manfred glanced at Barry before turning his attention back to the pickup. Its right blinker kept going, monotonously and without conviction. Of course, this driver did not want to turn. He'd just left the blinker on. "Asshole," muttered Manfred, and then returned to the conversation. "Yeah, I met her in Bon Temps," he said. "You from there, too? You related to her? I mean, is this hereditary or genetic or whatever?"

"Whatever," Barry said. "I thought I was the only one in the world until I met Sookie in Dallas."

"I can't picture her anywhere but Bon Temps."

"I'd as soon live in a shack in the slums of Mexico City," Barry said vehemently. "I had one of the worst times of my life in Bon Temps, and that's saying something. Got abducted and tortured."

"That's seriously bad," Manfred agreed. "So, if I called Sookie and asked her about Barry Horowitz, what would she say?"

"She'll probably remember me under a different name," Barry said. "But I'm not speaking it out loud in Texas."

"Because of your vampire problem."

"My *very serious* problem."

They rode for some miles in silence.

"You must be pretty devoted to your grandfather," Manfred said.

"If I'd been really devoted, it wouldn't have taken me so long to track him down. Due to my own troubles, I kind of lost track of him. Now that I've found him, I don't know what to do. He's not in good shape mentally. He's not a nice old guy. But he's all I've got left."

"I have a mother. Never knew my dad."

"My folks were pretty ordinary, but my dad's mother was something else, according to what I remember and what people have told me."

"Lawbreaker?"

"Not like Shorty," Barry said, and laughed. "Shorty was always in and out of jail. He was a thief. Not a violent guy, but he never thought the laws of personal property applied to him. My grandmother Horowitz was wild, and one minister told me he thought she was the spawn of Hell."

"Wow, pretty drastic." Manfred thought he would have liked to meet such a woman.

"Yeah, I only spent time with her once or twice. She disappeared after that, when I was in elementary school."

They'd both had unusual childhoods, Manfred thought. And when he looked over at Barry, Barry nodded.

"You scared Olivia pretty bad," Manfred said.

"She's got a lot of secrets."

And they rode in silence until Olivia called them to say Suzie needed to go to the bathroom.

23

Joe stepped out of the front of the Antique Gallery and Nail Salon and looked up and down the street. Chuy, who was reading a book since there were no customers, didn't even look up. Joe had been restless all morning, and now his antsiness was reaching a high level. He held open the door a little and said, "The town is empty."

With a sigh, Chuy closed his book and put it down. He came to the door. "Emptier than usual?"

"Yes. Olivia's gone. Manfred's gone. Two of the old people from the hotel. That young guy, the one who's been visiting his grandfather."

"You saw them leave?"

"Yeah. But I think I would have known anyway."

Chuy looked up at Joe, and Joe could tell he was worried. He didn't try to reassure his partner. He only got this feeling when things were about to go south.

Chuy said uneasily, "Our killers are gone."

That was true. Lemuel and Olivia were the most ruthless among them, and the quickest to action.

"I'm going to the store, just for a minute," Joe said. Leaving Chuy standing in the doorway, he went east and passed an empty storefront and then came to the corner gas station/convenience store. The bells over the door chimed as he went inside, and Teacher Reed, who'd been playing solitaire on the old computer, looked up gratefully.

"Hey, man," he said, getting off his stool. "I thought no one was going to come in today. Except maybe the holdup guy. You know three convenience stores have been held up in this area?"

"I read that in the county paper. I'd be surprised if the holdup man came in here. Not enough business."

"That's for damn sure. Some days I'm fairly busy, but today I haven't seen anyone since Olivia gassed up early this morning. If I have to do this job much longer, I'm going to go crazy."

"Any end in sight?"

"Yes, praise God and hallelujah."

Though Joe could tell Teacher didn't really mean those words, it felt good to hear them. "So you heard from headquarters?"

"Yeah, man, finally! There's a guy who's interested in taking it over. They're reviewing his background. If his financials and everything else check out, he could be moving in next month."

"He would live in the same house that the Lovells had?"

Teacher shrugged. "I guess. I don't care where he lives, as long as he takes this place over soon."

"You didn't have to take it on," Joe said mildly.

"But the money was so good." Teacher looked rueful. "Pays well enough to where I didn't feel like I could turn it down, with Madonna and Grady to feed."

"I think Madonna takes care of the feeding," Joe said.

Teacher laughed. "I don't hear you tell a lot of jokes, Joe," he said.

"Not a funny world," Joe said, after he'd thought about Teacher's statement. "Have you felt a little strange today?"

"Strange? How? Naw, I feel bored, and I feel restless, but I don't feel *strange*." Teacher looked from side to side, as if he might spot something odd creeping between the bags of potato chips and the dishwashing liquid. The fluorescent light in the store bounced off Teacher's dark skin, giving him shadows where there should have been none. "You feel strange? Like, weird?"

"Yes," said Joe. "I do."

"Does that mean something? I never would have asked that before we moved here."

"Why did you move here?" This was not a question you should ask in Midnight, but Joe had a great suspicion that the Reeds were not truly Midnighters.

"Well . . ." Teacher floundered. "The café was open to rent, Madonna thought she could run a place so small, and the man who sold it to us threw in the trailer. I don't know if you've ever been in the house on the other side of the Rev's, that's the house we could've taken, but it's in terrible shape. Madonna said it was bad enough me going out to work every day to fix other people's houses, she didn't want me coming home to work there, too. The trailer is in great shape."

This was too much explanation, and Joe felt sad. Madonna was truly a gifted cook, Grady was a charmer, and Teacher was literally a handy man to have around. He could fix almost anything. But Joe felt sure that the Reeds would not stay.

"I understand," Joe said. "Stay well, Teacher. I hope you get your replacement soon."

"See you, Joe," Teacher said. There was a definite guarded tone to his voice.

The last family who'd worked at Gas N Go hadn't worked out, either. Joe hadn't wondered at all (at the time) why the Reeds hadn't been summoned to the little meeting that presaged the Lovells' departure. He'd simply accepted it. But now he knew. As he returned to his shop, he wondered if there was some kind of curse on Gas N Go. He turned back to look at it in the magical spectrum. There was a smudge of sadness around the building but nothing permanent. He could hope that the next manager would be someone who fit into the town perfectly.

There was no point going over to talk with Lenore and Harvey Whitefield. There was nothing extranormal about them, and Joe had found he didn't even particularly like them. He knew that Mamie and Shorty were in the hotel, and he knew that they were both napping, and he knew that Mamie was very close to passing through the veil. He could also tell that two other people staying at the hotel (both doing contract work at Magic Portal) were both away for the day.

As uneasy as he felt, he hoped they'd stay away until late in the night. Or maybe they'd find someone to spend the night with, someone fun, and by the time they returned to the Midnight Hotel, whatever was going to happen—tonight, tomorrow night, soon—would all be done.

He could hope.

24

Olivia made it through lunch at the Cracker Barrel by the skin of her teeth. She hated the merchandise room, she hated the false harking back to a re-created past reflected in the wall decor, and she hated Barry and Manfred because they were oblivious to the fluffy sweatshirts and silly souvenirs and the faux farm implements. They simply enjoyed the food, as Suzie and Tommy did. Their waitress looked exhausted but kept smiling, and Barry told Olivia that the woman was a single mother and had two jobs to keep afloat.

"I don't want to be obliged to pity my server," Olivia snapped.

Barry turned his attention back to his menu pointedly. "Then don't. I just didn't want you to jump down her throat because she was slow bringing your coffee."

"So you go around being Mr. Compassionate?" Her voice was low but sharp.

He flinched. "No," he confessed. "Not always."

"Yeah, I thought so."

"Listen, I can tell you're mad at me for something I really can't help. But see if you can rein it in for today, all right? I'm not telling anyone any of your awful little secrets."

Olivia wanted nothing so much as to punch him in the face. "Be quiet now," she said, her voice so low and intense that people near them actually turned to look. "Really, really, be quiet."

Suzie said, "Everything okay here? You young people! Mind your manners!"

"Says the ex-hooker," Barry whispered, and suddenly Olivia wanted to laugh.

"Hey, Tommy, you need some more tea?" Manfred was down at the other end of the table, and he'd been very solicitous to Tommy and Suzie the whole meal. Maybe because he wanted to pretend she, Olivia, wasn't in a total rage? Olivia took a deep breath and reconciled herself to the fact that she could do nothing about what Barry had learned from her thoughts. *But,* she reassured herself, *I can kill him if he ever tells anyone. What about when he leaves? He might find my father and tell . . .*

She glanced sideways at the man next to her. She didn't want to have to kill Barry, but she might have to. It would be a pity. She could see so many times a gift like his would come in handy. If only somehow she could immunize herself against it!

"Is there anyone you can't hear? At all?" she asked, picking up a roll and taking a small bite.

"Vampires." He cut up his ham with precision. "And it's hard to hear people who can turn into an animal. Texas is better than Louisiana. Not so many of either one."

"And yet you have enemies here in Texas."

He chewed and swallowed. "Enemies with long memories."

He was reminding Olivia that she had a hold over him, too.

It was still true that if you didn't go looking for vampires, you'd have a good chance of never seeing one. But every large city had at least one vampire-oriented nightclub and a house or two where vampires were known to nest. For those reasons alone (the company of their own kind, the profitability of simply being undead, and the safety of numbers), it was hard to find a vampire who preferred to live on his or her own in a rural area; Lemuel was an exception. But he was an exception in more than one way. He didn't have to have blood. He could take energy instead, a sip here and a sip there, just enough to keep him going.

He could take from other vampires, too. And he defended his area vigorously.

That was why most undead would not come within miles of Midnight, unless they had to come to the pawnshop for something rare. Lemuel would not leech from a customer of the store.

"You won't be bothered by your enemies while you're in Midnight," Olivia said. "At least, when Lemuel is there."

"But he's not. Any idea of when he'll return? I'd like to stay to see Granddaddy settled in a real nursing home. With more supervision. But I'm not going to die to make that happen."

"Of course not," Olivia said. "He's had his turn."

Barry said, "When you put it like that, doesn't make me sound too good."

She raised her eyebrows. "But it's the truth."

He lifted his shoulders, let them drop. "Yeah, I guess so."

"You better take Tommy to the men's room. You never know what kind of conversation he's going to have with another customer."

Barry went with Tommy while Olivia took Suzie to the ladies' room and Manfred paid their bill. Olivia, glancing back at the wreck of the table, thought, *I didn't know old people could eat that much.* She remembered her own grandmother picking at the food on her plate. But her grandmother had been ill . . . her last illness.

Manfred and Barry loaded Suzie and Tommy into Manfred's car this time, and Olivia drove alone. The solitude was a huge relief. She listened to Yo-Yo Ma the whole way into Dallas. It cleared her mind and calmed her. She felt much better when they stopped for the final briefing, which took place at a filling station in Bonnet Park. But by then, she'd come to a decision.

"I have to go in," she said.

Everyone stared at her, but that didn't bother Olivia. She was used to it.

"But the maid might recognize you, you said yourself," Manfred said. "And I know Lewis would recognize me."

"Give me ten minutes at a Goodwill and she won't know me," Olivia promised.

"Where are you going to find a Goodwill around here?" Barry waved a hand. "I don't care if you come in or not. But I have to be out of Dallas by dark, and I'm not kidding. So if you've changed your mind, fine with me, but get your ass in gear."

"Okay, give me thirty, and I'll be back." She'd spotted a wig shop five blocks south, and she went in there first, emerging with short black hair. There was a consignment shop a block away, and she came out of it in a pair of very tight jeans and a tank top and sandals. She put on a lot of eye makeup with the help of the rearview mirror.

When she got back to the filling station, she found Tommy and Suzie sipping icy drinks while Manfred filled his gas tank and Barry stared at the sky and his watch alternately. There were hours of daylight left, but it was easy to see he was genuinely anxious.

Whatever he'd done to engender this terror, it must have been something pretty awful. Barry grew more and more interesting. *It's a real pity I hate to be in the same room with him.*

Manfred did a double take, and Barry raised one eyebrow in an irritating way. Tommy said, "You look smoking hot, young lady."

Suzie grinned. "I used to wear jeans that way," she said. "Believe it or not. But I was never tall like you, honey."

"So, do you think she'll recognize me?" Olivia said.

"No," Manfred said. "I don't know why you changed your mind about risking it. But I'm sure the maid won't know you."

"Okay, let's recap," Olivia said briskly. She felt much better, now that she knew she could take action. If there was one thing she wasn't good at, it was sitting and waiting. "We go over to the Goldthorpe house. You, Tommy, tell the maid, Bertha, and/or the asshole, Lewis, that Morton Goldthorpe had borrowed some books—rare books— from you. Naturally, they'll be in his study, or library, or whatever they call it. Lewis will already have gotten a letter from Manfred's lawyer stating this. I don't know how Lewis will react. He's a little crazy, after all."

"And when we're up there?" Tommy said. "On the second floor?"

"In the elevator," Suzie added hastily.

"When you go up to the study in the elevator, take your time looking. Pick out some likely books and tell him those are yours. Rick here is going to be listening in to Lewis's brain, to try to pick up information about the whereabouts of some jewelry."

Suzie and Tommy were clearly confused by this information. Tommy stared at Barry as if he had two heads, while Suzie made a sound best described as "*Tchah!*"

Since Olivia didn't want to address their skepticism, she decided to ignore it. "I'm going to be studying the layout to see if I can pinpoint good places to search if I have to return." If? When. No matter who lay in wait for her, she'd have to get back in the house. Olivia actually felt a little excited as she thought of whom she might encounter this time. She'd be so ready for them. They wouldn't have a chance.

She'd kill them all.

Leaving a visibly anxious Manfred behind, they drove to the

Goldthorpe house in silence. Suzie made one comment about how nice the neighborhood was, which no one could argue with. Tommy seemed to get more and more ornery, as if he were thinking himself into his role as a disagreeable old fart. (Olivia didn't think that was such a stretch for Tommy.) Barry, beside her, seemed detached. He was not as invested in this, and he was only interested in completing his role and departing a few hundred dollars richer.

Bertha answered the door. This time, the gardener was on a tall ladder in the foyer. He was replacing a bulb in the light fixture that hung down from the two-story ceiling. Bertha looked frazzled. Maybe having Lewis for a boss wasn't working out very well. Given Lewis's paranoia, Olivia was a little surprised he'd kept her on. Perhaps the answer lay in the For Sale sign they'd passed in the front yard.

"I'm Thomas Quick's grandson," Barry said, smiling pleasantly. "Mr. Lewis Goldthorpe should have gotten the letter from Mr. Quick's lawyer yesterday, saying Mr. Quick needed access to the library today."

Bertha stared at him, a crease between her brows. "I don't know," she said. "Let me call Lewis. He hasn't said anything to me about this. Please wait here." She shut the door in Barry's face, and he turned to Olivia. "She's not happy," he said. "Lewis has been acting crazy. She's nervous all the time. Visitors make him more nuts."

You don't have to be a mind-reader to know that, Olivia thought. "By the way," she said, "my name is Amanda today." It had been awfully careless, not thinking of that until now.

"Crazy man, huh?" said Tommy. His voice was loud and angry. "I want my books back!"

Tommy was a method actor, apparently.

"Yeah," said Suzie. "We need our books back. They're worth thousands! How come we didn't get a notice from Morton's estate when he died? That's what I wanna know!"

"Hams," Barry said, amused. But he said it very quietly.

"They're living it," Olivia agreed.

The front door flew open again, but this time so abruptly that it almost banged against the inside wall. Lewis was framed in the opening. Behind him was the maid, clearly unhappy and worried. The gardener was descending from the ladder, and he seemed to be glad as hell to be coming down.

Lewis was brandishing a piece of paper. Olivia was delighted to see it was the bogus letter from Manfred's lawyer. "What the hell is this about?" Lewis demanded. He wasn't exactly screaming, but his tone was not conversational, either. "My father never borrowed any books from anyone! Much less you!"

"Sir," said Barry with quiet dignity. "This is my grandfather, Tommy Quick, who was a friend of your father's. He'd just like to reclaim his property. He was really grieved to discover his friend Morton is dead, and he found out only because he read the obituary of Morton's widow. Please respect his age and grief."

It was as though he'd slapped Lewis in the face. The man got very quiet and still, so abruptly it was even more shocking than his previous pugnacity. "You're saying this man was my father's friend?" Lewis gave Tommy a very sharp once-over. "All right, come in. It's very hot outside. And these two . . . ladies . . . are?"

"I'm Rick's sister Amanda. This is my grandfather's intended, Suzie Lee." At the last second, Olivia had realized she had no idea what Suzie's true last name was, and she'd supplied one on the spur of the moment. Suzie looked up at Lewis with a smile, and Olivia had to admire the old woman's adaptability.

"I hope you don't mind me coming along," Suzie said, generating so much charm that Olivia almost had to take a step back. "Tommy and I go everywhere together."

"Let me go turn off the television," Lewis said abruptly, and vanished. When he reappeared, Bertha abruptly retreated to the back of the house. It was clear the maid was washing her hands of the situation.

Her son—he must be, their mouths and eyes were so alike—was folding up the ladder and giving the newcomers a comprehensive stare, starting with Olivia's tight blue jeans. But he left, too, carrying the ladder carefully down the hall to the back of the house.

Good. Now there were no witnesses, whatever happened.

Lewis reappeared, so changed it was like he'd taken a hit of laughing gas. He'd morphed into the gracious master of the manor. "There's an elevator right back here for you, if you'd prefer," he said. If he'd had mustaches, he'd have been twirling them. "I often take it myself."

"Thanks," said Tommy gruffly. "The little lady has a problem with stairs."

Every effort had been made to make the tiny elevator unobtrusive. Even the door was designed to look like a real wood door. Olivia said, "I'll just take the stairs."

She met them at the top and confirmed that the elevator door was right by the study door. She was smiling when the elevator door dinged open and they all appeared.

Lewis's new hospitality made Olivia deeply suspicious, and her anxiety was confirmed when she caught Barry's expression. Behind Lewis's back, he made an urgent face at her. She didn't know exactly what it meant, but nothing good. She went on full alert.

Tommy got off the elevator with extra care and turned to extend his hand to Suzie. She took it with a smile. Somehow, in the Goldthorpe mansion, they looked smaller and frailer and less in control of their destinies than they had in the Midnight Hotel. Tommy seemed to be aware of it, too. In a patronizing tone, he said, "This is a nice house, young man." He looked around him in a lordly way. "I haven't been here in years," he added, perhaps thinking that he should have visited at least a few times if he'd been such a good friend of Morton's.

"I'm so glad you like it," Lewis said smoothly.

Obviously, Lewis suspected they weren't what they seemed. Olivia didn't know what he suspected or what to do about it. For the moment, she decided to go along with the plan. Lewis was not a good pretender. She was.

"I'm really sorry about your mom," she said. Lewis's glasses winked as he swung his head around to glare at her.

And she saw Barry blink and look away, just for a second.

Lewis was more dangerous than he seemed, apparently.

"She never took good care of herself," Lewis said brusquely. "She was getting forgetful, too. She was hiding things from me."

"Hiding things," Olivia echoed in a murmur with just a hint of a question in it.

"Yes," he confirmed. "She was getting very . . . well, paranoid, I'm afraid, and she decided I was after her jewelry. Poor thing," he added unconvincingly. "I miss her so much."

"Of course," Barry said. "Grandpa, can you see the books you loaned Morton? Look carefully. We don't want to leave one behind."

Tommy had gone to the shelves to begin his "search." Suzie began a stilted conversation with Lewis about estate taxes, which only went forward fitfully, because Lewis was watching Tommy like a hawk. Did he think Tommy would try to stuff books down his pants?

Olivia looked around her, registering fact after fact. There was not much furniture. The room was lit from a window on the west wall, casting a pool of light on the large polished desk and the imposing chair behind it. There was an easy chair with a small table and lamp, and there was a huge globe standing in one corner of the room. It hadn't been visible from the door on Olivia's previous visit.

Olivia wondered if the globe was Morton Goldthorpe's idea or if some decorator had told him every man should have a globe in his library. Maybe a bit of both; it was a beautiful thing. The desk was handsome, too; cherry, she thought. The shelves on the south and north walls were stocked with books interspersed with a tennis trophy or two, some business awards, and family pictures. From those pictures, it was evident that Morton had been older than Rachel by at least ten years. He looked very proud of his wife and his children in those portraits of a time long past.

Olivia had the oddest feeling as she looked at those faces, including that of the boy who now stood before her grown into a peevish and unstable man, greedy and grasping. The couple must have been happy in those long-ago days, surely. They must have looked forward to meeting the people their children would partner up with, to loving the grandchildren that would result. How could it be that such anticipation would crash and burn so spectacularly in Lewis's case?

Had her parents ever looked at her, counted on her to comfort their old age, to present them with the little representations that would carry their name forward?

Not my mother, Olivia thought certainly. *Not even she would be capable of such hypocrisy.* As for her father, who knew? He'd proved himself capable of such willful blindness that there was no telling how far he'd deceived himself.

And for the first time, in the middle of a job and in a sunny room of a mansion she'd never visit again, Olivia thought, *If he'd had any balls at all, he'd have killed my mother when I told him what she'd done. I wouldn't have had to do it myself.* It was a truth that came at the worst possible moment.

"I see your father was interested in Rex Stout," she said, almost at random. She had no idea who Rex Stout was, but there were many books with that name on them, and they were all together, and they looked old.

"He has a complete set of first editions," Lewis said with massive indifference. "I'm trying to find a buyer for them."

"Those are hard to come by," Olivia said, trying to sound like she gave a shit.

"Yes." Lewis's limited patience was trickling away.

Olivia's brain was telling her to cut and run, that this was a fiasco. She wondered if Barry's was saying the same thing. There was a certain tension in the way he stood that alerted her. No such danger message had reached Tommy and Suzie, who were shuffling along the shelves, industriously looking for the fictional loaner books.

The front doorbell rang downstairs, and Lewis's head jerked in that direction. It was a busy morning at the Goldthorpe house. Olivia heard Bertha's plodding footsteps cross the foyer and the sound of the front door opening.

"I wonder who that can be?" Lewis said malevolently.

Tommy's head jerked around. He said, "Suzie, honey, these are the books." He pulled three books from a lower shelf, and Olivia could see they were a set because the bindings matched.

"*The History of Geography and Judaism in Western Europe,*" Suzie said. "Of course! It's been so long since you read them."

She was pretty convincing. Olivia almost believed Suzie spent her leisure time reading. Wait, she'd mentioned wanting to go to the library in Davy. Maybe it was true. Olivia dismissed that as irrelevant and concentrated on her job. The desk was an obvious place to search for the jewelry. Possibly it had a secret compartment, though those were usually easy to find. She looked hard at the shelves. She was sure Lewis had been all over them. Even if his sisters had already cataloged everything in the house, which she didn't believe, Lewis would still want to run his own inventory because he was so convinced that the house was his.

"I'm surprised you're selling such a beautiful place," she said, and

Lewis glared at her. "Not my idea," he snapped. "My sisters want to sell the place and divide the proceeds, though I offered to buy them out."

Not at fair market value, I'm sure, Olivia thought. But she shook her head in apparent amazement at his sisters' inexplicable stubbornness, while she looked from the desk to the shelves. The books were all aligned on the forefront of the shelves, not pushed back against the wall, so there was plenty of room behind them. But would that be a very safe place to hide anything? Only temporarily. Hadn't Rachel told them something else, at the séance?

The leather chair—nope. A table at its side, only a single shallow drawer. Nope. There were cabinets below the bookshelves on the north wall behind the desk. That was somewhere to look. Maybe one of the books was hollowed out?

Suddenly she had a great idea, a wonderful idea, just in time. There were two sets of feet mounting the stairs, and Detective Sterling, Bonnet Park PD, came into the room. Another man was with Sterling, and Olivia pegged him instantly as a cop.

Lewis smiled triumphantly.

Well, damn. This was not her day.

It had seemed so important to see the study for herself. Now she realized it had been stupid, though she was sure she'd identified the hiding place of Rachel's jewelry. While she was wondering if she could possibly go unrecognized, Lewis practically precipitated himself at the detectives.

"So glad to see you, guys!" Lewis was beaming from ear to ear. "I'm delighted you came so quickly." He pointed at the Midnight party in a dramatic way. "These people are frauds."

"I beg your pardon," Suzie said. She was unexpectedly fierce. "How dare you say that? We came to retrieve Tommy's books. Fraudulent, my . . . ! We haven't done a single thing that's incorrect or illegal."

If Olivia hadn't been so busy being mad at herself, and also elated, she would have been tempted to laugh.

Barry was looking intently at the policemen. He said, "I'm sorry Mr. Goldthorpe has caused you so much trouble today. We did send a letter ahead, telling him we would be coming. He could have called our lawyer if he had an issue with our visit." Barry looked very serious, very distressed, and not at all guilty of anything.

Olivia thought, *He's reading their minds. Follow his cues.* She tried to stand a little behind Barry. She was aiming for inconspicuous but not suspicious. It was a fine line.

Detective Sterling was definitely taken aback. Maybe he'd expected guilt, embarrassment, flagrant con artists; instead, he'd gotten feisty older citizens, an indignant grandson, and a quiet sister. Versus the demonstrably unstable (but Bonnet Park citizen) Lewis Goldthorpe. So he did what Olivia figured she would have done. He played for time to evaluate the situation.

"I'm Detective Sterling and this is Detective Woodward," Sterling said. "We're from the Bonnet Park police. You are?"

They all introduced themselves and shook hands, just a bunch of citizens who were completely aboveboard.

Detective Sterling had no choice but to follow through. Though Olivia was no mind-reader like Barry, she could tell that he had misgivings about this whole situation. "Mr. Goldthorpe has complained about your coming here today. He maintains none of these books were loaned to his father, who's been dead some time now. Since his mother died only recently, he's very sensitive about strangers making claims on the estate."

"Which I would definitely agree with," Tommy said. "If I were saying that I'd loaned my buddy books worth a lot of dough. But these books, about the faith of our people, they are worth nothing but some sentiment, gentlemen. Sentiment. Not money. And I'll tell you here and now, if this man here, Lewis Goldthorpe, if he tells me sincerely he'll read these books and learn from them, I am not going to stand in his way. My Suzie and I are deeply, I say deeply, offended by these accusations, and we are leaving now, with or without my books. Calling the police, young man? Your father would be astonished at you."

Tommy did offended dignity very well, if a little in the Foghorn Leghorn manner. Their little party began to move to the door of the study in a tight formation. Suzie clung to Tommy's arm, looking frail and tremulous, and Barry did his best to look offended, and Olivia strove to be invisible. She thought for one moment that Detective Sterling looked at her curiously. Would he figure out she'd been at Vespers?

But he didn't try to stop them. They reached the elevator. And crowded on. And punched the button to go down. It took for-fucking-ever for the doors to close. Olivia swore to herself the whole time.

Lewis began shrieking at the detectives.

"Bad move, Lewis," Olivia whispered. Then they were on the ground floor and the doors opened. Bertha and her son were nowhere in sight. The coast was clear. Moving a little faster than they should have been, considering the offended dignity they were trying to project, they got through the double front doors, all the time hearing the voices of the detectives, determinedly calm, counterpointing with the shrill tones of Lewis, demanding that they be stopped and searched and questioned and thrown in jail. And all manner of other things.

Then they were out into the scorching heat.

"Let's slow down a little," Barry suggested. "Tommy, hold on to the railing, okay? Suzie, let me give you a hand." Tommy didn't put up any protest, and neither did Suzie. Olivia swung around to get to the bottom of the steps in case they fell, standing ready to catch them. But despite the fact that Tommy and Suzie were both visibly angry—or maybe just excited—they managed the few steps down with no problem, and then all four of them crossed the gravel to the car. The detectives' sedan was parked behind them.

A whoosh of heat came out of the opened car doors, but they weren't going to wait for the car to cool. They climbed in, Barry and Tommy in the front, Suzie and Olivia in the back, and then they were going down the driveway.

"Whew," said Suzie. "That little fucker! Someone should clip his nuts off."

"*If* he has any," Tommy said.

Olivia couldn't stop the giggle. After a second, Barry joined her. They'd gotten away with it.

"But we didn't find out where the jewelry is," Tommy said.

"Yes, we did." Olivia smiled to herself. "I know where it is."

"Where?" Tommy demanded. "Hey, I think I deserve to know!"

"You do, but I have to tell Manfred first," she said. "This is his deal, after all."

"How are we gonna get 'em, now that he knows what we look like?" Suzie said. Suddenly they were a gang of jewel thieves instead of a group of newly met misfits.

"We'll think of something," Olivia said.

"After we get out of here," Barry said brusquely, and they all agreed it was time to leave Bonnet Park.

25

The Rev was in front of the chapel, looking up into the sky. Afternoon was drawing to a close, but the sun was still blazing away with implacable heat. He took his hat off and waved it in the air, whether to dry the sweat on the hatband or to create some air circulation, Joe had no idea. The boy was with him, and for the first time they looked like they belonged together. Diederik was slightly behind the Rev, as if he were trying to stand in the Rev's meager shadow. They both looked into the vast blue, their eyes narrowed against the glare, reading the sky to come.

Chuy had been ordering some nail polish online, but he came to look out when Joe beckoned. "Huh," Chuy said. "Let me check something." He returned to the laptop and typed something in a search engine. After a moment, he said, "Yep. The prediction is no clouds, for three nights."

"I figured," Joe said. There was a long moment of silence, while they both considered the fact.

"Still," Joe said, as if their thoughts had been spoken out loud, "as long as everyone stays inside . . ."

"Yeah. But isn't Manfred out of town now? With Olivia and two hotel people?" Chuy was anxious.

"They're not back yet. Right."

"Better text them." Chuy got out his cell phone. "Both of them?"

"Yes, I think so."

Joe could hear the tiny click of the keypad on the telephone. He and Chuy were tech titans compared to the Rev. The old minister ignored computers and wasn't even comfortable on his landline telephone. He had grudgingly agreed to have an answering machine attached to the one in his little house only after he had missed the opportunity of some pet burials because grieving pet owners couldn't get in touch with him.

The Rev and Diederik looked completely at home in their own world just at the moment.

As Joe watched, the older man turned to look at the boy and said something to him, something very serious. The boy nodded, looking nervous, looking excited. He was even taller than the day before, Joe realized. He looked as old as Dillon, the high school junior who bussed at Home Cookin.

That led Joe to think about the Home Cookin family. "Chuy, I have to go talk to Teacher and Madonna," he said.

Chuy said, "Sure. I'm waiting to hear back from our wanderers. Hey, take Rasta, so he'll get some exercise."

Joe put Rasta on his leash, and the little dog danced around, anxious to go on a walk. The sidewalk was hot for Rasta's feet, so Joe carried him most of the way but put the dog down to take advantage of a little strip of dirt between the sidewalk and the street. He let Rasta have a few happy moments of sniffing and peeing before they continued on their short way.

As Joe pushed open the glass door, he realized he could not remember ever entering Gas N Go twice in consecutive days. Teacher was making change for a customer who'd bought gas, and when the rancher had climbed back into his pickup and pulled out onto the Davy highway, Teacher said, "What an honor! What's up, Joe?"

"Close early tonight," Joe said.

"What? Come again?"

"Close before dark. Go home. Make sure Madonna and Grady are inside. Lock your doors. Don't go out. Tonight, and the next two nights."

"What's up?" Teacher wasn't as surprised to be given this message as he would have been a year ago. And he didn't question Joe's word.

"Will you do this?" he asked.

"Yeah, Joe. I'll do it. Do I need to get my rifle out?"

Joe sighed heavily. "If you don't go out, you won't need it," he said. "Will you tell Madonna, or do I need to go over to the restaurant?"

"She'll take this better if it comes from you."

Joe thought that was an odd thing to say, because as far as he knew, Madonna and Teacher had a companionable marriage, but he wasn't going to question Teacher any more than Teacher had questioned him. He nodded and left, going straight across the road to the hotel and walking west to the restaurant, taking advantage of another patch of shade to let Rasta get a bit of exercise. Madonna and Dillon were having a conversation about the nature of true barbecue, a discussion that could go on forever, especially in Texas. Madonna was sitting on one of the stools cutting up tomatoes in a leisurely way, and Dillon was wiping down the plastic envelopes that enclosed the menus.

Their heads turned to the door simultaneously when the bell chimed, and Madonna cast an anxious glance to one of the booths, where Grady was stretched out asleep. Dillon, who was always glad to see a customer, smiled in a surprised kind of way, because it was before five o'clock.

"Hey, Mr. Joe," he said. "You want a table? Or you want to sit up here with us? I can bring you some iced tea."

Joe shook his head.

Madonna put down her knife and wiped her hands on her apron. "Can I fix you something to take home for supper? Roast beef isn't ready yet, but I can come up with something."

"No, thanks. What time have you been closing?" Joe asked.

"By eight or maybe as late as eight thirty," she said. "Every now and then someone will linger that late."

"Close earlier tonight. Please."

"Klan going to come burn a cross?" She bared her teeth in a smile designed to show the boy, Dillon, that she was joking. Just a little bit. When Joe didn't smile back, she dropped her own quickly. "Seriously, Joe?" she said.

"Yes. I've already talked to Teacher."

She glanced over at her sleeping son. "Okay." She nodded. "I'll close by seven thirty at the latest."

He was pleased that she didn't ask more questions. "Seven thirty will be okay," he said. Sunset wasn't until eight thirty p.m. or thereabouts, but it would be wise to err on the side of caution. "Dillon, you drove your truck in, right?"

Dillon looked at Joe as though he'd grown another head. *Of course,* Joe thought. *He's a rural kid. He's been driving since he was thirteen, probably.* Now Joe remembered that Dillon had saved up to buy a secondhand Chevy 4x4, and he kept it as clean and polished as a vehicle in dusty Texas could be. "Of course you did," Joe said, with an apologetic smile. "When the restaurant closes, please go straight home." The Braithwaite ranch was ten miles due south of Midnight.

The boy's face was full of a thousand questions, but Joe knew if he answered one, he'd be there for ten more minutes. He was ready with a credible story. "A customer in the shop told me he'd seen a mountain lion on his property right outside of town. He said it was wounded, might attack people. I think we need to take serious precautions until they track it down."

That seemed to make sense to Dillon. To forestall any more questions from the boy, Joe nodded at both of them and left. He hesitated once outside, picking up Rasta and scratching the little dog's head. Rasta was panting but still glad to be outside with his human.

"What now?" Joe said to the dog. He'd just thought of Fiji when he heard her call his name. He looked far past her down the sidewalk and saw Mr. Snuggly sitting on the edge of her yard looking after her. When Fiji came up to him, he saw that her face was tight with anxiety. Though she was wearing a short denim skirt and a tank top, she was flushed and breathing heavily.

"Tonight," she said. "Something's happening tonight."

"Yes. I was just telling Madonna and Teacher to be inside early. I was going to call you."

"I went over to the chapel with some cookies for the Rev and Diederik. The Rev wouldn't come to the door, though I know they were in there. There's only that big ceiling fan in there, no air-conditioning. Silence. And I got a shivery feeling."

"Good thing you trust your feelings," Joe said approvingly. Fiji tried to smile back.

"Something's going to happen to the boy tonight," she said. "I think so, at least. He's been growing so much, and he seems so different from other boys, anyway. I don't know what it is, but I know he won't be the same after it."

Joe nodded. "Don't forget to tell your cat," he said. He'd put the dog down, and Rasta was prancing around Fiji's ankles, smelling the cat on her legs and shoes.

"Mr. Snuggly seems to know. Better than I do. He's already told me to get a litter box ready for tonight. Normally, he just goes outside."

"We'll take Rasta out at the last minute and then hope for the best," Joe said. "Remember, Fiji. I know you are strong, and I know you are powerful. But no running outside to pick some last-minute herbs for supper or to stand in the moonlight to cast a spell."

"Do I seem that scatterbrained to you?" Fiji shook her head. "Don't answer that. I promise, I won't try to rescue anyone. Have you talked to Bobo?"

Joe shook his head. "I'll leave that to you, if you have time. I need to get Rasta home. The heat's too much with all his fur."

"Okay, I'll stop in," she said. "I think Manfred and Olivia have been gone today? You've texted them?"

"They've been told," Joe assured her.

"Bye then, and thanks. Stay safe, Joe." She glanced both ways and then ran diagonally across the intersection and up the steps to the old door to the pawnshop.

It was gloomy inside as it almost always was, and she stopped to get her sight back.

"Hey, Feej," Bobo called from the back of the store, which was much larger than it looked on the outside. She began fumbling her way back. By the time she reached him she could see.

Bobo was examining a vest. He'd spread it out on the top of an ancient table with carved legs, which probably should have gone to Joe's antiques shop instead of his own business. That happened, from time to time.

"Is that leather?" she asked, sidetracked for a moment.

"Sure is," he said. "But I don't know what the leather is made from. What animal, I mean. Could be anything."

"Even a person?" She scrunched up her nose.

"I guess so." Bobo seemed mildly amused by the idea. "It looks pretty cool, though, so I hope not. Maybe when Lemuel comes back, he'd know."

"I don't even want to think about that," she said. "Listen, Bobo, I got a warning from Joe."

"Joe?" She had his full attention.

"He says to stay in after dark tonight, no matter what."

Bobo thought about that for a second. "Did he say why?"

"No, but it's got something to do with Diederik and the Rev."

"What about Manfred? His car hasn't been there all day."

"Joe texted him. Should be okay. I hope he's close."

"Maybe Olivia is with him. I haven't seen her all day, either, and I think her car is gone, too."

"Yeah, they went somewhere together. They took a couple of old people from the hotel. And the young guy."

"Weird. That doesn't seem very much like Manfred. Or Olivia."

"I know, right? Joe's probably heard back from them, but I may text Manfred myself, just to keep my mind at rest."

As it happened, Manfred and Olivia returned to town an hour and a half later, having treated Suzie and Tommy to a substantial mid-afternoon snack at an ice cream shop. While Manfred dropped off Barry, Olivia saw the two others into the hotel.

Manfred had driven back to Davy to pick up his dry cleaning, and he'd lingered to drive by Magdalena Orta Powell's office out of sheer curiosity. It did not have gold pavement outside, and the door was not set with gemstones. He'd also picked up some Mexican food for his own supper, and he was looking forward to heating it up. Though that put him much later than he'd planned, he was definitely in before his advised curfew.

Manfred responded to Fiji's text when he'd had time to feel alone again. "Here I am," he said when she picked up. "Way before dark."

She was looking out of her front window. She'd been pulled to it ever since she'd talked to Joe. "What are you doing?" she asked.

"Pouring a glass of V8," he said. "Why?"

"The sheriff is pulling up to your door."

"Oh, for God's sake!" Manfred felt he'd had as much tension as he could handle for one day.

"I'll let you go. If you need me, call me." She hung up and worried, pacing back and forth in the shop. She heard the cat door in the kitchen make its distinctive clatter, and Mr. Snuggly came to stand beside her.

"Is he getting arrested?" the cat asked her, mildly curious.

"I hope not," she said.

26

Maybe five minutes before Arthur Smith arrived at Manfred's, Joe told Chuy he was going to go for a run. He hadn't been going out since he'd hurt his ankle, but he was so restless waiting for the night to come that he didn't think he could stay indoors another moment.

Chuy looked at the clock doubtfully. "You warned everyone else in town," he said. "Do you really want to take a chance yourself?"

"I know when darkness falls tonight," Joe said impatiently. "You know the longest I've ever run is fifty minutes. I've got way more time than that."

Chuy gave him a very direct look. "Okay, you. No fooling around. You get back here in time, and don't overdo it on that ankle."

"Yes, Mom," Joe said, and went to change into his running clothes.

In ten minutes, he'd done his stretching and began to run. For the first few minutes, he brooded over the fact that he hadn't been kind to Chuy, and he promised himself he'd make up for it when he got back. And then the fact that he had no shadow, since he was running in the evening, was a bit spellbinding. He was used to seeing his shadow precede him, and he was constantly tempted to look back to make sure it was following him. He persuaded himself that was foolishness and pounded on with determination. It did feel good to be running again. It had been all too easy to take off days because of his ankle.

Which was beginning to throb again.

At first, Joe tried to ignore the burst of discomfort every time his foot hit the pavement. Then he admitted it but ran through it, because turning back so soon would mean he'd been foolish.

Then he admitted he'd let his anxiety provoke him into unwise behavior.

Then he fell again.

And he was down for several minutes. His ankle hurt far more than it had the first time, and that had been bad. This was terrible. He wondered if he'd broken a bone, for the first time in his long existence.

When he had gathered himself mentally, and the pain had subsided maybe a degree, Joe tried to get up. And failed.

He looked at his watch and began dragging himself back to Midnight.

After ten determined minutes, he had to admit he was not going to make it in time. If fate didn't intervene, he'd be wounded and disabled out here with nowhere to hide, close to Midnight, when darkness fell.

Chuy might appear at any minute with the Suburban, but he might not. Chuy would wait until the last second, so he wouldn't look like "Mom," as Joe had so carelessly called him. Chuy was not overly proud, but he knew Joe very well. Yes, he would wait.

Joe thought about any solution other than the one that had occurred to him, and he came up with nothing. He was going to have to break a promise, and it grieved him. But he felt the surge of excitement even as he felt the grief, and he knew the guilt even as he prepared for the glory.

He sat up straight and let his other nature rush in and fill him. He became more. He became much more. And his wings emerged, white and gleaming, indescribably beautiful. He caught his breath at the wave of joy that filled him, and he willed his wings to move.

He rose in the air, almost screaming with the sensation, and then he was flying. Each powerful flap made muscles in his back flex, muscles he had not used in years. Even on Halloween, when he and Chuy let their wings out for Fiji's party, they did not fly, because they had promised each other they would not. Now he was breaking that promise, and he would pay for it, but the moment was sublime. He circled high above Midnight, looking down, once, twice, and then he saw his beloved come out on the sidewalk in the gathering gloom to look anxiously to the west. With a sharp reluctance, he knew he must land, and he came down behind the store.

Chuy must have caught a glimpse of him passing overhead, because he was there in a second, his face a mask of distress. But when he saw Joe lying on the ground, groaning, he rushed to help him. With a lot of effort, he got Joe up, and somehow they made their way up the outside stairs to their apartment as darkness fell on Midnight. They paused to rearrange themselves about halfway up. From the darkness nearby, they heart a sort of chuffing noise. It came from some large animal. And without saying a word, they moved up the remaining stairs with a speed they hadn't thought they could achieve a minute before. They went in the door as fast as they could and locked it behind them.

Then the only light was the light of the full moon.

27

"Rachel Goldthorpe was murdered," Arthur Smith was telling Manfred, at the same time that Joe was putting on his running clothes.

Manfred sat down abruptly. "For sure? How?"

"The tox results show that she had taken six times the dosage of her blood pressure medicine. Almost certainly that wasn't on purpose. It had been dissolved in the water bottle she carried."

"She drank out of it while I was watching."

"Yeah, it was your telling the Bonnet Park police that detail that let them know to look for the bottle. Somehow in the attempt to save her, it got knocked off the table and rolled under the couch. One of the cops there found it just in time. The doctor says he suspected an overdose from the first, but now it's confirmed."

"She said she dropped it in the lobby," Manfred said. "She said people helped her pick up her stuff and put it back in her purse. I guess . . . could it have been put in there then?" He almost held his breath, waiting for the answer.

"It doesn't seem likely," Arthur said, and Manfred breathed again. "If someone wanted to poison her, surely they'd put the medicine in an identical water bottle and substitute that one for the one in her purse. And that would take a lot of foreknowledge. The appearance of the bottle, with all the butterfly decals on it. The type of medicine she'd been prescribed, the dosage that would kill her."

"What kind did she take?"

"The medical examiner says she overdosed on Cardizem."

"What exactly does that do?"

"That was her blood pressure medication."

"But she wouldn't have taken it like that. Crushed up and put in her water. Who would take their pills like that?"

"Some people—especially sick people, and especially elderly sick people—can forget they've taken a dose of their medicine and take another one. And maybe after that, they forget again. But not only was she comparatively too young and clearheaded to make such a mistake, the pills were actually ground up. Her daughters told the Bonnet Park police that she had no trouble swallowing pills the normal way. So the conclusion is, she was murdered. What was in her and what was left in the bottle was probably ten doses altogether. Enough to kill her."

"She took that big a dose that morning?"

"Yes. Some time that morning, before she walked through your door, Rachel Goldthorpe had taken at least six times the dose of Cardizem she should have had for the day. In consequence, she went into shock and died."

"Could her regular dosage of pills have had an unexpected effect on her because she was sick?"

"It was a deliberate overdose." Arthur said this with finality.

"I don't want to believe anyone would kill Rachel. Especially since it sounds like whoever did it, it had to be someone who knew her really, really well." Manfred shook his head vehemently. "She would never have killed herself."

"You sound pretty sure."

"She was so coherent," Manfred said. It was a relief to tell Arthur this; he hadn't realized until this moment how much he'd wanted to talk about Rachel. "She felt pretty bad, as I told you. Sick as a dog. And she looked it. But she was on top of things mentally, for sure. She was just worried about her son."

"Who still insists that you stole her jewelry."

"Which I did not. For God's sake, what would I do with it? You may not admire what I do for a living, but I'm not a thief."

"That's debatable," Arthur said. "Most people would say that you take money under false pretenses: that you can actually predict the future or advise the people who call you on how to make their lives better."

"I *could* debate that with you, but I'm not going to," Manfred said. "I wouldn't take jewelry, or . . . I don't know, stock and bonds, whatever . . . or anything but money for services rendered. I'm an honest man." He'd been sitting at his curving desk, and Arthur had taken the other office chair. Now Manfred rose to look outside. It was almost dark. "Twilight," he said. "Dusk. Gloaming."

"Are you trying to tell me something?" Arthur sounded amused.

"I don't want to sound all mysterious, but you need to get in your car and leave now," Manfred said. "It's not safe here tonight." He turned to face the sheriff. "Don't ask me questions. I can't answer them. You know this is a weird little town, right? Midnight has its own rules. Tonight's not a good night to be here. So can we continue this conversation tomorrow? I can even drive into Davy if you want me to."

"You're serious?" The sheriff joined him at the window. He looked out curiously, didn't see a thing except the deepening darkness. "I don't see the Yakuza coming down the street, or a giant lizard."

"Arthur. It's not really a good evening to be making fun."

The sincerity of Manfred's concern finally got through to Arthur. "Who told you this?" he asked. "What's the danger?"

"A very reliable source. And I don't know yet, but I know it's coming."

"If something is going to be on the streets that's so dangerous, shouldn't I be calling out a SWAT team or at least more deputies?"

"That would just put them in danger, too," Manfred said. He wasn't sure how he knew this, but he knew it was so.

There was a muffled sound outside, and both the men peered out the window. The Rev was leading a cow by means of a rope around its neck. The cow was not happy.

"What the hell?" Arthur said. "What's the minister doing with a cow?"

"Good-bye, Arthur," Manfred said hopefully.

"Just to keep you on an even keel, okay, I'll go," Arthur said, with a smile that said he was placating Manfred. Manfred had no trouble reading that.

"Okay, see you tomorrow," Manfred said. "Straight to your car, now." He tried to keep the anxiety out of his voice. He opened his door. If Manfred could have lifted Arthur and thrown him into the front seat, he would have. As soon as the sheriff was out of the front door, Manfred closed it to a crack and watched as Arthur walked to the crumbling driveway. He unlocked the car with a key fob as he walked, so he could climb in and start the motor as soon as he got there. Manfred could hear the little *thunk* that said the car doors had locked automatically.

Blowing out a sigh of relief, Manfred shut his own door and locked it. He drew the curtains closed.

He went into the kitchen to heat up his Mexican supper at about the same moment Joe was landing behind the Antique Gallery and Nail Salon. Outside it grew as dark as it was going to get on this night of the glowing moon.

Manfred didn't look out again, not even an hour later when he heard a sort of bellow. He thought it came from nearby, perhaps from across the road, and he thought it sounded like a terrified animal. But he only looked up from his book for a moment and then went back to reading with his jaw set. Much later, in the middle of the night, he woke. Despite the window air-conditioning in the front room, which served to cool the whole house, he had thrown off his sheet. He sat up to find the end so he could draw it back up. As he groped around the bed, he heard something pass by outside his house, something big, something that made an odd coughing noise. He closed his eyes and prayed, and the thing passed by. He sank back down on the bed, pulling the percale sheet up over him like a child.

Whatever had prowled around his house seemed to be going in the direction of the pawnshop.

In her basement apartment, with its windows right by the ground, Olivia watched the paws walk by outside. Her lights were all off. She felt safer that way.

Above the Antique Gallery and Nail Salon, Joe and Chuy looked out the front windows. For the most part, they were silent. Joe's ankle was hurting, but it was bandaged and he'd taken some pain relievers. He was as comfortable as he was going to be that night. They'd pulled up chairs and a small table for their wineglasses, and Chuy had gotten Joe a footstool to prop his ankle on.

They sat there through the night. They were keeping guard, in their own way. So they saw everything that happened.

"At least one more night, maybe two," Chuy said, as the darkness began to lighten. "You think we can do this two more nights?"

Joe said, "I think we have to. With the boy being so young." He shook his head. "Honey, you can sleep if you want to. Doesn't need but one of us. My ankle would keep me up, anyway."

"I'm not going to leave you watching by yourself," Chuy said.

Joe didn't answer out loud, but he reached over to take Chuy's hand.

Above the pawnshop, Bobo Winthrop tried to sleep, with little success. He was worried about so many things. Foremost in his mind was his concern about the pawnshop not being open at night during Lemuel's absence. Sometimes Olivia was able and willing to do the shift; sometimes she wasn't. When a business wasn't open regular hours, people tended to stop coming. And the night customers were the most profitable. What would happen if he couldn't keep his business afloat?

He turned over to try a new position, but his mind refused to turn off.

Lemuel and Olivia could find somewhere else to live, he supposed. Perhaps Lemuel would want to buy the business back from him. But Bobo didn't want to leave Midnight. He liked the town, liked the area, liked Texas. There were so many good things about living here: Fiji being across the road, so he could see her often. Manfred next door. Joe and Chuy down the street. And the Home Cookin Restaurant, where he'd passed some very contented hours eating and talking.

He hadn't realized the previous few months had been a Golden Age. Now the money wasn't trickling in, Manfred was in trouble with the law, and there was this big, bad thing outside trapping them indoors for the night. Of course he'd noticed there was a full moon. The moon would be as near to full as made no difference for the next two nights. He wondered if he'd have to stay locked inside all that time or if he could manage to stay up most of the night with the front doors unlocked to get the customers he often got during that moon phase. They were the customers better left to Lemuel—but he hadn't heard from Lem in weeks. Or would those customers be in too much danger? What made this full moon more dangerous?

And then he was back to his worry about the shop.

The worst thing about sleepless nights was the feeling of running in a hamster cage, at least mentally. The same thoughts, over and over . . . He tossed and turned for another half hour. Finally, he slept.

The Reeds drew all the shades in their trailer, double-checked to make sure all the windows and doors were locked, and got out their guns, which were loaded and ready for use. Madonna held Grady for a long time before she put him to bed, and she left the door of his room open so she could hear the smallest sound. They didn't turn on their television, either, which was a trial for both Madonna and Teacher. Instead, Madonna checked her Facebook page and some recipe websites, and Teacher read a backlog of mechanics magazines. By midnight, they were relaxed enough to crawl into bed to sleep.

In the Midnight Hotel, in their separate "suites," Suzie and Tommy slept the sleep of exhaustion, only rousing enough to go to the bathroom or get a drink of water. Just down the hall, Mamie had had to take some pain medication for her hip, and she was snoring in her room. Shorty Horowitz slept sporadically, waking to confused dreams that were set in his colorful past. His grandson, in a room upstairs, was worried about spending yet another night in Texas, and concerned about finding somewhere for his grandfather to settle. If only he had a sibling to share the load. Barry slept with silver around his neck and wrists.

Lenore Whitefield was exhausted, too. She was out the second her head hit her pillow. Her husband stayed up to look at porn on his laptop, unbeknownst to Lenore, who would have hit him over the head with that laptop had she known.

The two contract workers sat in their respective rooms upstairs playing a computer game with each other. They did not see anything odd about this behavior. They didn't pay any attention to the town, and they never knew that if they'd stepped outside the doors that night, they might have been eaten.

28

Manfred had to leave his work desk untended the next day to honor his promise to drive into Davy to see Arthur Smith. Though he grumbled internally about leaving his work, and he did need to talk more to Barry and Olivia about what had happened when they were in the Goldthorpe house (there'd been no chance for him to get the full story), he had to admit he was anxious to hear whatever Arthur had to tell him. Davy only seemed a large town in comparison to Midnight. Though it was just a few minutes' drive north, Davy had many more restaurants and shops. It was also the county seat, with the usual cluster of lawyers around the usual courthouse. Since Davy was also on a small river where rafting and canoeing were possible, the town conducted a brisk tourist trade in the summer and early fall.

The law enforcement agencies in the town had recently consolidated into one building, a renovated school. The sheriff's department, the jail, and two courtrooms were in the same building, and the ambulance service was one block away, the fire department a block after that. Manfred had expected a little district that ran on emergencies and crime to be bustling, but not in Davy. There were no fires, nor anyone in need of rescue at the moment. The sheriff's department seemed just as quiet. The jail had a separate entrance at the other side of the building, so Manfred didn't even have to share parking space with visitors. He was not at all tempted to find out if there was more bustle over on the jail side. He was nearly phobic about cages; he had not gone to a zoo since his first visit to the Memphis zoo with his school class.

The lobby of the sheriff's department was spick-and-span, thanks to an inmate who was mopping it with great vigor. Another inmate was dusting the leaves of the large potted plant by the door. They were both wearing traditional orange jumpsuits.

A female officer in uniform was behind the desk. Manfred's heart sank when he recognized Officer Gomez, who'd been to Midnight before and shown herself unsympathetic in the extreme. She glared at Manfred, her round face hardening with disapproval. They'd never talked, but apparently she recognized him. Or maybe she just hated small men with facial piercings.

"Officer Gomez, what a pleasure to see you. I hope you're doing well." Manfred didn't even try to summon up a smile, but he did manage to sound civil.

Arthur Smith came through an open doorway behind Gomez, just in time to hear her say, "Yeah, asshole, what do you want?"

There was a moment of silence that could only be described as pregnant. Manfred was fighting the sudden temptation to grin, Gomez was sharply aware that someone was behind her, and Arthur was furious. The mopping prisoner sniggered, and the dusting prisoner stifled a smile.

"Officer Gomez," said Arthur, the care he was taking to make his voice calm and smooth apparent in every syllable.

"Sir," she said. She didn't dare to turn around. She kept her eyes fixed down on the telephone at the desk.

"After I talk to Mr. Bernardo—a taxpayer and a citizen of this county who has never been charged with, much less convicted of, any crime—you and I are going to have a conversation. Is that clear?"

"Yes, sir."

Manfred could read Gomez's posture. She did not lift her eyes because she didn't want to meet Manfred's. She was afraid he would be triumphant or gleeful.

Not much, he thought. *Hardly at all.*

"Please come back to my office, Manfred," Arthur said, sounding close to normal.

"Thanks, good to see you." Manfred worked to make his own greeting nonchalant.

When they were in Arthur's very modest office with the door shut, Arthur said, "What was that about? Has she behaved this way before?"

"Short answer is yes. She's not a fan of Midnight. She answered a call out there when we were worried about motorcycles buzzing the streets, basically told us to go to hell."

"You didn't tell me about this."

"The motorcycles left when they saw the patrol car, so just the fact that she showed up worked. Telling you about her attitude seemed a little like tattling to Daddy, I guess. Besides, Fiji threatened Gomez with her cat."

Arthur smiled. "I would have liked to see that."

"We also figured, maybe the next time we called it might be Gomez who responded again. We wanted to stay on her good side, just in case."

"I apologize. I try to run a good department."

"I'm sure you do." Manfred shrugged. "Cops are just people. They have their likes and dislikes. It would be nice if she could be pleasant and respectful. But as long as she does her job, that's what we need." Manfred felt noble and surprisingly adult after his little speech.

"It doesn't sound like she did her job that day."

"You'll have to ask her about that."

"I intend to." Arthur nodded sharply, as though that topic was closed and they should move on to other things.

"Putting that aside," Manfred said agreeably, "you were telling me about what killed Rachel. And I have a question."

"What's that? I may or may not know the answer."

"Would it have been fatal even if she hadn't been sick?"

"Yes, probably. Of course, I haven't read the autopsy report or talked to the medical examiner. Not my place, not my case. But that's what the Bonnet Park cops say."

"So her blood pressure just dropped? Until she couldn't live anymore?"

"Essentially, yes." Arthur lifted some papers on the desk in front of him, then dropped them. "The important point as far as you're concerned is that unless something was radically different about Rachel Goldthorpe's metabolism, she ingested that medicine before she got to your room. Probably forty-five minutes to an hour before, but it could have been a little later."

Manfred felt overwhelmingly relieved. "How do you know?" he said.

"She died less than fifteen minutes after she'd entered your room. The toxicologist says that makes it almost a hundred percent certain that she ingested it earlier than that."

"So I'm off the hook for putting pills in her water bottle and causing her death. But I'm still on the hook for the theft of her jewelry."

"Based solely on Lewis's words." Arthur leaned back in his chair, which creaked alarmingly. They devoted a minute to thinking about that.

Footsteps went by outside, the telephone rang, voices rose and fell in conversation. A man laughed, full out, as if he'd heard the funniest joke ever. Manfred had the sense that life flowed all around them, that they were on an island in the middle of a stream. It was curiously comfortable and personal.

"I have to worry about the jewelry?" Manfred said.

Arthur spread his hands. "Lewis is acting so irrational that the Bonnet Park police hate to deal with him. But they have to take what he says seriously. And the jewelry is not in the house. There are six pieces that aren't accounted for. They're insured for quite a large amount."

"As I told the cops there, she told me she hid the jewelry from Lewis."

"As he told the cops there, she was carrying it in her purse and you stole it while she died. He said versus he said."

"They searched the room. They searched my luggage. They searched her purse. They searched her poor old body, I'm sure."

Arthur patted the air to tell Manfred to calm down. "Until it shows up, you need to be concerned. I wish you had a recording of Mrs. Goldthorpe saying those words." He stood up. "I'm sorry, Manfred, but they're bringing in a suspect in those convenience store robberies. I've got to question him."

"Sure, and thanks for the good news." It just wasn't good enough. Manfred hoped his talk with Olivia and Barry today was productive. He was ready to feel free again.

29

To Manfred's astonishment, he had a guest when he returned from Davy. And she was as mad as anyone he'd ever seen. Magdalena Powell pulled up in her car just as he got out of his, and Olivia (with perfect timing) came out of the side door of the pawnshop and walked across the dry brown lawn.

Magdalena shot out of her car and launched right in. "Forging my letterhead to send a bogus letter from me! Don't deny it. I'm seriously considering bringing a case against you. You'd never get out of jail once I got through with you."

"Hello, Ms. Powell," Manfred said, spreading a big dollop of calm all over his voice. "Before you get any more upset, let me tell you the circumstances."

"Ms. Powell, I have to confess," Olivia said, her voice so charming that Manfred turned to her with his mouth hanging open. "It wasn't Manfred. It was me."

It was hard to say who was more astonished by Olivia's confession.

"And you are?"

"Olivia Charity. I'm Manfred's neighbor. I've been so worried about him. In trying to get him out of this terrible predicament he's in, I confess I went overboard. But when you hear the result of the stunt I pulled, I think you'll forgive me. I had Manfred's welfare at heart." She looked at Manfred meaningfully. The ball was in his court.

Manfred made his jaw snap shut and said numbly, "Please come in. I can tell we need to talk for a while."

"We sure do," Magdalena said, though in a somewhat modified tone. She swept into the house when Manfred stood back, and Manfred gave Olivia a big, silent, questioning expression when Magdalena's back was to them. Olivia just smiled. Then Magdalena turned around and the moment was over.

"Um, please, come in and sit down," Manfred said. He'd had a lot of visitors lately, and he was beginning to wonder if Midnight was isolated enough. As he turned to close the front door, he saw a naked man walking on the sidewalk across the street. He froze for a second. The man was Diederik, and Diederik was definitely fully grown. Manfred pushed the door shut before Magdalena caught a glimpse. He thought, *What the hell?*

But he turned to face his guests, who hadn't seen. He did his best to act as though they were the sole focus of his attention.

"Can I get you a glass of water or some coffee or some tea?" he asked, not too surprised his voice came out funny.

"An explanation will be sufficient," Magdalena said, sounding every inch the lawyer.

"Please, let's sit in the living room," Manfred said, shepherding them farther into the house. Anything to get away from the front window.

With tactical precision, Magdalena sat in the armchair so that she could look at Manfred and Olivia at the same time. "All right," she said, her hands planted on her knees. "Let's have it."

Manfred was more than ready to leave the explanation to Olivia, since he had no idea what she was going to say. He was surprised when she gave Magdalena a factual account of their trip to Bonnet Park the day before—factual, that is, if you believed in telepathy and if you didn't know that Olivia had a lot of experience as a sort of covert operative.

To give the lawyer credit, she listened with every appearance of attention and interest. If her slight smile got tighter and tighter, that was only what Manfred expected.

At the end of Olivia's story, Magdalena said, "You know this is a bunch of bullshit, right?"

"I know to most lawyers it would sound like the chitchat of a total nut," Olivia said. "But I also know you've done legal work for my . . . boyfriend, Lemuel Bridger."

"Yes, well, Lemuel is a real person to whom I have spoken on more than one occasion," Magdalena said. "He's not a mind-reader or a psychic."

"But he *is* an energy-sucking vampire," Manfred said brightly.

Magdalena looked down, as if she didn't want to go on record as admitting even that much. "Lemuel is unusual," she conceded.

Olivia didn't even try to conceal her smirk. "Yeah, that's one way to put it," she said. "But the important thing is that Manfred is telling the truth. And if we hadn't gotten into the house to see for ourselves, I would never have known where the jewelry is. But now, I know."

That was what Manfred wanted to know. They hadn't had a chance to talk alone on the drive home. "Where?" he asked eagerly.

"Where is it?" Magdalena leaned forward.

"It's in the globe." Olivia leaned back, smiling triumphantly.

"Remember? Well, maybe you wouldn't, since you weren't yourself. Rachel told us she saw the world. World, get it?"

"The globe," he said blankly.

"The globe in Morton Goldthorpe's study."

"How do you figure that?" Magdalena was skeptical, to say the least.

"I've seen another one made by the same company, a globe that was designed to hold guns," Olivia said. "It has a fitted compartment inside so they won't shift around and make noise if someone spins the globe."

"But you haven't had an opportunity to open the globe to test this theory of yours?"

"No, I couldn't do it with Lewis standing by. He would turn around and accuse us of planting the jewelry to escape prosecution."

"Since you've been in the house, that is certainly what a police officer might assume." Magdalena wasn't as angry as she had been, but she wasn't thrilled about Olivia's information, either. She was thinking it through. "Say you're right, and the jewelry is in the globe. How will we go about proving that in a way that won't leave a shadow on my client?"

"Let me just add another detail here," Manfred said, feeling that the two women were settling his future without his input. "I just came from a conversation with the sheriff in Davy."

"You went to talk to the sheriff without me." Magdalena's temperature was rising again.

"Since he's not the Bonnet Park police, yeah. He had something to tell me that we didn't get around to yesterday," Manfred said. "Since he'd driven down here to tell me, it seemed like the least I could do. And what he told me was that apparently Rachel was murdered."

Both women were absolutely stunned. Manfred took care to look at Olivia directly, and he could swear that she was genuinely taken aback. Relief flooded him, but he was very careful not to show it.

"How?" Olivia asked. "How was she murdered? When I saw her in the lobby, she seemed to be unwell but not anywhere close to death."

"It's likely that someone crushed several of her blood pressure pills and put them in her water bottle. I guess there's a remote possibility she did that herself, but she was really sane, and she did not have a suicidal thought in her head."

"Someone who had access to the pills and the bottle," Magdalena said. "That limits the field considerably." She smiled. "In fact, that means it has to have been the maid or the son, right?"

"No, not exactly. I wish it were that clear-cut. When she dropped her purse in the lobby," Manfred said, "everything fell out of it, including the water bottle. So it's just possible that the bottle was switched there. It was pretty distinctive: a black refillable bottle with butterflies on it. I say it must have been a switch—I can't see how anyone could drop the medicine into the bottle she already had, not out there in public with so many eyes watching. To say nothing of the security cameras. To say nothing of having to ensure Rachel dropped her purse in the first place. To say nothing of the timing of the pill ingestion being wrong, according to the postmortem."

"I helped her pick her things up," Olivia said immediately. "She was really flustered and embarrassed. And I handed her everything I found. But I don't remember a water bottle. Either I simply didn't register it, or someone else must have picked it up." She looked momentarily abstracted, as if she were re-creating the scene in her head. "There were lots of people helping her, including a police officer. It took more time than you'd think. Stuff had rolled under the furniture."

Manfred gave himself permission to believe Olivia was innocent. What he said out loud was, "Since Lewis is going to be a hot suspect in his mother's murder, do we still need to worry about the jewel theft?"

"Yes, of course," Magdalena said, as if he were an idiot. "He hasn't been arrested yet. Even if he is, he's got a good lawyer, as I think you know, Mr. Bernardo."

Manfred winced. "Yeah, he sneaked my last lawyer out from under me, but I'm pleased with my representation now." He managed a weak smile, which Magdalena didn't bother to return.

"Besides," Magdalena said, pursuing her own train of thought, "his fingerprints could logically be on the bottle. So could the maid's. Maybe Rachel kept her bottle in the household refrigerator. They could have moved it from one side to another, innocently. They both had access to her pills. And thousands of people take that same medicine. Perhaps the pills could have been introduced into the bottle of water much earlier. She might not have used it in a while. You say she'd been confined to the house, sick, and maybe she only took the bottle with her when she was riding in her car. I'm sure there were many occasions when people were in the house prior to Rachel leaving for her appointment with you. Her entire family was surely in and out during her illness. All of those people might have a reason for wanting her dead at that point in time. Maybe her daughters got impatient for their inheritance."

Manfred wondered if he looked as dismayed as he felt. "But none of that is true," he protested feebly.

"It all *might* be true," the lawyer said. "There's plenty of doubt there. Unless the case against Lewis gets strengthened somehow . . . for example, if Bertha the maid says she saw him putting something into his mother's water bottle, or if he has a girlfriend who taped him confessing to killing his mother . . . there might not be enough real evidence to charge him with the crime."

Olivia nodded. "I'm afraid that's the case," she said. "Of course,

Lewis is so unpredictable that he might confess. Though I don't think so. I think he's all about Lewis, all about getting everything that's his due and then some."

"So really, I'm no better off? Even now that it really seems probable that Lewis killed his mother?"

Magdalena sighed heavily. "I don't think so. Plus, now you've made me angry with you, with good reason, though your friend Olivia is taking the blame. And we have to decide how to get the police to check the globe."

Olivia said, "Can I just apologize to you very sincerely for using a trick that seemed brilliant to me at the moment?"

"You can apologize, but I hardly think that's enough."

Manfred groped around for a response. "What else can we do, Magdalena?" He felt he had to include Olivia in the atonement, since she'd shouldered the blame.

Magdalena sighed again and looked off into the distance. "You can give my mother a reading. A personal reading."

Olivia looked away, too, to hide her smile, but Manfred saw it. He kept his own face solemn. "Your mom's a follower? I'm flattered."

"She is. It's the flaw in her character. Otherwise, she's a sane and rational woman. Active in her community and in her church. But she's a fan of the Great Manfredo. Every time you put on your website that you're going to do some personal readings in whatever city, she figures out the cost of going and having the reading, and every time she can't quite bring herself to part with the money. But if you would go to her home and give her a reading, I will forgive your deception in forging my letterhead. I'm choosing to blame you instead of Miss Charity, here, because it was done on your behalf. If you ever do such a thing again, I will sue your ass."

"Where does your mother live?" Manfred accepted those terms

happily. He was relieved. He didn't care if Magdalena saw that. In fact, he was glad she did.

"Mother lives in Killeen. Her name is Agnes. You'll have to set up a time with her. I'm telling her this is her belated Mother's Day present."

"I'd be delighted." Manfred wondered how long the drive to Killeen was, but he would start out right now if he had to. He was just relieved she didn't live somewhere even farther away.

He had a definite presentiment that he would meet Magdalena's mother, so at least he would live a little while longer. He wandered to the front window, where the curtains were drawn, to see what was happening now. The Rev was outside the chapel. He was pulling a long hose back to the fence enclosing the pet cemetery. He was fully clothed, though he was not wearing his usual black jacket. The boy— man?—was nowhere in sight, thank God.

"Now that that's settled," Magdalena said, her voice sharp to demand his attention, "have you and Miss Charity had an idea about how to tell the police where to look?"

"Anonymous phone call?"

"From where?"

"I could drive to a town between here and Dallas and find a pay phone." Olivia sounded doubtful.

"Yes, but there aren't any isolated ones anymore. At least, not any that you could assume would function. There are some at rest stops, but those are usually under camera surveillance."

"True," Olivia said. "Okay, cell phones are out. We could buy a phone, but I suppose they keep serial numbers somewhere?" Of course Olivia had a burner phone in her apartment, but she wasn't about to admit that to a lawyer. "What about an anonymous letter?"

Manfred grimaced in distaste. His grandmother had gotten some. That was a very bad memory. The viciousness of them, the coward- ice of people who wouldn't reveal their names, had nauseated him.

Of course, if he sent one, it wouldn't contain an accusation. It would be a statement. "The jewelry of Mrs. Goldthorpe is in the globe in her husband's study in her house." Something simple and declarative like that, with lots of nouns. But still . . . that was a last resort.

Magdalena said very reluctantly, "I have a client. The police say he sells illegal drugs. I say they haven't proved it. But he told me there's an app on his phone that can turn it into a burner. It's legal. He might show me how that works."

Manfred let out a gust of breath. "So, you'll call them soon?"

"He has an appointment this afternoon," she said. "If he keeps it, I just may ask him to show it to me."

Manfred had never appreciated how much more difficult sneaking around had gotten. Surveillance cameras, cell phone records that showed where you were when you made a call, advances in lab testing . . . but he wondered how much of the available technology (which must be expensive, both the investment in equipment and in technicians who understood how to use it) the average law enforcement department could actually finance and employ. Would this poor county have access to forensic labs that could tell you what ream of paper a sheet of computer paper had come from, and where it was sold? Would they view hours of surveillance footage to determine who'd bought that paper? Manfred was skeptical. He'd watched plenty of television shows where police departments not only could unearth this very specific information but could do it instantly. He didn't believe that could be the truth. So maybe this would be the right way to go: having his lawyer make a sneaky phone call. Simple enough.

"Okay," he said. "Let's do that. I'm ready to be rid of this situation and get back to work. Especially now that I owe my lawyer more money." He smiled, though he was pretty sure it wasn't a happy smile.

Olivia said, "So that's it? After all the trouble we went to, that's the end?"

"What else do you want to do, honey?" Magdalena asked, genuinely interested. "You want to break Lewis's neck?"

Olivia looked at Magdalena with an expression that chilled Manfred. "That would be a start," Olivia said.

"No need," Manfred said, though there'd been moments when he could have throttled Lewis himself. This had turned into a personal mission for Olivia, though he wasn't sure how or why. "We've got a plan, and if Magdalena will make the phone call, we should be seeing the result soon."

"We have a deal," the lawyer said, standing up. "I'm sending you my mother's phone number today, and you're honor-bound to call her and set up an appointment to meet in person."

"Honor-bound," Manfred agreed. He didn't believe he'd ever heard anyone say that out loud.

Without another word, Magdalena left.

"She didn't even let her car air out," Olivia observed. "Iron woman."

She began prowling around restlessly. "Did you ever get a chance to talk to Barry? After we started back yesterday?"

"No, but it looks like I will now. Here he comes."

Barry knocked on the door before Manfred could swing it open. "Hey, man," he said. "Listen, I was just going to tell you about yesterday."

"Please. Olivia was telling me you had some things to share. And I've got to pay you."

"It's really cool to tell stuff to someone who'll believe it." Barry stretched and yawned. "My grandfather came into my room to wake me up last night. He kept wanting to go home."

"Where to?" Olivia asked.

"That's the thing, he's lived about twenty different places. Texas. Nevada. California. Longest in Vegas, where he was a blackjack dealer at one of the casinos. Till Eva Culhane snatched him up and brought him here."

"I wonder why? It's like Tommy and your grandfather and the ladies are just camouflage for something."

"Those are good things to wonder about, but let me get this stuff off my chest first." Barry made a sweep with his hand, indicating he was ready to unload.

"Okay, man, go ahead."

"This is what I learned yesterday on our little trip to Bonnet Park. First, the maid, Bertha, is scared to death of Lewis, right? She thinks he's going to kill her one of these days. He's getting increasingly off the rails mentally and emotionally, and he's getting more and more specific. Like, he wants his tea in a certain glass with a certain type of straw and a sprig of mint with three leaves on it. Shit like that. So she's scared, and she's glad he's sleeping out in the pool house so she doesn't have to see him all day, every day. She thinks he's unworthy to inherit so much from his folks. She thinks her own son is far superior."

"So she's got no loyalty to Lewis," Olivia said.

"On the contrary. Bertha can't stand him. But she's also determined to stay with the job as long as she can, because she wants to know what Lewis is up to. Somehow, when Mr. Goldthorpe died, her son didn't get what she thought he would. She thought he'd get enough to start up his own landscaping business, buy a couple of trucks and mowers, and hire people. But instead, everything went to the wife. Rachel. There's some test that has everything hanging in the balance." Barry had closed his eyes while he related all of this, as if it would help him remember Bertha's thought better.

"So Bertha was expecting a legacy she hasn't received," Manfred said. "Anything more pertinent?"

"Here's the really good stuff. When we went into the study and Lewis was so upset, he was thinking about his mother and how scared he'd been that she would say something about Bertha to the psychic—you, Manfred. And he was wondering if Rachel's will was going to mention Bertha."

"Why would it?" Manfred sat for a minute. "What's the connection? Has Bertha's son been romancing one of Rachel's daughters? But they're both married women."

"And they're at least fifteen years older than him, going by appearances," Olivia said. "I guess the son and Lewis could be having a thing, though I can't imagine anyone being genuinely interested in Lewis sexually."

Barry snickered. "I can't, either."

"You can hear people's deepest secrets," Olivia said. "Manfred can talk to dead people. I feel very plain compared to your skill set."

"What I do has its weak points," Barry said. "People don't always think in an orderly way, with background. They know all the background. So you're left with lots of gaps. You have to be careful not to fill them in yourself."

Olivia said, "Your life must be one long trail of disillusionment."

He nodded. "You're about right. That's a good way to put it."

Manfred was trying to think of something positive to say when Barry stood up. "Okay," he said. "I think that's it. I just wanted to tell you that and collect my money. I got to get back to Shorty. He's not having a good day. I think moving him from Vegas was a mistake. Mrs. Whitefield says he's seemed mentally fuzzy ever since he arrived. When I'd call him in Vegas, he wasn't that off base."

Manfred got out his wallet (stocking up on cash was another thing he'd done in Davy) and handed Barry the agreed amount. As soon as the door closed behind the telepath, Olivia said, "What's really interesting is what they'll decide to do with Shorty once they've found he actually has to go into some kind of home and they can't really keep him in the hotel any longer. If all the old people are just window dressing, what's going to keep them from dumping them out in the desert? What could be the purpose of this?"

Manfred nodded. "I could swear Lenore Whitefield isn't a villain. She really believes she's there to keep her guests happy until they move on to their final destination. Ah . . . that sounds way more gruesome than I intended. What I'm trying to say is, she doesn't have any designs on them."

"Yeah, I get that, but the fact is that only the guests staying there who are doing contract work for Magic Portal are real, actual paying guests, and of course whoever is crazy enough to stop in Midnight. I guess the hotel might get to be a sort of destination place since it's been converted so cleverly, but it's not really a period piece, is it? It's a modern version of a motel, fitted into an old shell."

Manfred said, "This whole town is a shell."

"What?"

"There are more storefronts boarded up than open. How does any-one here live? How does Home Cookin stay open? How does the Rev survive on what he makes burying dogs and cats and performing wed-dings? How does the Antique Gallery and Nail Salon make a profit? You have to leave here to make your living. Why don't the others?"

"You left out Fiji and Bobo," Olivia said.

"Fiji inherited the house. She's got almost no overhead. And she sells some spells online, as well as the crap she carries in the shop. Plus, the Thursday night classes are paying propositions."

"She sells things online? Really?"

"Yeah, I helped her set something up about four months ago, and I got a friend of mine to design her website."

"You're a man of secrets." Olivia did not seem to think that was a good thing. There was a long moment of silence before she said,

"Sometimes I think about that, too. But I have no way of knowing how the others get along, and I'm not going to ask them. We don't ask many questions here, and I like it that way. Call me if the police actually get into the house and find the damn jewelry in the globe. I need to go do stuff."

And she left, too. Manfred said, "Dammit." He'd finally said things out loud that he'd wondered about for months—and said them out loud to Olivia, of all people. And she'd blown him off and gotten out the door as fast as she could.

30

The town fell silent again at dusk. Everyone did the same things they'd done the night before, even though some of the tension had gone. Fiji called Manfred to ask him if he wanted some home-made bread, and when he said yes, they met in the middle of Witch Light Road. There was still plenty of light; they talked a little. Though the heat radiated off the road, it was still pleasant to be outside, to be confident that nothing was lurking . . . yet.

"Mr. Snuggly won't come out of the corner of my bedroom," she said. "He's gone into scaredy-cat overload."

"One more night of this, you think? After tonight?"

"I think so."

"What, exactly, are we so afraid of?"

"Well," Fiji said, "it is the full moon." She looked at him significantly, obviously expecting Manfred to pick up her meaning.

"It's been the full moon lots of times since I moved here, and I've never had to do this before."

"Then you should ask yourself, 'What's different about this time?'"
she said patiently. "Here's the bread. There's beer in it. Enjoy." She
cast a quick glance over at the pawnshop, perhaps hoping that Bobo
would emerge. She turned to go back to her house, calling good-bye
over her shoulder.

Manfred raised the bread to his nose. It had the most wonderful
aroma. He wondered if baking might someday be included in his skill
set, because he would do anything to make his house smell like this.
He caught movement out of the corner of his eye. A police car was
driving very slowly down the street. The driver was looking from side
to side. There was someone else in the front seat. Manfred saw that
the passenger was Shorty Horowitz.

"Shit!" Manfred said. He flagged down the car. It pulled into his
driveway. He didn't know the driver, but it was a sheriff's department
uniform.

"You know this man, sir?" asked the deputy.

"Yes, where was he?"

"I found him on the Davy highway just north of here. He says he
has a grandson here? Someone named Barry Bellboy?" The deputy
said this very carefully, as if he suspected he was the butt of a joke.

"His grandson is over at the hotel," Manfred said. "I'll bet he's
going nuts."

He looked over at the hotel and saw Barry standing in the hotel
doorway, looking from one direction to another, obviously terrified.
Manfred waved his arms and pointed at the patrol car. Barry came
running across the intersection like there was no such thing as traffic, and in a second was standing by the car, panting.

"Oh, you've found him! Thanks so much."

"You Barry? He do this a lot?" asked the deputy.

At least it's not Gomez, Manfred thought.

"I'm Barry Horowitz. He's never done this before," Barry said. "God,

I couldn't find him anywhere. I was really, really . . . scared." He leaned down to look across the deputy at the errant Shorty. "Granddad, where've you been? Why did you leave?" His voice sound gentle, and he'd put the fear away somewhere.

"Barry?" Shorty turned to look at his grandson. He seemed puzzled.

"That was part of the problem," the deputy explained. "He kept telling us your name was Bellboy, and I put out a call to search for someone of that name. Of course, there wasn't anyone in this area called that."

Barry didn't seem to be able to speak. He looked stricken.

"You ready to take your grandpa back home?" the deputy said, looking a little worried.

Barry had recovered his vocal cords. "Okay, Grandpa, you ready to go back to the hotel?"

"All right. If they'll give me cake for supper and let me take a nap."

"I'm sure Mrs. Whitefield won't mind giving you some cake, if she's got one made, and you can sure take a nap in your room."

"Barry took a nap," Shorty said. "But it was time for me to go home."

"That was my big mistake," Barry told the deputy. He seemed to have recovered his wits. "He woke me up last night with this 'going home' theme, and I dropped off to sleep this afternoon. He gets worse the closer to night it becomes. Sundowner syndrome, they call it."

"*Sundown*," Manfred said significantly. The deputy looked at him oddly, but Barry got Manfred's drift.

It was very close to nightfall.

"Thanks so much, Deputy . . ." Barry paused.

"Nash. Glad to help. Glad we found the old guy before he came to harm."

After some well-meaning advice from Deputy Nash and more profuse thanks from Barry and more disjointed statements from Shorty, Barry and Manfred extricated Shorty from the car and waved while the deputy backed out and turned right to go back to Davy.

"Go, go, go," Manfred said. "Do you need to stay at my place?" He made the offer reluctantly, but he made it.

"We've got the time," Barry said. "I don't know what the urgency is, but we'll be inside in four minutes, maximum." He began to coax his grandfather toward the hotel, promising cake and ice cream and many naps. Manfred stood in his doorway watching.

Finally, the tall man and short man reached the double glass doors to the hotel.

Manfred heard a sound coming from somewhere close, a deep sound, one he could not identify. But it made him think of the zoo again.

In an instant, he was in the house with the door shut behind him. And he locked it. And he drew the curtains tight.

After he had gotten his breathing under control, he noticed that the message light on his cell phone was blinking. He had two messages. The first one was from Magdalena Powell. "I did the thing I said I was going to do," she said. "Have you called my mom yet?"

The second message was from Fiji. "What the hell is with the cop car?" she said.

Manfred returned her call.

"Yeah?" she said breathlessly.

"Barry's grandfather went walkabout," he told her. "The cops returned him. Deputy Nash was confused because Shorty kept telling him that his grandson's name was Barry Bellboy. Weird, huh?"

"He'll have to do something about Shorty."

"Yeah, I'm sure he's thinking about that right now."

"Did you tell Barry that? About the Bellboy thing?"

"The deputy did. Barry freaked out." Manfred reconsidered his terminology. "Actually, he was scared shitless."

"That's pretty strange. Well, have a good evening and enjoy the bread."

31

The next day was a strange one, right from the moment Manfred woke up. He glanced at his calendar and realized he had a dental appointment in Marthasville. Manfred hated going to the dentist almost as much as he hated zoos. This dentist in Marthasville was supposed to be especially good at treating jittery patients, and when Manfred had heard of her, he thought he'd give her a try before his teeth rotted out of his head. And he'd made an early appointment so his entire day wouldn't be ruined by the anxiety over the impending trip.

By the time he got back to Midnight, it was ten in the morning. The dentist had been good and kind, but he was frazzled and longed for nothing more than to drink something cold and soothing and to bury himself in work. The past few days had put him horribly behind.

Manfred noticed there were some cars at Fiji's shop, and he was glad that she had some business. There was a car outside Joe and Chuy's place, too. And the hotel. Lots of visitors to Midnight today. Weird.

Manfred unlocked his front door and got another unhappy surprise. Olivia was sitting in his kitchen. She leaped to her feet when he came in. "Who are they looking for?" she said.

Manfred's heart had stuttered when he saw her inside his house, and it took a few seconds for him to be able to process what she'd said. "Olivia, I'm plenty pissed that you broke into my house," he said, trying hard to make his voice even. He didn't want her to see how frightened he'd been.

"I'll apologize later," she snapped. "Who?"

"I don't know what you're talking about." He poured himself a drink with lots of ice and let it cool his sore mouth.

"There are people in Midnight," she said through clenched teeth. "Why are they here? They're looking for someone. I want to know who."

"They're just shoppers," he said, though he did not believe that.

"Bullshit!" She leaped from her chair, and he flinched. "How often have you seen four cars at one time in Midnight? Cars that stopped? With strangers inside?"

Manfred's phone rang. He held it to his ear. "Yes?" he said.

"Hi," said Fiji, in a bright, impersonal voice. He knew right away that something was wrong. "Mr. Bernardo, I did some research, and that was the correct reaction."

It took him a second to decipher that. Barry had been right to be afraid that the name "Bellboy" had been broadcast. "Yeah," he said. "I understand. That why you have visitors?"

"I am definitely not the only shopholder in Midnight who feels that way."

"I understand," he said again. "Are you okay?"

"Of course," she said with a smile in her voice. "We'll talk later, when you're at liberty." And she hung up.

"You're right," Manfred told Olivia. "They're not here to shop. But they're not looking for you. They're looking for Barry."

He stood at his window, assessing the situation. There was a sign across the way on the front door of the chapel.

"Can you read that sign, Olivia?"

She joined him. "It says, 'CLOSED today and maybe TOMOR-ROW.' With 'closed' and 'tomorrow' in caps."

There was now another car at Home Cookin. But the restaurant wouldn't be open for a while. A woman—at this distance he could only tell she was tall and thin and pale—crossed Witch Light Road after turning away from Home Cookin. She hesitated in front of Joe and Chuy's shop, and then walked to Gas N Go. He saw her push open the glass door, and he could almost hear the electronic buzz.

"They're everywhere," Olivia said.

"Olivia, I don't know who these people are or what they're doing here. Barry is the guy who probably knows all about it, and I'm pretty sure it's because of his senile grandfather that he's in a fix. I don't think this is connected to you."

"Tell me." She seemed to relax a little.

"In a nutshell, Barry Horowitz isn't his real name. It's Barry Bellboy, which is pretty strange, and I have to think that isn't the name he was born with. Yesterday in the evening, Grandpa got lost, told the deputy who found him what his grandson's name was, the deputy broadcast that name to find somewhere to return Grandpa, and apparently whoever Barry is so scared of heard it. They're in Fiji's shop now. You believed these people were looking for you?"

"Yes, I did believe that," she said. "They'll be here any minute. No matter who they're looking for, they'll go to every place in Midnight."

"Are you gonna let them see you?"

"Hell, no! I'm going to hide in your kitchen and listen to what they say to you."

"Thanks," he said bitterly. "Jump in and save my life, okay?"

"They're not going to kill you. At least, probably not. But if they get aggressive, I'll take action."

Manfred thought it was ominous she didn't say what that action might be. Maybe Olivia would run out the back door.

He was almost relieved when he saw her put a gun ready on the table. He didn't know anything about guns, and he didn't like them. It was worse than having a snake on the table. But at least now he knew she was not planning to leave him defenseless.

She sat, hands folded, waiting.

She was better at it than Manfred.

He took a cold drink to his workstation and began to answer personal e-mails. He never had very many. But today, he heard from Rain, and it was a significant message. She and Gary had gotten married. "Since we couldn't see the situation with his kids changing and we weren't getting any younger, we just eloped!" she wrote. Manfred sighed heavily. Rain Redding. He'd have to get used to it. And he'd have to have a conversation with Fiji about an appropriate wedding gift. He tried composing a reply, but after two abortive attempts, he decided he would call later. An unspecified "later." *When all this is over,* he thought.

Finally, he started real work. He turned on the psychic hotline phone, as he thought of it, and started taking calls. In between calls, he answered the paying e-mails. And if he caught up with those, there was the Amazing Bernardo website, and messages to answer there. The routine took over. He almost forgot about the woman with the gun behind him, and the strange people going around searching Midnight, and he worked. After all, the bill from Magdalena would be high, and his car wasn't any younger.

At least he wouldn't have to fly home for his mother's wedding.

A knock at the door broke his concentration. He sent the e-mail he was working on (*Your boyfriend gives off a very violent vibration, and you should take care of your own safety first*) before he went to the door.

And then looked down.

The man was less than five feet tall and looked to Manfred's uneducated eyes like an Indian. Manfred could not have specified what kind of Indian or his country of origin, but he was built broadly and he was very dark skinned. The whites of his eyes weren't actually white, but faintly yellow.

"Hello," Manfred said, hoping Olivia was primed to take action. "Can I help you?"

"Your name, sir?"

The Indian's voice was not the deep rumble Manfred had expected. It was a light tenor. Manfred felt ridiculously self-conscious and couldn't decide what a totally innocent response would be to what was actually a kind of strange question.

"You're the one who knocked," he said. "I'm working here, and I need to get back to it." He began closing the door, but there was a small boot in the way.

"Excuse me," said the Indian. "Perhaps I wasn't polite or clear. I am looking for someone, and I need to ask you a few questions."

"Maybe *I* wasn't clear," Manfred retorted. "I am working, and I am not obliged to answer your questions." He tried to close the door again. The boot didn't move.

"Is there anyone else in your house?" the Indian asked.

"No, there is no one else in my house."

"May I look and see?"

"No." Manfred was definite about that.

"Has there been a strange man in town lately? Tall, in his late twenties, perhaps using the last name Bell or Bellboy?"

"If there is, I haven't met him, but mostly I'm stuck here working, which I need to do now." Manfred deftly kicked the boot out of the way with his own and slammed the door, locking it as quickly as he could.

Then he walked back to his desk and threw himself into the chair to make it creak and roll noisily over the hardwood floor. And he waited. After an extremely long thirty seconds, the Indian moved away. Manfred exhaled slowly and deliberately.

"You heard?" he said.

"Yeah. I think he's a daytime guy, working for a vampire."

Manfred turned around. Olivia looked a lot more like the woman he knew than she had when he'd returned home that day. Some terrible emotion had leaked out of her to be replaced by practicality. "Why do you think that?" he asked.

"Was he wearing something around his neck?"

"Yeah," Manfred said. "A bandanna. Like he was part of an Old West pageant."

"Okay, then. He's a fangbanger."

"I don't know much about the vampire thing," Manfred said. "I've only been to Louisiana once, and that was in the daytime."

"They do keep a low profile almost everywhere else," Olivia said. "Especially since the were-animal disaster. I know there's an enclave in Dallas, though. I think these people searching Midnight were sent by that enclave. They all arrived about the same time, they're all strangers, they're all asking questions, I assume. They're going in and out of all the businesses in town. They're looking for Barry, so they've got a grudge against him for some reason, and he knows about it. Since they're after him, not me, I'm outta here. I have something to do in Dallas." And she was gone.

Manfred hardly noticed. Before he could think the better of it, he called Barry's cell.

"Hello." Barry's voice was low and cautious.

"Someone was here."

Barry said, still very quietly, "I saw them out the window. If they find me, I'm dead."

"Are you . . . well hidden? A short guy with a bandanna around his neck was here. He was very persistent."

"His name is Alejandro," Barry said. "Even for my grandfather, I shouldn't have set foot in Texas again."

Manfred was powerfully curious to learn the whole story, but this was not the time to ask to hear it. "We won't give you up," he said, aware that his own voice had hushed to match Barry's.

"You won't have a choice," Barry whispered. "They'll find me and take me to Dallas. I won't get away with it this time. Better keep back." And he hung up.

Manfred had an idea. There was a huge downside, but it might work, and he owed it to Barry, or Rick, or whatever the hell the man's name was, to try something. Barry had done him a good turn. True, he'd gotten paid. But he'd done it willingly.

Manfred spent some time on the phone with Magdalena Powell. Then he warned the other residents of Midnight. When a news van rolled up, they were as ready as they were ever going to be. As he'd hoped, Magdalena was eager to take the opportunity to be on television. This would be a tiny press conference, maybe the smallest in Texas history: with a reporter from the Davy paper, a reporter from the closest television affiliate, and the regional stringer for a Dallas paper. Manfred elected to hold it in front of the Inquiring Mind, with Fiji's permission. He reasoned that Fiji could use the publicity a lot more than he could. Besides, her lovingly created garden, with flowers blooming everywhere, was a much nicer backdrop than his barren little cottage.

Mr. Snuggly obliged by sitting on the porch and looking picturesque. One of the reporters almost stepped on him and then leaped to one side, looking wildly around to find the source of the tiny voice that said something very pointed to him.

Manfred, nervous and regretting his impulse already, let his gaze pan over the streets of Midnight. The strangers were popping out of the Midnight buildings, and they started to drift down to Fiji's. That was exactly what he'd wanted.

Magdalena looked at her watch, looked at the reporters, and said, "Time to get started."

Manfred would rather have waited another two or three minutes, but he didn't want to rouse any suspicion in Alejandro, who was standing like a very unfortunate statue by one of Fiji's rosebushes.

"I wanted to announce today," Manfred said clearly, "that I am innocent of the charges leveled against me by Lewis Goldthorpe. These charges relate to the disappearance of some jewelry of his mother's. Also, I understand that Lewis Goldthorpe has been hinting to his media connections that I am guilty of some kind of wrongdoing in the death of his mother, my friend Rachel Goldthorpe. The very idea of such a thing is repugnant to me, and I suggest that if Lewis keeps spreading this kind of terrible rumor, I will see him in court with my lawyer, Magdalena Orta Powell." Manfred felt relieved at getting through this statement, especially "repugnant," and he added, "Magdalena Powell can kick Lewis's butt legally."

There was some actual laughter, and Magdalena, who wanted to punch him, instead smiled in an arctic way. Manfred was relieved she didn't shove him off Fiji's porch.

"Magdalena," called the man who'd almost stepped on Mr. Snuggly's tail, "how are you gonna kick Jess Barnwell's butt?"

"Barnwell's a fine lawyer," Magdalena said seriously. "But he's got an unreliable client."

"As opposed to a phone psychic?"

"Ouch," said Manfred, smiling. "But I've heard much worse." He thought, *Barry, get out now! Now!*

He didn't know if Barry could pick up on Manfred's particular thought pattern, but he did sense that Barry was on the move, and he saw a car pull out of the alley running behind the hotel. It turned left to drive west on Witch Light Road. That would take him to the nearest highway north, which would get him into Oklahoma in a few hours.

Manfred turned his attention back to the here and now. "I may be a phone psychic, among other things, but I don't make false accusations against people to the police or the media," he said.

"You're saying Lewis Goldthorpe has slandered you?"

"I'm saying that he should remember that he lives in a glass house," Manfred said, and he thought Magdalena was going to blow a fuse. "It may be in Bonnet Park, and I may live in Midnight." He swept his hand around theatrically to indicate his surroundings. "He may be the son of a millionaire, and I may be the grandson of a great psychic." (He owed his grandmother Xylda that, he figured.) "But when he makes statements that besmirch the memory of his mother, he has forfeited his right to my respect and consideration."

That got their attention, and there was a lively back-and-forth between Manfred and "the media" until Magdalena shut it down with a graceful statement thanking them all for coming today. The little crowd dispersed, the fangbangers gathering to engage in a low-voiced conference, the reporters to straggle back to their vehicles and depart.

"That was a good idea," Magdalena said. "I think. What made you so determined to do it?" He'd only been able to get her to agree to show up by telling her he'd do it without her. Instead of dropping him as a client, she'd figured being on television was not so bad.

"It was a diversion, plus I wanted to get up in Lewis's face," he said. "He's tried to say I'm a thief. Well, maybe he's a murderer. He needs to be worried about himself."

"You baffle me," she said, looking at her client with frustration all over her face. "And if you think I did this for free . . ."

"That never crossed my mind," said Manfred honestly. "I expect your bill in the mail. Listen, as long as you're here, would you like to have an early dinner at Home Cookin?"

The lawyer's face was a picture of *startled*. She hesitated. "A regular gathering?" She was gauging the social texture of the meal. Manfred didn't blame her.

"It's almost always just us Midnight people," he said. "But I'm giving Arthur a call."

That decided her, as he had suspected it would. She looked at her watch. "I am through for the day," she said. "All right. As long as you know we're just . . . lawyer and client."

Magdalena was attractive, but he'd rather date a barracuda. "Of course," he said, hoping he sounded just a little regretful.

Fiji came out of her house, where she'd been secluded in the back during the press conference. He could tell she was feeling pretty today, though she always seemed pretty to him.

"Fiji, you coming with us?" he asked.

She smiled. "I guess so. I don't feel like cooking and making my kitchen hot, you know?" Her smile brightened when Bobo emerged from the pawnshop. He crossed the road to walk with them. "*Hola*, Magdalena," he called.

Manfred was not at all surprised to find that Bobo knew his lawyer.

"Hey, Feej, are you going to charge Manfred? Since he used your garden as a backdrop for his press thing?"

"Nah," she said. "The shop sign was probably in the photos."

Mr. Snuggly rubbed against Manfred's denim-covered leg before vanishing into the backyard in his mysterious cat way. They passed the closed chapel with its sign, and none of them said anything, though Magdalena gave it a curious look. Manfred, who'd been texting, grinned. "Arthur's showing up in a few minutes," he said.

"Cool," Bobo said. "I haven't had a talk with him in months."

"Okay," Fiji said. "I kind of like him." She sounded faintly surprised, as if she were not in the habit of liking law enforcement officers.

Fiji and Bobo walked ahead. While Manfred and Magdalena were out of hearing, he asked, "Just out of curiosity, can you find out the terms of Morton's will?"

"It's a matter of public record," Magdalena said. "If you want to pay for my time, of course I can get a copy."

"I do, and the sooner the better."

"I'll tell Phil tomorrow."

When they were about to cross the Davy highway, they saw Chuy and Joe emerge from their shop doorway. They, too, were eating out tonight. Now that the strangers were gone, and so was Rick Horowitz (né Barry Bellboy), everyone was happier except maybe Shorty Horowitz. Manfred was glad Barry was on his way to safety; he was glad no vampires would come to Midnight. Crisis averted.

And, he had to confess to himself, it was a relief to have the telepath gone from their midst, as much as he'd been curious about what Barry was "receiving" from his companions.

"By the way," Magdalena said.

"What?"

"I only agreed to your little press conference because the Bonnet Park police had already called me to tell me they'd found the jewelry. You'd just been cleared. So it was safe for you to deny all the charges in public."

Manfred stared at her, his mouth hanging open. "I should have wondered harder why you agreed to do it," he said. "You know what? I'm just happy it's over. I couldn't have killed her, and I didn't steal anything, and it's all public knowledge." He felt amazingly lighthearted.

Chicken and dumplings was on the menu that night, along with baked tilapia. These were new, so they were all more interested than usual in their food.

Manfred wasn't the only one to notice that Arthur chose a chair by Magdalena, or perhaps Magdalena had arranged to have an empty seat available. She was a lawyer and used to strategizing. But after Arthur had ordered, his phone buzzed, and he stepped outside to take the call. Dillon was in the kitchen getting another pitcher of iced tea, and Madonna was cooking.

Manfred had been able to see the tension in the way his landlord was sitting. There was something Bobo wanted to say, and since he couldn't get rid of Magdalena as well, he leaned forward with sudden resolution.

"I wonder where our missing citizens are," Bobo said. Since they were all seated around the big round table that dominated the little restaurant, they could all hear him even though he didn't raise his voice. He meant the Rev and Diederik.

"Just one more night," Fiji said, even more obliquely.

Manfred wasn't sure he really wanted to know what the Rev was up to. "I guess we'll find out if we're supposed to know," he said, and grabbed a piece of corn bread from the basket in the middle of the table.

Arthur came back in, Magdalena stopped looking from one to the other of them as though she expected them to speak in tongues, and Dillon eased through the swinging doors to the kitchen with a brimming pitcher of tea. He refreshed their drinks, but he seemed subdued. Manfred had a moment of doubt. Was the atmosphere of Midnight contagious? Dillon had always seemed like a normal ranch teenager. Now he was preoccupied.

"Dillon, you doing okay?" Bobo asked, just before Manfred could get the words out.

"Yeah, just broke up with my girlfriend," Dillon said, and smiled weakly. "I made her mad. I told her I saw . . ." He hesitated, and the smile faded away. "Well, never mind. She just got mad at me. When she cools off, we'll talk."

"That's a good plan, Dillon," Bobo said. "Give her time to come around."

He ducked his head. "Can I get you guys some more bread?" The basket for rolls and corn bread was almost empty.

"Sure," Manfred said, not because he wanted any more but because he wanted to give Dillon a reason to exit.

Arthur looked after the boy. He seemed lost in thought for a moment.

Magdalena was unexpectedly entertaining at table talk. She had a number of stories that Manfred suspected were stock stories, anecdotes she told to keep the social ball rolling: terrible clients, terrible judges, funny lawsuits. Arthur was more engaged in that world than any of the others, and he laughed the hardest. He was inspired to tell "best arrest" stories. And Bobo told a few "weird things people wanted to pawn" anecdotes—the used coffin, the grenade, the blank tombstones.

This was high entertainment for a Midnight dinner. Manfred looked at the smiling faces around the table: at Joe and Chuy, who were clearly enjoying themselves; at Fiji, who laughed out loud; at Olivia's guarded smile and Bobo's animated face. Dillon brought out a buttermilk pie with Madonna's demand that they all try it, since it was a new recipe. It was already sliced, and they each took a piece. It was rich and delicious, but Manfred thought it too sweet. However, Madonna was so formidable that he didn't say anything.

At eight thirty, the diners scattered for home as though they'd heard a warning bell sound. The glow in the sky was golden pink, and Magdalena's and Manfred's shadows preceded them as they strolled back to his house, where her car was parked. They didn't talk: It was hot, and they were full, and Manfred had things to think about. Apparently, so did his lawyer.

Magdalena unlocked the car and opened the driver's door. A blast of furnace-hot air gusted out. There was no question of leaning against the metal; she stood, shifting from foot to foot, a woman whose shoes were definitely pinching.

"You call my mom yet?" she asked.

"Nope, but tomorrow for sure."

She seemed to consider, her eyes on her feet, as if she could make them ache less by looking at them.

"You people here are all very odd," she said at last, and then she left.

32

The sun seemed to plummet; the light vanished abruptly, and only the glow of the moon illuminated Midnight. From time to time, it was obscured by clouds. Despite what the weather report had told Chuy two days before, the chance of rain was heavy in the air.

Fiji stood on her back porch, looking out over her garden, until the light was absolutely sucked away. She saw lightning cut through the darkness miles away to the south. She noticed a little piece of the darkness moving in the bushes, and then Mr. Snuggly was by her feet.

"Get in," he said, in his bitter little voice. "Foolish woman."

Fiji, who'd been mesmerized by the lightning, flung open the back door and skittered inside, Mr. Snuggly dashing in past her. She had the door shut and locked while he investigated his water and food bowl. He looked up at her with wide, sad eyes, and she could almost imagine tears.

"You piker," she said, not without affection, and opened a can of cat food. She put half of it in his food bowl and cleaned and refilled his water bowl. There was silence for a few moments, while Mr. Snuggly made his food disappear with a neat dispatch that had her shaking her head incredulously.

When the cat finished, he began to clean his paws. He paused for a moment to say, "Did you know Joe has wings?"

"Yes," she said. "I suspect he's an angel."

"Everyone else thinks they're fake," Mr. Snuggly observed, and resumed his cleaning program. "The wings, that is. The ones he and Chuy 'wear' at Halloween."

"They're just not always visible." She sat down in one of the chairs by the kitchen table. She scrubbed her face with her hands. "Did you see anything else out there that I should know about?"

He nodded. "The Rev and Diederik are out and about," he said. "Everyone else . . . besides you . . . is properly in a house."

"And now I am, too," she said, determined not to be miffed with the cat.

"The big man is almost back," he said. "Diederik was talking to him on the phone."

"Diederik's father? That's wonderful. The boy will be so happy. He's grown so much! I wonder if his dad knew he would." Fiji beamed at the cat.

"He told his son he was sorry to have missed the boy's first moon time. I have very sharp ears."

"I'm glad he's coming back."

"Tonight is very, very dangerous."

The smile vanished from Fiji's face. "More dangerous than the past two nights? Why?"

"Don't need to know," Mr. Snuggly muttered. "Long as you stay inside like a sane creature."

"Why would I not?"

Muttering something unpleasant under his breath, Mr. Snuggly stalked into the front room. Making his way between the display cases and chairs and the table, he went over to the window and jumped onto a padded stool Fiji had placed there just for him. The light was off in the big front room, and Fiji went to look out with the cat. There weren't any streetlights in Midnight, of course, and the traffic light and the moon were the only sources of illumination.

Fiji caught her breath.

In the middle of Witch Light Road (smack between Manfred's house and hers) stood a tiger.

It was huge.

When she finally exhaled, she whispered, "Bengal. Holy Goddess, look at those teeth!"

"Told you so," said Mr. Snuggly.

"But is that . . . ?"

The first tiger was joined by another. It was larger.

"The Rev? And Diederik?" she breathed.

"Maybe his dad is here by now," Mr. Snuggly said. "I can't tell 'em apart unless I smell 'em."

"Do they . . . Would they know me? If I went out there?"

"Do you want to risk them *not* knowing you?" the cat asked acidly.

"Ah. No."

"Then keep your butt indoors."

"I will."

She was glad the light in the shop was out, for though she didn't imagine the tigers would notice her at the window, she felt very strongly that avoiding their attention was better than drawing it. Shoulder to shoulder, the two huge cats paced slowly down the street until they reached the empty house two doors east of Manfred's, where they simply vanished into the shadows. Their smooth movements, their silence, the massive heads turning slightly from side to side to survey the night around them . . . it was as eerie and powerful as anything Fiji had ever seen.

Perhaps they'd vanished because they'd heard the car coming. The road was empty for only a few seconds before it appeared. It was an antique car with big tail fins. Fiji had no idea what make and model it was, and she was not interested. She didn't know the driver, who seemed almost irrelevant to the behemoth he was driving. He was a short, plump man with thick blond hair and a lot of rage. She could see it simmering and shimmering in the night like a red nimbus. He'd pulled into Manfred's driveway, blocking Manfred's car, and he got out of the car to walk rapidly to the front door, his arms pumping with energy. He banged on the door with his fist and began yelling.

"Oh, no," Fiji said. "Oh, no! This is awful!" She rushed over to her own door and suddenly felt a lot of needles sticking in her back. She shrieked.

Mr. Snuggly hissed, *"Do not open that door!"* He'd launched himself from the stool to land on her upper back, and he was clinging desperately to her with his claws.

"I have to stop him! He doesn't know!" she said. "Dammit, get off my back!"

"Just back over to the stool," Mr. Snuggly said. "I'll drop off."

Clumsily, she did so, and he landed on the stool, righting himself immediately and with as much dignity as he could.

"You silly woman," the cat said.

"I can't let—" Then a noise from outside made her look through the window.

One of the tigers was peering around the corner of Manfred's house at the newcomer, who was still banging and screeching. Above the pawnshop, in Bobo's apartment, a light came on. Bobo flung open a window. She could see the silhouette of his head.

"Get back in the car, man!" Bobo called.

"What?" The man stepped back and peered upward.

"Get back in your car and leave. Right now!" Bobo sounded very serious.

"See?" Mr. Snuggly said. "He has a whole floor between him and the creatures. Let *him* speak."

"I will not!" The man fairly twitched with indignation, and Fiji pulled up her own window.

"Get back in your car, you moron!" she yelled. "You're in danger!"

"Don't threaten me," he yelled back, and he banged on Manfred's door again.

The first tiger padded silently around the corner of the house. Perhaps the man smelled the tiger or caught its movement out of the corner of his eye. He turned his head to look. And he froze. Fiji hoped that was a good thing.

The tiger made a "chuff" noise, like a cough. Hearing it in the Texas night was hair-raising, literally. It was as out of place as a hyena's cackle.

Fiji was awed into silence, and she didn't hear a peep from Bobo.

She had never read a brochure advising her on what to do if she had to deal with a loose tiger. Or two.

The second one joined the first. Fiji could feel the fear emanating from the stranger. It had gathered in a tight black ball around him. The two tigers took a step or two closer to the man. Then several things happened as quick as a wink. Manfred's front door opened, his tattooed arm shot out, his hand grasped the man's shirtfront, and he yanked him in.

In theory, this should have worked like a charm, ending with the door slamming shut in the tigers' faces. In actuality, the stranger's feet got tangled, and he sprawled in the doorway, leaving it wide open.

Fiji leaned out her window and yelled, "Hey! Tiger!"

And Bobo did the same thing at the same moment.

Both tigers turned their heads, one to look up at Bobo and one to turn slightly to look at Fiji, and while they were distracted, the man was dragged inside. Manfred's door closed.

"Shut your window," Mr. Snuggly said. He was hiding somewhere in the room, Fiji could tell, but she couldn't see the cat. Hearing him was enough. She shut the window and locked it.

"I wonder who the idiot is," she said, collapsing into a chair.

"I expect," said Mr. Snuggly, "that's Lewis Goldthorpe."

33

The silence in Manfred's house was broken only by the ragged breathing of the man on the floor. Lewis Goldthorpe had wet himself, which Manfred supposed was not an unreasonable reaction to being faced with two tigers. But it didn't make the atmosphere any more pleasant, and it made Lewis even more angry.

"I hope you die," Lewis sobbed.

"I should have left you out there to be eaten." Manfred's grandmother had warned him about helping other people. He should have listened.

"Why are there tigers here? What's *wrong* with this place?" Lewis managed to sit up.

"The only thing wrong with this place is that you're in it right now," Manfred said. "Why the hell did you come here?"

"The police came back," Lewis said. "They took apart the globe. They found Mama's stuff."

Manfred said, "So now you know I didn't steal it. Now you know to leave me alone. I only wished your mother well. I liked her."

"You cheated her," Lewis said, and his voice began to rise. "You cheated her."

"Out of what? Hours of loneliness? I just saved your life, asshole!"

"She should have turned to me when my dad died." Now Lewis was snarling, and there was something in his face that made Manfred feel a flicker of fear. The man was down on the floor, and he was a mess, and his facial expressions were all over the place—fear, anger, some tears, a boatload of frustration. He was ridiculous. But he was frightening, too.

"But she didn't?" Manfred made his voice gentler. It took a huge effort.

"No, she became more and more 'Lewis, you need to stand on your own two feet,' and 'Lewis, you need to get another job.'"

"But you didn't feel that was right?" From years of talking to upset people, Manfred made himself sound as sympathetic and understanding as a good therapist. But it was a huge effort.

"Of course not! She needed someone on the spot, someone to keep the—the predators away from her. People like you and that whore Bertha."

"Bertha? The maid?"

"Yes, Bertha, the maid." Lewis tried to do a cruel imitation of Manfred, but he just succeeded in sounding more foolish.

"I thought Bertha seemed . . ." What had he thought? He hadn't really looked at Bertha with any interest. She was the maid.

"Seemed what? Grabby? Possessive? *Fertile?*" He spat out the last word.

"She didn't seem anything," Manfred said slowly. "She seemed like the background."

"Right! Right!" Confirmed in his judgment, Lewis crowed in triumph. "Always there. Always at Daddy's right hand. Waiting. Whispering. Always with John skulking around."

"John?" That was all Manfred could think of to say.

"Yes, *John*." Lewis sneered. "Couldn't name him Juan, I guess. Wanted to be *American*."

"She's not American?"

"Bertha? Oh, I guess, technically she is."

Manfred sighed. "So why are you upset that Bertha's son, John, came into the house?"

"Because she wanted my dad to love him. Because she wanted my dad to love him more than he loved me. And after my dad died, she started to work on my mother. But not telling my mom the big thing! No, waiting for the lawyers on that!"

Manfred had followed Lewis's narrative until that moment. "What the hell are you talking about?"

"John is Dad's son!"

"Are you kidding?" Manfred's amazement was genuine and complete.

Never ask a madman if he's kidding. For the next five minutes Manfred had to listen to an account of the affair between Bertha and Morton Goldthorpe. And the worst part was, Manfred couldn't tell if this was fact or fiction, because Lewis believed it absolutely. He thought that Bertha's son, John, was the product of that long-ago liaison.

"When my dad died," Lewis said, "his will said his estate was to go to Mother during her lifetime. And afterward it was to be divided among the heirs of his body. See? Of his body? Which includes John. But my mom didn't know about John. And maybe she could have changed the will."

"Is that why you put the pills in her water?"

"I did not." Lewis sounded definite and almost sane when he said that. "I did not poison my mother."

"Are you saying Bertha did?"

"That is what I am saying."

"Then why did you drag me into this?"

"You and Bertha worked together. She put the pills in Mama's water the only time Mama had gone out of the house in a couple of weeks. She thought Mama would have a car wreck on her way to see you, and that either you or I would be blamed."

"And how do you know this? And why on earth do you think I knew about it ahead of time?"

"I know it because Mama told me so. She's been whispering in my ear. She told me all this."

"That is total bullshit and you know it. Your mother is at peace with your father. She is not whispering in your ear." Manfred shook his head. "I'm willing to believe you have some kind of delusional situation going on here. But you can leave me out of it. I wished your mother nothing but good."

Lewis, amazingly, had no response to that. He struggled to his feet. Manfred offered no help. He didn't want to get that close to Lewis. He was wondering how to clean the wood floor, which was wet where Lewis had landed. Maybe one of those Swiffer things?

"So what do we do now?" Manfred asked. "Are you ready to run back to your car and get out of here?"

"I still think you conspired with Bertha," Lewis said. He was as tenacious as a pit bull but with half the brainpower and none of the looks.

Manfred sighed, and he made it gusty and obvious. "You're a jerk, and I don't know why your mother didn't put you in a straightjacket," he said, and then realized that had crossed the border into cruel. Did he mind? Not at this exact moment.

"There's someone outside," Lewis said. He was staring at the window. Skeptically, Manfred glanced in the same direction. There was a face at the window for real. Manfred gasped. But once the shock was over, he thought he knew who he'd glimpsed.

"Was that Bertha?" he said, astonished. She must have followed Lewis all the way to Midnight. "You weren't lying," he said, and there was a lot of wonder in his voice. "She really does have it in for you."

Manfred had a choice at that moment. (Afterward, he thought of it as his "The Lady, or the Tiger?" moment.) He could try to warn Bertha, grab her, and bring her into his house, just as he had Lewis— or he could leave her to the mercy of the tigers.

He felt something very like relief when the choice was taken out of his hands.

34

Outside, with the moon radiating a gentle glow—intermittently, since clouds were drifting through the sky—Olivia felt more alive than she had since Lemuel had left for New York. She'd been atop Manfred's roof since he'd left for Home Cookin with the lawyer. Since sunset, she'd been watching the tigers prowl through Midnight.

Olivia was almost certain she'd seen three. But like Fiji, she couldn't tell them apart, and they'd never been all together.

Only one of the big cats was in sight now, and it was right below her. The woman who'd been looking through Manfred's window had backed against the wall, and Olivia could hear her breathing—ragged, uneven breaths, almost like crying. Olivia hadn't been able to get a good look at the woman, but she was fairly certain it was Bertha, and she was delighted at Bertha's appearance here in Midnight.

Bertha stayed put until the tiger advanced and batted at her with a huge paw. Then Bertha bolted. Olivia watched, transfixed, as the tiger overtook her with one bound.

At least it was quick. The last shriek was cut off like a knife.

Olivia supposed that now the tiger would dispose of the corpse in the most practical manner.

But the tiger who'd made the kill didn't get to consume his prey. An even larger tiger suddenly appeared from the brush-strewn acres that lay between Midnight and the river. The new arrival shoved the killer away from the corpse. Olivia figured the larger tiger would now eat the corpse himself, but he didn't. He made a huffy, chuffy noise and rubbed up against the killer. Olivia thought, *He's telling him he shouldn't eat people.*

The killer tiger made a halfhearted lunge at the new arrival, but the larger tiger simply butted him back. Then a third tiger emerged from the shadows behind the pawnshop. But he didn't interfere. He turned silently and crossed Witch Light Road in a single bound.

As far as Olivia could tell, the tiger passed between Fiji's house and the fence around the pet cemetery. Then it vanished into the night, heading south, perhaps to the Braithwaite ranch. After some silent interaction, which was surely communication, the other two followed.

Olivia waited a few minutes before swinging down. She landed in a neat crouch and knocked on Manfred's door. "They're gone," she called.

The door opened. "Thank God," Manfred said. "You're okay, then? What about Bertha?"

"She's a mess," Olivia said. "Dead, of course. Was that Lewis pounding on your door? I couldn't tell."

"Yeah, he's in here." Manfred stood aside, and Olivia could feel herself smiling as she looked down at Lewis. "You're a mess, too," she said. And he was. He smelled like pee, his clothes were wet and dirty, and he was clearly very shocked by what had just happened. But she'd met a few Lewises before, and she knew that very soon he'd revert to being his disagreeable and unbalanced self.

She was right.

"You, you, you . . . crazy people!" Lewis was pulling himself up as he sputtered.

"Why'd you come here, Lewis?" she asked.

Manfred said, "Good question, Olivia. Lewis?"

"To tell you . . . to tell you . . ." he began, but he couldn't think of a good ending for his sentence.

"Do you think he came to kill me?" Manfred asked Olivia.

She patted Lewis down. It was unpleasant to touch him, but she was not one to flinch at unpleasant things.

"No," she said. "Unless words can turn to stones. I don't think Lewis has the balls to kill someone. He likes to screech at 'em, though."

"You people should be locked up," Lewis said. But it had no force behind it. He was exhausted, at least for the moment. He did muster up a spark of defiance, just enough to make him draw his hand back to slap Olivia, but she caught his arm with no trouble at all and bent it the wrong way. He began to sob.

"Olivia," Manfred admonished her. "I think we've heard enough from him for one night."

"I agree," she said. "Lewis, pipe down."

Lewis made a poor effort to do so.

She opened the door. "Just go home," she said. "And never talk to anyone about tonight. Or Manfred will bring charges for trespassing and assault against you. You know, I bet you'd really, really hate jail."

Lewis staggered out the door and to his car, moving with almost frantic clumsiness to pull open its door and dive inside. He locked the doors. In the quiet night, Olivia could hear the click. He didn't even glance over at the mangled corpse.

"I wouldn't want to be on the road with him driving tonight," she said, as they watched the car lurch backward and then go to the intersection. Lewis turned south, probably going to the interstate.

"And yet we're not stopping him," Manfred said. He sounded angry. Surprised, Olivia swung around.

"You have issues with the way I handled that?" She was beginning to get angry herself.

Manfred took a deep breath, and she watched him calm down. "No," he said. "And yes. I'm not happy that a woman is dead outside my house, and that she died in pain and fear. Also, I'm worried with how to conceal her corpse. I'm worried about further police investigation. And I'm sorry that since she's dead, there may not be justice for Rachel. No one will know what happened to her. Since the murderer has been murdered, there'll always be suspicion floating around."

Olivia felt depressed now. And that made her angrier. She'd done well, she thought, and this was the thanks she got: none at all.

"Listen, shrimp, no one can ever prove that you put her meds in her drink, because you didn't. Bertha did."

Manfred sat down abruptly. "Lewis just told me Bertha did it. But I didn't know whether to believe him."

"I looked up Morton's will," she said. "He did leave everything to his wife first, and after she died, to the heirs of his body. He had his money in a trust. Rachel had the use of the trust in her lifetime, but after that, yada yada yada."

"And John really is Morton's son?"

"Morton apparently suspected he was, or he wouldn't have worded the will that way. I found a way to read it online." She smiled with considerable pride.

"But why kill Rachel? If the money would eventually come to John anyway?"

"I'm just guessing, but John was arrested recently. That's public record, too. Not in Bonnet Park, but in Abilene. For vehicular manslaughter. He totaled his car and his passenger was killed. So he was facing a trial. And he had no *dinero* for a lawyer. I don't know if Bertha tried to get Rachel to cough up the money or if she even told Rachel what was going on. But John needs money, and he needs it now."

"But it would still have to go through probate, right?" Even his grandmother's meager estate had had to go through probate. "I needed money to keep the house running after Xylda died, and the lawyer let me have it."

"I bet he would have let you have money for an attorney if you were facing criminal charges."

"That . . . well, I just don't know." Manfred suddenly felt the whole day crash down on him like a ton of bricks.

"Where are you going?" Olivia asked sharply.

"To bed, Olivia," he said. "I just can't . . ." He never finished his sentence but went into his bedroom and closed the door.

And now, it seemed, Olivia would have to clean up Bertha's body all by herself. She had counted on the tigers doing their thing and eating most of Bertha, but she guessed that was not going to happen. She went outside again.

"When I called you and told you to follow Lewis, this is *not* what I expected," Olivia said to what was left of Bertha.

It hadn't been hard to incite Lewis into tearing over to Midnight. Not hard at all, especially after she'd told him about the newscast. She'd pretended to be a reporter, and she'd repeated everything Manfred had said, and embellished some. And once he'd threatened to confront the fiend who'd ruined his life, Olivia had called Bertha. The result had been pretty damn near perfect. *Except, of course, if the body is found and the law starts looking for tigers. Boy, the Rev won't like that at all. . . .* And this thought, which she admitted she should have had much sooner, worried Olivia quite a bit.

Okay, the body wouldn't be found. And Bertha's car wouldn't be, at least for a while. Olivia hoped she had another shower curtain and extra duct tape stockpiled in her apartment. They were the handiest tools for body disposal. And she'd have to keep a close watch out for the tigers, not a hazard at any body disposal site she'd ever attended. She went down to her apartment, humming.

When she came back out some twenty minutes later, Olivia was pleasantly surprised to find that the body was gone. Only a bloody patch showed where it had lain. In the interest of tidiness, she attached the Rev's hose to Manfred's outside water faucet and spent ten minutes hosing down the evidence. There was still a chance of rain, but better to get the process started.

She thought, *At least he can pay for the water.*

35

Joe went out to exercise the next morning for the first time since he'd hurt his ankle. He couldn't run, but he could walk. He turned east instead of west because he wanted to check on the death site. He and Chuy had heard the scream the night before, and they'd hugged each other. After a short time, he'd observed one of the tigers dragging something across the street and through the gate into the pet cemetery. And he'd seen Olivia cross the street to fetch the Rev's outside hose, so he figured she'd watered down the ground.

Joe was willing to bet that the Rev was in the pet cemetery now, digging a deep grave. There were several deep graves in the burial ground. The Rev put the illicit bodies very far down and buried the pets on top of them. It was his technique. "The exercise is good for me," he'd told Joe, back when he was talking more. As the years had gone by, the Rev spoke more and more seldom.

Before he'd gone far out of town, Joe heard someone running behind him. He half turned his head and glimpsed the tall man who'd left Diederik with the Rev. He was a little surprised that the man was up to running this morning, but then, were-animals were high-energy creatures. Joe was taking it easy on his ankle, and it wasn't long before the taller man had caught up with him. He passed Joe with a nod, which Joe returned.

Joe turned around a few minutes later, because he was feeling an unpleasant ache in his injured leg. When it began to nag at him, he slowed still more.

By and by, he heard footsteps behind him. The sun was beginning to hammer down, and Joe was streaming with sweat, and at first he thought he was just hearing his pulse hammering in his ears. But the tall man was coming up behind him, and after another moment he fell into step beside Joe.

"You may be thinking what a terrible father I am," he began.

"Let's stop by Fiji's. Maybe you should tell her this story," Joe said. "She's taken great care of your boy, more than any of us." After that they proceeded in silence.

Though it was early in the morning and her store had not yet opened, Fiji was dressed and working in her garden when they strolled up. She didn't seem surprised when Joe called to her; he thought perhaps she had seen both of them set out on their run, and put herself in their way. She rocked back on her heels and stood up, putting her hand over her eyes to look up at the two men. Though Fiji smiled, at her feet Mr. Snuggly glared up at the tall man.

The tall man squatted down. The sun gleamed on his bald head as he held out his hand to Mr. Snuggly. "Little brother, you have nothing to fear from me," he said. "And neither does Miss Fiji." The cat stared at the man's hand. Then he turned and strolled away, his tail straight up in the air. Giving the cat version of the finger, Joe figured.

After a moment, the man straightened and stood. He looked from Joe to Fiji, and Joe noticed his eyes were purple, like pansies.

Like his son's. "I'm Quinn," he said. "My son tells me that you've all been taking care of him. Especially you, Miss Fiji."

"Just Fiji will be fine. Diederik's a cute kid," she said slowly, as a preliminary. Joe thought she wasn't sure how to put what she wanted to say. "Really, we all helped to take care of him. The Rev . . ." She paused. Then she decided to be blunt. "What the hell," she said. "You gotta know, Mr. Quinn, that the Rev was not the best person to leave a little boy with. No matter how much he looks like he's in his teens, Diederik's still a kid. Especially in view . . ." She looked at Joe for support, and he nodded.

"We wonder what the story is," Joe said, simplifying.

"I deserve that," Quinn said. "And I want to explain. I didn't think there were any other weretigers left in North America. In fact, I was wondering if I was the last one in the world when I met Diederik's mother, Tijgerin. The first time she got pregnant, she told me she wanted to be a traditional mother. That means she would raise the cub on her own. I hated the idea, but she wanted to do things the way her own mother had. But Tijgerin lost the cub. We were sad. Really sad. But we both figured it wasn't likely that something else would go wrong with another pregnancy. So after a time, we made another baby. I was sure she would be different this time, but I was wrong. Tijgerin was still convinced she was right. She wanted to raise him old-school. Away from me." The big man shook his head. Joe could feel the sadness and regret emanating from him.

"She seemed healthy and so did the cub inside her. I felt I didn't have a choice. I couldn't force her, *wouldn't* force her, to do what I wanted. I'd been forced to do a lot of things myself, and I didn't want that for her. Tijgerin was a proud woman. A proud tiger."

Mr. Snuggly had crept out from the bush to look up at Quinn. Absently, Fiji scooped the cat up so he could see better.

Joe closed his eyes to guard himself against Quinn's pain.

"She delivered him by herself, in human form, as we two-natured do, in case you don't know that. She called me to tell me everything went well, that we had a son. I was so excited and started out to see him," Quinn said. "Just a quick visit. She was adamant. But while I was traveling, something went wrong inside her. By the time I tracked her down, she was almost gone, but she'd kept the baby alive."

Joe turned away. He pulled out a handkerchief and used it to mop his face. He was sad and burdened, and he longed for his apartment and Chuy. But he was here to bear witness.

"So you had the raising of the boy," Fiji said.

He nodded. He seemed intent that Joe and Fiji understand his story. "I had Diederik, and I did the best I could. I have a traveling job, so sometimes I had to leave him with my sister. She's human, and she's married. Soon she had her own baby on the way. She told me that she would find it hard to take care of Diederik and her own baby at the same time. I could understand that, especially when he began grow-ing. Once out of infancy, the growth really accelerates, until—well, you saw. So I started taking him with me, which wasn't ideal. But I couldn't leave him with someone who wouldn't understand."

"But why'd you have to leave him with the Rev?" Joe asked. "Did you know this would be his moon?"

"Let me make myself clear. I would *never* have left him if I'd been sure it was his moon," Quinn said, his voice hard. "But I knew it was getting close, and I knew he would start growing like crazy, so when I found out there was another tiger, I was . . . so relieved. Another tiger in this country! Finally, a safe place to leave Diederik, with someone who would understand, while I did my job one more time."

"But . . . this is going to be a problem forever, right?" Fiji looked troubled. "I mean, I hate to criticize, but . . ." She waved one hand as if to say, *This is permanent.*

"Now that he's had his first moon, we can plan together," Quinn said. "We're on the same schedule. I only wish I could have been here from the start of his moon. Last night was unfortunate."

"That's one way to put it," Fiji said.

Quinn took a deep breath. Joe could tell the weretiger wanted to leap in with some defense of his cub, but facts were facts. "I stopped him from eating her," he said finally. "He won't be a maneater. We went and took down a sheep afterward."

"The woman did not deserve to die like that," Joe said.

"And I feel as bad as you can imagine about it. But I didn't arrive, change, and get on Diederik's trail fast enough to prevent it happening. And the Rev was not fast enough. Since dawn, I've been comforting a boy who remembers sinking his teeth into a woman's throat."

There was a moment of silence. Joe regrouped. "So where is he now?" he asked, proud that his voice was mild and even.

"At the Rev's, asleep, finally." Quinn looked away. "I was too keyed up to sleep myself, so I came out for a run."

"If you take him with you everywhere you go now, what will happen about his schooling?"

"That's something I'll have to think about. He learns really quickly. He's smart." The pride shone through the words. "But were-animals have a hard time in human schools, especially the ones who grow extra fast, like Diederik. It's going to take a long time for his emotions to catch up with his body. At least, a long time in kid terms. Maybe a year or two, it varies. In the meantime, he looks like he should be in high school, but he hasn't been to any school at all. So he has none of the background or social conditioning."

"Please come in," Fiji said abruptly. "We don't need to be standing out in the heat."

They all trooped inside, and she sat them down in her cool kitchen. Mr. Snuggly retired to a basket in the corner, where he could keep an eye on Quinn. Fiji offered them beverages, and both the men took glasses of iced tea. She put a plate of raisin bread on the table, with a knife and some butter and napkins. Though Joe felt he shouldn't, he cut a slice and slathered it with butter and ate it slowly. *So much for my run*, he thought, before making himself concentrate on Quinn.

"So, Diederik," Fiji said. And waited.

"The Rev has offered to keep him here for a few months while Diederik gets his balance emotionally," Quinn said. "You can imagine how scary it is to go from being a little kid to being a teen in a very short time. It's hard enough, my friends tell me, to do it in human time. It's a dangerous time for Diederik. I'll come in every chance I get."

"That's the best you can do," Fiji said.

Joe nodded in agreement. Though he himself could not remember being a teenager, he was sure it must have been hard. He had only to think of the two teens who'd recently lived in Midnight to confirm that.

"And after that?" Joe said.

"This is a community that's not afraid to jump in and speak its mind," Quinn said, one corner of his mouth quirking up. "I guess I deserve that. I blew one of the biggest moment's in my son's life when I tried to take on one more job."

"And your mysterious job, the one that keeps you traveling so much, is?" Joe found himself curious.

"I'm an event planner for the supernatural community. I do vampire weddings and coming-of-age parties for were-animals . . . the ones who can predict more closely than tigers! Leadership struggles of one kind or another. And so on. Since the supernaturals are such a small percentage of the population and so scattered, that involves a lot of travel. I was hoping to put enough in the bank to retire after this year. At least I can afford to take some time off until I can figure out what to do next."

Fiji said, "So, now that Diederik's had his first change, it'll be monthly from now on?" She had cut a piece of bread for herself, and she was taking a bite every now and then. She rose to pour herself a cup of coffee and to refill the men's glasses.

"Yes," Quinn said. "Though illness and environment can change that with tigers, that's the ideal pattern."

"And ranchers would lose a cow a month? That's kind of hard for some people, don't you think?" Joe was picturing the ranchers who came into Home Cookin, men and women who lived on a very narrow financial margin.

"Sometimes the Rev needs to hunt," Quinn said. "We all do. Sometimes the instinct gets so strong you just have to. But mostly, he buys a cow and stakes it out in the open land just north or just south of town overnight."

Until he can jump on it and kill it and eat it, Joe thought. He could see that a hunt would be far more satisfying and natural than stalking a bought-and-paid-for domestic animal, furthermore one that was stationary.

He remembered, thousands of years ago, fighting. The feral thrill of finding his opponent, the flash of the bright sword. But memories only brought bitterness, and he was out of the bitterness business. He shoved that cycle of emotion aside to return to Fiji's kitchen, lit with sunlight and clean surfaces and good smells.

"You're the father, and I've never had a child," Joe said. "But surely the boy would be better off with you, instead of here. If, as you say, you're going to retire soon, can't his education wait until then?"

It was lucky that he'd put the question with so much gentleness. Joe saw that Quinn's face tightened and so did his shoulders, the signs of an irritated man.

"I'm sure you don't know this," said Quinn with equally good manners, "but a young weretiger is prized for his fighting ability. When I was the boy's age, I was in the pits, obliged to fight and kill, to clear a family debt." Without warning, he pulled off his T-shirt and rose, turning to show them the scars crisscrossing his back. There were plenty on the front, too.

"Oh," said Fiji, deeply distressed. "That's horrible. I'm glad you survived it."

The big man shrugged and put his shirt back on. "It's done. But more than anything else, I don't want the supes to start imagining Diederik as pit fodder, now that he's got his growth."

"They could get him away from you?" Joe said.

"If I were dead."

"So for now he'll stay here in Midnight," Joe said.

"Yes. Maybe a few months, maybe a year will see him strong enough, past the dangerous part. If he can make a name for himself doing something else, it won't be easy to abduct him, force him. He will find a job he can do."

Joe and Fiji looked at each other. "With the Rev?" she said finally. "You've been in the Rev's house?"

"Yes," Quinn said steadily. "I've seen it's barren. I was going to ask if there was somewhere else he could stay, though the Rev would be responsible for educating Diederik in the ways of the tiger and instructing him in our history. Of course, I would pay his room and board and other expenses. I understand that you . . . Fiji . . . have been buying him clothes, and I want to pay you back for that. I thank you for your generosity."

"*De nada*," she said, smiling. "If you want to, sure, but I did it to keep him decent and smiling. Kids got to have clothes and lots of food."

"Do you two have any ideas about who would host him?" Quinn looked from one to the other.

"I guess I could clean out my second bedroom. It's pretty crammed with stuff," Fiji said doubtfully.

"You've been great for Diederik, and he loves your cooking," Quinn said. He smiled again. "I can see why, after eating this bread. But you're also pretty and young, and sharing a house with an adolescent boy at such close quarters . . . well, it might not be ideal."

Fiji turned red. "Okay," she said.

"We have visitors," Joe said regretfully. "So our guest room gets some use." Chuy kept in touch with his human descendants, though they didn't know his true nature, of course. Joe did not chide Chuy for the elaborate fictions he fed them about their kinship. Chuy seemed to need the contact.

"That leaves Manfred or Bobo," Fiji said. "They're both good men."

Quinn stood. "I'll go talk to them after I shower. I owe both of you for your kindness to my son."

Mr. Snuggly raised his head and said, "Good-bye, big man."

Quinn seemed taken aback. "Well . . . good-bye, little brother." He shook his head and left.

"Joe, do you think this can work?"

"I hope so," Joe said. "This town seems to have adopted a child."

As he walked back to his apartment, looking forward to his shower, he was still thinking about the hard life Quinn had had, and the loss of the female Tijgerin.

Diederik was motherless, and his greatly accelerated growth rate had deprived him of a childhood. Yet the boy had always impressed Joe as being cheerful and willing and intelligent. For a moment, Joe almost resented Chuy's odd attachment to humans that made Diederik's boarding with them very unlikely. It would have been nice to have someone young around the place. He smiled to himself. It hadn't escaped his notice that Quinn had automatically assumed that Diederik would be attracted to a woman rather than a man. Well, he was probably right. Joe hadn't gotten any vibe that said otherwise, though a boy so young sometimes didn't know his own nature.

Joe wondered if Diederik's mother, Tijgerin, had really been the last female weretiger.

If so, Diederik was the end of the line. If he couldn't find another female, weretigers were extinct. For most of his life, Quinn must have assumed that he was the last one, and now he had a son. Joe hoped that Diederik would be even luckier and find a mate who lived.

The death of the woman the night before did not overly trouble Joe. It was done now. Past mending. He was not going to lament over it or ask God to smite Diederik.

And that was one reason he was in Midnight.

36

By the time lunch rolled around, there was a small crowd gath-ered in Home Cookin. Olivia was indulging herself with an open-faced roast beef sandwich. She cut the pieces very small and chewed them deliberately. Her fellow Midnighters were gathered around the table, and she smiled at them all. The action of the night before had left her feeling pleasantly relaxed. Aside from the absent weretigers and Teacher, perpetually on duty at Gas N Go, everyone else was there, though Madonna and Grady were in the kitchen and Dillon was at football practice.

Manfred came in later than the others, looking flushed and excited. Since he was normally the palest person in town (except, of course, for Lemuel), this was a notable occurrence.

"What's up?" asked Chuy, who was holding Rasta on his lap. Rasta had had a bad time of it the night before. The chuffing sound of the tigers had made him shiver and shake and whine. Long after the silence had fallen, Joe and Chuy had let the little dog in the bed between them, a behavior usually only indulged during thunderstorms.

Manfred paused to tentatively pat Olivia on the shoulder, something he'd never done before. (If he'd known why Lewis and Bertha had turned up at his door last night, he might not have.)

"I just stopped by the hotel to check on Mamie and Tommy and Suzie," Manfred said to the table in general. "Also, I wanted to see if Shorty had heard from his grandson. I found them all packed up and ready to go."

"What?" Olivia looked at him sharply, trying to believe this was some weird joke. "What did Lenore Whitefield say?"

"She said that places had opened up for all of them in Safe Harbor, that really fancy assisted-living place in Davy. They'll each have their own rooms with a little kitchen space, a television, a queen bed, and a La-Z-Boy. I'm quoting."

Everyone digested that for a minute.

"How'd they feel about it?" Olivia was almost angry.

"They said there was sure to be more going on in Davy. The residents there have dance lessons and bowling nights and yoga classes."

"So they were willing to go?" Olivia could hardly believe it.

"Yes, even after we took them to lunch at Cracker Barrel, they were willing to go," Manfred said, laughing. "But they want us to come and visit, and they said you'd promised to take them to the library, Olivia."

"I'm going to do exactly that," she said.

"And they weren't suspicious about it all being paid for?" Chuy said.

"I guess if you've been living in a roach motel in Las Vegas, you're ready to accept whatever good comes your way," Manfred said.

"What about the regular guests? The contract workers at Magic

Portal?" Bobo asked. One of them had come into Midnight Pawn the previous Saturday and tried to bargain with Bobo over an old tray. He'd been embarrassingly persistent.

"They're still in residence, as Lenore put it," Manfred said. "I asked her if more old people would be coming in, and she said that was out of her authority, or something like that. But the hotel's going to stay open."

"Very strange," Chuy said, scratching Rasta's head. "Two staff, plus the cook, for two guests."

Bobo said, "What does this mean for the future, I wonder?"

Of course, none of them knew the answer to that. It was unsettling, to say the least.

The electronic chime on the door made them all turn to see who'd come in.

"Hey, everyone," said Arthur Smith.

They were relaxed enough with the sheriff to say "Hey" back and to make room for him at their table. He eyed Olivia's roast beef sandwich with interest.

"I came to talk to you, Manfred, and I figured you'd be over here when I couldn't catch you at your place." Madonna brought Arthur a glass of water and some silverware, and he asked if he could have an open-face like Olivia. Madonna nodded impassively and left.

"What about? I'm not in more trouble, I hope?" Though Manfred tried to sound confident, he knew they could all hear the uncertainty in his voice.

"The Bonnet Park cops called me. They had a few things to say about Lewis Goldthorpe."

"Oh?" Manfred hoped Arthur didn't notice that everyone at the table had grown silent.

"Yeah. He came in to tell them today that he'd seen three tigers here."

"Tigers. Three." Manfred didn't have to struggle to sound amazed. He really was; how did Lewis believe this news would go over at any police department in America? "Ah, and why was he here, did he say that? Because I sure can't imagine it."

He hoped he wasn't imagining that Arthur's eyes were sharp and taking in his every twitch.

"He said they ate his housekeeper. Some woman named Bertha?"

"Bertha was here, too?" Manfred couldn't manage a laugh, but he did produce a passable sneer. "Aside from three tigers and Bertha, did he mention anyone else?"

Arthur smiled, just a little. "Nope. But since the jewelry was found and you couldn't have killed Rachel Goldthorpe, you're no longer part of the investigation."

"Cleared!" Manfred thumped the table. "That's what I've been waiting for all along. So did they give you a hint about who did kill her?"

"Don't know. Lewis says it was this Bertha and that she was his dad's mistress. I don't know if that's so or not. And no one can find Bertha. She's gone from home, her son doesn't know where she is, she didn't show up for work, and her car is nowhere to be found. Her son says he has a blood test to prove he's the son of Morton Goldthorpe. Annelle and Roseanna, the daughters, are pretty excited about that."

"They want another brother? Weird," Bobo said. "Well, the important thing is that Manfred is in the clear."

"The Bonnet Park police couldn't have told Manfred themselves?" Olivia looked properly indignant.

"They seem a little overrun with things to do right now," Arthur said. "What with Lewis acting crazy, an unsolved death on their hands, the missing woman, a potential new heir, and the resultant publicity. Lewis, as it turns out, has been going all over the place telling this story about the tigers, and the chief of police there says he thinks the sisters are going to try to have him committed."

"That's a relief," Manfred said. "He doesn't sound stable enough to be running around on his own."

Arthur nodded and began to cut up his sandwich. He closed his eyes for a moment to appreciate the aroma. "This is like heaven," he said, and put a bite in his mouth.

"Enjoy it. I've got to go," Olivia said, smiling all around. She folded her paper napkin and put it on her plate, pushing back from the table and rising in one smooth movement. She reached the glass door, where she paused. After a second, she said, "Arthur. Come here. Quick."

With a sigh, Arthur laid down his fork and joined her. "What's up?" he asked, making it clear he was none too happy.

"The Gas N Go is being robbed," she said, as quietly as if the robber could hear her. "That car just pulled up to the pump. The guy went in with a hoodie on. Like the guy who's robbed all the others. In this weather, a hoodie. He didn't start pumping any gas."

Madonna, who'd been clearing Olivia's plate, went straight into the kitchen and came out with baby Grady and a shotgun. "You keep this child," she said to Joe, handing Grady over. Grady and Joe were both a little surprised. Madonna went straight for the door with the shotgun in her hand. "No one is holding my husband up," she said simply, and she would have pushed out the door and gone over to Gas N Go if Arthur hadn't stopped her.

"Let me take care of this," he said. "It's my job. If I go down, feel free to take over. I've called for backup." He smiled—just a little—and left Home Cookin.

They were all gathered at the window by then, Bobo and Manfred, Fiji, Chuy and Joe and Rasta and Grady. Olivia was outside on the sidewalk, very fidgety.

Arthur Smith had his game face on. He drew his gun and ran across the road. When he got to the corner of Gas N Go, he edged forward until he could see through the window.

"He know where the back door is?" Madonna asked no one.

"Yes," Manfred said. "He does." Arthur had seen it a few months before when Manfred and Bobo had gotten jumped in the alley behind the store.

They all held their breath while Arthur left the window and hurried up the alley to the back door.

"Teacher, don't have locked that damn door," Madonna said out loud.

He hadn't.

Arthur slipped inside, and without saying a word, Madonna opened the door and crossed the street, shotgun at the ready.

"Ahhhh," Fiji said. Her hands were twitching.

"You can't go over there," Manfred said. "Arthur wouldn't understand."

Olivia said, "Showtime."

Like the diner, Gas N Go was fronted with glass, but it was at an angle to the street. There was no way the little crowd at Home Cookin could see inside as Madonna could. She pulled open the door and raised the shotgun, and they all drew in breath at the same moment. Joe held Grady's little face to his shoulder so the boy couldn't see.

There was no boom, no screaming, none of the sounds they were dreading they'd hear.

Instead, they heard sirens approaching from Davy.

"Oh, thank you, God," Chuy said.

"All's well that ends well," Olivia murmured. "Well, I'm out of here." As if nothing much had transpired, she strode down the sidewalk and crossed after the intersection to go back to her apartment.

Fiji had tears streaming down her face.

"Hey, what's up?" Manfred asked. Then he realized how stupid that was, and he shook his head at his own foolishness.

"I know it's dumb," she said. "I think it's just cumulative tension, you know? After last night?"

"Oh. You saw."

She nodded. "I need some drama-free time," she said. "And I'm going to go home and have me some."

"Good idea," Manfred said, but she was already out of Home Cookin and walking home. "And who knew Madonna kept a shotgun in the kitchen?" he asked Joe, who was rocking from side to side, Grady drowsing in his arms.

"Not me, for sure," Joe said. "Chuy?"

"Knock me over with a feather," Chuy said, and smiled.

The three weretigers, in their human bodies, of course, emerged from the Rev's small house and stood in a line on the sidewalk, watching the deputies, including Gomez and Nash, swarm all over Gas N Go. The three wandered over to stand by the angels and the psychic, who had stepped outside. Manfred was hoping the blood patch outside his house was really dispersed. Olivia had done a good job, but he wanted to check.

Madonna came stomping back across the street, holding the shotgun broken open in the crook of her arm.

"Let me put this up. I'll come back and get Grady," she said.

"Sure. He's no trouble," Joe said. "Everything okay over there?"

"Yeah. That Smith came through the back area just before I came in the front. Little jerk-off thief didn't know where to look."

"Anyone we know?" Joe asked.

"No, some punk from Abilene," she said. "Thought it would be easy to knock over a little store in a little town like Midnight. Huh. Not with me and Teacher here, it isn't." She gave the line of men a look that expressed her contempt at their inaction, and then she went in to put away the shotgun. "Thanks for all your help. Not."

"I guess we got put in our place," Quinn said, sounding amused.

The Rev shook his head. Diederik (now even taller, Manfred noted) smiled, not the big open grin of previous days, but a smile nonetheless. Joe and Chuy stood as close together as they could get, and Joe smiled down at the dark head resting on his shoulder.

"Yes, we're a sad bunch," Manfred said, and he smiled, too. He thought Diederik still smelled like blood. He watched as, out of nothing, a feather fluttered from Joe's shoulder and landed gently on the sidewalk.